A MEMORY
CALLED EMPIRE

ALSO BY ARKADY MARTINE

A Desolation Called Peace

A MEMORY
CALLED EMPIRE

ARKADY MARTINE

TOR

A TOM DOHERTY ASSOCIATES BOOK
NEW YORK

A MEMORY CALLED EMPIRE

Copyright © 2019 by AnnaLinden Weller

A Tor Book
Published by Tom Doherty Associates
120 Broadway
New York, NY 10271

www.tor-forge.com

Tor® is a registered trademark of
Macmillan Publishing Group, LLC.

The Library of Congress has cataloged the hardcover edition as follows:

Names: Martine, Arkady, author.
Title: A memory called empire / Arkady Martine.
Description: First edition. | New York : Tor, 2019. | "A Tom Doherty
    Associates Book."
Identifiers: LCCN 2018046933 | ISBN 9781250186430 (hardcover) |
    ISBN 9781250186454 (ebook)
Subjects: | GSAFD: Science fiction.
Classification: LCC PS3613.A786325 M46 2019 | DDC 813/.6—dc23
LC record available at https://lccn.loc.gov/2018046933

ISBN 978-1-250-18644-7 (trade paperback)

Our books may be purchased in bulk for promotional,
educational, or business use. Please contact your local bookseller
or the Macmillan Corporate and Premium Sales Department
at 1-800-221-7945, extension 5442, or by email at
MacmillanSpecialMarkets@macmillan.com.

First Edition: March 2019
First Trade Paperback Edition: February 2020

Printed in the United States of America

*This book is dedicated to anyone who has ever fallen in love
with a culture that was devouring their own.
(And for Grigor Pahlavuni and Petros Getadarj,
across the centuries.)*

Our memory is a more perfect world than the universe; it gives life back to those who no longer exist.

—Guy de Maupassant, "Suicides"

I would not have chosen life with Calypso rather than the smoke from Constantinople. I am absolutely possessed by the thought of the many sources of pleasure which are there on all sides: the size and beauty of the churches, the length of its colonnades and the extent of its walks, its houses and all the other things which enrich our image of Constantinople; gatherings of friends and conversation, and indeed the greatest of all—my gold-pourer, which is to say, your mouth and its flowers—

—Nikephoros Ouranos, *doux* of Antioch, Epistle 38

A MEMORY
CALLED EMPIRE

PRELUDE

IN Teixcalaan, these things are ceaseless: star-charts and dis-embarkments.

Here is all of Teixcalaanli space spread out in holograph above the strategy table on the warship *Ascension's Red Harvest*, five jumpgates and two weeks' sublight travel away from Teixca-laan's city-planet capital, about to turn around and come home. The holograph is a cartographer's version of serenity: *all these glitter-pricked lights are planetary systems, and all of them are ours.* This scene—some captain staring out at the holograph re-creation of empire, past the demarcated edge of the world—pick a bor-der, pick a spoke of that great wheel that is Teixcalaan's vision of itself, and find it repeated: a hundred such captains, a hundred such holographs. And each and every one of those captains has led troops down into a new system, carrying all the poison gifts she can muster: trade agreements and poetry, taxes and the prom-ise of protection, black-muzzled energy weapons and the sweep-ing architecture of a new governor's palace built around the open many-rayed heart of a sun temple. Each and every one of those captains will do it again, render one more system into a brilliantine dot on a star-chart holograph.

Here is the grand sweep of civilization's paw, stretched against the black between the stars, a comfort to every ship's captain when she looks out into the void and hopes not to see anything looking back. Here, in star-charts, the division of the universe into *empire* and *otherwise*, into *the world* and *not the world*.

Ascension's Red Harvest and her captain have one last stop before they begin their trip back to the center of their universe. In Parzrawantlak Sector lies Lsel Station: one fragile turning jewel, a toroid twenty miles in diameter rotating around a central spoke, hanging in the balance-point between a handy sun and its nearest useful planet. The largest of a string of mining stations that make up this small region of space, a region touched by the reaching hand of Teixcalaan but not yet subject to the weight of it.

A shuttle spits itself from the station's spoke, travels a few hours' distance to the waiting gold-and-grey metallic hulk of the warship, deposits its cargo—one human woman, some luggage, some instructions—and comes back again unharmed. By the time it has returned, *Ascension's Red Harvest* has begun ponderously to move on a vector toward the center of Teixcalaan, still subject to sublight physics. It will be visible from Lsel for a day and a half yet, shrinking slowly to a pinpoint of brightness and then winking out.

Darj Tarats, the Lsel Councilor for the Miners, watches that retreating shape: the vast slumbering menace of it, hanging like a weight and eating up half the horizon visible from the viewport of the Lsel Council meeting room. That omnipresent blotting out of familiar stars is to him just the latest evidence of Teixcalaanli hunger for Stationer space. There may soon come a day when such a ship does not retreat, but turns the bright fire of its energy weapons on the fragile metal shell that contains thirty thousand lives, Tarats's included, and spills them all into the killing chill of space like seeds from a smashed fruit. There is, Tarats believes, a kind of inevitability to empire unchecked.

No star-chart holograph glows above the strategy table around which the Lsel Council sits at meetings: only a bare metal surface, polished by a multitude of elbows. Tarats contemplates again the simplicity of how that retreating ship still feels like such a present threat—and stops looking out the viewport, retaking his seat.

Empire unchecked might be inevitable, but Darj Tarats has within him a quiet, determined, and conniving optimism that *unchecked* is not the only option available, and has not been for some time.

"Well, *that's* done with," says Aknel Amnardbat, the Councilor for Heritage. "She's off. Our new Ambassador to the Empire, as requested *by* said Empire, which I sincerely hope she keeps far away from us."

Darj Tarats knows better: he's the man who sent the *last* ambassador from Lsel to Teixcalaan, twenty years ago when he was still middle-aged and enamored with high-risk projects. There is nothing *done with* about sending a new ambassador, even if she's already been packed off in a shuttle, irretrievable. He puts his elbows on that table, as he's been doing for all of those twenty years, and rests his narrow chin in his narrower palms. "It would have been better," he says, "if we could have sent her with an imago that wasn't fifteen years out of date. For her sake, and ours."

Councilor Amnardbat, whose own imago-machine, a precisely calibrated neurological implant which allows her to carry in her mind the recorded memories of six prior Councilors for Heritage, passed down the imago-line one to the next, cannot imagine standing up to someone like Darj Tarats without the benefit of the most recent fifteen years of experience. If she was a new member of the Council, and fifteen years out of date, she would be *crippled*. But she shrugs, not precisely minding the idea of the newest Ambassador to the Empire being so deprived of resources. She says, "That's your problem. You sent Ambassador Aghavn, and Aghavn hasn't bothered to come back here more than once in his twenty-year tenure to give us an updated imago-recording. And now we've sent Ambassador Dzmare with only what he left us fifteen years ago to replace him just because Teixcalaan asked—"

"Aghavn's done his job," says Councilor Tarats, and around the table the Councilors for Hydroponics and for the Pilots nod in agreement: the job Ambassador Aghavn has done is keeping Lsel Station, and all the rest of the little stations in their sector, from being easy prey to a Teixcalaanli expansionist agenda, and in return for this they have collectively agreed to ignore his shortcomings. Now that Teixcalaan has abruptly demanded a new ambassador, without explaining what has become of the old one, most of the Council are delaying an accounting of Ambassador Aghavn's flaws until they know if he is dead, compromised, or simply fallen prey to some internal imperial shakeup of politics. Darj Tarats has always supported him—Aghavn was *his* protégé. And Tarats, as Councilor for the Miners, is first amongst the six equals on the Lsel Council.

"And Dzmare will do hers," says Councilor Amnardbat. Mahit Dzmare had been her choice, of the possible new ambassadors: a perfect match, she'd thought, for the out-of-date imago she'd carry. The same aptitudes. The same attitude. The same xenophilic love for a heritage that was not the heritage Amnardbat protected: a documented fascination with Teixcalaanli literature and language. Perfect to be sent away, with the only copy of Ambassador Aghavn's imago that existed. Perfect to carry that corrupt and corrupting imago-line away from Lsel— perhaps, for good. If Amnardbat herself had done right.

"I'm sure Dzmare will be adequate enough," says the Councilor for the Pilots, Dekakel Onchu, "and now can we consider the problem *currently* before the Council, namely what we are going to do about the situation at the Anhamemat Gate?"

Dekakel Onchu is exceptionally concerned about the Anhamemat Gate, the more distant of Lsel Station's two jumpgates, the one that leads into parts of space unclaimed by Teixcalaanli hands. Lately, she has lost not one scout-ship—which could have been an accident—but two, and both in the same spot of black. She has lost them to something she has no way to talk to. The communiqués sent back before those ships went dark, garbled and staticky with radiation interference, have made no sense; worse, she has lost not only the pilots of those ships, but the long imago-lines of memory that they belonged to. The combined minds of those pilots and their imago-lines cannot be salvaged and placed into new pilot-minds without the recovery of the bodies and imago-machines that had been destroyed—and that is impossible.

The rest of the Council is not so concerned, not yet, but they will be by the end of this meeting, after Onchu has played them the remains of the recordings—all but Darj Tarats. Darj Tarats has a terrible sort of hope instead.

He thinks: *At long last, perhaps there is an empire larger than the Empire that has been devouring us by inches. Perhaps now it comes. Perhaps now I will be able to stop waiting.*

But this he keeps to himself.

CHAPTER
ONE

And from behind the curve of the large gaseous planet at coordinate B5682.76R1, the Emperor Twelve Solar-Flare arose on the bow of her ship, and she was a radiant blaze flooding all of the void. The rays of her light, reaching outward like the spear-spokes of her throne, struck the metal shells which were the dwelling-places of human beings in Sector B5682, and illuminated them brightly. The sensors of Twelve Solar-Flare's ship recorded ten of them, each alike to the other, and this number has not increased since. Within the shells the men and women knew not seasons nor growth nor decay, but lived endlessly in orbit without benefit of a planetary home. The largest of these shells called itself Lsel Station, which in the language of its people meant a station that both listened and heard. But the people there had grown strange, and cleaved to themselves, though they were capable of learning language, and immediately began to do so . . .

> —*The Expansion History, Book V*, lines 72–87, anonymous but
> attributed to the historian-poet Pseudo-Thirteen River,
> writing in the reign of the Emperor of All Teixcalaan
> Three Perigee

*   *   *

In order to expedite your travel into the Imperium, Teixcalaan requests the following as proofs of identity: a) a genetic record stating your sole possession of your own genotype, unshared with clonesibs OR a notarized document stating that your genotype is at least 90 percent unique and that no other individual holds LEGAL claim to it; b) an itemized list of goods, chattels, currencies, and objects of idea commerce which you intend to bring with you; c) a work permit from a registered employer in a Teixcalaanli system, signed and notarized, with salary and maintenance information, OR a record of superlative performance on the Teixcalaanli Imperial Examinations OR an invitation by a person, governmental entity, bureau, ministry, or other authorized individual specifying your entrance and exit dates from Imperium space OR evidence of sufficient self-supporting currency . . .

—Form 721Q, Visa Application Made from Foreign Sectors
ALPHABETIC LANGUAGE VARIANT, page 6

MAHIT came down to the City, heart-planet and capital of the Teixcalaanli Empire, in a seed-skiff, a bubble of a ship hardly big enough for her body and her luggage both. She squirted from the side of the imperial cruiser *Ascension's Red Harvest* and burned atmosphere on her planetward trajectory, which distorted the view. Thus the first time she saw the City with her own flesh eyes, not in infofiche or holograph or imago-memory, it was haloed in white fire and shone like an endless glittering sea: an entire planet rendered into an ecumenopolis, palatially urban. Even its dark spots—older metropolises not yet clad in metal, decaying urban blight, the harnessed remains of lakes— looked *populated*. Only the oceans remained untouched, and they gleamed too, a brilliantine blue-turquoise.

The City was very beautiful and very big. Mahit had been on a fair number of planets, the ones closest to Lsel Station that weren't completely inimical to human life, and she was nevertheless overcome by awe. Her heart beat faster; her palms went clammy where they gripped her harness. The City appeared exactly as it was always described in Teixcalaanli documents and songs: the jewel at the heart of the Empire. Complete with atmospheric glow.

<That's what looking at it is meant to make you think,> said her imago. He was a faint staticky taste on the back of her tongue, a flash of grey eyes and sun-dark skin in her peripheral vision. The voice in the back of her head, but not quite her voice: someone around her age, but male, and quicksilver-smug, and as *excited* to be here as she was. She felt her mouth curve in his smile, a heavier and wider thing than the muscles in her face preferred. They were new to each other. His expressions were very strong.

Get out of my nervous system, Yskandr, she thought at him, gently chiding. An imago—the implanted, integrated memory of one's predecessor, housed half in her neurology and half in a small ceramic-and-metal machine clasped to her brainstem— wasn't supposed to take over the host's nervous system unless the host consented. At the beginning of the partnership, though, *consent* was complicated. The version of Yskandr inside her mind remembered having a body, and sometimes he used Mahit's as if it were his own. She worried about it. There was still so much *space* between them, when they were supposed to be becoming one person.

This time, though, he withdrew easily: sparking prickles, electric laughter. <As you will. Show me, Mahit? I want to see it again.>

When she gazed down at the City again—closer now, the skyport rising to meet her skiff like a flower made of scooping nets—she let the imago look through her eyes and felt his rush of exhilaration as if it were her own.

What's down there, she thought. *For you.*

<The world,> said her imago, who had been Ambassador from Lsel in the City when he was still a living person and not part of a long chain of live memory. He said it in the Teixcalaanli

language, which made it a tautology: the word for "world" and the word for "the City" were the same, as was the word for "empire." It was impossible to specify, especially in the high imperial dialect. One had to note the context.

Yskandr's context was obfuscating, which Mahit had come to expect of him. She coped. Despite all her years of studying Teixcalaanli language and literature, his fluency had a different quality than hers, the sort that only came from immersive practice.

<The world,> he said again, <but also the edges of the world.> *The Empire, but also where the Empire stops.*

Mahit matched his language and spoke out loud in Teixcalaanli, since there was no one but her in the seed-skiff. "You've said something meaningless."

<Yes,> Yskandr agreed. <When I was ambassador it was my habit to say all sorts of meaningless things. You should try it. It's quite enjoyable.>

In the privacy of her body, Yskandr used the most intimate forms of address, as if he and Mahit were clonesibs or lovers. Mahit had never spoken them out loud. She had a natural younger brother back on Lsel Station, the closest she would ever get to a clonesib, but her brother only spoke the Stationers' language, and calling him "you," intimate-otherself in Teixcalaanli, would have been both pointless and unkind. She could have said "you" to a few people who had been in those language and literature courses with her—her old friend and classmate Shrja Torel would have taken the compliment correctly, for instance, but Mahit and Shrja hadn't spoken since Mahit had been picked to be the new Ambassador to Teixcalaan and carry the imago of the previous one. The *why* of that little breakage between them was obvious, and petty, and Mahit regretted it—and it wasn't something she was going to get a chance to repair, except by apologetic letter from the center of the Empire both she and Shrja had wanted to see. Which almost certainly wouldn't help.

The City had come closer: it filled up the horizon, a vast curve she was falling into. To Yskandr, she thought, *I am the Ambassador now. I might speak meaningfully. If I wanted.*

<You speak correctly,> Yskandr said, which was the sort of compliment the Teixcalaanlitzlim gave to a still-crèched child.

Gravity caught at the seed-skiff and sank into the bones in Mahit's thighs and forearms, giving her the sensation of spin. It was dizzying. Below her the skyport's nets flared open. For a moment she thought she was falling, that she would fall all the way to the planet's surface and smear to paste on the ground.

<It was the same for me,> Yskandr said quickly, in that Stationers' language that was Mahit's native tongue. <Don't be afraid, Mahit. You are not falling. It is the planet.>

The skyport caught her with hardly a bump.

She had time to gather herself together. There was some business with the seed-skiff being shunted into a long line of other such vessels, moving along a great conveyor until each one could be identified and come to its assigned gate. Mahit found herself rehearsing what she would say to the imperial citizens on the other side as if she was a first-year student preparing for an oral examination. In the back of her mind, the imago was a watchful, thrumming presence. Every so often he moved her left hand, the fingers tapping along her harness, someone else's nervous gesture. Mahit wished they'd had longer to get used to each other.

But she hadn't undergone the normal process of having an imago implanted, complete with a year or more of integration therapy under the precise care of one of Lsel's psychotherapists: she and Yskandr had had a scant three months together, and now they were approaching the place where they'd need to *work* together—work as one person, compiled out of a memory-chain and a new host.

When *Ascension's Red Harvest* had arrived, hanging in parallel orbit around Lsel Station's sun, and had demanded a new ambassador to take back to Teixcalaan, they had refused to explain what had happened to the previous one. Mahit was sure there had been a great deal of politics on the Lsel Council as to what—and who—to send back, and with what demands for information. But this she knew was true: she herself had been one of the few Stationers both old enough for the job and young enough not to have already been brought into an imago-line—and one of the fewer still within that group who had any of the appropriate aptitudes or training for diplomacy. Of those, Mahit had been the best. Her scores on the Imperial Examinations in Teixcalaanli language and literature had approached those of an imperial citizen, and she'd been proud of that—spent the half year since the exams imagining that she would come to the City, sometime in her middle age, once she was established, and collect experiences—attending whatever salons were open to noncitizens that season—gathering up information for whoever she'd share her memory with after she died.

Now she'd get to the City, all right: more important than any Teixcalaanli examination, her scores on the imago-aptitudes had come up green, green, green for this match. Her imago would be Yskandr Aghavn, the previous Ambassador to Teixcalaan. Who was now somehow unsuitable to that empire—dead, or disgraced, or held captive if still alive. Mahit's instructions from her government included determining precisely what had gone so wrong with him—but she still had his imago. He—or, at least, the last version of him available to give her, fifteen years out of date—was the closest thing Lsel could provide to a native guide to the Teixcalaanli court. Not for the first time,

Mahit wondered whether or not there would be a Yskandr waiting for her in the flesh when she stepped outside. She was not sure which would be easier, having one—a disgraced ambassador? A competitor for her, but perhaps salvageable?—or not having one, which meant he had died without ever giving to any younger person what he had learned in his lifetime.

The imago-Yskandr in her head was hardly older than she was, which was both helpful in finding commonality and uncomfortable—most imagos were elders or victims of early-death accidents—but the last record of Yskandr's knowledge and memory had been taken when he'd last returned to Lsel on leave from his post in Teixcalaan, only five years after he had first gone down to the City. It had been another decade and a half since then.

So he was young, and so was she, and whatever advantage to integration that might have granted the two of them was belied by how short a time they'd been together. Two weeks between the courier's arrival and when Mahit learned that she'd be the next ambassador. Three more weeks for her and Yskandr to learn how to live together in the body that used to belong to her alone, under the supervision of the Station's psychotherapists. A long, slow time on *Ascension's Red Harvest*, traversing the sublight distances between the jumpgates that were scattered like jewels throughout Teixcalaanli space.

The seed-skiff peeled open like a ripe fruit. Mahit's harness retracted. Taking hold of her luggage in both hands, she stepped onto the gate, and thus into Teixcalaan itself.

The skyport gate had an airy utilitarianism constructed of wear-resistant carpet and clearly marked signage between glass-and-steel-paneled walls. Standing in the center of the gate's connecting tunnel, a precise halfway between the seed-skiff and the skyport proper, was a single Teixcalaanli imperial official in a perfectly cut cream suit. She was small: narrow at the shoulder and hip, much shorter than Mahit, and she wore her hair in a fishtail-braid queue of black that spilled over her left lapel. Her sleeves, wide like bells, shaded through flame-orange at the upper arm—<Information Ministry coloring,> Yskandr told Mahit—down to the deep red cuffs that were the privilege of the titled members of the court. Over her left eye she wore a cloudhook, a glass eyepiece full of the ceaseless obscuring flow of the imperial information network. Hers was sleekly decorative, much like the rest of her. Her large, dark eyes and thin cheekbones and mouth were more delicate than was fashionable on Teixcalaan, but by Mahit's Stationer standards she was *interesting,* if not quite pretty. She touched her fingers together politely in front of her chest and inclined her head to Mahit.

Yskandr lifted Mahit's own hands to make the same gesture— and Mahit dropped the two bags she'd been carrying on the floor with an embarrassing clatter. She was horrified. They hadn't slipped like that since the first week they'd been together.

Fuck, she thought, and heard at the same moment Yskandr say <Fuck.> The doubling wasn't reassuring.

The official's carefully neutral expression did not change. She said, "Ambassador, I am Three Seagrass, *asekreta* and patrician second-class. It is my honor to welcome you into the Jewel of the World. I will be serving as your cultural liaison at the command of His Imperial Majesty Six Direction." There was a long pause, and then the official gave a small sigh and went on: "Do you require some sort of assistance with your belongings?"

"Three Seagrass" was an old-fashioned Teixcalaanli name: the numeral half was low value, and the noun half was the name of a plant, even if it was a plant Mahit hadn't seen used in a name before. All of the noun parts of Teixcalaanli names were plants or tools or inanimate objects, but most of the plant ones were *flowers.* "Seagrass" was memorable. *Asekreta* meant she was not only Information Ministry, as her suit suggested, but a trained agent of rank, as well as holding the court title of patrician second-class: an aristocrat, but not a very important or rich one.

Mahit left her hands where Yskandr had put them, which was where they belonged no matter how angry she was at how they'd gotten there, and bowed over them. "Ambassador Mahit Dzmare of Lsel Station. At your service and that of His Majesty, may his reign be a radiant blaze upon the void." Since this was her first official contact with a member of the Teixcalaanli court, she used the imperial honorific she'd picked carefully in consultation with Yskandr and the Council government on Lsel: "radiant blaze" was the epithet for the Emperor Twelve Solar-Flare in *The Expansion History as Attributed to Pseudo-Thirteen River,* the oldest account of imperial presence in Stationer space. Using it now was thus a sign of both Mahit's erudition and her respect for Six Direction and his office; but "the void" carefully avoided any intimation of Teixcalaanli claim on parts of Stationer space which were *not,* in fact, space.

Whether Three Seagrass was aware of the implications of reference was somewhat difficult to tell. She waited patiently while Mahit scooped up her luggage again, and then said, "Keep a tight grip on those. You are urgently awaited in the Judiciary concerning the previous ambassador, and you may need to greet all sorts of people along the way."

Fine. Mahit wouldn't underestimate Three Seagrass's capability to be snide, *nor* her capability to be clever. She nodded, and when the other woman turned smartly and walked up the tunnel, she followed.

<Don't underestimate any of them,> Yskandr said. <A cultural liaison has been at court for half as long as you've been alive. She earned the post.>

Don't lecture me when you've just made me look like a flustered barbarian.

<Do you want me to apologize?>

Are you sorry?

Mahit could imagine his facial expression all too easily: arch, as calm as a Teixcalaanlitzlim, the lusher mouth she remembered from holographs of him dragging her own lips up and askew. <I wouldn't want you to feel like a barbarian. You'll get enough of that from them.>

He wasn't sorry. It was marginally possible that he was embarrassed, but if he was, he wasn't feeling it with her endocrine system.

———

Yskandr got her through the next half hour. Mahit couldn't even resent him for it. He behaved exactly like an imago ought to behave: a repository of instinctive and automatic skill that Mahit hadn't had time to acquire for herself. He knew when to duck through doorways built for Teixcalaanlitzlim instead of Stationers; when to avert her eyes from the rising glare of the City reflected in the glass of the elevator that crawled down the outside of the skyport; how high to step to climb into Three Seagrass's groundcar. He performed courtesy ritual like a native. After the incident with the luggage he was careful about actually moving Mahit's hands, but she let him have charge of how long she maintained eye contact and with whom, the degree to which her head was inclined in greeting, all the little ways of signaling that she was less of an alien, less of a barbarian, something that might belong in the City. Protective coloration. Going native without ever having to be a native. She could feel curious eyes slide off of her and fixate on the far more interesting court dress of Three Seagrass, and wondered how much Yskandr had loved the City, to be this good at being in it.

In the groundcar, Three Seagrass asked, "Have you been within the world long?"

Mahit needed to stop thinking in any language but Teixca-laanli. What Three Seagrass meant was a standard bit of politesse small talk, a *have you ever been to my country before,* and Mahit had heard it like an existential question.

"No," she said, "but I have read the classics since I was a very small child, and I have thought often of the City."

Three Seagrass seemed to approve of this answer. "I wouldn't want to bore you, Ambassador," she said, "but if you'd like a brief and verbal tour of what we're passing by, I'd be pleased to recite an appropriate poem." She flicked a control button on her side of the car, and the windows faded to transparency.

"I couldn't be bored," Mahit said honestly. Outside, the city was a blur of steel and pale stone, neon lights crawling up and down the glass walls of its skyscrapers. They were on one of the central ring roads, spiraling inward through municipal build-ings toward the palace itself. Properly, it was more of a city-within-a-city than a palace. By statistics, it had several hundred thousand inhabitants, all of whom were responsible in some minute fashion for the functioning of the Empire, from the gar-deners on up to Six Direction himself: each of them plugged into the information network that was guaranteed to imperial citizens, and every last one bathed in a constant flow of data that told them where to be, what to do, how the story of their day and week and epoch would go.

Three Seagrass had an excellent voice. She was reciting *The Buildings*—a seventeen-thousand-line poem which described the City's architecture. Mahit didn't know the precise version she'd picked to declaim, but that might have been Mahit's own fault. She had her own favorite narrative poems from the Teix-calaanli canon, and she'd memorized as many of them as she could in imitation of Teixcalaanli literati (and to pass the oral portions of the examinations), but *The Buildings* had always seemed too dull to bother with. It was different now, hearing

Three Seagrass recite it as they passed the structures being described. She was a fluent orator, and she had enough command of the metrical scheme to add amusing and relevant original detail where improvisation was appropriate. Mahit folded her hands across her lap and watched the poetry going by through the glass windows of the groundcar.

This was the City, then, the Jewel of the World, the heart of the Empire: a collapse between narrative and perception, Three Seagrass making adjustments on the fly to the canonical *Buildings* when some building had changed. After some time she realized that Yskandr was reciting along with Three Seagrass, a dim whisper in the back of her mind, and also that she found the whisper reassuring. *He* knew this poem, and thus she knew it too, if she needed to know it. That was what imago-lines were for, after all: making sure useful memory was preserved, generation to generation.

They traveled through forty-five minutes and two traffic snarls before Three Seagrass concluded her stanza and stopped the groundcar at the base of a needlelike pillar of a building, quite near the center of the palace grounds. <Judiciary complex,> Yskandr said.

Good sign or bad sign? Mahit asked him.

<It depends. I wonder what I did.>

Something illegal. Come on, Yskandr, give me a general sense of the possibilities here. What would you do to get yourself thrown in jail?

Mahit got the impression of Yskandr sighing at her, but also the queasy sensation of someone else's nervousness setting off her adrenal glands. <Mm. Sedition, mostly.>

She wished she could be sure he was joking.

Surrounding the pillar of the Judiciary was a perimeter of grey-uniformed guards, clustered more closely at the door: a security checkpoint. The guards carried long, slim dark grey sticks rather than the energy weapons that the Teixcalaanli legions favored. Mahit had seen a lot of the latter on *Ascension's Red Harvest,* but not these.

<Shocksticks,> Yskandr said. <Electricity-based crowd control—these were *not* here when I was last here. They're anti-riot gear, or at least they are in tabloid entertainments.>

You're fifteen years out of date, Mahit thought. *A lot might have changed—*

<This is the center of the palace. If they're worried about riots at the Judiciary, something hasn't *changed,* something is *wrong.* Now go find out what I did.>

Mahit wondered what had gone sufficiently wrong to create security theater at the door of the Judiciary, and if Yskandr had *helped* it go that wrong—felt prickles go up the back of her spine and down through her arms, the ulnar nerves crawling unpleasantly—and then had no time for more distressing reflection, as Three Seagrass was escorting her through. She offered up her thumbprints as well as Mahit's, and stood with her eyes politely averted as a Teixcalaanli security guard patted chastely at the pockets of Mahit's traveling jacket and her trousers. Her luggage was decorously placed in their custody, and she was promised that she could have it back on her way out.

Once the guard was done breaking all of Mahit's personal space taboos, she advised Mahit to avoid wandering off without escort, as her identity was neither recorded on cloudhook nor otherwise authorized to be present within the Judiciary. Mahit raised an inquiring eyebrow at Three Seagrass.

"There were questions of speed," Three Seagrass said, proceeding briskly through a multiplicity of irising doors into a cool, slate-floored interior, toward the elevator bank. "Your registration and permission to move about the palace complex will of course be taken care of as soon as is possible."

Mahit said, "I've been in transit more than a month, and there are questions of speed?"

"*We* have been waiting for *three* months, Ambassador, since we sent for a new representative from the Station."

<I must have done something quite spectacular,> Yskandr said. <Down below are secret courts and interrogation chambers, or so the palace rumors always went.>

The elevator chimed in fourths. "And one more hour matters, after three months?"

Three Seagrass gestured for Mahit to precede her into the elevator, which was a sort of answer, if not an informative one.

They descended.

Waiting for them below was a chamber that could have been a courtroom or an operating theater: blue-metal floor, and amphitheater-style benches arrayed around a high table on which lay some large object covered in a sheet. Floodlights. Three Teixcalaanli strangers, all broad-cheekboned and broad-shouldered, one in a red cassock, one dressed identically to Three Seagrass in the orange-and-cream of the Information Ministry, and one in a dark grey suit that reminded Mahit of nothing so much as the metal sheen of the shocksticks. They stood around the table, arguing in low, rapid voices, and blocked Mahit's view of whatever was lying on it.

"I still would like to make my own examination, for my Ministry, before he's returned," said the Information Ministry courtier, annoyed.

"There's not a single good reason to just turn him back over to them," the Teixcalaanlitzlim in red said, with some finality. "It won't do us any *good* and might spark an incident—"

Dark Grey Suit disagreed. "Contrary to the opinions of your Ministry, *ixplanatl*, I am entirely certain that any incident they could induce wouldn't be more trouble than an insect bite, and as easily soothed."

"Oh for fuck's sake, argue *later*," said the one from Information, "they're here."

The man in red turned toward them as they entered, as if he had been anticipating their arrival. The ceiling was a low dome. Mahit thought of a bubble of gas, trapped under the earth. Then she understood the shape on the table as a corpse.

It lay under a thin sheet drawn midway up its bare torso, hands resting on its chest, fingertips touching as if it was preparing to greet some afterlife. Its cheeks were sunken and its open eyes were filmed over with a hazy blue. The same color had infiltrated its lips and nailbeds. It looked like it had been dead a long time. Perhaps . . . three months.

As clearly as if he had been standing next to her, Mahit heard Yskandr say <I got old,> with wondering horror. She was shaking. Her heart raced, drowning out the sound of Three Seagrass introducing her. A dizzying rush, worse than falling toward the planet, panic out of nowhere. Not her panic: Yskandr's, her imago flooding her with her own stress hormones, enough adrenaline to taste metallic. The mouth of the corpse was slack, but she could see the smile lines at its corners, feel on her own mouth how Yskandr's muscles would have formed them over time.

"As you see, Ambassador Dzmare," said the man in red, whose name Mahit had completely failed to catch during the introductions, "a new ambassador was necessary. I apologize for preserving him in this fashion, but we did not want to disrespect any funereal processes which your people might prefer."

She came closer. The corpse stayed dead, stayed still and limp and empty. <Fuck,> Yskandr said, a fizz of nauseating static. Mahit was horribly, helplessly sure she was going to throw up. <Oh, fuck, I can't do this.>

Mahit thought (or Yskandr thought—she was having trouble keeping them apart, and this wasn't how the integration was supposed to go, she was never supposed to be lost inside his biochemical panic response hijacking her own endocrine system) about how the only place that Yskandr existed now was *inside her head.* She'd considered that he was dead, when Teixcalaan had demanded a new ambassador, thought about it intellectually, planned for it, and yet—here he was—a *corpse,* a hollow rotting shell, and she was panicking because her imago was panicking and an emotion-spike was the easiest way to fuck up an integration that wasn't finished, an emotion-spike would burn out all the tiny microcircuits in the machine in her mind and *oh fuck he was dead* and *oh fuck I am dead* and the *blur,* the nauseating blur of everything.

Yskandr, she tried, aiming for comfort and missing by a long distance.

<Get closer,> he told her, <I need to see. I'm not sure—>

He moved them before she could decide to do what he asked. It was like she'd blacked out for the space of time it took to approach the corpse, blinked and *was there,* and this was going so very, very awry, and she couldn't stop it—

"We burn our dead," she said, and didn't know who to thank for the fact that she'd said it in the right language.

"How interesting a custom," said the courtier in dark grey. Mahit thought he was from the Judiciary itself; this was likely to be his morgue, even if it was the man in red who was the mortician.

Mahit smiled at him, too wide for her face and too uncontrolled for Yskandr's, an expression that'd horrify any serene Teixcalaanlitzlim. "Afterward," she said, searching for the correct vocabulary, a spar to cling to through the roiling waves of adrenaline, "we eat the ashes as a sacred thing. His children and successors first. If he had any."

The courtier had the grace to blanch and the stubbornness to repeat himself. "How interesting a custom."

"What do you do with yours?" Mahit asked. She came nearer Yskandr's corpse, drifting. Her mouth seemed to be under her control for the moment, but her feet belonged to Yskandr. "Excuse my inquiry. I am, after all, not a citizen."

The man in red said, "Burial is common," as if it was a question he answered every day. "Do you wish to examine the body, Ambassador?"

"Is there some reason I should do so?" Mahit said, but she was already pulling down the sheet. Her fingers were sweating, slick on the fabric. Underneath, the corpse was naked, a fortyish man with all of his skin tinged that same blue at its most translucent points. An injectable preservative, all through him. The injection points were strikingly visible, holes surrounded by a halo of pale, swollen flesh—at the carotid, and in the ulnar veins of both arms. There was an extra injection site at the base of the corpse's right thumb, distorting the shape of the hand. She found herself staring at it, in another one of those blanked-out moments—she'd been looking at his face, and now she was looking at his wrist, as if the imago needed to see every place his former body had been altered. Even if Mahit had wanted to claim her rights as his successor to the dust of his flesh—and she wasn't sure she wanted to—she thought that it might be a very stupid idea to ingest whatever the man in red had filled him up with. Three months without rotting. She could taste bile in her throat, under the metallic endocrine cascade. Bodies should *decompose,* and be recycled.

But the Empire preserved everything, told the same stories over and over again; why not also preserve flesh instead of rendering it up for decent use?

She was touching the wrist, the imago tracing her fingertip over the injection site, and then further, into the palm, following the line of some scar. The flesh was rubbery, plasticky, too much give and not enough all at once—*her* Yskandr hadn't gotten that scar yet; her Yskandr wasn't *dead* yet—there was another one of those dizzying nauseous waves, the edges of her vision irising to fizz and sparks, and she thought again *We are going to blow out all the circuitry,* **stop it**—

<I can't,> Yskandr said again, an enormous negation inside her mind, an avulsion that felt like a spark gone to ground— and then he was *gone.*

Dead quiet. Not even the feeling of him watching through Mahit's eyes. She felt gravityless, full of endorphins she hadn't produced on purpose, and horribly alone. Her tongue was heavy. It tasted like aluminum.

Nothing like this had ever happened to her before.

"How did he die?" she asked, and was amazed that she sounded entirely normal, entirely unfazed; asked for the sake of continuing to *talk.* None of the Teixcalaanli knew about imagos, none of them would even be able to understand what just happened to her.

"He choked on the air," the man in red said, touching the corpse's neck with a practiced span of two fingers. "His throat closed. It was very unfortunate; but the physiologies of noncitizens are often so different from ours."

"He ate something he was *allergic* to?" Mahit asked. This seemed absurd. She was shock-numb, and apparently Yskandr had died of anaphylaxis, and if she wasn't careful she was going to have a hysterical laughing fit.

"At dinner with the Minister for Science Ten Pearl, no less," said the last courtier, the one from Information. This one looked like he'd climbed out of a classical Teixcalaanli painting: his features were unbelievably symmetrical: lush mouth, low forehead, perfectly hooked nose; eyes like deep brown pools. "You should have seen the newsfeeds afterward, Ambassador; it was quite the tabloid story."

"Twelve Azalea means no disrespect," said Three Seagrass from where she stood by the door. "The news went no farther than the palace complex. It would be inappropriate for the general population."

Mahit pulled the sheet back up to the corpse's chin. It didn't help. He was still *there*. "Was the story also inappropriate for the stations?" she asked. "The courier who asked for my service within the City was unnecessarily vague."

Three Seagrass shrugged, a minute shift of one shoulder. "Ambassador, while I am *asekreta,* not every *asekreta* is privy to the decisions of the Information Ministry as a whole."

"What would you like done with his body?" inquired the man in red. Mahit looked up at him; he was tall for a Teixcalaan-litzlim. His eyes, an unnervingly friendly green, were almost even with hers. She had no idea what to do with a corpse. She had never burnt anyone herself; she was too *young.* Her parents were both still living. And besides, what you did was you called the funeral manager and *they* handled it, preferably while someone you loved held your hand and cried with you over the mutual loss.

She had less idea what to do with this corpse. No one was going to cry over Yskandr, even her, and there weren't any funeral managers in Teixcalaanli space who would know where to begin.

She managed, "Nothing yet," and swallowed hard against the remains of the nausea. Her fingers felt electric, all prickle-shimmer where they had touched the dead man's skin. "I will of course make arrangements once I am better acquainted with the facilities available. Until then, well, he's not going to rot, is he?"

"Only very slowly," the man in red said.

"Sir—" Mahit looked to Three Seagrass for help; she was a cultural liaison so she could damn well *liaise*—

"*Ixplanatl* Four Lever," Three Seagrass said obligingly. "Of the Science Ministry."

"Four Lever," Mahit went on, dropping the man's title—it meant "scientist," in a very general sense, scientist-with-credentials—entirely on purpose, "when will the rot be noticeable? Another two months, perhaps?"

Four Lever smiled enough to show off a sliver of teeth. "Two years, Ambassador."

"Excellent," Mahit said. "That will be plenty of time."

Four Lever bowed over the triangular press of his fingertips, as if she'd given him an order. Mahit suspected she was being indulged. She'd take it. She had to. She needed space enough to think and she wasn't going to get it here, in the bowels of the Judiciary with three courtiers and a *ixplanatl* morgue attendant all waiting for her to make some irrevocable error and end up like Yskandr had.

Betrayed by his own physiology. After twenty years of living in the City, eating what the Teixcalaanlitzlim ate. Did she believe it?

Yskandr, she thought at the blank place where the imago ought to be, *what did you get us into before you died?*

He didn't answer. Reaching for the blank spot made her feel like she was falling even though she knew her feet were steady on the floor.

"I would like," said Mahit to Three Seagrass, slow and even and in the correct language, trying to hide the vertigo and the fear, "to be registered as the legal Ambassador from the stations to Teixcalaan, and also to see to my luggage." She wanted to get *out* of here. As fast as possible.

"Naturally, Ambassador," said Three Seagrass. "*Ixplanatl.* Twelve Azalea. Twenty-Nine Infograph. As ever, your company is a pleasure."

"As is yours, Three Seagrass," said Twelve Azalea. "Enjoy the Ambassador."

Three Seagrass did that one-shoulder shrug again, as if nothing anyone had said could affect an *asekreta* of the court in a fashion that mattered. Mahit liked her, abruptly, and was aware that the liking was more of a desperate grasp at an ally than anything else. She was so *alone,* without the imago talking to her. Surely he'd come back in a moment. Once the shock was over. Once the emotion-spike had faded. It was fine. She was fine. She wasn't even dizzy anymore.

"Shall we, then?" she said.

CHAPTER
TWO

**urgently direct your attention! / novelty and importance
characterize what comes next / IMMEDIATELY
on Channel Eight!**

Tonight, Seven Chrysoprase and Four Sycamore bring you a report
from Odile-1 in the Odile System, where the Twenty-Sixth Legion
under sub-yaotlek Three Sumac are preparing to break orbit
now that the insurrection in Odile-1's capital city has been
quelled—in a moment we will have Four Sycamore, on site in the
capital's central square, with an interview with the newly reinstated planetary governor Nine Shuttle—trade through the Odile
Gate is expected to return to normal levels within the next two
weeks . . .

> —Channel Eight! nightly newscast, as broadcast on the
> City's internal cloudhook network, 245th day, 3rd year in
> the 11th indiction of the Emperor of all Teixcalaan Six
> Direction

*   *   *

JUMPGATE APPROACH PROTOCOL LIST, PAGE TWO
OF TWO

> . . . reduce speed to 1/128th of craft's maximum sublight, to
> enable evasive maneuvering if the jumpgate is simultaneously
> being accessed by non-Stationer ships from the far side.

17. Signal impending jump by local radio broadcast
18. Signal impending jump to crew and passengers

19. At 1/128th speed, approach area of greatest visual dis-
tortion . . .
    —Lsel Station pilot training manual, page 235

THE ambassadorial suite was as full of Yskandr as Mahit felt
empty of him: like she had been turned inside out, surrounded
by the *things* of her imago rather than suffused with his memory. The suite had been aired out before Mahit arrived—or at
least she hoped it had, and assumed it had by virtue of the open
windows and the antiseptic scent of cleaning fluid that the air
coming in through those windows and blowing their draperies
back hadn't managed to dispel—but it was nevertheless very
much a place someone had *lived in,* and for a long time.

Yskandr-the-man had liked the color blue, and expensive-
looking furniture in some dark sheeny metal. The industrial
lines of the workdesk and low couch would've made anyone
who grew up on a station or a ship, unplaneted, feel right at
home, but the floor was covered in silky deep-piled rugs run
through with patterns. Mahit thought—gleeful fleeting desire—
of going barefoot at home for the sheer physical pleasure of it,
and thought again about how imago-successors matched even
on *aesthetic* preferences with their predecessors. Yskandr had
liked being barefoot on woven fiber; apparently she did, too, despite having never before had the opportunity.

Beyond the suite's inner door was a sleeping chamber.
Yskandr had hung a metalwork mosaic of the Teixcalaanli star-
chart for Stationer space on the ceiling over his bed like an
advertisement. *Sleep here and you'll be sleeping with the resources
of this entire sector!*

It was such a beautiful piece of work that it almost didn't seem
gauche. Almost.

On the bedside table was a small pile of codex-books and

plastic infofilm sheets, neatly squared. Mahit doubted Yskandr was the type to line up the edges of his bedtime reading material, as *she* certainly wasn't. It would be easier if he were here to *ask,* and what was she supposed to do if he didn't come back? If that horrible spike of emotion had burnt out the connections between her imago-machine and her brainstem, before she and Yskandr had ever had a chance to fully become one person? If they'd had longer, the machine wouldn't *matter*—she'd be Yskandr, or Yskandr would be her, or they'd be a new, more complete thing called Mahit Dzmare which knew what Yskandr Aghavn had known, intimately, muscle memory and compiled skill and instinct and his voice and hers in a blend— how it should be, a new link in the imago-line. But now? What was she supposed to do? Write home for repair instructions? *Go* home, and leave all this work undone, including understanding why he'd died? At least she wasn't going to have language problems without his help—she dreamed in Teixcalaanli half the time; had dreamed *of* the City often enough—but reaching for the place where she'd felt the weight of him since he'd been joined to her made her feel that dizzying, horrible *falling* sensation again. She sat down on the edge of the bed and looked at the squared-off edges of the codexes until she was sure she wasn't going to faint. Whoever had cleaned the rooms had arranged them, which implied that anything obviously incriminating had been removed.

She was already thinking about *incriminating.*

Of course she was thinking *incriminating.* Assume deception, she told herself. Assume foul play and double meanings. *Choked on the air.* Allergies, or breathing something too rarefied. Politics, always. This was the *City.* Every person here had a cloudhook whispering a story into their eyes. Intrigue and triple-crosses and she'd spent her childhood reading those same stories and telling them herself—oh pale imitation, talking in perfect meter to the blank dumb metal of station walls, and hadn't that made her a popular and cheerful childhood companion—not that it mattered.

Think like a Teixcalaanlitzlim.

Incriminating information would have been removed or made innocuous.

Or Yskandr had hidden it, if he'd known what was about to happen to him, or suspected. If he was smart. (The imago was smart; but the imago was out of *date*. A man might change in fifteen years.)

Mahit wondered what she'd be like, if she lived that long in this place. Especially *without* the imago—more important than *out of date,* the imago was *gone.* Unless he came back (of course he'd come back, this was a minor flicker, an *error,* she'd wake up tomorrow and he'd be here) she was going to have to think about *sabotage* right along with *incriminating.* Something had gone wrong with her imago-machine—either sabotage or mechanical failure. Or *personal failure to integrate.* It could be her own fault. Her own psychology, rejecting his. She shuddered. Her hands still felt prickly and strange.

"Your luggage is processed and yours again," said Three Seagrass, coming through the irised door of Yskandr's bedroom. Mahit sat up very straight and tried to look like she was absolutely not having a possible neurological incident. "Not a single bit of contraband. You are a very dull barbarian so far."

"Were you expecting excitement?" Mahit asked.

"You're my very first barbarian," Three Seagrass said. "I am expecting everything."

"Surely you've met noncitizens before. This is the Jewel of the World."

"Meeting is not the same as liaising-for. You're *my* noncitizen, Ambassador. I open doors for you."

The verb form she used was just archaic enough to be

idiomatic. Mahit risked sounding less fluent than she hoped she was and said, "Door-opening seems beneath the responsibilities I'd expect of a patrician second-class."

Three Seagrass's smile was sharper than most Teixcalaanli expressions; it reached her eyes. "You don't have a cloudhook. You *can't* open some doors, Ambassador. The City doesn't know you're real. Besides, without me, how will you decrypt your mail?"

Mahit raised an eyebrow. "My mail is encrypted?"

"And three months late in being answered."

"That," said Mahit, standing up and walking out of the bedroom—*this* door knew her, at least—"is Ambassador Yskandr Aghavn's mail, not mine."

Three Seagrass trailed behind her. "There isn't a difference. Ambassador Dzmare, Ambassador Aghavn," she said, tilting one hand back and forth. "It's *the Ambassador's* mail."

There was less of a difference than even Three Seagrass knew. Or would be, if the imago would ever come back. Mahit was, she realized, *pissed off* at him, besides being worried about mechanical failure. All he'd done was panic at seeing himself dead, run her through an adrenaline crisis, and give her the strangest headache of her life, and now she was alone with all of the unanswered mail his fifteen-years-more-Teixcalaanli self had abandoned via being almost-certainly-murdered, and a cultural liaison with a sense of humor.

"And it's encrypted."

"Of course. It wouldn't be very respectful to not encrypt an ambassador's mail." Three Seagrass retrieved a bowl brimming with infofiche sticks, little rectangles of wood or metal or plastic surrounding circuitry, each one elaborately decorated with its sender's personal iconography. She fished out a fistful, holding them between her fingers like her knuckles had sprouted claws. "What would you like to start with?"

"If the mail is addressed to me, I ought to read it myself," said Mahit.

"Legally, I'm an absolute equivalent," Three Seagrass said, pleasantly enough.

Pleasantness wasn't sufficient. Just because Mahit wanted an ally—wanted Three Seagrass to be helpful and useful and not an immediate threat, considering the woman had to live in the next room and *open doors* for however long she'd been assigned to mind Mahit, considering that Mahit was beginning to realize how trapped she was going to be in the City, considering that she was *not real* to that City's panopticon eyes—just because Mahit *wanted* wasn't enough to make Three Seagrass an actual extension of Mahit's will, no matter what she said she was.

"Perhaps by Teixcalaanli law," Mahit said. "By Stationer law, you are nothing of the kind."

"Ambassador, I hope you aren't assuming I'm not trustworthy enough to guide you through the court."

Mahit shrugged, spreading her hands wide. "What happened to my predecessor's cultural liaison?" she asked.

If Three Seagrass was disturbed by the question, the disturbance didn't reach her face. Impassive, she said, "He was reassigned after his two years of service were up. I believe he is no longer in the palace complex at all."

"What was his name?" Mahit asked. If Yskandr was with her she would have known, those two years of service would have been his first two years in the City, well within the five years that the imago remembered.

"Fifteen Engine, I think," said Three Seagrass, easily enough—and Mahit had to clutch at the edge of Yskandr's desk, hang on to it, flooded with a complex of emotion out of nowhere: fondness and frustration, the echo of a face wearing a cloudhook set in a bronze frame that filled up his entire left eye socket from cheekbone to browbone. Fifteen Engine, as Yskandr the imago remembered him. Memory-flash, memory-*swarm*, and Mahit reached for the imago, thought *Yskandr?* And got nothing.

Three Seagrass was staring at her. She wondered what she looked like. Pale, probably, and distracted.

"I would like to speak to him. Fifteen Engine."

"I assure you," said Three Seagrass, "I have extensive experience and really unusually excellent scores on all the necessary aptitudes for working with noncitizens. I'm sure we'll be fine."

"*Asekreta—*"

"Please call me Three Seagrass, Ambassador. I'm *your* liaison."

"Three Seagrass," said Mahit, trying very hard not to raise her voice, "I would like to ask *your* predecessor about how *my* predecessor conducted his business here, and perhaps also about the circumstances of his extremely untimely, and based on the quantity of this mail, inconvenient death."

"Ah," said Three Seagrass.

"Yes."

"His death was quite, as you say, inconvenient, but entirely accidental."

"I'm sure, but he was my *predecessor,*" Mahit said, knowing that if Three Seagrass was as Teixcalaanli as she seemed, a request to know the intimate details of the person who had held one's own position in society would be culturally compelling, like asking to know about a prospective imago would be on Lsel Station. "And I would like to speak to someone who knew him as well as we are going to get to know one another." She tried to remember the muscle memory of the precise degree to which Yskandr had widened her eyes in a Teixcalaanli-style smile, and imitated it by feel.

"Ambassador, I have every sympathy with your current— predicament," said Three Seagrass, "and I'll have a message sent to Fifteen Engine, wherever he might be now, *along with the rest of the answered mail.*"

". . . which I can't answer myself, because it is encrypted."

"Yes! But I can decrypt nearly any of the standard forms, and most of the nonstandard ones."

"You still haven't explained why my mail is encrypted in a fashion *I* can't decrypt."

"Well," said Three Seagrass, "I don't at all mean to be disparaging. I'm sure that on your station you are an extremely educated person. But in the City, encryption is usually based in poetic cipher, and we certainly don't expect noncitizens to have to learn that. And an ambassador's mail is encrypted for the sake of showing off that an ambassador is an intelligent person, well-acquainted with courts and court poetry—it's customary. It's not a real cipher, it's a game."

"We do have poetry out on Lsel, you know."

"I know," said Three Seagrass, with such sympathy that Mahit wanted to shake her, "but here, look at this one." She held up a scarlet lacquered infofiche stick, its two parts held closed with a round gold wax seal embossed with the stylized image of the City—the Teixcalaanli imperial symbol. "It's definitely for you, it's dated today." She cracked the seal and the infofiche spilled into the air between them, a stream of holographic word-shapes in Teixcalaanli script that Mahit felt like she *ought* to be able to understand. She'd been reading imperial literature since she was a child.

Three Seagrass touched her cloudhook and said, "I bet you could decrypt this kind by hand, actually—do you know political verse?"

"Fifteen-syllable iambic couplets with a caesura between syllable eight and syllable nine," said Mahit, realizing only as she spoke that she sounded more like a candidate in an oral exam than a knowledgeable subject of Teixcalaan, but having no idea how to stop sounding so. "It's easy."

"Yes! So, the cipher for most communication at court is a

straight transposition, with the opening four couplets of whoever's written the best encomiastic poem—that's praise poetry, which I'm sure you do know if you can count syllables and caesuras—from last season. It's been Two Calendar's 'Reclamation Song' for *months* now. I can get you a copy, if you *really* want to decrypt your own mail."

"I would certainly like to hear what the City thinks is the best encomiastic poetry going," Mahit said.

Three Seagrass snorted. "You're *great*. You could have been *born* here, with that attitude."

Mahit did not feel complimented. "What does it say?" she asked.

Three Seagrass narrowed her eyes—her pupils tracked to the left and up in tiny jerks, micromuscular instructions to her cloudhook—and peered intently at the infofiche. "Formal invitation to the Emperor's own salon and oration contest, hosted within a presentational diplomatic banquet, in three days. I'll assume you want to go?"

"Why wouldn't I?"

"Well, if you want to insult all your predecessor's contacts and establish that Lsel Station is hostile to imperial interests, not coming to dinner is a wonderful start."

Mahit leaned in quite close, close enough that she could feel the warm pulse of Three Seagrass's breath on her face, and smiled with all her teeth, as barbaric as possible. Mahit watched her try to stay still and not flinch back; spotted the moment when she succeeded, rationalized what was happening.

"Three Seagrass," Mahit said then, "how about we assume that I'm not an idiot."

"We could do that," Three Seagrass said. "Do your people invade personal space as a reprimand on a regular basis?"

"When necessary," Mahit said. "And in exchange I will

assume you're not involved in an obvious attempt at diplomatic sabotage."

"That seems like a fair trade."

"So I'm accepting His Imperial Majesty's gracious invitation. Send the message and I'll sign it. And then we need to get through the rest of this backlog of infofiche."

The backlog took the rest of the afternoon and stretched on into the evening. Most of it was the usual sort of communication for a minor but still politically significant ambassadorial office—information requests from the chancellery and from universities concerning the habits, economics, and tourist opportunities available at Lsel, protocol queries. Repatriation requests from Stationers who had been living in Teixcalaanli space and wanted to stop—Mahit signed those—and a smaller batch of entrance queries, which she approved and sent onward to one of the imperial offices concerned with "barbarian entry visas." An unexpectedly high number of half-authorized safe-passage-through-Stationer-space visas for Teixcalaanli military transport—all of them stamped with Yskandr's personal seal, but few of them actually *signed* by him. The half-authorized copies didn't mean anything: they weren't done. It was as if Yskandr had been interrupted in the process of officially allowing half a legion's worth of Teixcalaanli ships into Lsel territory. Mahit spared a moment to wonder at the sheer *number* of them, and why they hadn't all been sealed and signed at the same time, and set them aside for a quieter moment of contemplation. *She* wasn't prepared to send Teixcalaanli warships through her Station's sector without doing *some* research as to why they wanted to move in such quantity, no matter what Yskandr had been doing when he died.

None of the requests were for *Ascension's Red Harvest*. Someone other than Yskandr must have approved *that* ship's journey to pick her up. But then Yskandr had already been dead by the time that request needed to be processed. Mahit felt mildly ill. *Someone* had sent that ship—she should find out who—

But Three Seagrass handed her the next infofiche stick, which turned out to be a thoroughly distracting mess concerning import fees on a shipping manifest that would have taken half an hour to sort out had it been answered when it was originally asked, back when Yskandr had been alive. It took nearly three times that long for Mahit to solve, considering one of the parties had left the planet—that was the Stationer—and another had married into citizenship and changed his name during the lag time. Mahit made Three Seagrass hunt down the new-made Teixcalaanlitzlim under his new name and issue him a formal summons to the Judicial Department of Interstellar Trade Licensing.

"Just make sure he shows up to pay the import fees on the cargo he bought from one of *my Station's citizens,* whatever his name is," Mahit told her.

The name the man had chosen, it turned out, was Thirty-Six All-Terrain Tundra Vehicle, a revelation that produced in both Mahit and Three Seagrass a kind of stunned silence.

"No one would actually name a child that," Three Seagrass complained after a moment. "He has no taste. Even if his parent or his crèche was from a low-temperature planet with a lot of tundra in need of all-terrain vehicles."

Mahit wrinkled her eyebrows in sudden puzzlement, remembering—vividly—the part of her early language training on Lsel when her entire class had been encouraged to make up Teixcalaanli names to call themselves while they were learning to speak. She'd picked Nine Orchid, because the heroine of her then-favorite Teixcalaanli novel, about the adventures of the crèchemate of the future Emperor Twelve Solar-Flare, had been called *Five* Orchid. It had felt very Teixcalaanli, picking a name based on one's favorite book. She'd thought the names the other children had chosen were *much* less successful, at the time, and had felt very superior. Now, in the center of Teixcalaanli space, the entire episode seemed not only appropriative but absurd. Nevertheless, she asked Three Seagrass, "Just how *do* you Teixcalaanlitzlim name yourselves?"

"Numbers are for luck, or the qualities you want your child to have, or fashion. 'Three' is perennially popular, all the low numbers are; Threes are supposed to be stable and innovative, like a triangle. Doesn't fall over, can reach pinnacles of thought, that sort of thing. This person picking 'Thirty-Six' is just trying to look new-money City-dweller, it's a little silly but not that bad. The bad part is 'All-Terrain Tundra Vehicle.' I mean. Blood and *sunlight,* it's technically permissible, that's an inanimate object or a piece of architecture, but it's so . . . *nice* names are plants and flowers and natural phenomena. And not so many syllables."

This was the most animated Mahit had seen Three Seagrass be so far, and it was really making it difficult for Mahit not to like her. She was funny. Thirty-Six All-Terrain Tundra Vehicle was funnier.

"When I was learning the language," she said, deciding all at once to share, to offer something back for this little bit of cultural exchange—if they were going to work together they should work together—"we had to pretend to have Teixcalaanli-style names, and one of my classmates—the kind of person who scores perfectly on exams and has a terrible accent—called himself *2e Asteroid.* The irrational number. He thought he was being clever."

Three Seagrass contemplated this, and then snickered. "He was," she said. "That's *hilarious.*"

"Really?"

"*Enormously.* It's like turning your whole persona into a self-deprecating joke. I'd buy a novel written by a *Two-E Asteroid,* it'd probably be satire."

Mahit laughed. "The person in question wasn't subtle enough for satire," she said. "He was a dreadful classmate."

"He sounds it," Three Seagrass agreed, "but he's *accidentally* subtle, which is even better." And then she handed over the next infofiche stick, and began to decrypt the next problem Mahit needed to solve.

The whole afternoon was—work. Work Mahit was good at, work she had been trained to do, even if the forms of it were obscure and Teixcalaanli and required Three Seagrass's decryption skills. At sunset Three Seagrass ordered them both small bowls of a spiced meat in dumpling wrappers, covered in a creamy semi-fermented sauce laced with red oil, assuring Mahit that it was extremely unlikely that she would be allergic to anything in the meal.

"It's *ixhui,*" she explained. "We feed it to babies!"

"If I die, no one will answer the mail for *three more months,* and then where will you be," Mahit said, stabbing a dumpling with the two-pronged fork the meal had come with. It burst when she bit into it, tangy and warm. The red oil was finely spiced, just hot enough to linger on her tongue and make her wonder about neurotoxic effects before it faded to pleasantness. She was abruptly starving. She hadn't eaten since the cruiser.

It was somewhat gratifying to see Three Seagrass devour her own bowl of *ixhui* with a similar level of enthusiasm. Mahit waved the fork at her. "This is too good for babies," she said.

Three Seagrass widened her eyes in a Teixcalaanli version of a grin. "Work food. Anything that's too delicious to eat slow."

"And then you get back to the job faster?"

"You're getting the idea."

Mahit tilted her head to the side. "You're the sort of person who works all the time, aren't you."

"It's in the job description, Ambassador."

"Call me Mahit, please," Mahit said, "and surely there are cultural liaisons less helpful."

Three Seagrass nearly looked *pleased*. "Oh, lots. But cultural liaison's my assignment. *Asekreta*'s the job."

Intelligence, protocol, secrets—and oratory. If all the literature about the City Mahit had ever read hadn't lied to her. "And that job is?"

"Politics," said Three Seagrass.

A close enough correspondence to the literature. "Why don't you tell me about these military transport visas, then?" Mahit started, just as the door to the suite chimed in a chord that made Mahit wince but seemed not to strike Three Seagrass as lacking any euphony.

Three Seagrass went to the door and punched in a code on the wall-keypad next to it. Mahit watched her fingers and tried to internalize as much of the sequence as possible. Surely she would be able to operate the door codes to her own suite. (Unless she was more of a prisoner than she thought. How narrow *were* the City's definitions of real people who could move through it? She wished she could ask Yskandr.) The wall-keypad, satisfied, projected an image of the face of the person waiting outside, his name and string of titles floating above his head in blocky gold-limned glyphs. Young, broad-cheeked, bronze skin, a thick dark hairline over the short forehead all the imperial art seemed to prefer. Mahit recognized him from the mortuary viewing hall. Twelve Azalea, Indistinguishable Courtier Number Three, except for how looking at him gave Mahit the impression of being in the presence of some other culture's impeccably observed standard of masculine beauty. She felt a little peculiar about her lack of response. He was like an art object. *Twelve*

Azalea, patrician first-class, Three Seagrass had said, which meant she knew him by name at least, and possibly by something closer to reputation.

"I haven't any idea what *he* wants," Three Seagrass said, which did suggest that reputation was somewhat of a factor.

Mahit said, "Let him in."

Three Seagrass pressed her thumb to the wall-keypad firmly (what if it was *fingerprint-locked*? But surely the Teixcalaanli wouldn't use technology that primitive) and the door admitted Twelve Azalea in a sweep of orange sleeves and cream lapels. Mahit braced herself for the full sequence of greeting protocols without any help from Yskandr (she was supposed to not have to *worry* about these things), but had only begun to introduce herself when Twelve Azalea said, "I came to your suite, we really don't have to bother," brushed past Three Seagrass, leaving an affectionate kiss on her temple and a look of profound annoyance on her face, and sat down on the divan.

"Ambassador Dzmare," he said, "welcome to the Jewel of the World. A pleasure."

Three Seagrass settled next to him, wide-eyed, the corners of her mouth visibly tilted up. "I thought we weren't doing formalities, Petal," she said.

"Lacking formalities hasn't robbed me of being polite, Reed," Twelve Azalea said, and then turned a large, un-Teixcalaanli smile on Mahit. It made him appear slightly unhinged. "I hope she hasn't been too rude to you, Ambassador."

"Petal, must you," Three Seagrass said.

They had pet names for one another. It was . . . cute, and simultaneously hilarious and embarrassing. "Not rude at all," Mahit said, earning her a theatrically grateful look from Three Seagrass. "Welcome to the diplomatic territory of Lsel Station. How might I help you, other than letting you renew your acquaintance with my liaison?"

Twelve Azalea took on an expression of concern, which Mahit suspected was a thin veil over a more unsavory—and more honest—excited interest. It was inconvenient in the utmost that every single Teixcalaanlitzlim was going to assume she was as astute as an airlock door, recognizing only the surface images of people: uniforms, and expressions of concern. She wondered how long it would take before anyone at all would take her seriously.

"I have some worrisome information," said Twelve Azalea, "concerning the corpse of your predecessor."

Well. Perhaps *seriously* began now. (And perhaps she'd been right to immediately assume Yskandr could not have died by accident; it wasn't *like* him. And it wasn't like the City, to be so straightforward.)

"Is there a problem with his body?"

"Possibly?" said Twelve Azalea, gesturing as if to suggest that there was certainly a problem and it was a matter of determining its exact nature.

"As if you'd get involved in my business for just *possibly*, Petal," Three Seagrass said.

"I would suggest that the body of my predecessor is *my* business," Mahit said.

"We covered this, Mahit," Three Seagrass said briskly. "Legal equivalency—"

"But not moral or ethical equivalency," said Mahit, "especially involving a Lsel citizen, as my predecessor certainly was. What is the problem?"

"After *ixplanatl* Four Lever left the operating theater I stayed a little while with the corpse, and availed myself of the theater's imaging equipment," Twelve Azalea said. "My current assignment within the Information Ministry—I have been working with noncitizens on their medical and accessibility needs while they are visiting us here—has made me quite curious about the physiologies of noncitizens—some are quite different from human people! Not that I'm implying Lsel Station isn't human, Ambassador, nothing of the kind. But I am insatiably curious, you can ask Reed, she's known me since we were cadet *asekretim* together."

"Insatiably curious and often in large amounts of trouble, especially if it involves interesting forensics or peculiar medical practices," Three Seagrass said. Mahit could see the lines of tension in her jaw, the sharpening angle of her mouth. "Get to the point. Did Two Rosewood send you to check up on me?"

"As if I'd run errands, Reed, even for the Minister for Information. The *point* is that I stayed behind and examined the corpse of the Ambassador's predecessor. And that corpse is not entirely organic."

"What?" said Three Seagrass, at the same time as Mahit found herself struggling to keep her mouth shut around a Stationer expletive.

"How so?" she asked. Perhaps Yskandr had replaced a failing hip joint. That would be innocuous and explicable, and more easily noticeable than the implant nestled at the base of his skull that had first given him his *own* imago and then had recorded an imprint of his knowledge and self and memory—the imago-imprint, which was meant to be passed on down the line.

"His brain is full of metal," Twelve Azalea said, denying her even that brief moment of hope.

"Shrapnel?" Three Seagrass inquired.

"There were no wounds. Trust me, *wounds* would have been noticed by the morgue attendant. A full-body scan on the imager is much more complete. I can't think why it hadn't been done previously—perhaps it was just so obvious that the Ambassador had died of anaphylaxis—"

"I am interested in your immediate assumption that shrapnel is a possibility," said Mahit quickly, trying to steer the conversation away from its most dangerous aspects. It would help if she knew what, if anything, Yskandr had exposed about the imago process—but she couldn't even ask her version of him, and how was that version to know what his . . . continuation? His continuation, that would do—what he had done in the time which had elapsed between them?

"The City is occasionally hostile," said Three Seagrass.

"There are accidents," added Twelve Azalea. "More lately. A person mis-operates their cloudhook, the City overreacts . . ."

"It isn't a problem you'll ever need to deal with," Three Seagrass said, with a blithe reassurance that Mahit did not believe at all.

"Did my predecessor have a cloudhook?" she asked.

"I have no idea," said Three Seagrass. "He'd have to have been granted permission to use one from His Majesty, Six Direction, himself. Noncitizens don't have them—it's a *right*, having a connection to the City; it comes with being Teixcalaanli."

It came with being Teixcalaanli, and having one *opened doors,* and also, apparently, brought a person into a certain sphere of heightened risk. Mahit wondered just how well the cloudhooks tracked Teixcalaanli citizens as they moved around, and who exactly kept track of that information.

"What the former Ambassador has got, cloudhook or not," Twelve Azalea interrupted, "is a very large quantity of mysterious metal in his brainstem, and I thought perhaps you, Ambassador, would like to know, before someone tries to install some in yours."

"Cheerful as always, Petal."

"Who else knows about this?" Mahit asked.

Twelve Azalea said, "I haven't told anyone," and folded his hands demurely in the long sleeves of his jacket. Mahit could hear the "yet" implicit in that statement, and wondered what this person wanted from her.

"Why did you tell *me*? The Ambassador might have had all sorts of implants—an epileptic pacemaker, for instance—those are common, if epilepsy develops late in life," she said, deploying the standard lie about an imago-machine to someone who wasn't from Lsel. "I assume you have them here in a civilization as great as Teixcalaan. You could have looked up the Ambassador's medical records and found out, without going to all this trouble."

"Would you believe me if I said I wanted to see what you'd do? Your predecessor was—mm. Quite a political man, for an ambassador. I am curious to see if all Lsel people are."

"I'm not Yskandr," Mahit said, and felt, as she said it, acutely ashamed—she should have been *more* Yskandr. If they'd had time to integrate—if he hadn't disappeared inside her head. "'Political' varies. Does the *ixplanatl* know, you think?"

Twelve Azalea smiled enough to show his teeth. "He didn't mention it to you. Or to me. But he is a *ixplanatl* of the Medical College of the Science Ministry—who is to say what he thinks is important?"

"I want," said Mahit, standing up, "to see this for myself."

Twelve Azalea looked up at her, delighted. "Oh. You *are* political after all."

CHAPTER
THREE

Within each cell is a bloom of chemical fire
[DECEASED'S NAME] committed to the [earth/sun]
shall burst into a thousand flowers, as many as their breaths in life
and we shall recall their name
their name and the name of their ancestor(s)
and in those names the people gathered here
let blood bloom also from their palms, and cast
this chemical fire as well into the [earth/sun] . . .

> —Teixcalaanli standard funeral oration (partial), modeled
> on the Eulogy for the *ezuazuacat* Two Amaranth, earliest
> attested date second indiction of the Emperor of All
> Teixcalaan Twelve Solar-Flare

* * *

[static]—repeat, lost all attitudinal control—I'm tumbling—
unknown energy weapon, I have fire in the cockpit [garbled] [gar-
bled] [expletive] black—black ships, they're fast, they're holes in
the [expletive] void—no stars—there's [garbled] can't—[expletive]
more of them [sound of scream for 0.5 seconds followed by
roaring sound, presumed explosive decompression, for 1.8 seconds before loss of signal]

> —last transmission of Lsel pilot Aragh Chtel, on
> reconnaissance at sector-edge, 242.3.11 (Teixcalaanli
> reckoning, reign of Six Direction)

THIS time, Mahit approached the Judiciary complex on foot, Three Seagrass and Twelve Azalea walking in an ever-shifting pattern around her. She felt like a hostage, or someone who was worried about political assassination, both of which were too close to accurate for her to be particularly sanguine. Besides, she was on her way to break into a morgue. Or help someone with legitimate access to the morgue bring people without that access inside. Either way. She was being *political*.

She wished she had better instructions from the Stationer Council as to just *how* she should be political. The majority of her instructions, after *find out what happened to Yskandr Aghavn*, were on the order of *do a good job, advocate for our citizens, try to keep the Teixcalaanli from annexing us if the subject arises*. She'd gotten the impression that about half the Council—particularly Aknel Amnardbat, the Councilor for Heritage, which tended to take diplomacy and cultural preservation within its purview— had been hoping she'd like Teixcalaanli culture just enough to enjoy her assignment and *dislike* it sufficiently to discourage further cultural interpenetration into Stationer art and litera- ture. The other half of the Council, led by Councilor Tarats for the Miners and Councilor Onchu for the Pilots (what Mahit thought of as the practical half of Lsel's six-person governing board, and so much for Aknel Amnardbat's hopes for her, really) had harped on *keep the Empire from annexing us and also continue to make sure we are the prime source of molybdenum, tungsten, and osmium—not to mention information and travel access to the An- hamemat Gate*. Was "my predecessor has been murdered and I suspect I am involving myself in an under-table investigation in order to protect Stationer technology" a case of "try to keep the Teixcalaanli from annexing us"? Yskandr would have known. Or at least have had a strident opinion.

The part of the City which contained the imperial government was enormous and old, shaped like a six-pointed star: sectors for East, West, North, and South, and two more: Sky, extending out between North and East, and Earth, pointing out from the middle of South and West. Each sector was composed of needle-sharp towers jammed full of archives and offices, tied together by multilevel bridges and archways. Stacked courtyards hung in midair between the more populated towers, their floors translucent or inset with sandstone and gold. At the center of each was a hydroponic garden, with photosynthesizing plant life floating in standing water. The unbelievable luxuries of a planet. The flowers in the hydroponic gardens seemed to be color-coded; as they moved closer to the Judiciary, their petals shaded redder and redder, until the center of each courtyard looked like a pool of iridescent blood, and Mahit caught sight of the building that had been her first destination, a practically unthinkable number of hours earlier that morning.

Twelve Azalea brushed a burnished green-metal plate next to the door with his index finger, tracing a sweeping figure that Mahit thought might have been a calligraphic signature—she caught the glyph for "flower" hidden in the middle of it, and his name written out would have "flower" along with one of the glyphs for "twelve" and some adjustment for the *type* of flower. The doors to the Judiciary hissed open. When Three Seagrass raised her hand to touch the plate too, Twelve Azalea caught her around the wrist.

"Just come inside," he said under his breath, shooing them both through and letting the doors seal shut behind them. "You'd think you'd never snuck in anywhere before . . ."

"We have legal access," Three Seagrass hissed. "And besides, we're on the City's visual record—"

"Which our host doesn't want us to associate with *his* access," Mahit said pointedly, just loud enough to be heard.

"Exactly," said Twelve Azalea, "and if we get to the point that someone is scraping City audiovisual for 'who went into the Judiciary today,' we have *such bigger problems,* Reed."

Mahit sighed. "Get on with it; take us to my predecessor."

Three Seagrass's mouth compressed into a thin, considering line, and she slipped back to walk at Mahit's left shoulder while Twelve Azalea led them underground.

The morgue looked the same. The air was chill and smelled forcibly clean, like it was being churned through purifiers. The *ixplanatl*—or Twelve Azalea, after he was done *investigating*—had covered Yskandr's corpse with the sheet. Mahit was abruptly consumed with crawling dread: the last time she'd stood here, her imago had sent up terrible flares of emotion and endocrine-system hormones and then *vanished*. And she'd come back anyway. A nasty flicker of *sabotage* reoccurred: Was this room somehow inimical? (Did she want the *room* to be inimical, so that the sabotage could not be either her own failure or from someone on *Lsel?*)

Twelve Azalea peeled the sheet down again, revealing the dead face of Yskandr Aghavn. Mahit came close. She tried to see the corpse as a material shell; a physical problem of the present world, instead of something which had housed a person like she housed a person. The same person.

Twelve Azalea pulled on a pair of sterile surgical gloves and gently lifted the corpse's head, turning it in his hands so the back of its neck faced Mahit, hiding the largest of the preservative in-jection sites, the one in the great veins of the throat. The corpse moved like something fresher than three months dead: supple and floppy.

"It's quite difficult to see—a very small scar," he said, "but if you press down at the top of the cervical spine, I'm sure you'll feel the aberration."

Mahit reached out and pressed her thumb into the hollow of Yskandr's skull, directly between the tendons. His skin was rubbery. Too much give, and the wrong kind. The small imago-scar was a tiny irregularity under the pad of her thumb; beneath it was the unfolded architecture of the imago-machine, a firmness as familiar as the skull bones themselves. Her own was identical. She used to rub her thumb against it while she was studying. She hadn't done that since the imago-machine containing five years of Yskandr's experience had been surgically installed inside her. It wasn't one of his habitual gestures, and it was a tell, outside of the Station, and so she'd let it dissolve into the new combined person they were supposed to be becoming.

"Yes," she said. "I feel it."

"Well then." Twelve Azalea smiled. "What do you think it is?"

She could tell him. If he had been Three Seagrass, she might have—an impulse she knew was dangerous even as she felt it; there was no appreciable safety in confession to one Teixcalaanlitzlim over another, not after a single day—but she was *desperately* alone, without Yskandr, and she *wanted*.

"It's certainly not organic," she said. "But he's had it for a long time." A sidestep. She needed to get through this unwise bit of corpse-handling and back to her rooms and shut a door and *deal with* wanting . . . friends. A person wasn't friends with Teixcalaanli citizens. A person especially wasn't friends with *asekretim*, the both of them were Information Ministry—

"I never heard of him having spinal surgery," said Three Seagrass. "Not in all the time he was here. Not for epilepsy or anything else."

"Would you have noticed?" asked Mahit.

"With the amount of time he spent at court? He was very visible, your predecessor. If he disappeared for a week someone would have commented that His Majesty must be missing him—"

"*Really*," said Mahit.

"I did mention he was a political man," Twelve Azalea said. "So you'd say the metal was, perhaps, inserted before he became Ambassador."

"And what does it *do*?" Three Seagrass said. "I am far more intrigued by that possibility than when it was *installed*, Petal."

"Does the Ambassador know such technical matters?" Twelve Azalea said, lightly. Teasingly, Mahit thought. Perhaps even *insultingly*. He was baiting her.

"The Ambassador," she said, gesturing to herself, "is not a medical practitioner nor an *ixplanatl*, and could not possibly explain the neurological effects of such a device in any detail."

"But it is neurological," said Three Seagrass.

Twelve Azalea said, "It's in his brainstem," as if that was a sufficient answer. "And it is certainly not Teixcalaanli; no *ixplanatl* would adjust the functioning of a person's mind in such a way."

"Don't be insulting," said Three Seagrass. "If noncitizens want to stuff their skulls with metal it is their own business, unless they plan to become citizens—"

"The Ambassador was certainly *involved with the functioning of Teixcalaan*, Reed, you know that, it's practically why you applied to be this new one's liaison—so it *does* matter that he had some kind of neurological enhancement—"

"I am entirely fascinated by this information," Mahit said pointedly, and then cut herself off as both Three Seagrass and Twelve Azalea abruptly straightened and composed their faces to formal stillness. Behind Mahit the morgue door opened with a shallow hiss. She turned around.

Coming toward them was a Teixcalaanli woman dressed entirely in bone-white: trousers and many-layered blouse and a long asymmetrical jacket. The planes of her face were dark bronze, her cheekbones wide, her nose knifelike over a wide and narrow-lipped mouth. Her soft leather boots were soundless on the floor. Mahit thought she was the most beautiful Teixcalaanli woman she'd ever seen, which likely meant that she was mediocre to ugly by local standards. Too slight, too tall, all dimension in the face in the nose, and difficult to look away from.

She catches all the light in the room and bends it around herself.

That didn't feel like Mahit's own observation. It had floated up in her mind the way an imago-borne skill would, like knowing how to gesture like a Teixcalaanlitzlim or do multivariable calculus—perfectly natural and perfectly alien to Mahit's own experiences. She wondered if Yskandr had known this woman and was again *angry* that he wasn't here to ask. That he'd absented himself when she needed him, left nothing but these shreds of thought, brief impressions.

Three Seagrass stepped forward and lifted her hands in precise formal greeting, her fingertips just touching, and bowed deeply.

The newcomer did not bother to return the gesture. "How unexpected," she said. "Here I thought I'd be the only one coming to visit the dead at this hour of night." She did not seem perturbed.

"May I present the new Ambassador from Lsel Station, Mahit Dzmare," Three Seagrass said, using the highest formal construction of the phrase, as if they were all standing in the Emperor's receiving hall instead of a sub-basement of the Judiciary.

"My condolences on the loss of your predecessor, Mahit," said the woman in white with perfect sincerity.

No one else in the City had called Mahit by her given name without considerable prompting. She felt suddenly exposed.

"Her Excellency, the *ezuazuacat* Nineteen Adze," Three Seagrass went on, and then murmured, "whose gracious presence illuminates the room like the edgeshine of a knife," one fifteen-syllable-long participial phrase in Teixcalaanli, as if the woman in white came with her own premade poetic epithet. Perhaps she did. The *ezuazuacatlim* were the Emperor's sworn confidantes, his closest advisors and table companions. Millennia ago, when the Teixcalaanli had been planetbound, the *ezuazuacatlim* had also been his personal war band. It was, according to the histories available on Lsel, a less violent title in recent centuries.

Mahit was not so sure of "less violent," considering the epithet. She bowed. "I am grateful for Your Excellency's sympathies," she said, during the process of bending from the waist and getting upright again, and then pulled herself straight, imagined herself as someone who could *loom,* perhaps even loom over unfashionably tall Teixcalaanlitzlim with dangerous titles, and asked, "What brings a person of your responsibilities to, as you said, visit the dead?"

"I liked him," said Nineteen Adze, "and I heard you were going to burn him."

She came closer. Mahit found herself standing elbow to elbow with her, looking down at the corpse. Nineteen Adze straightened out Yskandr's head from how it had been turned and pushed back his hair from his forehead with gentle and familiar hands. Her signet ring glinted on her thumb.

"You've come to say good-bye," Mahit said, implying the doubt she genuinely felt. An *ezuazuacat* did not need to sneak around like a common ambassador and her miscreant *asekretim* companions, not to look at a corpse. She had some other reason. Something had shifted for her when Mahit had arrived, or when Mahit had informed the *ixplanatl* that Yskandr's body should be burnt. She had expected that the presence of a new ambassador would certainly set off some political maneuvering— she wasn't an *idiot*—but she hadn't thought the ripples of disturbance would reach as high as the Emperor's inner circle. *Yskandr,* she thought, *what were you trying to do here?*

"Never good-bye," Nineteen Adze said. She looked at Mahit sidelong, a brief gap of smiling white visible between her lips. "How impolite, to imagine a permanent farewell for such a distinctive person, let alone a friend."

Were her hands, so careful on the corpse's flesh, looking for that same imago-machine Twelve Azalea had noticed? She could be implying that she knew all about the imago process; perhaps she imagined she was even talking to Yskandr, inside Mahit's body. Too bad for the *ezuazuacat* that he wasn't hearing her; too bad for Mahit, too.

"You've certainly picked an unusual hour for it," Mahit said, as neutrally as she could manage.

"Certainly no more unusual than you. And with such fascinating company."

"I assure Your Excellency," Twelve Azalea broke in, "that—"

"—that I have brought my cultural liaison and her fellow *asekreta* here to be witnesses in a Lsel ritual of personal mourning," Mahit said.

"You have?" said Nineteen Adze. Behind her, Three Seagrass gave Mahit a look which clearly expressed, despite fundamental cultural differences in habitual facial expressions, a chagrined admiration of her nerve.

"I have," Mahit said.

"How does it work?" Nineteen Adze inquired, in the most formal and delicately polite mode Mahit had ever heard someone use out loud.

Perhaps when Mahit received a fifteen-syllable poetic epithet of her own it would involve *following through on initial poor ideas*. "It's a vigil," she said, inventing as she went. "The successor attends the body of her predecessor for a full half rotation of the station—nine of your hours—in order to commit to memory the features of the person she will become, before those features are rendered to ash. Two witnesses to the vigil are required, which is why I have brought along Three Seagrass and Twelve Azalea. After the vigil the successor consumes whatever of the burnt remains she desires to keep." As imaginary rituals went, it wasn't a bad one. Mahit might even have liked to have such a ceremony done as part of the integration process with an imago. If she ever went back to Lsel she might even suggest it. Not that it would have made a difference for *her*.

"Wouldn't a holograph do just as well?" Nineteen Adze inquired. "Not to disparage your culture's *habitus*. I am merely curious."

Mahit just bet she was. "The physicality of the actual corpse adds verisimilitude," she said.

Twelve Azalea made a small, choked noise. "Verisimilitude," he repeated.

Mahit nodded with solemnity. Apparently she was trusting the *asekretim* after all, or at least trusting them to not break character. Her heart was racing. Nineteen Adze glanced with undisguised delight between her and Three Seagrass, who looked entirely composed aside from the wideness of her eyes. Mahit was sure that the entire invention was about to come crashing down around her. At least she was already inside the Judiciary; if the *ezuazuacat* decided to arrest her, there wasn't all that far to go.

"Yskandr never mentioned such a thing," Nineteen Adze said, "but he was always reticent about death on Lsel."

"It's usually much more private than this," said Mahit, which was only partially a lie. Death was private except for where it was the beginning of the most intimate contact two people could have.

Nineteen Adze pulled the covering sheet midway up the corpse's chest, smoothed it once, and stepped away. "You're so little like him," she said. "Perhaps the same sense of humor, but that's all. I'm surprised."

"Are you?"

"Very."

"Not all Teixcalaanli are the same, either."

Nineteen Adze laughed, a single sharp sound. "No, but we come in *types*. Your *asekreta* here, for example. She's the precise model of the orator-diplomat Eleven Lathe, except a woman, and too thin through the chest. Ask her; she'll recite his entire oeuvre for you, even the parts where he unwisely got involved with barbarians."

Three Seagrass gestured with one hand, the motion both rueful and flattered. "I didn't think Your Excellency had been paying attention," she said.

"Never think that, Three Seagrass," said Nineteen Adze. Mahit couldn't quite tell if she meant to be threatening. It might just be how she said *everything*.

"I am fascinated to meet you, Mahit," she went on. "I'm sure this won't be the last time."

"I'm sure."

"You ought to return to your vigil, don't you think? I sincerely wish you a joyous union with your predecessor."

Mahit felt quite near to hysterical laughter. "I wish that also for myself," she said. "You honor Yskandr with your presence."

Nineteen Adze seemed to be having some sort of complex internal reaction to that idea. Mahit wasn't familiar enough with Teixcalaanli facial expressions to decipher hers. "Goodnight, Mahit," she said. *"Asekretim."* She turned on her heel and walked out as unhurriedly as she'd come in.

Once the door was shut behind her, Three Seagrass asked, "How much of that was true, Ambassador?"

"Some of it," Mahit said wryly. "The end bit, where she wished me a joyous union and I agreed. That part, absolutely." She paused, mentally gritted her teeth, and got on with it. "I appreciate your participation. Both of you."

"It's quite unusual for an *ezuazuacat* to be in the morgue," said Three Seagrass. "Especially *her*."

"*I* wanted to see what you'd do," Twelve Azalea added. "Interrupting you would have ruined the effect."

"I could have told her the truth," Mahit said. "Here I am, new to the City, being led astray by my own cultural liaison and a stray courtier."

Twelve Azalea folded his hands together in front of his chest. "*We* could have told her the truth," he said. "Her friend, the dead Ambassador, has mysterious and probably illegal neurological implants."

"How nice for us, that everyone lies," Three Seagrass said cheerfully.

"Cultural exchange by mutually beneficial deception," said Mahit. She lifted one shoulder in a shrug.

"It won't stay mutually beneficial for long," said Twelve Azalea, "unless we three make an agreement to keep it so. I still want to know what this implant does, Ambassador."

"And I want to know what my predecessor was doing being friends with Her Excellency the *ezuazuacat* and also *the Emperor Himself*."

Three Seagrass slapped both her hands down on the morgue table, one on each side of the corpse's head. Her rings clicked on the metal. "We can trade truths just as well as lies," she said. "One from each of us, for a pact."

"That *is* out of Eleven Lathe," Twelve Azalea said. "The truth pact between him and the sworn band of aliens in book five of *Dispatches from the Numinous Frontier*."

Three Seagrass did not look embarrassed, though Mahit thought she might have reason to. Allusions and references were the center of Teixcalaanli high culture, but were they supposed to be so obvious that any one of your old friends could pick up the *precise* citation? Not that she'd read *Dispatches from the Numinous Frontier*. It wasn't a text that had ever reached Lsel Station. It sounded like one which probably hadn't got past the Teixcalaanli censors—religious texts, or texts that could be read as statecraft manuals or unsanitized accounts of Teixcalaanli diplomacy or warfare, rarely did.

"Nineteen Adze isn't *wrong* about me," Three Seagrass said, serenely enough. "It worked for Eleven Lathe. It'll work for us."

"One truth each," Mahit said. "And we keep each other's secrets."

"Fine," said Twelve Azalea. He shoved a hand backward through his slicked-down hair, disarraying it. "You first, Reed."

"Why *me* first," Three Seagrass said, "you're the one who got us into this."

"*Her* first, then."

Mahit shook her head. "I hardly know the rules of truth pacts," she said, "not being a citizen, and never having the pleasure of reading Eleven Lathe. So you'll have to demonstrate."

"You're really enjoying that, aren't you," said Three Seagrass. "When you can make a *point* of being uncivilized."

Mahit was, in fact. It was the only enjoyable part about being alone and alternately entranced and terrified by being surrounded by Teixcalaanlitzlim, who up until today had been both much less upsetting and much more approachable by virtue of primarily appearing in *literature*. She shrugged at Three Seagrass. "How could I be anything but distressed at the great distance which separates me from a Teixcalaanli citizen?"

"Exactly like that," Three Seagrass said. "*Fine,* I'll go first. Petal, ask me."

Twelve Azalea tipped his head slightly to the side, as if he was considering. Mahit was almost sure he'd already come up with his question and was delaying for effect. Finally, he asked, "Why did you request to be Ambassador Dzmare's cultural liaison?"

"Oh, unfair," Three Seagrass said. "Clever, and unfair! You're better at this game than you used to be."

"I'm older than I used to be, and less awestruck by your charms. Now go on. Tell a truth."

Three Seagrass sighed. "Vainglorious personal ambition," she began, ticking off her reasons on her fingers, beginning with the thumb, "genuine curiosity about the former Ambassador's rise to the *highest* favor of His Majesty—your station is very nice but it is quite small, Mahit, there is no *sensible* reason for the Emperor's attention to have come so firmly upon your predecessor's shoulders, however nice the shoulders—and, mm." She paused. The hesitation was dramatic, but Mahit suspected it was also genuine. All the embarrassment that had been lacking in Three Seagrass earlier was now visible in the set of her chin, in how she avoided everyone's eyes, even those of the corpse. "And, I like aliens."

"You *like aliens*," Twelve Azalea exclaimed, delighted, at the same time as Mahit said, "I'm not an alien."

"You're pretty close," Three Seagrass said, ignoring Twelve Azalea entirely. "And human enough that I can talk to you, which makes it even better. Now it is absolutely no longer my turn."

Clearly Three Seagrass hadn't wanted to admit that in front of another member of the Information Ministry, and Mahit could almost imagine why—to *like,* in the sense of having a preference for, persons who weren't civilized. It was practically admitting to being uncivilized herself. (Never mind how it was also *suggestive.* That verb was distressingly flexible. Mahit would think about it later.) She decided to be merciful, and go on with her part of the game, and leave Three Seagrass alone.

"Twelve Azalea," she said. "What was my predecessor's political situation directly before his death?"

"That's not a truth, that's a university thesis," Twelve Azalea said. "Narrow it down to something I *know*, Ambassador."

Mahit clicked her tongue against the roof of her mouth. "Something you know."

"Something *only* he knows," Three Seagrass suggested. "For parity."

"*Truthfully*," Mahit said, choosing each word carefully, "what have you to gain from knowing what sort of implants the Lsel Station Ambassador has in his brainstem or anywhere else?"

"Someone murdered him and I want to know why," Twelve Azalea said. "Oh, don't look so shocked, Ambassador! As if you weren't thinking the same thing yourself, no matter what Reed and the *ixplanatl* told you this morning. I know better. It's all over your face, you barbarians can't hide a thing. Someone murdered an ambassador, and no one was admitting it. Even Information isn't talking about it, and I do have some medical training—I was *almost* an *ixplanatl*, once—so I thought I'd be the best possible candidate to find out *why* the court was covering it up. Especially if the cover-up came from Science rather than Judiciary; Ten Pearl in Science has been feuding with Two Rosewood for *years*—"

"That's the Minister of Science and our Minister for Information," Three Seagrass murmured, quite imago-like in her adroit filling in of information.

Twelve Azalea nodded, waved a hand for quiet, went on. "I got myself assigned to this investigation to make sure Ten Pearl wasn't pulling one over on Information, and I came down here and investigated on my own because *ixplanatl* Four Lever was *annoyingly* aboveboard and I still didn't know why the Ambassador was dead. Finding the implant was chance. Now that I've enticed you down here I think the one is connected to the other, but that's hardly where I started." He shook out his sleeves, set his palms flat on the table. "And now it's my turn to ask."

Mahit braced herself. She was more prepared to tell the truth—she was even *predisposed* to confess, just now, with the relief of Twelve Azalea admitting that Yskandr *had* been murdered coming close on the heels of Three Seagrass being so publicly embarrassed, being so *un-Teixcalaanli* and recognizably human—she was falling into the Teixcalaanli patterns, now, dividing everyone into *civilized* and *uncivilized* except inverse, backward. She was as human as they were. They were as human as she was.

She'd tell some of the truth, then. When Twelve Azalea inevitably asked. And deal with the consequences afterward. It was better than making a blanket decision that no one could be trusted because they were Teixcalaanli. What an absurd premise, from someone who'd spent their whole childhood wishing she could *be* an imperial citizen, if only for the poetry . . .

"What does the implant do, Ambassador?"

Hey, Yskandr, Mahit thought, reaching for the silence where the imago should be, *watch me. I can commit sedition too.*

"It makes a record," she said. "A copy. A person's memories and their patterns of thought. We call it an *imago*-machine, because it makes an *imago,* a version of the person that outlives their body. His is probably useless now. He's dead, and it's been recording brain decay for three months."

"If it wasn't useless," Three Seagrass said carefully, "what would you do with it?"

"*I* wouldn't do anything. I'm not a neurosurgeon. Or an *ixplanatl* of any kind. But if I was, I'd put the imago inside someone, and nothing Yskandr had learned in the last fifteen years would ever be lost."

"That's obscene," Twelve Azalea said. "A dead person taking over the body of a living one. No *wonder* you eat your corpses—"

"*Try* not to be insulting," Mahit snapped. "It's not a replacement. It's a combination. There aren't that *many* of us on Lsel Station. We have our own ways of preserving what we know."

Three Seagrass had come around the table and now she laid two fingers on the outside of Mahit's wrist. The touch felt shockingly invasive. "Do you have one?" she asked.

"Truth pact time is over, Three Seagrass," Mahit said. "Guess. Would my people send me to the Jewel of the World *without* one?"

"I could present convincing arguments for both options."

"That's what you're *for*, aren't you? Both of you." Mahit knew she should stop talking—emotional outbursts weren't appropriate in Teixcalaanli culture and were a sign of immaturity in her own—and yet she wasn't stopping. All the helpful, mitigating voices she ought to have had with her were silent anyhow. "You *asekretim*. Convincing arguments and oratory and truth pacts."

"Yes," said Three Seagrass. "That's what we're for. And information extraction, and getting our charges out of unfortunate or incriminating situations. Which this is becoming. Are we done here, Petal? Did you get what you wanted?"

"Part of it," said Twelve Azalea.

"Good enough. Let's go back to your quarters, Mahit."

She was being *gentle*, which was . . . There was no part of that which was good. Mahit took her wrist back, stepped away from her. "Don't you want to extract more information?"

"Yes, of course," Three Seagrass said, as if saying so didn't matter. "But I've also got professional integrity."

"She does," Twelve Azalea added. "It's infuriating, occasionally. 'Likes aliens' or not, Reed is really quite a conservative at heart."

"*Goodnight,* Petal," Three Seagrass said, sharp, and Mahit was not proud of how grateful she was to know she wasn't the only person rattled.

———

The message-box had filled up with infofiche sticks again by the time Three Seagrass had led Mahit back to her quarters. Mahit looked at them with a dull and inevitable sense of despair.

"In the morning," she said. "I'm going to sleep."

"Just this one," Three Seagrass said. She held up an ivory stick set with a golden seal. It was probably real ivory, from some butchered large animal. Sometime earlier Mahit might have been offended, or intrigued, or both. Now she waved a hand at it: *If you must.* Three Seagrass snapped it open and it spilled its holographs in pale gold light all over her hands, reflecting off the cream and red and orange of her suit.

"Her Excellency the *ezuazuacat* wants to meet with you at your earliest convenience."

Of course she did. (Of course she'd have an infofiche stick made out of an animal.) She was suspicious and smart and she knew Yskandr, and she'd been prevented from getting what she wanted in the morgue, so she'd try to get it another way.

"Do I have a choice?" Mahit asked. "No, don't answer that. Tell her yes."

———

Yskandr's bed smelled like nothing, or like Teixcalaanli soap, an empty smell with just the suggestion of mineral water. It was wide and had too many blankets. Curled up in it, Mahit felt as if she was a collapsing point at the center of the universe, sinking in on herself in recursions. She didn't know what language she was thinking in. The starfield art above the bed glimmered in the dark—it *was* gauche—and she *missed* Yskandr, and she wanted to be angry with someone who would understand how she was angry—and the Jewel of the World made the small settling noises of any city around her outside the window—

Sleep hit her like a gravity well, and she gave in.

chapter FOUR

In-City cuisine is as varied as a visitor to any planet might expect: the City, despite being urbanized to nearly 65 percent of land area, has as many climates as any other planet, and there is excellent cold-weather food (this author kindly recommends the thin-sliced loin of small-elk, wrapped around winter vegetables, at Lost Garden in Plaza North Four—if you're willing to make the trip!). Nevertheless classic in-City food is the food of the palace complex: subtropical, focused on the vast variety of flowers and pool-grown plants which are characteristic of the palace's famous architecture. Begin your day with fried lily blossoms, their petals cupping fresh goat-milk cheese—almost every street vendor sells these and they're better hot—before heading out on a culinary tour of Plaza Central Nine's many interplanetarily celebrated restaurants . . .

—from *Gustatory Delights of the City: A Guide for the Tourist
In Search of Exquisite Experiences* by Twenty-Four Rose,
distributed mostly throughout the Western Arc systems

*   *   *

[. . .] anticipate the ability to authorize up to five hundred nonreplacement births in the next five years, due to the greater efficiency of the zero-gravity rice crop in its newest iteration. Births should be accounted first to individuals who have been on the registered-genetic-heritage list for more than ten years; then to the Councilor for the Miners, in anticipation of producing children

likely to score highly on aptitudes for mining and engineering-
line imagos . . .

> —statement by the Councilor for Hydroponics on
> "Strategic Life-Support Reserves and Anticipated
> Population Growth," excerpt

YSKANDR was not back in the morning.

Mahit woke as empty-minded as she'd fallen asleep. She felt
cavernous and echoing, a glassy fragility that was like the very
beginning stages of a hangover. She put her hands out in front
of her, held them flat. They didn't shake. She tapped her fingertips against her thumb in alternating rhythmic patterns: it was
as easy as it ever had been. If she had neurological damage—if
her imago-machine had fucked up irrevocably and burnt out the
neural pathways that were supposed to have inscribed Yskandr
permanently into her, made them one individual out of two—
it wasn't showing up on the kind of basic workup she could do
for herself. She bet she could walk toe-to-heel on a painted line,
too. Not that it *helped*.

On Lsel, now would have been *past* time to go see her integration therapist and be very distressed. This sort of thing—the
cascading failure in the morgue, the blackouts and emotion-
spikes and then *silence*—she had never heard of an imago integration going wrong like hers was going wrong. On Lsel she
would have checked herself in to the medical decks. Now she
was sitting on Yskandr's bed in the center of Teixcalaan and
being *infuriated* that he wasn't here with her, instead. And if she
was suffering neurological failure it didn't seem to be having
effects that a Teixcalaanli medical professional would notice,
even if she wanted to see one.

Yskandr's bedroom had narrow, tall windows, three of them
in a row, and the dawn sunlight came in in floodlight beams.

There were tiny floating motes in them, dancing weightlessly—perhaps she *was* having neurological symptoms, or some kind of ocular migraine.

She got up, walked over (heel-toe, just to see) and swept her hand through them. *Dust. Dust motes.* No air scrubbers in the Jewel of the World. There was a *sky*, too, and plants. Just like other planets she had been on, those brief visits. She was being ridiculous. It was only that everything was strange and she was so *alone* that was making her have these flights of paranoid fantasy.

Three months wasn't enough time for *anyone* to integrate properly. She and Yskandr were supposed to have had a year, a period to grow into each other, for her to absorb everything he knew and for him to dissolve from a voice in her mind to an instinctive second opinion. There were meditation practices and therapy sessions and medical checks and she had none of that here in the place she'd always wanted to be most.

Yskandr, she thought. *Your precursor has gotten you and me and the whole Station in more trouble than any of us strictly deserve, and you'd enjoy it, you'd love this whole mess, so where the fuck are you?*

Nothing.

Mahit slammed the heel of her hand into the wall between two of the windows, hard enough to hurt.

"Are you quite all right?" Three Seagrass inquired.

Mahit spun around. Three Seagrass, already impeccably dressed as if she'd never removed her suit in the intervening night, leaned against the doorframe.

"How wide is the Teixcalaanli concept of 'you'?" Mahit asked her, rubbing her hand where she'd hit it. She'd probably bruised herself.

"Grammatically or existentially?" Three Seagrass asked. "Get dressed, Ambassador, we have *so many* meetings today. I've found you Fifteen Engine—your predecessor's former liaison—

and pinned him down for a late breakfast in the Central City. And you would not *believe* the things that Information has in his file. If you want to make him nervous, ask him about his 'charitable donations' to humanitarian organizations which have been implicated in supporting that nasty little insurrection out in Odile."

"Do you sleep?" Mahit asked dryly. "Grammatically or existentially, as you prefer."

"Occasionally, on both counts," Three Seagrass said, and vanished into the outer suite as swiftly as she'd arrived, leaving Mahit to think about what little she knew of Odile—there was *some* kind of petty rebellion there, but it had been kept quiet on the versions of Teixcalaanli newsfeeds which arrived on Lsel, as such things tended to be. Odile was on the Western Arc—one of the *last* systems annexed by Teixcalaan, at the beginning of Six Direction's reign, when he'd been a military emperor first and foremost, a starship captain. Why there would be an insurrection there, Mahit wasn't sure. But if she could pressure Fifteen Engine with having *bad politics,* she might have an advantage—if she needed one.

Three Seagrass was rather determined to be useful, wasn't she.

Mahit dressed in her most neutral Stationer greys, trousers and blouse and short jacket that would only be out of place in the City by virtue of not being Teixcalaanli, which was to say, *incredibly conspicuous but not overt about it,* and spent the whole time wondering if she'd live long enough to get imperial-style clothes made. In the outer room of the suite, she discovered that Three Seagrass had come up with bowls of some sort of creamy yellow porridge.

"Not poisonous, promise," she said, sucking a mouthful off a spoon. "The paste is processed for *sixteen* hours."

Mahit accepted a bowl with only mild trepidation. "I am

convinced you aren't deliberately trying to get me killed, if only for reasons of your vainglorious personal ambition," she said. Three Seagrass made an undignified noise through her nose. "What would happen if the paste *wasn't* processed?"

"Cyanide," Three Seagrass said cheerfully. "Natural antinutritional factor in the tubers. But delicious. Try yours."

Mahit did. There wasn't much point to refusing. There was nothing *safe*; there were only gradations of exposure to danger. She felt deliriously unmoored, and that was *before* any cyanide exposure. The porridge was faintly bitter, rich and delicious. She licked the last of it off the back of her spoon when she was done.

They took the subway out of the palace complex. Three Seagrass led Mahit down four levels and across a plaza swirling with lower-level functionaries in pale cream with no red patrician shading on their suits—*tlaxlauim,* Three Seagrass explained, *accountants, they travel in swarms*—before descending into the station she claimed would take them out of the palace complex and into the City itself. Someone had plastered the walls of the subway entrance with what looked to Mahit like political posters: the Teixcalaanli battle flag, a fan of spears against a starry backdrop, rendered in lurid red and with its spears turned into part of a graffiti-style glyph that Mahit had to peer at to decipher. It might have been the word for "rot," but she wasn't sure. "Rot" had fewer lines than six.

"Those'll be taken down by the time we get back," Three Seagrass said, plucking at Mahit's sleeve to redirect her down the stairs. "Someone will call for maintenance. Again."

"Not your favorite . . . political party?" Mahit guessed.

"I," said Three Seagrass, "am an impartial observer from the Ministry of Information, and have no opinions at all about the sort of people who like putting up anti-imperial propaganda posters in public spaces and then don't bother to participate in local government or apply to take the examinations and join the civil service."

"Is there a lot of that going around?"

"There's *always* a lot of that going around; it's only the posters that change," said Three Seagrass. "These ones aren't holographic, which is sort of a pleasant difference—not walking *through* them." At the bottom of the staircase was a sleek train platform, its walls decorated—where there weren't more posters—with mosaic-tile images of roses in a hundred colors, shading white to gold to shocking pink.

"This is Palace-East Station," Three Seagrass explained. "There are six stations in the palace complex—six for the cardinal points of the compass, except flat." She gestured at the subway's map, where the palace complex appeared as a six-pointed star. "It's more symbolic than practical, considering that you get off at Palace-Earth for the imperial apartments and cosmology says it ought to be Palace-Sky."

"What's at Palace-Sky?" Mahit asked. The train carriage, when it came, was as spartan and clean-lined as the spaceport had been, full of Teixcalaanlitzlim in white. Most of them looked like the Teixcalaanlitzlim in paintings and photographs—brown and short with wide cheekbones and broad chests—but there were people from all sorts of ethnic backgrounds, all kinds of planetary systems. She even thought she'd spotted a freefall mutant, all long limbs and codominant pallor and red hair and exoskeleton to hold him upright under gravity. But all of the subway riders were dressed the same, save for the colors on their cream sleeves that indicated what branch of the civil service they belonged to. All employees of the palace, of the City. All Teixcalaanli, more so than she'd ever be, no matter how much poetry she memorized. She held on to a metal pole as the train began to move, at first hurtling through a dark tunnel and then emerging into the open air of an elevated track. The City swept by through the windows, buildings blurring.

"Archives, the Ministry of War, and the Imperial Censor Office," said Three Seagrass, answering her earlier question.

"That's not wrong, cosmologically."

"What an opinion you have of what we send out into the universe," Three Seagrass said.

"Literature, conquest, and things that are forbidden. Isn't that accurate?"

The doors hissed open; half the Teixcalaanlitzlim exited. The ones who got on in their place were more colorfully dressed; some were children. The smallest children stared at Mahit unabashed, and their minders—parents or clonesibs or crèche caretakers, it was hard to tell—did little to redirect their attention. They all stood well back from Mahit and Three Seagrass, despite the crowdedness of the carriage, and Mahit wondered about touch-taboo, about xenophobia. When Yskandr had been here—when *imago*-Yskandr had been here, so, fifteen years ago—there hadn't been obvious avoidance of physical interaction with foreigners, and it wasn't in any of the cultural context *she* knew for Teixcalaan.

Changes in comfort levels with strangers were indicative of insecurity; she knew that from the very basic training in psychological response that all Lsel citizens had as part of their aptitude testing. Something had *changed* in the City, and she didn't know what.

"We took the Palace-East line and we're headed to Plaza Central Nine," Three Seagrass said, shrugging, as if that was an answer to what Mahit had asked, and pointed out the interlocking subterranean lines on the carriage's wall map. The subway laced through the City like ice crystals on a pane of glass: a fractal merging of multiple lines, an impossible complexity. And yet the Teixcalaanlitzlim used it with impunity and ease; there

had been a precisely calibrated countdown clock on the platform, saying when their train would arrive, and that countdown clock had been *correct*.

————

Plaza Central Nine had more people than Mahit had ever seen
in one place. Every time she thought she understood the scale
of the Jewel of the World she realized she was wrong. There
were no points of useful comparison with Lsel. Lsel—the largest of the ten stations—could support at most thirty thousand
lives. There were a quarter that many Teixcalaanlitzlim moving through this singular plaza, uncontrolled, unguided by
corridor-lines or shifting gravitational field strength, going
wherever they wished. If there was an organizing principle to
their movement it was something out of fluid dynamics, which
had never been Mahit's area of educational expertise.

Three Seagrass was an exemplary guide. She hovered at Mahit's left elbow, close enough that no curious Teixcalaanli could
take it into their heads to approach the barbarian foreigner with
inopportune questions, but far enough to preserve a modicum
of Mahit's personal space. She pointed out architectural features
and points of historical interest, falling automatically into poly-
syllabic couplets when she wasn't paying enough attention not
to. Mahit envied her that effortless fluidity of referents.

In the center of the plaza the bright steel and gold and glass
of the buildings peeled outward like the petals of a flower, revealing a burst of bright blue atmospheric sky. Mahit made
Three Seagrass pause in the direct center so she could tilt her
whole upper spine back and *look* at it. The vault of it, dizzying—
endless—it seemed to spin. She was the center of the world and—

—*her hand bleeding bright red into the gold sun of the ritual
bowl (his, not her, Yskandr's hand), the sky shaped like this, a vault
glimmering with so many stars as he looked up at it through the*

petal-explosion roof of a sun temple, and through the sting and the
dizzy whirl of the sky he said, "We're sworn to a purpose, now, you
and I—your blood and mine—"

Mahit blinked, hard, and the flash was gone. Her spine hurt
from the bending, so she straightened up. Three Seagrass was
smiling at her.

"You're *sunstruck*," she said.

(imago-struck)

"I ought to take you to a temple and have a divine throw gold
and blood at you. Haven't you ever been on a planet?"

Mahit swallowed. Her throat was dry, and she could still
smell the coppery blood from *ago,* a scent afterimage. "The sky
was never this color on any planet I've visited," she managed.
"Don't we have a meeting to get to? Side trips to religious officials will *surely* make us late."

Three Seagrass shrugged expressively. "The sun temples
aren't going anywhere. There are litanies at every hour. More,
if you're going out-of-City or joining the military, and you want
to shore up your luck and earn the favor of the stars. But the
restaurant's just over there, if you can bear to stop standing in
the exact middle of Central Nine." She pointed, straight-armed.

The restaurant in question was open and bright, with shallow bowls of water glistening with floating many-petaled pale
blue flowers set as centerpieces on each white-stone tabletop.
Mahit found it terribly ostentatious, and suspected that Three
Seagrass didn't realize that that much wasted water was even
something to remark on.

Fifteen Engine was waiting for them at a corner table. He was
middle-aged, broad shoulders over a high barrel of a stomach,
steel-grey hair combed back from an aristocratically low hairline and tied in a tail bound with a metal ring. His cloudhook
was exactly as she'd remembered it—as Yskandr had remem-

bered it—an oversized bronze structure that ate up his left eye socket, cheekbone to browbone. She felt an echo of the flash of emotional intensity she'd gotten off of just Three Seagrass saying his name: distant fondness, distant frustration. But shadowed, half remembered. Perhaps she hadn't felt them at all. Ghost memory, not the imago giving her anything useful.

Mahit realized she'd thought Fifteen Engine would be younger, someone only five or ten years her senior. But he'd been Yskandr's cultural liaison when Yskandr had arrived, twenty years ago, and only for a brief time: her imago might be young, but her imago was also fifteen years out of date, and whatever Fifteen Engine knew of him would be similarly aged.

Mahit lifted her hands to greet him, nevertheless. The pressure between her fingertips felt electrical, like she could feel all the nerves in her arms, an echo of all the times Yskandr had done this motion. Almost as if he was back with her.

When Fifteen Engine lowered his palms, he looked her over and said, wryly, "Stars, Yskandr, she's a quarter of your age. What does that *feel* like?"

"I knew it!" Three Seagrass said, shoving Mahit in the shoulder. "You've got one of those machines, and of *course* you'd have the brain of your predecessor stuck in your head—"

"Hush," Mahit said, and sat down. She did it like she'd sat when she was eighteen: awkward, girlish, too-long limbs folding into her chair, and she watched Fifteen Engine's hopeful expression change to wariness.

"Yskandr may have somewhat exaggerated the degree of carryover," she said, clipped.

"But you are in there—"

"Not at the moment he isn't," Mahit said, and hoped that Three Seagrass would understand that statement as something that intentionally happened with imago-machinery, not as a fundamental error. "In addition, I am fascinated to know that my predecessor was so profligate with sharing what is proprietary technology."

"I see it's taken your liaison approximately thirty-six hours to get the same information out of *you*," Fifteen Engine said.

"Extenuating circumstances, patrician, considering that Yskandr is dead."

"Is he," Fifteen Engine said, dust-dry.

"The man you knew, yes."

"I have no reason to be speaking with you, then," Fifteen Engine said. "I have been out of interstellar politics for the better part of two decades. I resigned from the Information Ministry more than ten years ago. I live quietly and pursue my own work away from the vicissitudes of the central government." He gathered himself to stand, pushing back his chair from the table. The bowl of flowers and water shook; some of the water slopped over the side and ran across the stone to drip onto the restaurant floor.

Transfixed by the waste, Mahit said, "He must have trusted you," trying to salvage something of the meeting, but Fifteen Engine took a step back, avoiding the puddle adroitly—and the world flashed white and roared.

———

She was lying on the ground, her cheek wet in the spilled water. The air roiled with thick, acrid smoke and shouting in Teixcalaanli. Part of the table—or part of the wall, some heavy immobilizing marble—had come down on her hip and pinned her with a radiating spike of pain when she tried to move. She could only see a partial visual arc—there were chair legs and debris blocking her—but in that arc was fire.

She knew the Teixcalaanli word for "explosion," a centerpiece of military poetry, usually adorned with adjectives like "shattering" or "fire-flowered," but now she learned, by extrapolation from the shouting, the one for "bomb." It was a short word. You could scream it very loudly. She figured it out because it was the word people were screaming when they weren't screaming "help."

She couldn't see Three Seagrass anywhere.

Wetness dripped onto her face, as wet as the spilled water but from the other side. Dripped and collected and spilled over the hollow of her temple and across her cheek and her eye and was *red*, was *blood*. Mahit turned her head, arched her neck. The blood flowed downward, toward her mouth, and she clamped her lips shut.

It was coming from Fifteen Engine, collapsed back into his chair, the front of his shirt—the front of his torso—torn open and away, his throat studded with shrapnel. His face was pristine, the eyes open and glassily staring. The bomb must have been close. To his right, from the angle of the pieces she could see.

Yskandr, I'm sorry, she thought. No matter how much she disliked Fifteen Engine—and she had been developing a very direct and powerful dislike, just a moment ago—he was someone who had been Yskandr's. She was Yskandr enough to feel a displaced sort of grief. A missed opportunity. Something she hadn't safeguarded well enough.

A pair of knees in smoke-scorched cream trousers appeared in front of her nose, and then Three Seagrass was wiping the blood off her face with her palms.

"I would really like you to be alive," Three Seagrass said. It was hard for Mahit to hear her over the shouting, and even the shouting was being drowned out by a rising electric hum, like the air itself was being ionized.

"You're in luck," Mahit said. Her voice worked fine. Her jaw worked fine. There was blood in her mouth now, despite Three Seagrass's efforts to smear it away.

"Great," said Three Seagrass. "Fantastic! Reporting your death to the Emperor would be incredibly embarrassing and possibly end my career and also I think I'd be upset—are you *going* to die if I move the piece of the wall that's fallen on you, I am not an *ixplanatl,* I don't understand anything about non-ritual exsanguination except not to pull arrows out of people's veins and I learned that from a really bad theatrical adaptation of *The Secret History of the Emperors*—"

"Three Seagrass, you're hysterical."

"Yes," said Three Seagrass, "I *know,*" and shoved whatever was pinning Mahit to the ground off of her hip. The release of pressure was a new kind of pain. The hum in the air was growing louder, the space between Three Seagrass's body and her own beginning to shade a delicate and terrifying blue, like twilight approaching. The marble restaurant floor had lit up with a tracery of aware circuits, all blue, all glowing, coloring the air with light. Mahit thought of nuclear core spills, how they flashed blue as they cooked flesh; thought of what she'd read of lightning cascading out of the sky. If it was ionized air they were already dead. She struggled up on her elbows, lunged for Three Seagrass's arm, and catching it, hauled herself to sitting.

"What's wrong with the air?"

"A *bomb* went off," Three Seagrass said. "The restaurant is on fire, what do you think is wrong with the air?"

"It's *blue!*"

"That's the City noticing—"

A section of the restaurant's roof shuddered and fell, ear-shatteringly loud. Three Seagrass and Mahit ducked simultaneously, pressed forehead to shoulder.

"We have to get out of here," Mahit said. "That might not

have been the only bomb." The word was easy to say, round on her lips. She wondered if Yskandr had ever said it.

Three Seagrass pulled her to her feet. "Has this happened to you before?"

"No!" Mahit said. "Never." The last time there had been a bomb on Lsel was before she was born. The saboteurs—revolutionaries, they'd called themselves, but they'd been saboteurs—had brought the vacuum in when their incendiaries exploded. They'd been spaced, afterward, and the whole line of their imagos cut off: thirteen generations of engineering knowledge lost with the oldest of them. The Station didn't *keep* people who were willing to expose innocents to space. If an imago-line could be corrupted like that, it wasn't worth preserving.

It was different on a planet. The blue air was breathable, even if it tasted like smoke. Three Seagrass had hold of her elbow and they were walking out into Plaza Central Nine, where the sky was still the same impossible color, as if nothing had gone wrong. A stream of Teixcalaanlitzlim fled across the square toward the safety of other buildings or the dark shelter of the subway.

"Is it possible," Three Seagrass asked, "that Fifteen Engine brought the bomb with him? Did you see—"

"He's dead," Mahit interrupted. "Are you suggesting he was some kind of—self-sacrifice?"

"Badly managed, if he was. You're not dead. Neither am I. And nothing about Fifteen Engine's record, ties to Odile or *no* ties to Odile, suggests he'd be in with domestic terrorists or suicide bombers or the kind of activists for whom posters are *definitely not enough*—"

"What would be the point of killing us? He wanted to talk to me—well, to Yskandr—and you're the one who asked him to breakfast for me in the first place."

"I'm trying," said Three Seagrass, "to figure out just how badly I have misread the situation and determine how much danger you're actually *in*—or if this is just terrible luck—or if something's set off another rash of bombings—"

"Another?" Mahit asked, and instead of answering, Three Seagrass stopped walking. Froze, her hand on Mahit's elbow, jerking her to a standstill.

The center of the plaza unfolded in front of them. What Mahit had thought were tiles and metal inlay when she'd walked across them were instead some kind of armature, emerging from the ground and corralling the crowd inside walls of gold and glass, crackling with that same blue light. Words scrolled up their transparent sides as they drew closer, pinning Mahit and Three Seagrass in the center of a little group of smoke-stained, shocked Teixcalaanlitzlim. The words were printed in the same graphic glyphs as the street signs and subway maps. A four-line quatrain, repeating over and over. *Stillness and patience create safety,* Mahit read, *the Jewel of the World preserves itself.*

"Don't touch the City," Three Seagrass said. "It's keeping us confined until the Sunlit get here. The Emperor's police." The corners of her mouth curved down. "It shouldn't be holding me—I'm a patrician—but it probably hasn't noticed yet."

Mahit didn't move. The walls crawled with gold poetry and blue shimmering light.

"What happens to people who can't read?" she said.

Three Seagrass said, "Every citizen can read, Mahit," as if Mahit had said something incomprehensible. She reached up to her cloudhook, tapping the frame of it where it rested over her left eye, adjusting. The thin pane of transparent plastic that covered her eye socket lit up red and grey and gold, like an echo of the patrician colors on her sleeves. "Hang on," she said. "That should do it."

She shoved her way to the front of the crowd. Mahit followed in her wake. Walking hurt, a bruised and insulted ache that spread from her hip across her lower belly. Three Seagrass went right up to the unfolded section of plaza, her nose inches from the glass, and said, "Three Seagrass, patrician second-class, *asekreta*. Request to transmit Information Ministry identification, City."

A tiny section of the glass wall and her cloudhook both swarmed with words, reflecting one another. Communicating. Three Seagrass muttered something subvocal—Mahit thought it might be a string of numbers, but she wasn't sure—and then the glass printed a word she could read quite clearly.

Granted, it said. Three Seagrass stuck out her hand and did exactly what she'd told Mahit not to do: she touched the wall, as if she expected it to part like a door in front of her. The gesture was so casual, so instinctively comfortable, that Mahit didn't understand when Three Seagrass made a noise like she'd been punched, and fell backward, stiff-limbed. A line of blue fire connected her outstretched fingertips to the City.

Mahit caught her. She was very small. Teixcalaanlitzlim all were, but Three Seagrass was the size of a half-grown Stationer teenager, barely coming up to Mahit's breastbone, and absurdly light for someone wearing as many layers of suiting as she was. Mahit sat on the ground. Three Seagrass fit in her lap, stunned and breathing in ugly gasps, her eyes rolled back in her skull. The crowd backed away from them both.

The City was still saying *Granted*, where the door wasn't. Mahit entertained a vivid and horrific fantasy of the entire artificial intelligence that kept the Jewel of the World in operation, all the sewers and the elevators and every code-locked door, having been programmed by whomever Yskandr had so deeply offended for the specific purpose of killing her and anyone so unlucky as to be associated with her. The concept felt absurdist: she was *one person*, even if she was also the inheritor of all of Yskandr's plans, and there were so many Teixcalaanlitzlim in the City to be accidentally hurt. So many *citizens*. Too many real people for the Empire to sacrifice for the sake of one barbarian. And yet she was entombed in glass, her cultural liaison electrocuted for performing a routine action. Absurd possibilities made too much sense, when so much had gone wrong so quickly.

"Do any of you have water? For her?" she asked, looking up. The faces of the Teixcalaanlitzlim surrounding her didn't change: tear-streaked or burnt or untouched, none of them looked *upset*, not the way a Stationer would. Her own face felt like a mask, scrunched up with emotion. Abruptly she was afraid she had spoken the wrong language; she didn't know what language she was thinking in. Either, or both. "Water," she said again, helplessly.

A man took pity on her, or on Three Seagrass, still limp and unresponsive; he came forward and squatted down. His hair was coming undone from a thick braid, tendrils sticking sweatily to his forehead, and he wore a large, tacky shoulder pin shaped like a sprig of purple flowers on the left lapel of his suit. "Here," he said, speaking both loudly and slowly as he held out a plastic bottle, "some water."

Mahit took it. "I'm Mahit Dzmare," she said, "I'm an ambassador—I don't know what's happening." *I am absolutely alone.* She flipped open the top of the bottle, poured water into her cupped palm, and tried to decide if it would be better to throw it into Three Seagrass's face or drip it into her mouth. "Thank you, sir. Can you inform the palace that one of the *asekretim* is hurt? Send a . . . a doctor vehicle." There was a better word for that and she couldn't find it.

"She's an *asekreta*?" the man asked. "You should wait. The Sunlit will be here soon—the City will call them. It's better if they take care of you."

Mahit wondered if by *take care of* he meant *finish murdering*.

She supposed it didn't matter. She wasn't about to run. There wasn't anywhere to run *to*. "Thank you for the water," she said.

"Where are you *from*?"

Mahit choked on a noise that wanted to be a laugh. "Space," she said. "A station."

"Really," said the man. "I'm sorry. You shouldn't worry. No one will think the bomb is your fault. This isn't that kind of neighborhood." He reached out to pat her on the forearm and she flinched away.

"Whose fault is it?" Mahit asked him.

She hadn't expected him to answer. But he shrugged, and said, "Not everyone in the City loves the City," and then stood up again, leaving her with the water bottle.

Not everyone in the City loves the City. Not everyone in the world loves the world, civilization is not coextensive with the known universe for someone, *someone with a bomb who doesn't care about civilian deaths . . .*

The water dripped through her fingers and onto Three Seagrass's mouth; it rolled down her cheek like Fifteen Engine's blood had rolled down Mahit's. Mahit couldn't watch it. She handed the bottle back to its owner like she'd hand back a knife, handle-first, careful not to spill. Three Seagrass made a noise like a thin hum in the back of her throat, and Mahit decided it was a good sign: she wasn't dead. She might not even die.

Surrounded by Teixcalaanlitzlim, Mahit felt nearly invisible. Not a one of them knew that she ought to have been *more* Yskandr, or what Yskandr might or might not have done. Not a one of them, unless one was the bomber—and there was nothing she could do about that, except to wait.

———

The Sunlit arrived like planetrise over the Station: slowly and then all at once, a distant intimation of gold shimmering through the occlusion of the City's confining walls, which crept closer and closer before resolving into a platoon of imperial soldiers in gleaming body armor, a vision out of every Teixcalaanli epic Mahit had ever loved as a child and every dystopian Stationer novel about the horrors of the encroaching Empire. The wall which had shocked Three Seagrass came down for them, sinking back into the plaza seamlessly, and Mahit remembered the man with the water saying *the City will call them.*

Mahit got to her feet, Three Seagrass tucked under her arm and propped on her hip. Her head lolled back, semiconscious, against Mahit's shoulder. Her hands came up to nearly press fingertip to fingertip, an automatic gesture that seemed to Mahit to be more instinctive or—if such a thing were possible—imago-supplied than something that originated in Three Seagrass's own mind. Neurological puppetry.

The leader of the Sunlit returned that half-gestured greeting with perfect and unconcerned formality. Their face, like all the faces of the troop, was obscured by a cloudhook large enough to cover them from hairline to jaw, an opaque reflective gold shield. Mahit could make out no distinguishing features, which she suspected was the point.

"Are you Mahit Dzmare?" the Sunlit asked. Behind Mahit, the man who had given her water, and all of his companions, had vanished. Fleetingly she wondered if somehow they'd been *responsible,* and were now hiding from law enforcement. *Not everyone in the City—*

"Yes," she said. "I am the Lsel Ambassador. My liaison is hurt and I would like to return to my chambers in the palace."

If the Sunlit officer reacted, favorably or unfavorably, Mahit couldn't tell. "On behalf of the Teixcalaanli Empire," they said, "we regret the physical danger that you were subject to within our territory. We are sure you'll be pleased to know that an investigation has begun into the origins and purposes of the explosive device."

"Entirely," Mahit said, "but I'd be more pleased with medical help and safe return to my diplomatic territory."

The Sunlit went on as if Mahit hadn't spoken. "For your own safety, Ambassador, we request that you come with us into the custody of the Six Outreaching Palms, where the Light-Emitting Starlike Emperor Six Direction's *yaotlek*, One Lightning, and the Minister of War Nine Propulsion can provide you with adequate protection."

The Six Outreaching Palms was the Teixcalaanli military establishment: fingers stretched out in every direction to grasp the known universe and reach its farthest edge. The name was mostly archaic; even Teixcalaanlitzlim talked about "the fleet" or named a particular regiment or division epitomized by the great deeds of its *yaotlek*, the supreme commander of a group of legions. That the Sunlit used it now made Mahit think she was being *formally* arrested; arrested with appropriate procedure applied. Arrested not just by the City and the Emperor, but by the *Ministry of War*.

Not arrested; taken into custody for her own protection.

And how different were these two descriptions? Not different enough, no matter who was arresting her.

She pulled the most formal modes of address out of the miserable culture-shocked sludge of her mind, and hoped she sounded vicious and in all of the control she wasn't. "The custody of the esteemed *yaotlek* One Lightning is not Lsel diplomatic space. If I am in danger, I'm sure someone can be assigned to guard the door to my chambers."

"We are no longer sure such measures are sufficient," said the Sunlit, "considering the unfortunate accident which befell your predecessor. You'll come with us."

Mahit was almost sure that had been a threat. "Or?" she asked.

"You *will* come with us, Ambassador. Your liaison will be taken to a hospital to have her cloudhook adjusted after this regrettable interface with the City, of course. You shouldn't worry." The Sunlit took a step forward, and the rest of the troop followed, like an echo. There were ten of them, each indistinguishable from the others. Mahit stood her ground. She wished Three Seagrass was awake and coherent enough to maneuver them around this—to tell her if this One Lightning was a petty military bureaucrat or a political force, whether the Sunlit were usually in the employ of the Ministry of War or if they were making an exception for acts of terrorism in high-end restaurants.

She was spending so much time wishing her sources of information weren't incapacitated. Wishing wasn't helping. She *didn't* know. She knew enough to be sure she didn't want to be taken into custody. Knew enough about the Teixcalaanli military to know she couldn't run. Knew enough about herself to know that she would have to abandon Three Seagrass if she tried and that she wasn't willing to do that.

How else to stop them?

"I'm afraid I won't be able to go with you," she said, to buy time. Used the extra few seconds to remember her technical diplomatic vocabulary, the most official forms, and then prepared—feeling as if she was about to deliberately step outside an airlock without checking the oxygen volumes on her vacuum suit—to claim sanctuary. "I am compelled by prior agreement to keep my appointment with the *ezuazuacat* Nineteen Adze, whose gracious presence illuminates the room like the edgeshine of a knife, this afternoon. I believe that she would be exceptionally displeased if I instead attended a meeting with the most respected and admired One Lightning without first fulfilling my obligation to her. The tragic situation in the restaurant should not be allowed to disturb the functioning of your government and its negotiations with mine."

She hoped she'd gotten the damned epithet right.

The Sunlit officer said, "One moment, Ambassador," and turned to the others. Their faceplate-cloudhooks glowed blue and white and red under the gold-tone reflective mirror surface that hid their faces from view as they talked to one another on some private channel.

One of them came back over to her. It wasn't the same one who had been speaking before, Mahit was nearly sure. "We will be making contact with the *ezuazuacat*'s office. If you would be patient."

"I can wait," she said. "But I would appreciate if you would also make contact with an ambulance for my liaison." Now she remembered the word. It was good to know that years of vocabulary drill and diplomatic training *would* kick in when she needed them, even if she was soot-stained and covered in mostly-dried blood. Now she just had to hope that Nineteen Adze *wanted* her—wanted Yskandr, more truthfully, wanted whatever Yskandr had promised her—enough to claim precedence over a military commander who could control the City's police.

It was probably best not to think about whether Nineteen Adze had been the one to arrange for the bomb. Not yet. One problem at a time.

That second Sunlit slipped back into the whole group of them. Mahit lost which one it was—she concentrated on standing quite still, on holding up Three Seagrass, on keeping her face expressionless and displeased at once by remembering how Yskandr could transform her mouth into a withering sneer of imperial-style contempt just by shifting the wideness of her eyes. She waited, and imagined she was invincible, like the First Emperor clawing her way off-planet or Three Seagrass's beloved Eleven Lathe, philosophizing amongst aliens—and wasn't she *just.* Doing that. Right here. The minutes droned on. The Sunlit conversed with each other through their faceplates. Three Seagrass made a nearly intelligible *what?* sound and buried her face in Mahit's shoulder, which was almost *sweet.*

The first Sunlit, or an indistinguishable Sunlit from that first, made a gesture to the others. They dispersed into the remains of the crowd, talking in low voices, taking statements from the bystanders. Mahit took it as a good sign: they weren't going to subdue her by brute force.

"An ambulance has been called," the Sunlit said.

"I will wait until it arrives before keeping my appointment with the *ezuazuacat.*"

There was a pause; Mahit imagined that the Sunlit's expression under that faceplate was quite annoyed, and felt pleased at the imagining.

"You may wait," the officer said, "and then we will escort you to the *ezuazuacat*'s office ourself. It would be inappropriate for you to use public transportation at this time. Many of the subways are in fact closed, and service has been suspended in this sextant during our investigation."

"I do appreciate the investment of your personal time," Mahit said.

"We do not have personal time. There's no inconvenience."

The Sunlit use of the first-person plural was unusual and slightly disconcerting. That last "we" ought to have grammatically been an "I," with the singular form of the possessing verb. Someone could write a linguistics paper, for girls on stations to gush over late on sleepshift—

It didn't matter. It wouldn't happen. The ambulance was arriving, a sleek grey bubble of a vehicle, flashing with white lights and a sharp piercing high note, repeated as a siren. It disgorged medical *ixplanatlim* in their scarlet tunics. None of them were Yskandr's morgue attendant, and Mahit was glad of it. They took

Three Seagrass away from her with gentle hands and were re-assuring about her recovery prospects. City-strikes happened all the time, they said. More now than a few years ago. It was just neurostunning, a mistake in the wiring, a fluctuation in the numbers of the enormous algorithmic AI that ran the City's autonomic functions.

"Are you ready to go, Ambassador?" said her Sunlit.

Mahit wished she could get a message to Nineteen Adze: something along the lines of *incoming with police escort, terribly sorry, hope you enjoy political mess, if I don't show up I've been disappeared*, but she couldn't quite think of how she'd manage to do it.

"I wouldn't want to be late," she said.

CHAPTER
FIVE

Before the Teixcalaanlitzlim broke orbit in force—while we were still bound to a single resource-diminished planet, studded with what cities we were able to scrounge out of steppe and desert and salt-laden water, but nevertheless a shell we had outgrown—before the First Emperor took us into the black and found for us the paradise which would become the City—it was common practice for leaders of men and women to select from amongst their closest companions a *sworn band,* tied together with blood sacrifice: the best and most trustworthy friends, the most necessary compatriots, who would if necessary spill all their veins into the cup of an emperor's hands. And these sworn companions were called the *ezuazuacatlim,* as they are today, when their reach extends the emperor's will throughout the stars. The first *ezuazuacat* to the First Emperor was called One Granite, and her life begins as follows: she was born to the spear and the horse, and did not know the city nor the spaceport . . .

> —*The Secret History of the Emperors,* 18th edition, abridged for crèche-school use

* * *

. . . the Council shall be comprised of no less than six (6) Councilors, who each receive one vote on matters of substance, with ties being broken by the Councilor for the Pilots, in recognition of that Councilor's symbolic representation of the initial Captain-Pilot who led the stations into Bardzravand Sector. The Councilors shall be appointed in the following ways: for the Councilor for the Pilots, an election by single vote amongst active and retired pilots; for the Councilor for Hydroponics, appointment by the previous Councilor for Hydroponics, or if such a member is deceased, by their will, or if no will exists, by general popular vote amongst the people of Lsel Station; for the Councilor for Heritage, the inheritor of the previous Councilor's imago . . .

—from the bylaws of the governing Lsel Council

NO one disappeared her.

The trip back to the palace in the passenger seat of the Sunlit's vehicle was anticlimactic enough, after the rest of the morning, that Mahit had time to feel shaky and exhausted with spent adrenaline. She wanted very much to shut her eyes, rest her head against the lightly padded seatback, and stop thinking or reacting or *trying* very hard at all. If she did that, this Sunlit— and possibly every other Sunlit, she'd have to ask Twelve Azalea, or someone else who collected peculiar medical facts, about them if she ever got a chance to—would *know* she was doing it. So she sat very straight and watched out the window ahead of her as they rose vertically through the levels of the City. The buildings thinned, became more elaborate, more tightly strung together with bridges made of gold-shot glass and steel, until they were back in the palace complex and Mahit almost knew where she was. Not well enough to give directions, but perhaps well enough to not get entirely lost on her own.

Her Sunlit stuck to her elbow all the way through two plazas and a mess of corridors inside the largest building in Palace-North, a rose-grey semitranslucent cube that hunkered on itself like a glowing fortress and bustled with grey-suited Teixcalaanlitzlim, shading to pink or to white for symbolic reasons Mahit couldn't entirely discern without her imago's help. They watched her with expressions of bemused interest, which she assumed she deserved: she was still covered in Fifteen Engine's blood. What Nineteen Adze, in her perfect whites, would think, Mahit neither knew nor particularly cared.

The *ezuazuacat*'s offices—which Mahit suspected were also her apartments, if her own were any model for City architecture—began with a wide, bright room behind a code-locked door of that same rose-grey, which had slid open as soon as the Sunlit had announced that Mahit Dzmare was here for her *meeting*. Mahit didn't miss the sarcastic twist of intonation. Her plan was quite transparent, really. Subtlety was for when you had more time to think. Beyond the door the floor was slate and there were enormous windows, rose-shaded to keep the sky from blazing too much across all the many holograph screens floating in a wide arc of a workspace that surrounded Nineteen Adze in a rough corona. She was still all in white, but her coat had been left somewhere and she'd rolled her sleeves halfway up her forearms. There were other Teixcalaanlitzlim in the room—her servants or assistants or functionaries—but she glowed in the middle of them, drawing the eye. Mahit wondered how young she'd been when she'd started to dress like that, thought to ask Three Seagrass, remembered that Three Seagrass was in a hospital somewhere in the City. Tried to draw herself up straight against the bruising ache where the restaurant wall had fallen on her hip.

Nineteen Adze banished three holographs with a flick of her wrist: two in text, one that might have been a scale model of Plaza Central Nine from above. Their afterimages glowed. "My thanks," she said to the Sunlit, "for delivering Ambassador Dzmare safely to her meeting with me. Your platoon is to be commended; I'll make sure of it. You're dismissed."

The Sunlit melted away back through the door without protest, and Mahit was alone inside the *ezuazuacat*'s territory. With grim professionalism she lifted her hands to greet her formally.

"Look at you," Nineteen Adze said. "Still so correct after the morning you've had."

Mahit discovered she was out of patience. "Would you prefer I be rude?"

"Of course not." She left her displays and scrolling transparent windows of information to be fussed over by her assistants, and came over to Mahit. "Getting yourself here was well done. The first *smart* move you've made since you arrived."

Mahit bristled, began, "I didn't come here to be insulted—"

"Nothing of the kind is meant, Ambassador. And lest you worry, this is only the first time you've been *smart*; you've been *clever* quite a bit."

The distinction in vocabulary was unkind; that word for "clever" was the one meant for con artists, hucksters, an animal sort of cunning. "Like any barbarian, I assume," Mahit said.

"Not *any* barbarian," Nineteen Adze said. "And better than some other young persons have done, when arriving at court at a particularly agitated moment. Relax, would you? I'm hardly inclined to interrogate you while you're still wearing someone else's body fluids, and besides, you've practically asked for sanctuary."

"Not asked," Mahit said.

"Found, if you'd like." She twitched her eye behind the white-smoked glass of her cloudhook, summoning one of the assistants to materialize at her side. "Five Agate, if you'd show Ambassador Dzmare to a shower and provide her with some clothing appropriate to her height."

"Of course, Your Excellency."

What else was there to do but surrender? At least, Mahit thought, she'd be a *clean* hostage.

The shower was not palatial or ostentatious. It was tiled in soothing black and white, and had a wall caddy filled with hair products that Mahit didn't touch—were they Nineteen Adze's own? Or was this some sort of collective shower for all her assistants? She seemed the type to make them all *live* with her, but no, that was a literary trope, and Teixcalaanlitzlim were people no matter how hard they tried not to be—and the water was hot. Mahit stood under it and watched what remained of Fifteen Engine sluice down her arms and into the drain.

She reached for the soap—a cake of it rather than a liquid dispenser like station showers used—and in the moment when her hand entered her field of vision, fingers extended, a perfectly standard motion, her hand was not her hand, it was a rougher, larger hand, the nails flat and square and manicured, *Yskandr's* hand reaching toward this soap, in this shower. The water hit lower on his shoulders than on hers—four inches in height would do that. The shape of his torso and his center of gravity, in the chest rather than the hips, overriding her sense of herself. She'd remembered like this when they had first been integrated, just briefly, the shape of his *body* rather than hers, superimposed—but why would he ever have been in the shower of the *ezuazuacat* Nineteen Adze?

Yskandr? she tried, again. Silence. The ache of muscles that weren't hers, a kind of exquisite tiredness.

And was herself, her own body, the doubled flash of memory gone: alone in the shower with only the bruised pain of her hip and none of that other body's shape, thinking of how Nineteen Adze had said *he was my friend,* how she'd touched Yskandr's dead face with such strange tenderness.

It would be exactly *like* Yskandr to have slept with a woman who called herself the Edgeshine of a Knife. That flashfire ambitious person who had been giving himself over to the new combination of him and Mahit Dzmare, a person who would say *sedition, probably,* when asked what he might have done wrong—it seemed the sort of thing he'd have done.

And it might explain Nineteen Adze's willingness to offer sanctuary. Or Mahit might be superimposing a moment of neurological failure, some electric signal in her imago-machine flashing and telling her that her body was Yskandr's body, onto the experience she was having right now. It was possible that she couldn't trust *anything* the imago gave her right now—if she and he were *damaged* (sabotaged—she shuddered under the water).

Mahit scrubbed her arms with soap and rinsed them clean. The whole shower smelled of some dark wood, and roses, and she thought she knew that scent too, or at least remembered it.

Afterward she dressed in the clothes Five Agate had left her, all aside from the undergarments: she wasn't about to wear someone else's panties, the ones she'd come in with would suffice, and the bra they'd given her was sized for a woman with more need for bras than Mahit strictly had. The rest of the clothes were soft and white and well made, both pants and blouse. Mahit wished she could put her own jacket back on over them, but it was irreparably stained. She'd have to walk out, barefoot, in what she suspected were Nineteen Adze's *very own* garments.

A hostage, but a clean one.

Someone had set out a tea service by the time she made her way back to the central office.

Nineteen Adze was immersed in her workspace, rearranging holographs and projections around her with a fluid rhythm, so Mahit sat down at the low table where the tea was and waited. It had a light scent, floral and faintly bitter. There were only two bowls, shallow ceramic, sized for cupped hands. Tea on Lsel Station was not nearly so formal: tea drinkers had tea bags and mugs and microwaves to heat the water. Mahit drank coffee, when she drank stimulants at all, which was the same process except with freeze-dried coffee grounds instead of the tea bag.

"There you are," said Nineteen Adze. She sat down across from Mahit and poured the tea into the bowls. "Feeling better?"

"Thank you for your hospitality," Mahit said. "I do appreciate it."

"It'd hardly be reasonable of me to expect you to talk before you had a chance to gather yourself back together. From the news coming out of Plaza Central Nine, I imagine you've had a traumatic sort of morning." She picked up her tea and sipped it. "Drink the tea, Mahit."

"I won't disparage your hospitality by worrying about poison or drugs."

"Good! That saves me the time of reassuring you that there are neither, and unless Lsel has vastly changed its conception of *human* since Yskandr got here, it should also be entirely harmless to you physiologically."

"We're still just as human as you," Mahit said, and drank. The tea was bracing, a bittersweet green flavor that persistently clung to the back of her throat.

"Twenty years is hardly long enough for significant genetic drift, I do agree. And all the other definitions are quite arbitrary, culture to culture."

"I'm sure you'd like me to ask what Teixcalaan arbitrarily considers inhuman, now."

Nineteen Adze tapped her index finger against the side of the tea bowl. Her rings clicked, metal on porcelain. "Ambassador," she said, "I was a friend of your predecessor. Perhaps one of his only friends, though I do hope that wasn't as true as I suspect. For his sake, I am offering you a conversation. But we can skip to the end, if you'd prefer to forgo the process of building a mutual edifice of common ground." Her smile, when it came, was that edgeshine-brightness that had gotten into her epithet. "I would like to talk to Yskandr. Either stop pretending to be Mahit Dzmare, or allow him to speak."

Quite exactly like a knife, Mahit thought.

"With all respect, *ezuazuacat,* I can't do either of those things," she said. "The first is impossible, as I am not pretending to be myself. The second is more complicated than you are suggesting."

"Is it," said Nineteen Adze. She pressed her lips together. "Why aren't you him?"

"On Lsel you'd be a philosopher," Mahit said, and promptly wished she hadn't. Even with the formal-respectful "you" she'd used, that was a much too intimate statement in Teixcalaan—but she didn't know another way of phrasing it which wasn't the suggestion of selecting a model for allusion and imitation, as Three Seagrass had apparently selected Eleven Lathe.

Nineteen Adze said, "How flattering. Now explain, Mahit Dzmare—I do believe the body you wear was once called that, so it will suit me fine to call you what you like to be called—explain why you are not my friend."

Mahit put down the bowl of tea and left her hands palm-down on the white linen of her borrowed trousers. Nineteen Adze's grasp of imago theory was amazingly perverse: the idea that Yskandr would be walking around *inside her body,* with her own self pushed out or vanished or killed, and only her name remaining to her flesh? The Station didn't waste its children like that. It was nauseating to contemplate—and reminded her far too much of that moment in the shower, where she hadn't quite felt like *her* at all. Not her, and not the combined person she and Yskandr were meant to become, either. "I will," she said, "but tell me first: was the bomb in Plaza Central Nine for *me* or for *Yskandr?*"

"I don't think it was for either of you," Nineteen Adze said.

"At worst it was for Fifteen Engine, and that's a conjecture I would not put weight upon. The victims of domestic terrorism are most often suffering from being in the wrong place at the wrong time. A mild case of political malaise like Fifteen Engine's links to the Odile insurrection are hardly a reason for someone to blow him up, especially as our local bomb-throwers tend to be *for* insurrections," Nineteen Adze said.

Mahit bit back the question she'd meant to ask Three Seagrass, this morning—*the Odile insurrection? What is going on in Odile?*—thinking, almost sure, that the *ezuazuacat* was trying to redirect her. She wouldn't be redirected, not yet. She could ask about Odile and the local bomb-throwers in good time; she needed to know what Nineteen Adze wanted with her before she could deal with the larger troubles of the City.

Nineteen Adze watched her, took in her silence. And went on. "Which does not answer your question about whether anyone *save* me knows about your Station's imago-machines, I know."

She was too sharp. Too *old*. How long had she been at court? Decades. Longer than Yskandr. And half that time at least in the perilous innermost circle of the Emperor. Clearly subtle misdirection and leading questions weren't going to *work*.

Like a knife, Mahit reminded herself, and tried to be a mirror.

"What did he tell you would happen to him after he died?" she asked.

"That it would be unthinkable of Lsel to not send the next ambassador carrying his imago. That it would be—how did he put it. An unimaginable waste."

"That sounds like Yskandr," Mahit said dryly.

"Doesn't it just? Arrogant man." Nineteen Adze sipped at her tea. "You do know him, then."

Mahit lifted one shoulder in a shrug. "Less well than I'd like," she said, which was true even if it was deceptive. "And what did he tell you the next ambassador would *be* like? When she got to the City, carrying his imago."

"Young. Not completely informed. Fluent in Teixcalaanli, to an *unusual* degree for a barbarian. Happy to see his friends again and get back to work."

"The term we'd use," Mahit said, "is 'out of date.' The Yskandr I know is not the Yskandr *you* knew."

"Is that the problem we're having?"

Mahit exhaled, slowly. "No. It is a very small subset of the possible problems we *might* have had."

"It is in fact my job to solve problems, Mahit Dzmare," Nineteen Adze said, "but I tend to find it easier to do so when I know what they are."

"The problem," said Mahit, "is that I don't trust you."

"No, Ambassador. That is *your* problem. *Our* problem is that I am still not speaking to Yskandr Aghavn, and that, despite his apparent death, the same unrest which is an ongoing problem in my City and which surrounded him—even and unto his more *distant* contacts, like Fifteen Engine—has surrounded *you* as well."

"I don't know anything about other bombs, if there have been any," Mahit said. "Or Fifteen Engine's involvement with the sort of people who'd set them, or the sort of people who'd set them against him." *The same unrest.* What had Yskandr *done*? Though, if she knew that, she might know who had killed him, or at least why he had died. And whether it was the sort of thing which would require retaliation in the form of multiple civilian casualties. That didn't seem—he'd said *sedition,* when she asked him what he'd most likely done, before he vanished, but *sedition* was one thing and *meaningless death* another and she could not quite imagine sharing sufficient aptitudes to have an imago made from anyone who would accept casual terrorism as a reasonable side effect of political action.

"Bombs in pricey restaurants in the City's center are an escalation, in my opinion," said Nineteen Adze. "Other similar incidents have kept themselves to the outer provinces. Thus my conjecture that Fifteen Engine may have gotten himself involved with those sorts of people, to his detriment and eventual dismemberment."

Mahit wondered if Nineteen Adze had just made a joke. It was difficult to tell—the humor of it cut so sharply, if it was humor. A joke like that could flay a person open before they noticed the pain.

"You and he *might* merely be collateral damage, Mahit," Nineteen Adze went on. "But I knew Yskandr, and thus I wonder."

"What *I* wonder," Mahit said carefully, "is what this level of domestic terrorism escalated from. In terms of local unrest. How many other bombings have there been?"

Nineteen Adze didn't answer her directly. Mahit hadn't precisely expected her to. She said, "Because you are 'out of date,' mm?"

"Yes. The imago that I accepted"—and here Mahit was committing sedition again, twice in twenty-four hours, maybe she and Yskandr had been right for one another after all, this was *easy*—"was made from Yskandr when he had only been Ambassador for five years."

"That *is* a problem," said Nineteen Adze, quite sympathetically, which made it worse.

"But not *our* problem," Mahit went on. "I don't think you understand, Your Excellency, what an imago *is*."

"Enlighten me."

"It's not a re-creation. Or a double. It's a—think of it as a mindclone language and protocol program."

Like an afterimage, Yskandr in the back of her mind: <*You wish.*>

Frantic, she thought, *Are you there?*

Nothing. Silence, and the *ezuazuacat* talking again, and Mahit didn't have the attention to spare and she'd probably imagined the whisper anyway, called it up like a ghost or a prediction.

"—that is not how Yskandr described the process," Nineteen Adze was saying.

"An imago is live memory," Mahit said. "Memory comes with personality. Or they're the same thing. We found that out very early. Our oldest imago-lines are fourteen generations as of when I left, and might be fifteen now."

"What role is worth preserving over fifteen generations on a mining station?" Nineteen Adze asked. "Governors? Neurobiologists, to keep making the imago-machines?"

"Pilots, *ezuazuacat*," said Mahit, and found herself vividly and suddenly proud of the Station, a sort of upwelling patriotism she hadn't considered part of her emotional vocabulary. "We, and the other stations in our sector, haven't been tied to a planet since we colonized the area. There *aren't* planets to *live* on in our sector, only planets and asteroids to *mine*. We're Stationers. We will *always* preserve pilots first."

Nineteen Adze shook her head, a wry, humanizing gesture; some of her short dark hair fell across her forehead and she pushed it back with the hand that didn't hold her bowl of tea. "Of course. Pilots. I ought to have guessed." She paused; Mahit thought it was more for effect than anything else, an indrawn breath to mark that moment of delighted mutual discovery and then to discard the connection it had made between them. "Memory comes with personality, then. Let's grant that. Which makes it all the more interesting that you still haven't told me why I'm not talking to Yskandr right now."

"Ideally the two personalities integrate."

"*Ideally.*"

"Yes," Mahit said.

Nineteen Adze reached out across the low table between them and put her hand on Mahit's knee. The touch was heavy, grounding, firm. Mahit thought of being pinned beneath an entire planet's mass, the gravitational fall of descent. "But this is not ideal, is it," Nineteen Adze said, and Mahit shook her head, no. No it wasn't.

"Tell me what's gone wrong," Nineteen Adze went on, and the worst part of it wasn't that it was a demand, but that her voice had become so endlessly, vastly sympathetic. Miserably, Mahit thought she was learning something about interrogation techniques. The kind that worked on angry, exhausted, culturally isolated people.

"He was here," she said, wanting more than anything to get it over with. "*My* Yskandr, not yours. *We* were here. And then he wasn't. He shut up on me; I can't reach him. Which is why I'm not able to oblige you, Your Excellency. At this point I wish I could. It'd be simpler, considering how thoroughly my predecessor has dismantled the secrecy of our state secrets. No point in hiding it."

Nineteen Adze said, "Thank you, Mahit, I do appreciate the information," and took her hand away from Mahit's knee; took the weight of her attention away in the same motion, all of the intent pressure vanishing somewhere internal to her. Mahit felt . . . she wasn't sure. Relieved, and angrier now that she was relieved. Now that there was space across the table *for* relief. She took two breaths, deliberately even.

"I would have been Mahit Dzmare even if my imago was as present as we'd both like," she said. "The pair always takes the name of the newest iteration."

"The habits of Stationer culture suit Stationers," Nineteen Adze said, which was a dismissal if Mahit had ever heard one.

She tried again, differently. (A mirror. A *clean* hostage.) "I'd like to know why someone thinks blowing up Fifteen Engine was an appropriate escalation of hostilities. In your most-estimable opinion, *ezuazuacat.*"

"There are always people who don't love being Teixcalaanli," said Nineteen Adze, dry and sharp. "Who wish we'd never broken atmosphere, never stretched out our hands across the jumpgates from system to system and had stayed . . . oh, something that isn't an everlasting state ruled by a man like Six Direction under the guidance of the brilliant stars. They'd like us to be a republic, or to stop annexing new systems even when those systems ask us to, or—any number of things which look sane on the surface and aren't, when one looks at them closely. Some of those people become Ministers, or think they could be Emperor themselves, and change everything to be as they see fit. Teixcalaan has always had problems with that sort, as I'm sure you're well aware. If you're as much like Yskandr as you claim his successor would have to be, you'll know all our histories."

Mahit did. She knew a thousand stories, poems, novels—bad film adaptations of poems—all of which told the stories of people who had tried to usurp the sun-spear throne of Teixcalaan, and mostly failed—or succeeded, and been acclaimed Emperor, and by virtue of their success declared the previous emperor a tyrant, unfavored by the sun and the stars, unworthy to hold the throne, and justly replaced by a new version of himself. The Empire survived the transfer of power, even when the emperor didn't.

"I have some idea," she said. "What's the other sort of person? Since domestic terrorism doesn't usually lend itself to a glorious return to ideal rulership, as most of the populace can't possibly enjoy it enough to like their new emperor afterward."

Nineteen Adze laughed, and Mahit felt an outsize satisfaction. Like making this woman laugh was a victory, hard won, long sought-after, each time a prize. Perhaps Yskandr *had* been

Nineteen Adze's lover—and even if Mahit was lacking his voice and his memory, she still had his endocrine system response.

"The other sort of person," said Nineteen Adze, when the laughter had subsided, "doesn't want power; they want the destruction of what power currently exists, and nothing else. We only *sometimes* have problems with them. But we have been having one now, for some span of years. We are a very *large* empire, as of late, and peaceful, and it gives men and women a great deal of time to think about what displeases them." She got to her feet. "Come over to the infographs, Ambassador. Work waits for nothing, even interesting young barbarians like yourself and our Yskandr."

Our? Mahit thought, startled—and didn't ask. Watched.

Nineteen Adze's servants reappeared as if they'd merely been waiting for a signal; one clearing away the tea service, another— the same one who had brought Mahit to the shower, Five Agate— surrounding herself with her own arc of holographs. Returning to the work, now that her boss was finished with extracting the sensitive information from the hostage. Nineteen Adze said, "Summarize it, Five Agate, and get me the Sunlit's reports on the survivor interviews," and Five Agate made an elegantly abbreviated version of one of the gestures for acquiescence.

"Mahit," Nineteen Adze went on, just as if she was one of her servants—her *apprentices*, perhaps, that was better, more accurate—"what did you intend to ask Fifteen Engine about? Your meeting with him was the most public he'd been since he retired. He moved out of the palace and practically vanished into the outer boroughs. He *looked* like he was living quietly, even if he was dissatisfied with the direction in which His Brilliance the Emperor was taking us."

That must be what she'd meant, earlier, when she'd talked about Odile—Fifteen Engine being *unsatisfied* with how the

Odile insurrection, whatever it was, was being handled. Mahit said, "I intended to ask him about how Yskandr died."

"Anaphylaxis due to allergies."

"*Really,*" Mahit said.

"Suspicion will certainly serve you well at court," Nineteen Adze said, perfectly straight-faced. Behind her busy screens, Five Agate might have snickered.

"We've been so direct with each other so far," Mahit said, daring a little. "I had to make an attempt."

Nineteen Adze flicked her wrist, vanishing one set of holographs and calling up another. "I don't know the precise physiological process that killed him. The *ixplanatl's* report said *allergies.*"

"For someone with your illustrious career at this court, Your Excellency, I would have assumed you'd be more suspicious."

Nineteen Adze laughed. "I do like you, Ambassador. I think Yskandr would also have."

That hurt to think about, in a way Mahit hadn't expected. A sort of loss she hadn't thought to expect, to go along with missing the Yskandr she *did* know. Not every link in an imago-sequence knew their predecessor personally, but it was always considered a sort of honor if one *had*—if a person had been chosen, not just come up all green on the aptitude tests and the practical exams. She'd thought that she didn't care: she was going to be an *ambassador,* she was significant and necessary, and of course it'd never be personal for her, hardly anyone came *back* to Lsel from Teixcalaan, and all her aptitudes had been aimed at getting her to the City even before she knew whose imago she'd receive or if she'd even earn one at all.

But all the same, she wished she could have met the Yskandr who had been embodied here, whose corpse she had been presented with. And she missed *home,* missed planetrise above the

Station, and being clever and ambitious and *not responsible yet*, talking to Shrja Torel and her other friends in the ninth-tier station bars, imagining what they *might* do and not actually having to do it.

All she said was, "We are carefully selected for compatibility with our predecessors, yes."

"Did Fifteen Engine like you, then?" Nineteen Adze asked. "If you're that compatible." Mahit thought she might be amused, or that interest was close enough to amusement for her that the two had become essentially indistinguishable.

"No," she said. "I asked too many questions, while simultaneously failing to be the person he worked with twenty years ago, before he retired. Did you like Fifteen Engine?"

"He was secretive, combative, and deeply connected to several patrician families that have little taste for me. During his tenure in Information he was often a thorn pricking my thumb. I was glad he retired, though I found it suspicious and still do— but he'd been *quiet* after his retirement. On the surface, at least. I will attend his memorial out of respect for a good opponent, an erstwhile drinking companion, and a former friend of *my* friend, the former Lsel Ambassador."

She paused, and looked directly at Mahit, expressionless, like a dark glass wall. Her cloudhook glowed in her eye. "Does that count for *like,* on Lsel?"

"Close enough," said Mahit. Of course Yskandr would be sufficiently charming to collect friends both assigned and attracted, and keep both kinds even when they weren't to each other's taste. "Who benefits from Fifteen Engine's death, *ezuazuacat?*"

"Anyone who didn't want you to know Yskandr's old friends," Nineteen Adze said, calling up a fresh infograph and annotating it with rapid small shifts of her fingertips, forming a list of word-glyphs in the surface of the air. "But more likely: anyone who wants people who quietly speak out against imperial methods of quelling insurrection to stop thus speaking. Or someone attempting to foment public fear, of which there is a great deal lately, much encouraged by incidents like this one and the anti-imperial activists who claim responsibility for them. So *who benefits*—what an interesting way of phrasing it, Mahit. Add half the *ezuazuacatlim,* particularly Thirty Larkspur, who'd like to shut down any trade which doesn't come from a system where his family has an economic interest, and will take *xenophobia* as a happy excuse to do so, and xenophobia is easily stoked when Teixcalaanlitzlim get exploded while at lunch . . . oh, and you. If you wanted to eliminate your predecessor's allies in order to take a radically new position on Teixcalaan–Lsel diplomatic relations."

"I didn't set that bomb," said Mahit, trying to remember *Odile* and *Thirty Larkspur,* trying to remember *public fear*—commit them to memory now, so that later she could hold the whole puzzle up in her mind, spin it, look for how it fit together.

"Did I say I thought you did, Mahit?" said Nineteen Adze, and there was that weight of her attention again, the intimation of sympathetic total intimacy. Mahit imagined her and Yskandr in bed, a flash of possible-memory that might just have been desire. Skin on skin. Something more than a political friendship. (Would it matter, if they had? *Mahit* had no intention of—not that she *wouldn't,* Nineteen Adze was—)

"If I might interrupt, Your Excellency," Five Agate broke in, to Mahit's considerable relief. "But you should look at the feeds from Plaza Central Seven."

Nineteen Adze lifted both eyebrows. "Shove them over here, then," she said. Five Agate did, with a broad sweep of her palm that caught the trailing edge of one of her infographs and sent it sailing over to Nineteen Adze's workspace. Nineteen Adze caught it through a combination of hand and eye gestures, positioned it, expanded its borders until it hung like a window in midair. Mahit stepped closer, standing at Nineteen Adze's left elbow like Five Agate stood at her right.

Plaza Central Seven, rendered in transparency from some high-up camera—planted by Nineteen Adze's agents? By the Emperor? The Sunlit? Or did the City itself watch itself?—looked much like Plaza Central Nine, if less grand by an order of magnitude. It had the same spread-petal shape that Mahit now knew could unfold into barrier walls; it was lined with shops and restaurants and what she suspected was either a government building or a public theater, from its size and from the statues arrayed in front of it. It was also full of Teixcalaanlitzlim.

Some of them had placards.

They were shouting. The sound came through the feed like a distant roar, indistinct.

"Can you—" Mahit started.

"Turn it up, yes," said Five Agate. "A little. It'll depend on what they're shouting, how clear it is—"

"They'll be shouting 'One Lightning,'" Nineteen Adze said. "I will buy you a new suit for the Emperor's banquet this week if I'm wrong, Five Agate. But turn it up."

They *were* shouting "One Lightning"—the name of the *yaotlek* who had been mentioned by the Sunlit while they'd been trying to arrest her. The *yaotlek* who was commander of the fleet nearest to the City right now. They were shouting his name, and a four-line snatch of iambic doggerel that Mahit made out primarily as rhythm, built around an excited repetition of "Teixcalaan! Teixcalaan! Teixcalaan*li!*" that ended the verse.

"Are they trying to acclaim him without a military triumph?" asked Five Agate wonderingly.

Nineteen Adze said, "Not *yet.*" She spread her fingers away from her palm like a starburst, and the feed zoomed in, onto the faces of the demonstrators. Some of them had streaked their foreheads horizontally with red paint. Mahit thought of the sacrificial crowns that returning Teixcalaanli generals wore in poetic epics: not paint but blood, their own mixed with that of whoever they'd defeated. Entirely symbolic, now, in this age of interplanetary conquests.

"I was under the impression that such things were illegal," she said.

"*Ineffective,* not illegal," Nineteen Adze said. "Five Agate, the purpose of military acclamation. For the edification of the Ambassador."

Five Agate coughed and caught Mahit's eyes sidelong. Mahit thought she looked slightly apologetic. "To confer legitimacy upon a prospective emperor of Teixcalaan, who does not ascend by congruence of blood or by the appointment of the previous emperor, a military acclamation is public demonstration of his virtue—which is to say, public demonstration of the favor of the ever-burning stars."

"And the form of that favor?" asked Nineteen Adze, prompting.

"Traditionally, a major military victory. Or a great number of them. Preferably a great number."

Nineteen Adze nodded. "Quite right. The great number of victories is the proof; all else is shouting, and a functional bureaucracy or a marginally intelligent citizenry—both of which we are blessed with—can strip all legitimacy from mere shouting."

"You'd like me to ask why they're shouting for One Lightning anyway," Mahit said. "Since he does not have the military achievements that would make him a viable emperor. Or at least such achievements have not reached the distant and uninformed regions where Lsel Station lies."

Five Agate's expression looked slightly shocked; more than slightly intrigued. "He's ambitious," she said, and when

Nineteen Adze nodded at her she went on. "He's the sort of ambitious which looks for opportunities. He's won skirmishes out in some of the wilder sectors, not to mention a small campaign or two to quell local unrest or head off out-Empire incursions—and his troops have spectacular morale reports. He wasn't at Odile, but he trained the commander who *is* there, Three Sumac, and she remembers to thank him every time she is on the newsfeeds. He *wants* significant military achievements, and he has enough backing to assure his soldiers that they'll have an opportunity to get them under his command."

"An acclamation based on *belief in the future*," Mahit said dryly. *An acclamation based on needing a war to fight.* "I wish him the greatest of personal success. Since he apparently lacks significant military achievements aside from taking credit for there not being *more than one* bomb in Plaza Central Nine today."

"A person might suspect you of being a diplomat, Ambassador," said Nineteen Adze.

"A person might."

"And she'd be right, if she suspected. But there is one significant factor you are missing, diplomat or no—and you've missed it only by having spent your first forty-eight hours here so *eventfully*."

Mahit tried to navigate between feeling insulted and feeling amused, and came up with sarcastic. "Enlighten me, *ezuazuacat*. If it wouldn't trouble you too much to *skip to the end*." After the conversation over the tea she oughtn't to have been able to manage sarcasm—but perhaps that was part of the point of Nineteen Adze: that the glittering quick-spoken politician who made you *want* to toss quips back and forth with her was the same creature who could slice a conversation to ribbons and make you want to weep that she *understood*.

She wished for Three Seagrass again: for anyone at all who could be a distraction or a covering shield. A *friend*. Her own friend, not some ghost-emotion friend of Yskandr's.

Nineteen Adze had zoomed the camera feed out. The whole mass of cheering Teixcalaanlitzlim hung in the center of the air between them and rotated slowly around a central axis when she inscribed the turn with a twist of her wrist. "The Emperor Six Direction, our light-emitting starlike ruler, brighter than jewels and more kind, he to whom I am sworn and for whose sake I would spill the last drop of my blood: he is eighty-four years old and has no biological offspring. *That* is what you're missing, Ambassador."

"You have a succession problem," Mahit said, because she couldn't say *I'm so sorry that you'll soon lose your friend*; it seemed—unkind. Unnecessary. Not on topic. And how was she to know whether an *ezuazuacat* was *really* a friend of the Emperor, or just a symbolic one? This was the problem with an entire society that obsessively re-created its own classical literature, and wouldn't she have liked to explain *that* to herself two weeks ago. Or to talk to Yskandr about it. She was sure he'd have something to say.

"One Lightning's shouters certainly think we do," Nineteen Adze said. She flicked her hand at the feed and it folded in on itself and faded out. "I am reserving judgment, myself. But you picked a fascinating moment to arrive at court, Ambassador."

"I didn't pick," Mahit said. "I was summoned."

Nineteen Adze tilted her head to the side. "With urgency?" she asked.

"With unseemly urgency," Mahit said, thinking of herself and Yskandr, shoved together with only hope and three months of meditation to make them one agent of the Station.

"If I were you," said Nineteen Adze, "I would find out who authorized your entrance permit. I suspect it would be quite revelatory."

Was it a leading question? Did she intend to have Mahit go through some laborious investigative process only to come up with *the* ezuazuacat *Nineteen Adze* as her answer? No, Mahit decided—she was too canny to want to watch Mahit squirm on the long-line of a tether. Tricks like that were for stock villains, melodramas, and even Teixcalaanli obsession with narrative was mostly reserved for *good* narrative. This was worse: this was Nineteen Adze giving her an assignment, like she'd give one of her servants. *Go find out, tell me what you know.* As if Mahit belonged to her. (As if Yskandr had belonged to her—but she was beginning to believe he *hadn't*, not entirely, not even if she'd shared her bed with him, and that had been part of the problem the two of them had had with one another.)

She said, "An interesting idea. When I return to my own workstation, in my own apartments, I'll be sure to look into it."

"Don't wait so long," said Nineteen Adze. "After all the work you did to get yourself to a place of relative security, do you imagine I'd send you back out into the palace alone? While we still don't know who is willing to blow up innocent citizens right next to you?"

"My cultural liaison—" Mahit began, intending to argue that she certainly was not alone.

"Should be out of the hospital soon enough. I have more than enough infograph displays to spare one, Mahit. I'll have Seven Scale set up a temporary office for you."

Right here, where I am not on Lsel diplomatic ground, Mahit thought, but she schooled her hands into one of the gestures of formal thanks—and when the young man who had disposed of the tea service came to lead her away into the further depths of Nineteen Adze's territory, she went with him.

————

The office—Mahit was doing her best to not think of it as a prison cell, and mostly managing—was flooded with late-afternoon light, shaded pink through a bay window. Tucked into its curve was a low, wide couch. Seven Scale showed her how to open her very own infograph display and provided her with a stack of blank infofiche sticks in neutral, impersonal grey. He was calm and incurious and efficient, and everything about him was a relief in comparison to Nineteen Adze. Which had likely been designed. She introduced comfort and withdrew it like a master interrogator, and Mahit was agonizingly tired of the emotional swing. When Seven Scale left, closing the door behind him, she lay down on the couch, turned her face to the wall under the windowsill, and drew her knees up to her chest until her bruised hip ached.

If she stared at the blank white paint, and stretched one hand over her head to touch the curving sill around the top of the couch, she could imagine she was in her room on the Station. The safe three-by-three-by-nine tube of it, the gentle eggshell cup of its walls: tiny and inviolate and hers, hanging in rows with everyone else's rooms. Soundproof. Lockable. You could curl up with a friend there, spine to spine, or belly to belly with a lover, or— It was *closed*. It was safe.

She made herself sit up. Outside the window a Palace-North courtyard was a riot of blue lotuses floating in ponds and star-shape paths, busy with Teixcalaanli feet marching on Teixcalaanli business. She considered first the impulse to go out the window herself, and second the equally unsuitable impulse to try to write fifteen-syllable verse about how she felt.

Hey, Yskandr, she thought, like throwing a stone into the dark water of one of those ponds. *What did you miss most about home?*

Then she turned on the infograph display and signed into it like she'd been instructed. As she did so, she realized that it was the first time she'd signed into her own equivalent of a cloud-hook, instead of having Three Seagrass *open doors* for her. So strange, to have as much freedom as she'd demanded in her own apartments—her own diplomatic territory—and only to receive it here, where she was some very complicated kind of prisoner. With perfect knowledge that Nineteen Adze was almost certainly recording everything she did, Mahit got to work.

The interface was, when one wasn't trying to decrypt basic communication, more intuitive than Mahit had expected. She gestured and the infograph responded—spreading her hands and twisting her wrist spawned multiple transparent workscreens, and she could make her own halo of information. She found Nineteen Adze's preset camera feeds and called up the one that was still trained on the demonstration in favor of One Lightning—let the *ezuazuacat* think what she wanted about Mahit's continuing interests—and set it to run off to her right side. Over her left shoulder she put a window full of a running stream of tabloid headlines, and resolved to improve her vocabulary of casual and insulting vernacular—and perhaps also to learn something more about anti-imperial activists, or Thirty Larkspur, or just what Teixcalaanli tabloids thought about bombings in restaurants. In the center she found a basic text input and began composing messages, routing them through her own accesses as Lsel Ambassador.

She'd probably have to encrypt them with that encomiastic verse, wouldn't she. If she wanted to be taken *seriously*—

No. She'd leave them unadorned. Uncivilized. Written in unseemly haste and urgency by a woman away from her home office (she thought, with absurdist longing, of the basket of unanswered infofiche sticks that was probably overflowing in her apartment right now) who was a *stranger* to the City. A mirror could reflect more than one thing—she'd been a knife, when she reflected Nineteen Adze. Now she'd be a rough stone: inescapable, blunt, barbaric. Expected, except for those people who had expected her to be Yskandr, and wouldn't she find out who they were, now?

In plain language, the sort that she'd discarded after her first trip through the aptitude exams in Teixcalaanli language, she wrote to the last man who had ever seen Yskandr alive. The Minister of Science, Ten Pearl. She asked for a meeting. She expressed a desire for normalization of relations—took out "normalization" and put in "I hope our offices will be on good terms in the future," since wishes didn't require any more specialized grammar than the future tense, and "to normalize" was a resumptive verb and required the speaker to have more than a passing acquaintance with tense sequencing and the subjunctive.

Teixcalaanli was a terrible language, sometimes, even if it did sound beautiful in fifteen-syllable verses. But there was nothing in that message to suggest that she was interested in investigating the death of her predecessor—nothing to suggest that she was even a marginally competent political operator.

So deeply in over her head, the new Lsel Ambassador. Did you hear? She had to ask Her Excellency Nineteen Adze to keep her from getting *arrested*.

Mahit snickered to herself. The sound was loud in the room, even over the muted roar of the feed from the demonstration. She schooled her face to imperial impassivity, as if she'd been caught in a compromising position.

The other messages were easier to compose. One to Twelve Azalea, asking him to check on Three Seagrass—surely he'd be interested in his friend Reed being hospitalized, and might even be inclined to let her know if her liaison was going to recover from that neurological insult. One to *herself,* copying both of the previous two messages so that she'd have a record delivered into the marginal *physical* safety of Lsel diplomatic territory, not just the limited safety of her electronic access—and one final message, to the Ministry of Information, addressee unspecified, requesting an account of who had approved her entrance permit.

Let Nineteen Adze watch what she did.

After Mahit had impressed her letters onto the infofiche sticks she'd been provided, and checked that each one would spill out her message when cracked open, she sealed them with hot wax. The wax came out of a sealing kit on the endtable by the office door, and had to be melted with a handheld ethanol lighter. Mahit burned her thumb, pouring it. So perfectly imperial, to have messages made of light and encrypted with poetry, and require a physical object for propriety's sake.

Such a waste of resources. Time and energy and material.

She could wish it didn't delight her.

CHAPTER
SIX

Remains of an accident on Chrysanthemum Highway are still being cleared as of early morning; commuters should be aware of heavy traffic . . . delays on Central Line expected to continue; Central Nine stop remains closed for Sunlit investigation into bombing; reroute through North Green Line for Central City stops beyond Central Nine; leave extra travel time for checkpoints when entering the palace or entertainment venues until further notice . . . the Circumpolar Maglev train will add an extra service every third day to accommodate winter tourisms, beginning D260, tickets now purchasable at municipal train stations throughout the City . . .

—METRO AND SUBWAY CLOSURES AND SERVICE
CHANGES, DAY 248 (Y3-I11)

* * *

. . . five Teixcalaanli warships transiting through our sector without presenting evidence of permits; while I expect their negligence is not only theirs but also the failure of our then-Ambassador Yskandr Aghavn, and that proper permits will soon again be issued, I submit this report to the Council on behalf of Heritage as a point of information: the security of our sector is limited to our own ships and there is nothing we can do to these Teixcalaanli

vessels but issue them fines, which they seem to have no difficulty
in paying cheerfully . . .

> —portion of report submitted to Lsel Council as new
> business, 248.3.11 (Teixcalaanli reckoning) by the
> Councilor for Heritage

THE problem with sending messages was that people responded
to them, which meant one had to write more messages in reply.

The sun slipping up over the horizon was bright and chilly
through the unshaded windowpanes, inescapable; it drove Mahit
out of what scraps of sleep she'd managed. It was barely dawn,
and yet there were three new infofiche sticks resting in the bowl
outside the office door, sealed shut. Did Nineteen Adze have the
mail delivered on the hour, every hour, even in the night? Mahit
wrapped the enormous feather-filled quilt—presented to her at
sundown the night before by the hyper-efficient hands of Seven
Scale—around her shoulders. She was awake. Awake, and still
alone inside her mind. It looked to be a permanent condition.

Sitting up hurt. Her hip had stiffened more in the night, and
when she peeled down her borrowed pajama trousers she could
see the bruise there—black-purple, paling to a sick green at the
edges—was as large as her spread hand. She wondered if there
were painkillers to be had in her new, elaborate prison, as well
as the delivered quilt and last night's tray of serviceable but unremarkable vegetable slices and more of that fibrous paste Three
Seagrass had served her for breakfast. Otherwise Nineteen Adze
had left her alone. As if Her Excellency was waiting for her new
pet to settle, so she wouldn't snap at outstretched hands.

Still encased in the quilt, and wincing as she stood up and got
the hip moving, Mahit went to fish out the infofiche sticks and
open them.

The first was as anonymous as the one she'd sent: grey and

sealed with undyed wax. She snapped it open, shook it to make it disgorge its light-spun glyphs.

> *Your friend composes warily on the subject of enclosures*
> *Boundaries, demarcations, edges of knives*
> *But thinks also of you, subject to lonesomeness*
> *And sends twelve flowers as a promise if you need them.*

It was poetry. It wasn't very *good* poetry, but it seemed to be an allusion meaning *oh fuck did the edgeshine-of-a-knife* ezuazua-cat *throw you in prison and can I help?*

It was unsigned.

Not that it *needed* to be signed. Mahit had only sent three messages, and neither the Minister for Science nor the multitude of minor functionaries in the Information Ministry would reply in blatant code. This was Twelve Azalea, and he was probably simultaneously sincere in his desire to effect a rescue if she needed one, and having *far too much fun.* Coded messages! Anonymous communiqués across departmental lines! And Mahit thought that *she* had an untoward degree of affection for the genre conventions of political intrigue in Teixcalaanli literature.

Was it untoward if one *lived* it, in one's own culture? Yes, she decided. It was untoward when one *reenacted* it for the sake of the convention. But a Teixcalaanlitzlim wouldn't think that.

No one had blown up Twelve Azalea, or even tried to do so. His friend might be hospitalized, and his new dangerous political acquaintance might be writing to him from rarefied captivity, but he was still perfectly within his rights to act like he'd walked out of *Red Flowerbuds for Thirty Ribbon* or some other palace romance.

She wrote a couplet back, thinking at least she wouldn't be any worse at poetry than he was, and probably better: *What encloses me I chose / I seek only what I asked of you: information.* And when she sealed the infofiche, she didn't bother to sign her name either. *Someone* should have a good time; it might as well be Twelve Azalea, for as long as he could manage it.

The second infofiche stick was not anonymous in any fashion. It was transparent glass aside from its electronic innards, and sealed with deep green wax stamped with a white glyph of a sun-wheel: Science Ministry. When she opened it, it unfolded into an elegant and condescending little letter: Ten Pearl congratulated her on her appointment as Ambassador, expressed formulaic regrets for Yskandr's unfortunate demise—so formulaic that Mahit instantly knew he'd copied those regrets from one of the practical rhetoric manuals, perhaps the very one she'd learned to write from herself. She had a very Teixcalaanli moment of being insulted at his lack of effort in allusion, and then a very personal moment of satisfaction at having successfully played the dull barbarian, trying so hard to emulate a citizen's education and only achieving an awkward and pitiable imitation.

At the close of the letter Ten Pearl suggested that of course he would be pleased to greet the Lsel Ambassador socially, perhaps at the upcoming imperial banquet in a day's time.

A *public* meeting, then. Safer in some ways; if Ten Pearl thought he was under any suspicion of having killed Yskandr outright, then meeting Yskandr's successor in public would allay any scurrilous publicity about trying to have that successor similarly eliminated. There couldn't be any secret murders of foreign dignitaries when the entire court was watching! Safer, for Ten Pearl's reputation (and Mahit's actual safety, if he *had* been responsible for Yskandr's death), but also politic: it would demonstrate to *everyone* that there were no hard feelings between Lsel and the Science Ministry.

Well. It wasn't like Mahit hadn't already said she'd go to the banquet. What was one more political hazard to negotiate, at this rate? And if she could corner Ten Pearl for a second, more direct meeting *after* the public bows and smiles he clearly wanted from her, so much the better. She put his message aside and turned to the last of the mail. (The last of the mail that she could get at—the sticks must be piling up inside her apartment in terrible little drifts of undone work.)

The final infofiche stick was another anonymous bit of grey plastic—but this one was flagged with a red tag marked with a black starfield. Off-world communication, routed somehow to her through her own office in Palace-East and Nineteen Adze's in Palace-North. Not for the first time Mahit wondered if she was being *watched* by the City, and thought again of the shimmering rise of those confining walls in Plaza Central Nine. Then she cracked the infofiche open, and stopped thinking of the City at once and entirely.

The message inside was not a spill of Teixcalaanli ideographs rendered in holographic light. Coiled into the stick was a machine-printed slip of semitransparent plastic, and when Mahit pulled it free and spread it out to read, the characters on it were alphabetic: her own alphabet. This message had come from Lsel Station.

And it was not addressed to her. Nor was it addressed to *The Ambassador from Lsel to Teixcalaan*. It was addressed to Yskandr Aghavn, and dated 227.3.11—the two hundred twenty-seventh day of the third year of the eleventh indiction of the Emperor Six Direction. About three weeks ago.

For Ambassador Aghavn from Dekakel Onchu, Councilor for the Pilots, it began.

If you are receiving this message you have personally queried your electronic database since the request for a new ambassador was delivered to Lsel Station. This message serves as a double warning, from those who would still be your allies on the station which was once your cradle and your home: firstly, someone is trying to replace you at the imperial court. Secondly, your replacement may have been sabotaged; she bears an early imago-recording of you which neither the Councilor for the Pilots nor the Councilor for Hydroponics was able to verify the condition of before integration. She was sponsored by Heritage—and by Miners. Be wary. Onchu for the Pilots suspects Amnardbat for Heritage is behind sabotage if same exists and originates on Lsel. Destroy this communication. Further communication may follow if possible.

The message must have been triggered when she'd accessed the Lsel Ambassador's electronic database the night before, composing her messages.

Mahit read it twice. Three times, to memorize it—automatic habit, born out of years of knowing how to study Teixcalaanli texts, knowing how to pack a collection of phrases and words into her mind, like a heat-compressed diamond of meaning. *If sabotage exists and originates on Lsel. Unable to verify the condition. Your cradle and your home—*

She found herself thinking—thinking to *not* think, thinking to let herself *feel* and exist through the shock and the distress. Practicalities like a veil over the way her stomach twisted, the way she automatically reached for the comfort of the imago that should have been in her mind and wasn't, and got that dizzy vertigo again for her trouble. Thought that she was going to have to burn Yskandr's corpse soon. While she thought she tore the plastic sheet into small pieces, and melted them with the handheld lighter she'd used to melt the sealing wax for the infofiche sticks. She hoped she could burn the corpse with full knowledge of who had killed him. It would be a strange, pale form of justice—but even if he never came back to her, she owed him that much. Most successors knew how their imago-predecessors had died: age, or accident, or illness, any of the thousand small ways a station could kill a person. You couldn't exact justice on a cancer or a failed airlock. There wasn't any *point*. But there was a point in knowing how the last person to hold all the knowledge you held had died, if only so that you could correct the mistake and keep your line alive a little longer, a little better. To stretch the continuity of memory just a bit farther, out on the edges of human space where it feathered away into the black.

Mahit folded the quilt evenly at the foot of the couch she'd slept on, dressed—awkward and in pain when she had to lift her leg higher than the height of the opposite calf—again in the same white borrowed trousers and blouse as yesterday, and considered when she'd begun to feel so strongly about Lsel ethical philosophy. Since her imago had abandoned her, probably. If she was being poetic about it. Since she had come unmoored from one of those long, long lines of memory.

She and her predecessor were never supposed to be *enemies*. And yet she could still hear Onchu's message (and when had it been *sent*? How long had it been waiting for Yskandr—dead Yskandr—to read it, and take care?) echoing like the best poetry: *if sabotage exists and originates on Lsel*—if she was without her imago because of some sabotage engendered by Aknel Amnardbat—but hadn't Amnardbat wanted her to be the new ambassador? Hadn't Amnardbat *pushed* for her, wanted her presence on Teixcalaan, insisted that she be granted the out-of-date imago of Yskandr to help her? Why would she do that, if she meant for Mahit to lose that imago, to be alone in the Empire, to be cut off from everything? Had she been sent to do *harm* to Yskandr, or to correct his policies? Or neither one?

It *hurt*, how much she didn't know. How alone she was. Hearing a voice from home should have made her feel comforted, even if it was the acerbic voice of the Councilor for the Pilots, but instead Mahit found herself sitting back on the edge of the couch, her head in her hands, still dizzy. The absence of Yskandr in her mind felt like a hole in the world. And now—now she couldn't *trust* herself, her own motives—

Be a mirror, she told herself again. *Be a mirror when you meet a knife; be a mirror when you meet a stone. Be as Teixcalaanli as you can, and be as Lsel as you can, and—oh, fuck, breathe. That too.*

She breathed. Slowly the dizziness passed off. The sun had just barely risen above the level of the windowsill. Her stomach growled. She was still here. She knew a little less (about what she was meant to *do*, as Ambassador to Teixcalaan) and a little more (about what might have been done to her, and why, and from where) than she had before she'd read Onchu's message. She would *compensate*.

———

Mahit left the infofiche sticks on which she'd written her replies in the outgoing basket and padded barefoot out into the warren of Nineteen Adze's office complex. Most of the doors were shut to her—blank panels that wouldn't budge for any cloudhookless gesture. If only she had Three Seagrass to open doors, she thought, and was bleakly amused at the difference a single day made in how she felt about that necessity. Fifteen minutes of wandering showed her the front office she'd seen yesterday, still empty of everything but dawnlight, all the infographs quiescent. She passed it by, turned left down a new corridor, and waded deeper into unfamiliar territory. Somewhere in this complex—it must be a floor of the building at least—Nineteen Adze slept. Mahit imagined her denned like a giant hunting cat, the sort that was too large to have retractable claws. Her sides rising and falling in huge, even breaths; eyes slit open even asleep.

Oh, but Mahit hadn't come to the City to be a poet.

(Why *had* she come—and under whose control—*no*. Not now.)

She hadn't come to the City to be trapped inside the home of an *ezuazuacat*, either, but here she was.

The corridor ended, opening up through a wide archway into a room that must have been on the opposite side of the building from the front office, judging by the dimmer, softer diffusion of morning light. It was clearly a library: all the walls lined with codex-books and infofiche where they weren't hung with starcharts. On a broad couch in the center, Five Agate sat with her legs folded under her, lotus-fashion. Above her knee she spun a brightly colored holograph of the City's local solar system, the orbits marked out in glowing-gold arcs and each planet labeled in glyphs Mahit could read from across the room—and standing in front of the holograph, his small hands busy pulling the planets apart and watching them snap back to their appropriate gravitational wells, was a child who couldn't be more than six.

"Good morning," Mahit said, to let them know she was there.

Five Agate looked up, her face flat and unsurprised. "Ambassador," she said, and turned to the boy. "Map, say hello to the Ambassador from Lsel."

The child gazed at Mahit critically, and pressed his baby hands together above his heart. "Hello," he said. "Why are you in the library before breakfast?"

Mahit came forward out of the archway, feeling ungainly and tall. "I couldn't sleep," she said. "I like your solar system. It's very beautiful."

The child stared at her, unmoved. Teixcalaanli expressionlessness on a person that age was more than a little unsettling.

"Oh, sit down," said Five Agate. "You're looming."

Mahit sat. The boy stuck his hand into the center of the holograph and grasped the sun in his palm, pulling the whole holograph out of Five Agate's lap. "It's mine," he said.

"Map, go work on the orbital maths, won't you?" Five Agate said. "Just for a moment. You can take the model."

Mahit thought for a moment he would resist—she'd hated being locked out of adult conversations when she'd been small—

but he nodded and retreated to the other side of the couch willingly enough.

"That's Two Cartograph," Five Agate said. "I'm sorry. Usually no one *is* in the library at this hour."

Two Cartograph, and called *Map*. Mahit smiled. "It's not a problem," she said. "Lsel has lots of children running around— usually in big crèchemate agegroups—I got into all sorts of things when I was that age. I don't mind. Is he yours?"

"My son," Five Agate said, and then, with a little bit of pride: "My son by my own body."

That was unusual on Teixcalaan—*unheard of* on Lsel. A woman using her own uterus rather than an artificial womb to grow a child was a luxury of resources the Station simply didn't have—women *died* doing that, or destroyed their metabolisms or their pelvic floors, and women were people who could be doing work. Mahit had been given her contraceptive implant at the age of nine. When she'd learned that Teixcalaanlitzlim sometimes bore their own children inside themselves, she'd thought of it the way she thought about the water spilling out of one of those flower bowls in the restaurant in Plaza Central Nine. To have that much to *easily spend* felt both offensive and compelling.

"Was it difficult?" she asked, genuinely curious. "The process."

Five Agate's eyes went smugly wide in a Teixcalaanli-style grin: "I spent two years getting into the best physical shape of my life beforehand," she said. "And it was still difficult, but I was a good home for him, and he came out exactly as healthy as he would have from an artificial womb."

"He's beautiful," Mahit said, with complete honesty. "And clever, if he's doing orbital mechanics that young." It was so *gratifying* to have a conversation with a Teixcalaanlitzlim that wasn't immediately, entirely politically barbed. Especially here in Nineteen Adze's offices. "Do you live here, the both of you?"

"Recently, we do," said Five Agate. "Her Excellency is *very* good to us."

"I wouldn't imagine she would be anything else," said Mahit. It was even true. "You're her people, aren't you?"

"For a long time now. Since far before I had Map."

Mahit wanted to ask Five Agate several questions, each more intrusive than the last: *what do you do for her* was the first one, and then *how did she make you hers,* and possibly on to *did she want you to have a child?* But what she asked was, "What changed? Recently, before you moved in."

Some of the openness in Five Agate's face shuttered, like an anti-glare coating coming down over the viewport of a shuttlecraft. "We're all working late, nowadays," she said. "And the commute was very long. I wouldn't want my son to be alone so much. And Her Excellency thought Map would be—better. Here. Close by."

Better. Mahit heard that word as *safer,* and thought about long commutes by subway, and how a bomb might devastate a subway car just as easily as it had a restaurant yesterday.

Her expression must have betrayed something of what she was thinking, because Five Agate changed the subject. "Were you just looking for the library, or . . . ?"

"Looking for anyone who wasn't asleep."

"Two Cartograph gets up with the sun, so I do the same." Five Agate shrugged one shoulder. "Do you need anything, Ambassador? Tea? A particular book?"

Mahit spread her hands open on top of her knees. She didn't want to treat Five Agate like a servant; and she couldn't afford to forget that this woman, as barefoot and casually dressed as herself, was Nineteen Adze's prize assistant. And therefore at least half as dangerous as her master. "No. Unless you'd like to tell me about the Emperor," she said. "I was watching the newsfeeds all last evening, but newsfeeds assume a kind of familiarity with local political emotion that someone from outside the City *can't* have—let alone someone who isn't Teixcalaanli."

"What do you want to know that I would know? I'm not even a patrician, Ambassador." Five Agate had a way of speaking—when she wasn't talking about her son—which was so dryly self-deprecating that the humor was nearly invisible. Not even a patrician, but instead an *ezuazuacat*'s servant—a much more important post, even if it had lower rank at court.

"Based on yesterday I'd take you for an analyst, which perhaps benefits from not being a patrician," Mahit said. It was like fencing; but a friendlier version than with Nineteen Adze. So far.

"All right," Five Agate said with a trace of a Teixcalaanli-style smile, her eyes widening. "If I'm an analyst. What do you want to know that I would know?"

And that you would tell me, Mahit thought. "Why doesn't His Brilliance Six Direction have a certain successor? Surely even if he hasn't got a child of his body he could have a child of his genetics. Or name a designate unrelated heir."

"He could," Five Agate said. "In fact, he has."

"He has?"

"He's associated *three* people to the Imperium. Three designate co-imperial heirs, none of whom have any superiority over the others—they're *all* co-emperor. Do Stationers not get centralized broadcast? The last time he designated anyone, Thirty Larkspur, there was nothing else but the ceremony on any newsfeed for months."

"We're not Teixcalaanli," Mahit said, thinking all the while of Thirty Larkspur, who Nineteen Adze had said was both an *ezuazuacat* like herself and benefiting from public fear. Public fear and trying to control import-export trade to benefit his own family's planetary holdings. "Why would we get centralized broadcasts?"

"Still. Just because you live two months out by ship—"

Mahit said, pointedly, "We manage," and watched Five Agate curl her lip up, wry, noticing that she'd slipped—the unconscious assumption that everyone in the universe would want exactly the same things as a Teixcalaanli person would want. Mahit took some pity on her, and said, "Though we remain ignorant of why Thirty Larkspur was worthy of being associated."

"His Excellency Thirty Larkspur is the most recent member of the Emperor's *ezuazuacatlim*. He has risen *quite* quickly in court, based on his wisdom—and," Five Agate said, tilting one of her hands ambivalently, "perhaps also for his strong family connections to the patricians from the planets on the Western Arc of the Empire."

"I see," said Mahit. She thought she did, actually. When Six Direction had made Thirty Larkspur an imperial associate, he was shoring up his support from the wealthy inhabitants of the Western Arc systems. Thirty Larkspur's family, along with the other patrician families who made the Western Arc— a distant string of resource- and manufacturing-wealthy systems all linked heavily together with jumpgates—would be assured of having a voice not only in the current government but in the next one. And—if Mahit understood the centripetal nature of the kind of usurpation attempt that *did* get celebrated in Teixcalaanli histories—the Emperor was also preventing those wealthy-but-distant aristocrats from throwing their support behind anyone *but* Thirty Larkspur. Revolts led by *yaotlekim* (like One Lightning's almost-revolt happening right now, being shouted about in the City) came from the outer corners of the

Empire, where people were more loyal to their own commanders than to some distant figure in the palace. They were often bankrolled by just the sort of people like the Western Arc families. By giving Thirty Larkspur power, the Emperor ensured that his family was loyal to the man who had *given* him that power: His Brilliance Six Direction.

"You'll see if you meet Thirty Larkspur, Ambassador."

"And the other successors? You said there were three."

"Eight Loop, of the Judiciary—she is nearly as old as His Brilliance Himself, they were crèchesibs together—"

Mahit had read enough novelizations of Six Direction's early life to recognize Eight Loop; his sister by either blood or emotion, the brutal politician behind Six Direction's military brilliance and sun-given favor. She nodded. "Of course, Eight Loop."

"And Eight Antidote, who is hardly older than my Map," said Five Agate. "But who *is* a child of Six Direction's genetics. A ninety-percent clone."

"A very disparate crowd."

From behind them, Nineteen Adze said, "Who could replace His Brilliant Majesty, after all?"

Mahit scrambled to her feet. "It takes three people?" she said, trying to feel less like she'd just been caught.

"At least," Nineteen Adze said. "Have you been interrogating my assistant?"

"Mildly," Mahit said. It seemed better to lead with self-awareness.

"Did you learn what you wanted?"

"Some of it."

"What else would you like to know?"

That was a trap, baited and set with something as sweet and easy as the infinite weight of Nineteen Adze's concerned regard, and Mahit decided to step into it anyhow. "How a succession would work in an ideal time, at an ideal place. The histories, Your Excellency, tend to focus on the exciting variants."

Nineteen Adze smiled, as if Mahit had answered entirely sufficiently. "An emperor has a child, of their body or their genetics, and the child is of age and mental capacity, and the emperor crowns them co-emperor. And thus, when the old emperor dies, there is already a new emperor, who the stars know and love and favor; made in blood, acclaimed in sunlight."

"How often does *that* happen," Mahit said dryly.

"Less often than some military commander backed by a hundred thousand loyal legionary soldiers claiming that the good regard of the universe has designated *them* emperor. The histories, Ambassador, are both exciting and all too accurate."

And how often does an emperor appoint a ruling council of three to succeed him? Not very often, I suspect, Mahit thought. *Only when there is something not quite right. No suitable successor. Not entirely. Even if Thirty Larkspur and Eight Loop are meant to stand as regents for the ninety-percent clone, that's going to be a long and contentious regency.*

"If you've had enough of politics," said Nineteen Adze, "there's tea. And you have acquired a visitor. In the front office."

"I have?" Mahit asked, surprised.

"Go see," Nineteen Adze said, and snapped her wrist, as if Mahit was an infograph in the wrong place.

———

Three Seagrass looked terrible, but it was a version of terrible that had improved relative to the last time Mahit had seen her, half catatonic after a City-induced seizure. Now she was ashen in the face and bruised under the eyes, but upright, impeccably dressed in her Information Ministry suit, her hair raked back from her forehead and knotted in an unfashionable but functional tail. Mahit had no idea what had possessed her to come *here* after the hospital had let her out instead of going home like a sensible person who had suffered a substantial neurological event.

Nevertheless, seeing her standing in the middle of Nineteen Adze's front office hit Mahit with a wave of relief—some small bit of familiarity here in Mahit's new prison-sanctuary, some kind of continuity. And she *had* apparently cared enough to come find Mahit, instead of going home, however unsensible it might be.

"You're not dead!" Mahit said.

"Not yet," said Three Seagrass, "but it's only a matter of time."

Mahit stopped short. "Are you serious? You should go back to the hospital—"

"Mahit, I am making a joke in poor taste about the inevitability of mortality," Three Seagrass said with a brittle gaiety. "And here you were telling me you were fluent in Teixcalaan."

"Humor is the last thing anyone learns in a second language," Mahit said, but she knew she was blushing, embarrassed—as much for the overt concern as for the linguistic slip. "What are you doing here?"

"When he came to pick me up at the hospital, Twelve Azalea implied you were being held against your will and forced to send unsigned infofiche messages through the palace maildrop. I thought I'd—rescue you? Being as you're my responsibility, and I nearly got you blown up yesterday."

"Twelve Azalea may have overstated slightly," Mahit said.

"Only *slightly*," said Three Seagrass, with a pointed look at Mahit's all-white borrowed outfit.

Mahit protested, "I was covered in Fifteen Engine's blood. It's not—"

"You've spent the night with the most dangerous woman at court and you're *wearing her clothes*."

Mahit pressed two fingers to the space between her eyebrows, trying not to laugh. "I swear, Three Seagrass, between your insinuations of impropriety and Twelve Azalea's unsigned messages, I really *will* feel like I'm a character in *Red Flowerbuds for Thirty Ribbon*."

"Putting aside how I'm not sure how *that* ever got past the imperial censors and out to Lsel," Three Seagrass said dryly, "and that I would never accuse an *ezuazuacat* of taking advantage of a foreign dignitary, at least not while in the recording range of that same *ezuazuacat*'s own front office, and certainly not an *ezuazuacat* who I personally respect and admire—Her Excellency isn't letting you leave, is she?"

There was a hectic flush in Three Seagrass's cheeks, beneath the hollow shadows under her eyes. Mahit wished she'd sit down. But no, she stood in the center of the room like the reed Twelve Azalea called her, narrow and wind-whipped and still doing her job: warning Mahit that they were most certainly being observed. Mahit said, "There were demonstrations in Plaza Central Seven. Acclamations."

"A very good excuse to keep you off the streets. I'm not *arguing*, Mahit. It's . . . the City is strange this morning, even this close to the center. Bombings do that, I imagine."

Mahit sat down herself, on the same couch she'd been interrogated on the evening previously, and made sitting an invitation for Three Seagrass to join her. It was gratifying when she did: sympathetic mirroring, and also not having to *look* at her, standing so very still and looking half shattered. She wondered if there were aftereffects of being attacked by the City itself. Physical, or psychological. Both, she'd guess, from how Three Seagrass carried herself.

"Tell me how it's strange?"

Three Seagrass tilted one hand back and forth in the air. "Not enough pedestrians. It's like a collective case of nerves. And of course Central Nine is blocked off, and the subway isn't running—"

Running, Mahit heard, an echo from a long distance off. A sensation like electric sparks ran from her shoulders through her elbows to hover in her outmost fingers, buzzing.

"*—keeps your new integrated subway running at all hours without operators,*" *Yskandr Aghavn is saying. He leans his elbows on the inlaid wood table that Ten Pearl—new-made Science Minister Ten Pearl, who wears a mother-of-pearl ring on each of his fingers like a living pun on his name—has installed in his office.* "*There's surely some methodology the City used when the lines were separate, and some new methodology of yours now, and I admit to a profound curiosity.*"

Ten Pearl has refined Teixcalaanli expressionlessness to a high art: he conveys utter disdain with the tiniest of sighs, but Yskandr knows this kind of person—what he really wants is to show off his project. And his project was connecting every part of the transit of the entire planetary City, subway and rail both, and rendering them seamlessly autonomous. It had won him his ministry—he headed Science now.

"*Ambassador,*" *says Ten Pearl,* "*I cannot imagine that you need a subway on Lsel Station.*"

"*We do not,*" *Yskandr agrees, willingly enough,* "*but an automated system that can be trusted to move hundreds of thousands of people, without error and without conflict—that, you must imagine, is of enormous interest to anyone who lives in a less-perfect automated system, as those of us who are planetless do. Have you embedded minds within the City's extant AI? A corps of volunteers, like the Sunlit, all together watching over this system?*"

Ten Pearl warms to the subject: Yskandr watches him thaw by inches. Yskandr has said something to him which is almost *right, but just wrong enough that his natural desire to inform and educate a barbarian is going to override his much more prudent wish to keep his new technology safely under wraps. His eyes widen a fraction. Yskandr waits for him: this is like drawing out a hungry animal from its lair.*

"Not like the Sunlit," says Ten Pearl at last, "the City is not a collective mind."

That is already interesting, as it implies that the Sunlit are such a collective: and yet Yskandr had recently met a young Teixcalaanlitzlim who was very excited about joining the imperial police, and was very much an individual person. It implies a process, a making of the Sunlit, and Yskandr wonders whether it is anything like an imago process, and how an empire so completely opposed to neurological enhancement thought about it. None of this is worth asking; all of it would expose his own interests too obviously. What Yskandr asks is, "If not a collective, is there a mind?"

"If you consider an artificial, algorithm-driven intelligence a mind, Ambassador—then yes, the City now has a mind, and that mind watches the subway for conflicts."

"How remarkable," Yskandr says, with only the faintest edge of mockery. "An infallible algorithm."

Ten Pearl says, "It hasn't failed me," implying that it is good enough to have made him Science Minister, and Yskandr thinks: It hasn't failed you yet.

More electric prickles swam in Mahit's fingers. Her nose filled with the remembered scent of ozone, the blue flash of light from the City's algorithm going very, very wrong and catching Three Seagrass unawares and—

She was back, alone again in her body instead of remembering some conversation Yskandr had had more than a decade ago.

Three Seagrass was still talking. Mahit thought she'd missed perhaps a half second, nothing more—a half second with an entire flash of memory in it, minutes of it. "—and the acclamation in Central Seven wasn't the only mass gathering, there was an old-fashioned sacrifice out in Ring Two, it showed up in the Information Ministry Bulletin this morning—"

"You checked that from the hospital?"

"Decryption's good for making sure I still have all my higher brain functions," Three Seagrass said, and Mahit began to get a sense of what had scared *her* worst about the scene in Plaza Central Nine. She could sympathize. The echoes of the imago-flash were still buzzing in her smallest two fingers. Ulnar nerve damage, or the facsimile of it.

"And I was bored until Petal came by with your *unsigned communiqués,*" finished Three Seagrass.

"I think he's having fun," Mahit confessed.

"I know he is," Three Seagrass said, and sighed. "He brought me *chrysanthemums.*"

Mahit was trying to remember what chrysanthemums meant in Teixcalaanli symbolism, and coming up mostly blank—eternal life? Because they were star-shaped?—when Nineteen Adze, emerging from the doorway like a sudden apparition, said, "How sweet of your friend, *asekreta*. I'm pleased to see you've survived yesterday's unfortunate accident."

Three Seagrass made to get to her feet and Mahit put her hand on her forearm—personal space norms or not—and held her still. "If I'm Your Excellency's guest," she said to the both of them, "then Three Seagrass is mine, and she's welcome where I am."

Nineteen Adze laughed, a short, bright sound. To Mahit she said, "Of course, Ambassador, as if I would be so rude to the guest of my guest," and then, sitting across from them, she looked Three Seagrass plainly in the face and told her, "Three days and you've got her loyalty. I'll remember *you*."

To Three Seagrass's credit, she didn't flinch, and she didn't take her arm away from Mahit's hand. "I'll be honored by your recollection," she said.

Mahit thought she ought to say *something*, if only as an attempt to reclaim some control over the conversation, if such a thing was even possible with Nineteen Adze and Three Seagrass both in the room. "What makes a sacrifice old-fashioned?"

She sounded like an ignorant barbarian, but she hardly had a choice about that. Not here. Not now.

"Someone died," Three Seagrass said.

"Someone *chose* to die," Nineteen Adze corrected her. "Some citizen made opening cuts from wrist to shoulder and knee to thigh and bled out in a sun temple, calling on the ever-burning stars to take them up in exchange for something they wanted."

Mahit's mouth was dry. She thought of the vivid spill of Fifteen Engine's arterial blood over his shirtfront and her face. A sacrifice for no particular reason. A Teixcalaanlitzlim would describe it that way. Not a death he chose. A waste of a sacrifice. "What does a citizen get, in exchange for their life?" she asked.

Three Seagrass, whose arm was still under Mahit's fingers, said, "Remembered," sharp and sure.

Nineteen Adze had that same expression as she'd had when Mahit had wished aloud for a joyous reunion with her predecessor back when they'd all stood in the morgue around what was left of Yskandr. That twist of emotion that Mahit couldn't parse. "The *asekreta* is right. Such a citizen is remembered as long as sacrifices are named in sun temples. You should attend a service, Mahit, and hear the litany of names. It'd be a cultural experience." She settled back onto the couch. "All aside from its memorial applications, dying in a temple is not in fashion. It is an extreme response to perceived threat."

"Domestic terrorism is perceived threat," Three Seagrass said.

"So are rumors of impending war," said Nineteen Adze.

Three Seagrass nodded. "The situation in Odile—the troop movements lately—*everyone* knows someone in the fleet, and everyone in the fleet knows the fleet is mobilizing."

"Even so," Mahit interjected, thinking again *Odile,* thinking *the Empire is less stable than it seems,* "I didn't know you held

One Lightning's shouting partisans in such high esteem—they can't *force* the *yaotlek* to begin a war, just wish he'd already had one to celebrate." When Nineteen Adze nodded to her, acknowledging the point, she was savagely pleased—pleased, and then angry at herself for being pleased. Nineteen Adze was using her; was using the both of them to think through the politics aloud. They *weren't* her retinue.

They were her *guests*. Her hostages. And how many stories, in Teixcalaanli literature, described the fate of children traded to one court or another before the Empire, one system to another within the Empire, hostages and guests both, made Teixcalaanli *enough* and then discarded when it was politically expedient. Enough that Mahit should stop trying to impress the *ezuazuacat*. There wasn't a point. There was the *narrative* which said she was being used—

Three Seagrass had no such qualms. "A blood death in a temple was how we used to ensure the success of a war, Mahit," she said. "One death from every regiment, hand-selected by the *yaotlek*. No one does it anymore. Not for hundreds of years. It's terribly selfish, for one citizen to take away the responsibility of calling on the favor of the stars from everyone else."

"Selfish" wasn't how Mahit would have described it. She'd say "barbaric," if she was speaking a language where that would be an intelligible sequence of words to describe a Teixcalaanli religious practice.

"What I'd like to know," she said, "is where the war will be, considering those troop movements that Three Seagrass mentioned." Some of those troop movements were detailed in those unsigned-but-sealed documents that had been in her initial pile of infofiche: requests to move Teixcalaanli warships through the Lsel jumpgates, on the way to *somewhere*.

"You're not alone in wondering," said Nineteen Adze. "His Brilliance has been remarkably closemouthed about his current thinking on that matter." She looked pointedly at Three Seagrass, as if she was a synecdoche for all of the secrets held by the Information Ministry, and might have an opinion.

"Your Excellency, even if I knew where His Brilliance had decided Teixcalaan was next looking to expand, I couldn't say. I'm an *asekreta*."

Nineteen Adze spread her hands wide, one palm-up, one palm-down, like a set of scales. "But the Empire expands. First principles, *asekreta*, not to mention evidence. So there *is* a where."

"There is always a *where*, Your Excellency."

A *where* and a *why now*. Mahit thought she knew the *why now*—the uncertainty around Six Direction's succession. Three equal associated-heirs, each with their own agenda—and one a child who was too young to have an agenda—was no stable mode of government. Something would have to bend; Thirty Larkspur or Eight Loop would emerge with the chief share of authority, or declare themselves regent for the ninety-percent clone, or—

Or One Lightning would declare himself Emperor by right of conquest and public acclamation.

(And somewhere in the midst of it, Yskandr had tried to intervene—she knew him too well to think he could have left *this* alone. She was turning it over and over, like tumbling a stone inside her mouth, and Yskandr was *more* political than she was. More political and more dead. The inheritor of an imago-line was supposed to learn from her predecessor's mistakes.)

"Perhaps we'll find out at the banquet tomorrow," Mahit said.

"We'll find out *something*," Three Seagrass replied, with some of that same brittle delight Mahit had heard in her voice earlier. "And as long as I don't actually get you blown up this time—"

Nineteen Adze laughed. "Of course you both are attending."

"Yes, Your Excellency," said Three Seagrass. "The Ambassador was invited. And I wouldn't miss one."

"Certainly not. Are you presenting a composition?"

"My work is in no way the equal of someone like Two Calendar," Three Seagrass said, theatrically self-deprecating in her comparison to the poet whose work was providing the mail decryption cipher this month, "and more importantly I'm not at the banquet as an orator, but as Mahit's cultural liaison."

"The sacrifices work asks of us," said Nineteen Adze. Mahit couldn't tell if she was joking.

"Will we see you there?" Three Seagrass inquired.

"Naturally. You both can join me on the walk to Palace-Earth tomorrow evening."

When Mahit, envisioning the political statement that entering the banquet in Nineteen Adze's company would make, opened her mouth to protest, Nineteen Adze gestured to cut her off and said, "Ambassador, the City is quite disturbed. I have plenty of guest space. Did you really think you would be leaving?"

INTERLUDE

AGAIN, the vast reach of space: the void and the pinpoint brilliantine stars. Ignore the map; leave it behind. No maps are adequate for what has happened here, at the Anhamemat Gate in Lsel Station's sector of space. Surrounding the discontinuity which marks the existence of the jumpgate—that small stretch of unseeable space, the place the eye and the instrumentation glance off of—there is wreckage. Some ships have died here, along with their pilots. Some ships have been killed here.

The thing which has killed them is vast, and shaped like a wheel within a wheel within a wheel; it has tripartite spin and a sleek dark grey metallic sheen, and a sort of intelligence. Enough for hunger, at least. That the dead ships attest to: hunger and violence. What they do not attest to is an intelligence that can be spoken to or negotiated with. Not yet. As of yet, what Lsel Station has learned from the predator beyond the Anhamemat Gate is how to run. The last ship to see it has made it all the way back to the Station, and not led it after them, either: if it hunts, it does not chase prey back to the den. It has some other purpose for the ships it kills with such impunity.

Dekakel Onchu, Councilor for the Pilots, sits in the medical facility across from the pilot who has seen that hunting thing: he is being very thoroughly examined by a doctor, but he has the wherewithal to tell Onchu exactly what he saw, three times. She makes him repeat it three times. She will need to remember every word. She will remember also the drawn horror in her man's face, how the shadows under his eyes have spread in deep pools. She knew this man—Pilot Jirpardz—before he was himself; she knew also the imago he carried, a brave woman named Vardza Ndun. Vardza Ndun, who had trained Onchu herself, before she died and gave her memories to the imago-line that Jirpardz inherited. Onchu is having trouble imagining anyone even partially made up of Vardza Ndun being this frightened, and that frightens *her*. (It frightens as well Onchu's own imago, long-absorbed into an echo-flicker of warmth and a voice she thinks of as her better self, her better reflexes—the man who taught her not to *fly* but to *soar* through space, who knew his ship like he knew his own body, and who gave to her that skill. Now she feels him like a spasm, an ache of upset in her gut: gravity's wrong, something is out of phase.)

What frightens her more: just this morning she had news come to her desk from a freighter captain who had docked briefly at Lsel to refuel and take on a cargo of molybdenum, and had just enough time to discreetly inquire if there had been any reports of large, three-ringed ships moving through this sector, like they were moving—like they were *massing*—in the sector he had come from, three jumpgates away.

It isn't just Lsel Station's problem, Onchu thinks, her hand wrapped around Jirpardz's hand, pressing it in thanks. The freighter captain hadn't figured out how to talk to the three-ringed devouring ships either. But he was adamant that they weren't human enough to talk to, and Onchu isn't entirely sure *anything*'s not human enough to talk to.

There's only one other Councilor she can bring this information to and have hope of keeping it secret while they decide what to do with it, and she wishes it was anyone but the one she's got. She is going to have to speak to Darj Tarats. She needs what allies she can get, even suspicious ones.

Dekakel Onchu is not a conspiracy theorist: she is a practical, experienced woman in her sixth decade, infused with the memory of ten pilots before her, and she thinks she can manage Darj Tarats, even if he *is* playing games with Teixcalaan, and has been for decades. He sent the Empire an ambassador, and Aghavn had sent back—oh, an open line of trade, which had enriched Lsel—and an open line of imperial culture, flooding back through the jumpgate, which had aligned Lsel more closely with Teixcalaan than ever before. And yet, Tarats—if she gets the man alone, or tipsy and alone—has a vicious, philosophically grounded *hatred* of Teixcalaan. He is playing some kind of very *long* game, and Onchu wishes she could have nothing to do with it. But she needs an ally: the Pilots and the Miners have traditionally been allies, from the inception of the Lsel Council. Pilots, Miners, and Heritage. The representatives of the oldest imago-lines, spaceflight and resource extraction, and the representative whose purpose was to guard imago-lines and Lsel culture in general.

Lately, Heritage under Aknel Amnardbat has realigned itself. Not *philosophically,* Onchu thinks, walking grimly away from the medical facilities and toward her offices, taking the longest loop around the outer edge of the station, just to feel the faint play of gravitational forces against her body. Not *philosophically* realigned: Amnardbat is as pro-Lsel as anyone Onchu has ever met, and fierce in her defense of it; nor has she made choices of imago-assignment which are disturbing or even unusual. What Onchu has discovered about her is worse than ideological or philosophical differences.

Heritage should never attempt to *damage* what it is meant to preserve. Onchu believes this, and thus she has sent a warning to Yskandr Aghavn, if he is still capable of receiving warnings: *What we have sent to you may be a weapon pointed at you.*

But right now, while Aghavn takes his own sweet time in replying, Onchu needs *someone* to help her deal with what is coming through the Anhamemat Gate, and if Heritage is not to be trusted, Tarats will have to do, games with empire or not.

CHAPTER
SEVEN

the heart of our stars is rotten
don't put weight on it
solidarity with Odile!
—flyer, with graphic illustration of defaced imperial war
flag, collected as part of cleanup efforts after the 247.3.11
incident in Plaza Central Nine; to be destroyed along
with all other seditious literature

*   *   *

[. . .] while Teixcalaanli literature and media remain a mainstay of the 15–24 age group's entertainment preferences, this survey also reports large numbers of Lsel youth whose primary reading material is by Lsel or Stationer authors. Particular emphasis should be placed on short fiction, both prose and graphic, distributed in pamphlets or perfect-bound codexes, both of which are easily constructed by every tier's plastifilm printer. These pamphlets and codexes are often composed by the same people who consume them as entertainment (i.e., the 15–24 age group), without the approval or intervention of the Heritage Board for Literature . . .
—report on "Trends in Media Consumption,"
commissioned by Aknel Amnardbat for Heritage, excerpt

THE fan-vaulted roof of the Palace-Earth ballroom was full of streaming lights: each rib made of some translucent material that a river of gold sparks rushed through. Teardrop chandeliers hung from the apexes, like suspended starlight. The black marble of the floor had been polished to a mirror sheen. Mahit could see her own reflection in it; she looked as if she'd been set in a starfield.

So did everyone else. The room was as crowded with patricians as it was with lights, clustering and unclustering in conversational knots, one enormous Teixcalaanli organism that shifted only in configuration. At Mahit's elbow, Three Seagrass—impeccable in her *asekreta*'s cream-and-flame suit, but deliberately dimmed to a functionary's normalcy in the vastness of the room and the sparkle of its inhabitants—asked, "Ready?"

Mahit nodded. She drew her shoulders back, straightened her spine; shook out the cuffs of the grey formal jacket she wore. Nineteen Adze had had someone fetch it from her luggage that morning, and wasn't she glad that the only state secrets she had were inside her own body and not hidden in one of her suitcases. It was drab, compared to the riot of metallics and mirrors the Teixcalaanli court displayed, but at least she looked like the Ambassador from Lsel, and not anything else. Even if she had walked over with Nineteen Adze, glittering in ice-white, and her entire entourage—even if spies and rumormongers and gossips would remember *that* walk and not this one down into the company of the court.

"The Ambassador Mahit Dzmare of Lsel Station!"

Three Seagrass was *loud* when she wanted to be. She'd planted her feet, lifted her chin, and called out Mahit's name like she was beginning a verse of a song—one long, clear, pitched shout. *Orator,* Mahit thought. *She did say if it wasn't for me she'd be reading poetry tonight.* There was a gratifying and intimidating stir of interest from the massed courtiers—a shifting of attention, hundreds of cloudhook-obscured eyes settling on her. She held still just long enough for them to look—long enough for a first impression. A tall, narrow person in a barbarian's foreign-cut trousers and coat, her reddish-brown hair cropped low-grav short, her forehead high and bare. Different from the last one of her kind: female, unknown, unpredictable. Young. *Smiling,* for whatever reasons an ambassador might smile.

(Also, not dead. That was another difference.)

Mahit moved out of the raised central doorway and descended the stairs to the floor, Three Seagrass just in front of her and to her left, just as she'd promised she'd be. She oriented herself toward the rear-center of the ballroom, the place where she knew the Emperor would appear. She had to get there by the evening's end; and she had to make her way across all of this glittering space without committing any social or geopolitical errors that she didn't intend to make. Somewhere the Science Minister, Ten Pearl, was waiting to have their oh-so-public meeting. Every time Mahit thought of him now she remembered that flash of Yskandr, of the two of them arguing—talking—*negotiating* around the nature of the City and the City's mind, if it had one. She kept coming back to it, how the memory had flooded her, interrupted her. She couldn't afford to have that happen again now, in front of all of the assembled court of Teixcalaan, and she also had absolutely no idea how to prevent it.

Behind her, Nineteen Adze had framed herself in the entranceway like a pillar of white fire, and Mahit could *feel* the attention in the room shift. She exhaled.

She liked parties—a certain level of extroversion and sociability was a basic part of the aptitude tests that had made her compatible with Yskandr—but she was still grateful for the chance to catch her breath, to make an approach of her own choosing. To not have all those eyes on her in case something went wrong in a more visible fashion than it had done thus far.

"Where to?" asked Three Seagrass.

"Introduce me to someone who writes poetry *you* like," Mahit said.

Three Seagrass laughed. "Really."

"Yes," Mahit said. "And if they have an official dislike of our most-esteemed *ezuazuacat* hostess, so much the better."

"Literary merit and diversifying political options," Three Seagrass said. "Got it. We *are* going to have fun, aren't we?"

"I am trying not to bore you," Mahit said dryly.

"Don't worry. The hospital trip was sufficient to relieve me of boredom, Mahit, and this part is what I'm *for*." Three Seagrass's eyes were bright, a little glassy, like she'd drunk too much of Nineteen Adze's stimulant tea. Mahit worried about her, and wished she had the time or energy to do something about that worry. "Come this way, I think I saw Nine Maize, and if Nine Maize is giving a new epigram tonight, Thirty Larkspur will be there to hear it. All the political diversity you could want."

———

Three Seagrass's friends were a mix of patricians and *asekretim,* some in Information Ministry cream and some in gleaming court dress that showed no particular affiliation that Mahit could decode—*this* was what she needed Yskandr for, even fifteen years' worth of out-of-date fashion observation would be better than *it's all very shiny* and a suspicion about anyone wearing purple flowers as a decorative motif. There were too many of them: worked in as embroidery on sashes, made of mother-of-pearl or quartz on jeweled hairpieces and lapel pins, more sophisticated versions of the one that helpful stranger in Central Nine had been wearing. They meant *something.* Three Seagrass wasn't commenting on it, which didn't tip the balance of meaning in any direction at all.

Instead she introduced Mahit formally, and Mahit bowed

over her fingertips and was an extremely proper barbarian—respectful, occasionally clever, mostly quiet in the midst of the sharp chatter of ambitious young people. She could follow about half of the allusions and quotations that slipped in and out of their speech. It made her jealous in a way she recognized as childish: the dumb longing of a noncitizen to be acknowledged as a citizen. Teixcalaan was made to instill the longing, not to satisfactorily resolve it, she *knew* that. And yet it wormed into her every time she bit her tongue, every time she didn't know a word or the precise connotations of a phrase.

Nine Maize turned out to be a sturdy man with a slim beard, paler than most Teixcalaanlitzlim, his eyes wide set over flat, broad cheeks. Mahit hadn't seen many people from this ethnic group—northern, cold-weather adapted, *blond*—in the City. There'd been a few on the subway, and a few in Central Nine, but they were the eighth most common in the census numbers—she'd done her research before she'd arrived. People who looked like Nine Maize might have been born here on the City, or come from a planet with more cold weather and less subtropical heat—or his parents might have. Or his genetic material might have, and had latterly been selected by some City-dweller as being suitably interesting and compatible with their own, when it was time to make a child. Three Seagrass had introduced Nine Maize as *patrician first-class*—unfashionably pale or not, he was Teixcalaanli.

"Is it true," Mahit asked him, "that you are reciting a new work tonight?"

"Rumors travel so quickly," Nine Maize said, looking not so much at Mahit as at Three Seagrass, who blinked at him as if the very suggestion of her complicity made no sense to her.

"Even to foreign ambassadors," Mahit said.

"How flattering," Nine Maize said. "I do have a new epigram, it's true."

"On what subject?" said another of the patricians eagerly. "We're due for an ekphrasis—"

"Out of fashion," Three Seagrass said, under her breath but just loud enough to be heard. The patrician made a little show of ignoring her. Mahit tried her best not to spoil the effect by smiling like a foreigner, wide and genuinely amused. An ekphrasis—a poetic description of an object or a place—*did* seem to be old-fashioned. None of the Teixcalaanli poetry which had come to Lsel lately had been in that style.

Nine Maize spread his hands and shrugged. "The buildings of the City have been described by better poets than me," he said, which Mahit suspected was a slightly more politic version of exactly what Three Seagrass had said. "Do you like poetry, Ambassador?"

Mahit nodded. "Very much," she said. "On Lsel, the arrival of new works from the Empire is celebrated." She wasn't even lying—new art *was* celebrated, passed around through the Station's internal network; she'd stayed up late with her friends to read new cycles of the latest imperial epics—liking Teixcalaanli poetry was just being *cultured,* especially when one was barely an adult and still spending all one's time getting ready for the language aptitudes. Nevertheless she disliked Nine Maize's acknowledging smile, the condescension in his nod: of course new works were celebrated in backwater barbarian space. For that dislike, she went on, "But I've never before had the honor of hearing one of your pieces, patrician. They must not be distributed off-planet."

The way Nine Maize's expression shifted—he couldn't *answer* that insult, not from a barbarian—was perfectly satisfying.

"You're in for a treat, then, Ambassador Dzmare," said a new voice.

"I'm sure I am," Mahit said automatically, and turned around. Thirty Larkspur was unmistakable. The multistranded braids of his hair were woven through with ropes of tiny white pearls and glittering diamonds; another strand made up the band around his temples, to imitate the bottommost part of a Teixcalaanli imperial crown. He had the wide Teixcalaanli mouth and the low Teixcalaanli forehead and the deep hook of the Teixcalaanli nose: the model of an aristocrat. Pinned to his lapel was an actual fresh-plucked purple flower: a larkspur.

How obvious, Mahit thought. She should have realized. (And realizing, noticed that she felt *no* echo of Yskandr while looking at this man: he hadn't known him, not during the five recorded years her imago had lived here. Thirty Larkspur was a mystery to her: she didn't even have an emotional ghost to rely on. The *dead* Yskandr must have known him, but he was dead—and she was both damaged (sabotaged!) and out of date.)

Maybe she'd get to come up with her own opinion. That felt frightening, and a little exhilarating, as a possibility.

She bowed deeply. "Your Excellency," she said, and then let Three Seagrass run through Thirty Larkspur's titles for her. He had his own epithet, of course. *He who drowns the world in blooms.* Mahit wondered if he'd *picked* it.

Straightening, she said, "It's an honor to meet a person associated to the Imperium such as yourself."

Thirty Larkspur said, "I know, it's the only thing anyone can think when they look at me in this getup. Trust me, Ambassador, Nine Maize's epigrams are more interesting than a co-heir—I'm sure I'm not the only one you'll meet tonight."

"But you're the first," Mahit said. It was difficult not to flirt back with the man, no matter how actually uninterested she was in everything but what opinions Thirty Larkspur held concerning her predecessor and Lsel.

"I do have that pleasure, Ambassador. I assume I'll have to make a decent showing of myself. Is this your liaison?"

"The *asekreta* Three Seagrass," Mahit said.

"We miss you at the salons, Three Seagrass," said Thirty Larkspur, "but I assume everyone has to work sometime."

"Invite me when I'm off-duty," said Three Seagrass, serene and too expressionless for Mahit to know if she was flattered or insulted or pleased, "if you can't do without my orations."

"Of course." Thirty Larkspur extended his arm to Mahit. "You won't be able to hear properly from the center of the floor, Ambassador," he said. "Perhaps you'd like to come with me and stand where the acoustics are better."

Mahit couldn't come up with a good reason to refuse, and there were several good reasons to say yes: further distancing herself from being seen as Nineteen Adze's pet prisoner, a chance to ask Thirty Larkspur something about Yskandr, actually hearing the poetry itself instead of everyone's commentary on the poetry. She put her palm on Thirty Larkspur's proffered forearm—the blue-and-silver fabric of his jacket was stiff with metallic thread—and let him pull her away from the group, Three Seagrass at her heels. "It's very kind of you," she said.

"Can't a person want to show off the best of his culture to a stranger?" Thirty Larkspur asked. "This *is* your first night at court properly."

"It is."

"The previous ambassador was such a mainstay! We miss him. But perhaps you like poetry more than he did."

"Was my predecessor not fond of epigrams?" Mahit said lightly.

They had stopped further toward the central dais. Thirty Larkspur made a gesture that reminded her of nothing so much as Nineteen Adze dismissing an infograph, and summoned up an attendant with a tray of drinks in deep-belled glasses. Mahit bent her head over hers to smell it: *violets,* and alcohol, and something she thought might be ginger or another aromatic root that only grew in soil.

"I believe Ambassador Aghavn preferred epics," said Thirty Larkspur. He raised his glass. "To his memory, and to your career, Ambassador Dzmare."

Mahit imagined drinking and dying, poisoned, in the middle of this enormous room—drank, and was only poisoned so much as to discover that she absolutely hated the taste of violet liqueur. She swallowed and kept her face appropriately expressionless. "To his memory," she said.

Thirty Larkspur spun his glass in his hand; the violet swirled. "I'm glad that Lsel Station has provided us with a new ambassador," he said. "Let alone one who is genuinely interested in epigrams. But you should know, Ambassador Dzmare—the deal is off. There's nothing I can do about it. Do trust me that I made an attempt."

The deal is off?

What deal? Mahit pressed her lips together—surely she could express disappointment visually—buy time—everything still tasted of violets—*What deal, Yskandr! And with who!*—and nodded. "I appreciate your candor," she said.

"I knew you'd be reasonable about it."

"Could I be otherwise?" Mahit said.

Thirty Larkspur raised both of his eyebrows so that they nearly met his hairline. "Oh, I imagined all sorts of unfortunate reactions."

"How pleasant for you that I'm not inclined to hysteria," Mahit said, as if she was operating on autopilot. *What deal,* and *why would Thirty Larkspur be the person to tell me it was off,* and all the time just talking in proper high-register Teixcalaanli, like a glittering veneer over her distress.

"I hope I haven't ruined your evening," Thirty Larkspur said. "It really is going to be a wonderful epigram—Nine Maize is something special."

"Perhaps he'll take my mind off of it," said Mahit.

"Fantastic. To your enjoyment of your first imperial oration contest, then." He lifted the violet again, drank again, and Mahit imitated him. She was never going to get the taste out of her mouth.

The glimmering lights in the ribs of the vaulted ceiling dimmed to twilight and then brightened again, a flickering and rapid migration of glowing points. The loud chatter of the courtiers diminished. Mahit looked over her shoulder at Three Seagrass, who nodded reassuringly—this was expected, then—and back over at Thirty Larkspur. He put his drink down on the tray of a passing attendant and murmured, "I ought to go stand in the right part of the room, Ambassador. So good to make your acquaintance!"

"Of course," Mahit said, "go—"

He did. Three Seagrass came closer. Mahit said, "Please get me another drink?" at approximately the same moment as Three Seagrass said *"What deal?"*

"I don't actually know."

Three Seagrass looked at her with an expression that Mahit hoped wasn't pity. "A stronger drink than that, then."

"Also without violets?"

"In a minute," Three Seagrass said. "You don't want to miss this." Very gently she took Mahit's elbow and turned her to where the imperial dais was—

—to where the imperial dais, which she had thought was a slightly raised oval on a raked floor, was rising from the ground, unfolding. Mahit thought of the City, trapping her in Plaza Central Nine—thought of Thirty Larkspur's epithet, *the world in blooms*. The throne rose on soundless hydraulic engines, an unfurling sunburst like a thicket of golden spears, a reified echo of the lights running through the ribbed vault of the ceiling. To the right of it Thirty Larkspur stood exalted in refracted illumination; to the left was a woman Mahit assumed was Eight Loop, stooped in the shoulders and balanced on a silver cane but not any less illuminated—her version of the imperial-associate partial crown glowed bright even against her silvered hair.

In the center of the sun-spear throne, revealed like a seed in a flower or the core in the heart of a burning star, Mahit got her first glimpse of the Emperor Six Direction.

She thought, *He's not imposing except by position*—he was short, sunken-cheeked, the long fall of his hair more dirty steel than silver even if his eyes were sharp—and then *The position is more than enough, I am being devoured by my own poetic imagination.*

Six Direction was old, was small, looked fragile—brittle-boned, too thin, as if he'd been ill and was now just barely recovered. And Six Direction was in command of all this ceremony, or commanded by it—the emperor and the empire were the same, weren't they? As close as the words for empire and world were, or nearly—and he claimed the attention of every Teixcalaanlitzlim. The exhalation of breath that sagged through the room when he lifted his hand in benediction was like a physical blow.

Smoke and mirrors and refracted light, and the weight of history in a glance—Mahit knew she was being manipulated and couldn't find a way to *stop* being. At Six Direction's side was a child who must be the ninety-percent clone. A small, serious boy with enormous black eyes.

And if that wasn't a declaration of where the succession would eventually fall, Mahit didn't know what was. It wasn't going to be a true tripartite council: it was going to be a child-emperor and two regents for him to fight with. That poor child, with Thirty Larkspur and Eight Loop for co-regents. Abruptly she wondered which people in the ballroom were One Lightning's supporters—if any of the people so prominently wearing

purple larkspurs were in fact covering for a less politic choice—
and, for that matter, where Ten Pearl from the Science Ministry
was, and when he'd approach her.

"Are you ready to be presented to the Emperor," Three Seagrass asked archly, "or are you going to stare for a while first?"

Mahit made a wordless noise, helplessly amused. "What did
you feel like, the first time you saw the throne rise?"

"Terrified that I wasn't good enough to be here," Three Seagrass said. "Is it different for you?"

"I don't think I'm terrified," Mahit said, finding her way
through how she felt as she framed the sentence, "I think I'm . . .
angry."

"Angry."

"It's *so much*. I can't *not* feel—"

"Of course not. It's meant to be like that. It's the Emperor,
who is more illuminate than the sun."

"I know. But I *know* I know, and that's the problem." Mahit
shrugged. "I will be very honored to meet him. No matter how
I feel."

"Come on then," Three Seagrass said, holding on to her
elbow more firmly. "It's one of your ambassadorial duties,
anyhow! You need to be formally acknowledged and invested
with your post."

There was a receiving line at the foot of the dais, but it was
shorter than Mahit assumed it would be, and His Majesty Six
Direction spent no more than a minute with each petitioner.
When it was her turn, Three Seagrass announced her again—
more quietly this time, but no less clearly—and she climbed the
steps to the center of the many-petalled sun-spear throne.

A Teixcalaanlitzlim would have dropped forehead to the
floor, bent over their knees in full proskynesis. Mahit knelt but
did not fold—bowed only her head, stretching her hands out in
front of her. Stationers didn't bow, not to pilots nor to the gov-

erning Council, no matter how long their imago-lines were, but she and Yskandr had come up with this solution in the two months they'd spent in transit to the City. She'd seen illustrations of the pose in infofiche scans of old Teixcalaanli ceremonial manuals: it was how the alien diplomat Ebrekt First-Positioned had greeted the Teixcalaanli Emperor Two Sunspot on the bow of the ship *Inscription's Glass Key,* during the official first contact between the Teixcalaan and the Ebrekti people. (Or, at least, how a Teixcalaanli artist had rendered the pose of a person whose limbs were arranged for quadrupedal locomotion.)

That had been four hundred years ago out on the edge of known space, after *Inscription's Glass Key* had leapt through a new jumpgate unexpectedly, while Two Sunspot was fleeing the usurper Eleven Cloud (Two Sunspot had eventually beaten her and her legions back, and remained Emperor—there were *several* novels about it, and Mahit had read them all). The Ebrekti had been good neighbors ever since: quiet, keeping to their side of the one gate that connected their space and Teixcalaan. She and Yskandr had calculated what it would say, to bow like this—a respectful statement of distance from the Empire.

Yskandr had told her that he'd chosen the same pose himself, when he was presented to Six Direction.

Only now, with her hands stretched out, supplicant but straight-spined, did Mahit wonder if she was repeating a mistake, making all of Lsel *inhuman* by virtue of one symbolic allusion—

The Emperor closed his hands around her wrists and lightly pulled her to her feet.

She was still two steps below the throne, which made her his equal in height. His fingers wrapped around the bones of her wrists were shocking, unexpected. They were *hot*. The man was burning with fever, and yet Mahit would never have known if he hadn't touched her. He was wearing some kind of citrus and woodsmoke perfume. He looked straight at her, straight *through* her—Mahit found herself smiling, helplessly, fighting back a rush of *familiarity* that wasn't hers. She thought for a moment it was the beginning of another memory-flash, her failing imago-machine spinning her out of time, back to *Yskandr*—but no, no, this was all endocrine response.

Sense memory was one of the strongest carryovers down an imago-line. Scents. Sound, sometimes—music could cue memory—but scent and taste were the least narrative, the most encapsulated kinds of memory, the most easily shifted from one person to the next down the line. Perhaps Yskandr was—was less gone than she'd thought, she could *hope* for that, through the dizzy strangeness of someone else's neurochemical mirroring.

"Your Majesty," she said. "Lsel Station greets you."

"Teixcalaan greets *you*, Mahit Dzmare," said the Emperor. Like he meant it, like he was glad to see her—

What the *fuck* had Yskandr done here?

"And invests you with your diplomatic office," Six Direction went on. "We are gratified by the choice of ambassador, and express our wishes for your service to us to be to our mutual benefit."

He was still holding her wrists. There was a thick scar on his palm, pressed against her skin, and she thought vividly of that first memory-flash, of Yskandr slicing his own palm open to swear an oath, and wondered how many oaths an emperor swore with blood over the course of his life. The hot pressure of his hands was intense, and she was still caught in the rush of oxytocin happiness that *didn't belong to her* and wouldn't she just like to interrogate Yskandr as to what exactly he'd meant to the *Emperor of all Teixcalaan*? Somehow she managed to nod, to thank Six Direction with correct formality, to bow and back down the steps of the dais without tripping.

"I need to sit down," she said to Three Seagrass.

"Not yet you don't," Three Seagrass told her, not without

sympathy. "Ten Pearl is headed straight for us. Are you going to faint?"

"Do people faint after audiences often?"

"It's more a thing in daytime dramas that come over the newsfeeds, but the strangest things end up being repeatable—"

Mahit said, "I'm not going to faint, Three Seagrass."

Three Seagrass actually took her hand and squeezed it. "Excellent! You're really doing fine."

Mahit wasn't exactly sure of that, but she could damn well pretend to be for the length of some political theater. She squeezed Three Seagrass's fingers back, and let them go. Walked a little farther away from the dais, into an open space in the glitter of the crowd. She could feel the focus of the room shift around her—from the Emperor on the dais, sitting back now and murmuring something to his tiny clone, audiences over, to where the barbarian ambassador had put herself right under the lights in an open space, a public declaration that *something important was about to happen* and maybe they should watch.

Ten Pearl, for an *ixplanatl*—and surely the Science Minister was a scientist, and not just an appointed bureaucrat—had enough theatricality in him to know that Mahit had taken his offer of a public meeting and accepted the gambit. This was as public as was available in Palace-Earth. He had to know it. The next five minutes would be all over the newsfeeds in the morning, right next to holographs of Mahit with her wrists in the Emperor's hands, and he came striding up to meet her in a swirl of deep-red coattails, a bony man with a scientist's hunched shoulders. He was older than he'd been in the memory-flash—more stooped—but he still wore a ring on each finger: thin bands of mother-of-pearl, stoneless. For his name—ostentatious, but in a self-deprecating sort of way. Mahit admired it. As Yskandr had admired it, the same rueful appreciation of a joke. Whether the feeling was genuine to Mahit she honestly didn't know.

"Ambassador," Ten Pearl said. "Congratulations on your investiture."

Mahit bowed over her fingertips. "Much appreciated," she said, a full level of formality lower than she ought to have kept to at court. But she'd planned to play the wide-eyed foreigner at this meeting and she was going to go through with it, even if she was still buzzing with imago-induced neurochemicals—the oxytocin rush from meeting the Emperor, the echo of Yskandr's conversation with this man fifteen years ago. The *subway*. The City as a mind, an algorithm that watched where everyone was, and ran seamlessly in response.

"I'm terribly sorry for the unfortunate incident that befell your predecessor," Ten Pearl went on. "I feel personally responsible; I ought to have inquired after his biological sensitivities."

His biological sensitivities! What a way to phrase it. Mahit hoped fervently she was not about to dissolve into hysterical giggling; it would wreck the play for the newsfeeds. "I'm sure there was nothing you could have done about it," she said, managing to stay straight-faced. "Lsel Station bears no enmity toward the Science Ministry, of course." Even a barbarian would know *enmity*; it was a rote diplomatic phrase. It was what you had before you started a war.

"You're quite understanding," Ten Pearl said. "A credit to your government. They've certainly made a solid choice with you."

"I hope so," Mahit said. Fawning, wide-eyed, a credulous provincial. Not a political threat. Not at all, not even with how the Emperor had greeted her. Of course it wouldn't hold up for long—Ten Pearl was the only one she was playing this particular game with—but this was the game for the newsfeeds, and it might give her some cover. A few days. A week, before someone tried to kill her like they'd killed Yskandr, who had clearly been *quite* dangerous.

She hadn't really thought of it like that before. That she was buying time.

It knocked the remains of the neurochemical high right back down to baseline.

"Ambassador Aghavn did not leave very many notes," she went on, shrugging as if to say *what can be done about the errors of the dead,* "but I would of course like to continue to explore whatever projects he was working on with the Science Ministry." A quick breath, and then she let her face fall into the pattern of Yskandr's expressions, the familiar-unfamiliar stretch of wider muscles, deeper-set eyes, and said: "Automated systems—without error and without conflict—such algorithms have certainly persisted."

Ten Pearl looked at her a fraction too long—had she been too obvious, leaving bait for a more private meeting than this? Using what Yskandr had said, so long ago—but it had felt *correct*—and then Ten Pearl nodded, saying, "Perhaps we can resurrect a little of what Ambassador Aghavn wanted to achieve, between the two of us—he was so interested in our automated systems, and how they might be applied on your station. I'm sure you are as well. Have your liaison arrange a time and place. I'm sure we can fit you in sometime this week."

Resurrect was a terrible choice of word. "Of course," Mahit said. She bowed again. "I hope for many future accomplishments for both of us."

"Naturally you do," said Ten Pearl. He stepped closer, a fraction past the norms of Teixcalaanli personal space, into that precise zone of closeness that Mahit was most comfortable with: how friends stood on Lsel, where there wasn't enough space to be standoffish. "Do be careful, Ambassador," he said.

"Of what?" Mahit asked. She wouldn't break the illusion of incompetence.

"You're already attracting a thousand eyes, just like Aghavn did." Ten Pearl's smile was perfectly Teixcalaanli, mostly in the cheeks and in a widening of the eyes, but Mahit could tell it was a show regardless. "Look around. And think of the eyes of that automated system you and your predecessor so admire."

"Oh," said Mahit. "Well. We are in front of the imperial throne."

"Ambassador," said Three Seagrass, materializing at Mahit's side, "I recall you wanted to watch the oration contest. It is about to begin. Perhaps Minister Ten Pearl would also like to hear the newest compositions from our court's poets?"

She'd spoken very slowly and clearly, as if she didn't know that Mahit could understand Teixcalaanli at full speed. Mahit could have picked her up and spun her around in gratitude for understanding and *participating,* without instruction. Was this how she'd been supposed to feel all this time, if Yskandr had remained with her? How an imago should make their successor feel: two people accomplishing one goal, without needing to consult. Perfect synchronicity.

"I wouldn't want to distract the Ambassador," said Ten Pearl. "Go on." He waved a hand at where Nine Maize and a cluster of other courtiers had begun to assemble, off to the left of the dais. Mahit expressed her gratitude to him again—tripped deliberately over the pronunciation of the most formal thanks, even though she knew she was pushing her luck, but it was so *satisfying* to see him try to figure out if she was lying. And *how* she was lying.

When she and Three Seagrass were safely out of his earshot, she leaned down and murmured, "I thought that went well."

"*I* thought you said you needed to sit down and rest, not that you needed to play at uncivilization with the *Science Minister,*" Three Seagrass hissed, but her eyes were glittering-bright.

"Did you have fun?" Mahit said, realizing as she said it that she wasn't as done with the neurochemical imago-effect as she'd thought—she still felt sparkling, giddily pleased. She hadn't exactly felt that way during the conversation with Ten Pearl, but now, with Three Seagrass hanging on her arm—

"Yes, I had fun! Are you going to be like this *all the time*? He isn't a fool, Mahit, he'll have you figured out by the time I set up that meeting."

"It's not for him," Mahit said. "It's for the audience. The court and the newsfeeds."

Three Seagrass shook her head. "No other job is ever going to be this interesting, is it?" she said. "I promised I'd get you a drink. Come on. They're about to start."

———

Somewhere in the middle of the second oration, an acrostic ode that simultaneously spelled out the name of the poet's hypothetical lost beloved via the opening letters of each line and told a heart-wrenching story of his self-sacrifice to save his shipmates from a vacuum breach, Mahit had the sudden realization that she was standing in the Teixcalaanli court, hearing a Teixcalaanli poetry contest, while holding an alcoholic drink and accompanied by a witty Teixcalaanli friend.

Everything she had ever wanted when she was fifteen. Right here.

She thought it should probably have made her feel happy, instead of abruptly unreal. Disconnected—*depersonalized*. Like she was happening to someone else.

The orations were good. Some of them were better than good—driving rhythms over clever internal rhyme, or an orator whose delivery of that particular Teixcalaanli style of half-sung, half-spoken rapid-fire chant was exceptionally fluid. Exquisite imagery washed over Mahit in waves, and she felt nothing. Nothing aside from wishing that she could have copies of every poem written down, confined to glyphs that she could read on her own someplace quiet and silent and still. If she could just read the poems—speak them in her own voice, try out the rhythms and the cadences, find how they moved on her tongue—surely she'd feel the power of them. She always had before.

She drank from her glass. Three Seagrass had brought her some spirit distilled from a grain she didn't know. It was the pale gold color of all the swarming lights, and burned going down her throat.

Nine Maize's oration, when it came, was the epigram Three Seagrass had promised it would be. He'd hardly begun—only took his place, cleared his throat, and recited a three-line stanza:

Every skyport harbor overflows
Citizens carry armfuls of imported flowers.
These things are ceaseless: star-charts, disembarkments

when he hesitated just long enough to signal a shift, a caesura. Mahit felt the entire room catch on his held breath. No matter how little she had liked him, she saw why he was the toast of the court's literati: what charisma he had was amplified the instant he spoke in verse. It was what he was made for. On Lsel he'd have been a candidate for an imago-line of poets, if Lsel had had such a thing.

"The curl of unborn petals holds a hollowness," said Nine Maize.

Then he sat down again.

There was no release of tension. The sense of unease remained, floating like a miasma. The next orator came forward in the midst of the awkward silence, the scrape of her shoes on the floor audible. She fumbled the first line of her own composition and had to begin again.

Mahit turned to Three Seagrass, questioning.

"Politics," murmured Three Seagrass. "That was . . . a critique. In several ways. I really thought Thirty Larkspur had Nine Maize under his thumb, but people can be so surprising."

"I'd think it was most critical of Eight Antidote?" Mahit said. "The child. *Unborn petals* . . ."

"Yes," Three Seagrass said, her eyebrows knit together, "but Thirty Larkspur's the heir who is most responsible for increasing importation of in-Empire goods to the City. It's why he has money—he's bringing it in from the Western Arc systems, that's where his family is from. And there's that suggestion of corruption for every citizen carrying a flower . . . every import being somehow *poisoned* . . . as if Thirty Larkspur's wealth is as bad as importing objects from outside Teixcalaan entirely."

Politics by means of literary analysis. Were there aptitudes that tested for *that,* or was it something a Teixcalaanlitzlim would learn through intense exposure? Mahit could imagine Three Seagrass as a child, deciphering the political messages in *The Buildings* with her school peers at lunch. It wasn't difficult to picture.

"Critical of everyone save Eight Loop, then," she said.

"She only survives pillory by overt omission," Three Seagrass said. "I think it's deeper than just *which heir is best,* Mahit. Why else would Nine Maize make such a dangerous choice in topics?"

Mahit thought of the fundamental assumption of Teixcalaanli society: that collapse between *world* and *Empire* and *City*—and how if there was such a collapse, *importation* was uneasy, *foreign* was dangerous, even if that importation was just from a distant part of the Empire. And barbarians like herself oughtn't be able to conceptualize why a poem about the perilous corruption of some other planet's flowers might be, in fact, designed to make a Teixcalaanlitzlim nervous.

But if a system was no longer *foreign*—if the world was large enough, the Empire large enough, to encompass and subsume all that was barbaric about that world—well, it wasn't barbaric anymore. It wasn't threatening anymore. If Nine Maize was pointing out the threat of *importation,* he was calling for—or at least suggesting—that Teixcalaan act to normalize that threat. To *civilize it.* And Teixcalaan had always civilized—had always *made something Teixcalaanli*—with force. Force, like a war. Nine Maize wasn't really talking to Thirty Larkspur; Nine Maize was shoring up whatever political factions were preparing for war. All those troop movements. One Lightning, with his legions and his shouting partisans—but also Six Direction, setting the fleet into the kind of readiness that had marked his early reign, when he'd been a star-conquering emperor himself.

"Where are One Lightning's supporters tonight, Three Seagrass?" she asked. "They're who that poem was for. For anyone who is interested in a stronger, more centralized, less importation-focused Teixcalaan."

"He's a populist and this is court, it's not fashionable. But I'm sure—*oh,*" Three Seagrass said. "Oh. Well. We were looking for the war."

"A war very soon," Mahit said, uneasily thrilled with discovery. "An annexation. A conquest war. For the purpose of making places *less foreign.*"

Three Seagrass reached over and plucked Mahit's glass of alcohol out of her hand, took a large sip, and returned it. "We haven't had an annexation war since before I was born."

"I know," said Mahit, "we do have history on the stations. We were enjoying Teixcalaan being a *quiescent* neighboring predator—"

"You make us sound like a mindless animal."

"Not mindless," Mahit said. It was as close as she could bring herself to an apology. "Never that."

"But an animal."

"You do devour. Isn't that what we're talking about? A war of *annexation*."

"It's not—*devour* would be if we were xenophobes or genocides, if we didn't bring new territories *into the Empire*."

Into the world. Shift the pronunciation of the verb, and Three Seagrass could have been saying *if we didn't make new territories real,* but Mahit knew what she meant: all the ways that being part of Teixcalaan gave a planet or a station prosperity. Economic, cultural—*take a Teixcalaanli name, be a citizen.* Speak poetry.

"Let's not argue, Three Seagrass," she said. "I don't want to."

Three Seagrass pressed her lips together. "We're going to argue. I want to understand what you *think*. It's my job. But we can argue later. The Emperor is going to announce the contest winner soon, look."

The orations were finished. Mahit had missed the last few entirely. None of them had disturbed the room the way Nine Maize had. Now the Emperor stood up, his *ezuazuacatlim* flanking him—had they conferred, chosen a winner together? She doubted that they could so *quickly* come to a conclusion, not when the group of them included Thirty Larkspur, two Teixcalaanlitzlim Mahit hadn't met, and Nineteen Adze, resplendent still in white. Quite nearly a relief to look at, in all of the gleaming lights.

Six Direction gestured, pointing out a poet who had made absolutely no impression on Mahit. She looked as surprised by her honor as the rest of the crowd, which hesitated on the verge of the expected acclamatory cheering as if they weren't certain of what had happened either.

"Who is that?" Mahit whispered to Three Seagrass.

"Fourteen Spire," Three Seagrass said. "She's exquisitely dull in her basic competence and always has been. She's never won anything before."

Nine Maize's face was impassive. Mahit couldn't tell if he was pleased to be so obviously snubbed or angry about it; whether he'd meant to ruin the evening so firmly. Fourteen Spire prostrated herself before the Emperor and received a blown-glass flower as her prize. Got up again. The assembled courtiers managed to shout her name, and Mahit joined in—it would have been stranger not to.

"Are you going to finish the drink?" asked Three Seagrass when the noise had died away.

"Yes. Why?"

"Because I am going to have to talk about Fourteen Spire's use of assonance for the rest of the evening, and you're going to have to listen, and we should both be slightly more inebriated."

"Oh," said Mahit. "When you put it like that."

CHAPTER
EIGHT

SIX OUTREACHING PALMS (TEIXCALAAN HIGH COM-
MAND) to FLEET CAPTAIN THREE SUMAC, 249.3.11-SIX
DIRECTION, code 19 (TOP SECRET): Prepare for immediate
withdrawal of Battle Groups Eight through Thirteen of the
Twenty-Sixth Legion from active engagement in Odile. Battle
Group Nine will remain in place under the command of *ikantlos*
Eighteen Turbine. Proceed immediately with Groups Eight
through Thirteen to the following coordinates to rendezvous with
the rest of the Third Imperial Fleet and prepare for imminent
jumpgate travel toward the Parzrawantlak Sector. Expedite. MES-
SAGE ENDS. COORDINATES FOLLOW.

> —message received by Fleet Captain Three Sumac in orbit
> around Odile-1 249th day, 3rd year, 11th indiction of the
> Emperor Six Direction of Teixcalaan

* * *

Lsel Station thanks you for your interest in serving our people in
our deepest tradition: movement through space. We of the Pilots'
Guild are proud to welcome prospective pilots to this informa-
tional session. This pamphlet summarizes how to adequately
prepare for application to the Pilots' Guild during the period approaching aptitude testing. Prospective candidates should keep in
mind the following requirements: mathematical preparation in
classical and quantum physics, basic chemistry, engineering; physical condition rated Excellent-2 with capacity to reach Excellent-4 in

hand-eye coordination; high scores on aptitudes in spatial aware-
ness and proprioception; high scores on aptitudes in group co-
hesion as well as independent initiative . . .

—pamphlet distributed to youth considering application to
the Lsel Guild of Pilots (age 10–13)

SOMEWHERE in the middle of her third glass of the pale
spirit Three Seagrass kept bringing her (Three Seagrass herself
was drinking something milky-white that she called *ahachotiya,*
which Mahit was convinced meant "spoilt burst fruit"—at least
from her understanding of the roots of the unfamiliar word—
and couldn't quite figure out why it was in any way desirable to
consume, let alone consume multiple instances of), Mahit found
herself standing on the edge of a circle of Teixcalaanlitzlim,
watching them have what she could only describe as not a
poetry *contest* but a battle of wits conducted entirely in extem-
poraneous verse. It had begun as a sort of game: one of Three
Seagrass's evanescently clever friends took up the last line of
Fourteen Spire's dull and prize-winning poem, said "Let's play,
shall we?" and proceeded to use that last line as her first one,
composing a quatrain that shifted the rhythm from the standard
fifteen-syllable political verse form to something that was absolutely stuffed full of dactyls. And then she'd pointed her chin
at another one of Three Seagrass's friends, in challenge—and
he took her last line, and apparently came up with a perfectly
acceptable quatrain on his own, with no preparatory time.
Mahit caught a few of his references: he was imitating the style
of a poet she'd read, Thirteen Penknife, who used the same
vowel-sound pattern repeated on either side of a caesura.

Imitating Thirteen Penknife seemed to be the order of the
day, after that—Three Seagrass took a turn, and then another
woman, and then a Teixcalaanlitzlim of a gender Mahit didn't

recognize, and then it was back to the initial challenger—who changed the game *again*, adding another element: now each quatrain had to start with the last line of the previous one, be in dactylic verse with a vowel-repeated caesura, *and* be on the subject of repairs made to City infrastructure.

Three Seagrass was annoyingly good at describing repairs to City infrastructure. She was lucid even through many glasses of *ahachotiya*, laughing, saying lines like *the grout seal around the reflecting pool / lapped smooth and clear-white by the tongues of a thousand Teixcalaanli feet / nevertheless frays granular and impermanent / and will be spoken again, remade in the image / of one department or another / clamoring,* and Mahit knew two things: first, that if she wanted to take a turn at this game, all she needed to do was step forward into the circle, and someone would challenge her, same as any other Teixcalaanlitzlim—and second, that she would *fail at it completely*. There was no way she could do this. She'd spent half her life studying Teixcalaanli literature and she was just barely good enough to *follow* this game, recognize a few of the referents. If she tried herself she'd—oh, they wouldn't *laugh*. They'd be *indulgent*. Indulgent of the poor, ignorant barbarian playing so *hard* at civilization and—

Three Seagrass wasn't paying the slightest bit of attention to her.

Mahit slipped back, away from the circle of clever young people, and made herself disappear into the great ballroom under the glittering starlit fan-vaults, and tried not to feel like she was going to cry. There wasn't any *point* in crying over this. If she wanted to weep she should weep for Yskandr, or for how much political trouble she was in, not over being unable to describe pool grout while referencing a centuries-old poem on departmental conflict. *One department or another, clamoring.* She'd read that poem in one of her collections, on the Station, and thought she'd *understood*. She hadn't.

The hall was still packed with inebriated courtiers; there seemed, if anything, to be more of them than before, a secondary tier of people who had come for the party now that the Emperor and his oration contest had finished—Six Direction himself was nowhere to be seen, and Mahit was glad of that. Glad, because he was hard to look at without wanting to go *near*. Glad, because he'd been so *fragile,* under all that power, and some part of her which she assumed was mostly Yskandr wanted him to be able to rest, and not waste time on entertaining this mess of shimmering Teixcalaanlitzlim. She got herself another drink (one more was not going to make a difference at this point, and she'd figured out how to avoid any of the ones that tasted of violets or milk-rotted flowers), and struck out across the floor.

Most people avoided her, or greeted her with the formality her office deserved, and that was absolutely fine. That was actually pleasant. She could do courtesy ritual, even without Yskandr's help, and she could be *personable*—these were all amongst her talents, these were the talents she had been specifically selected for, possessed *aptitude* in, and no Lsel imago-compatibility test ever looked for *fluid improvisational verse.* That was just a barbarian child's dream of a desire.

She was *wallowing.* Also she was slightly drunk.

And because both of these things were true, she was not at all expecting when a very, *very* tall person, wearing a long dress made out of bias-cut pale grey-gold silk, put her hand on Mahit's arm and spun her around. The room kept spinning for just a moment after Mahit stopped, and she should probably be worried about that.

The woman who had accosted her was not Teixcalaanli, not by features and certainly not by dress. Her arms were bare save for heavy silverwork cuffs, a bracelet on each wrist and one more wide band high on the left arm, and she was wearing a type of makeup Mahit wasn't familiar with: she'd covered all of her eyelids with red and pale-gold creams, like a painting of clouds at sunset on some distant planet.

Mahit bowed over her hands, and the other person did the same—awkwardly. With great unfamiliarity.

"You're the Lsel Ambassador!" she said brightly.

"Yes?"

"I'm Gorlaeth, the Ambassador from Dava. Come have a drink with me!"

"A drink," said Mahit, playing for time. She couldn't remember where Dava was. It was one of the most newly annexed planets in Teixcalaanli space, she was sure of *that,* but was it the one which exported silk or the one which had a famous mathematical school? This was what an imago was for. To help you remember things you needed to know that you hadn't known you needed to know.

"Yes," Gorlaeth said. "Do you drink? Do you have drinks on your station?"

Oh, Mahit thought, for *fuck's sake.* "Yes, we have drinks. Lots of them. What kind do you like?"

"I've been going through the bar. Local culture, you understand. You understand!" Gorlaeth's hand was back on Mahit's arm, and she felt a distant kind of disgusted pity for the other woman: she'd been sent here by her government, and her government was newly a protectorate of Teixcalaan, and she was *alone* (like Mahit was alone—but Mahit wasn't *supposed* to be alone), and being alone in Teixcalaan was like drowning in clear air.

A person might try all the drinks at a bar and call it *experiencing local culture.*

"How long have you been here?" Mahit asked. The same phrase Three Seagrass had used in the groundcar during her first minutes within the City. *How long have you been inside the world?*

Gorlaeth shrugged. "A few months. Now I'm not newest anymore—you are. You should come to our salon—several of the ambassadors from farther systems get together every other week—"

"And do what?"

"Politics," said Gorlaeth. When she smiled, she stopped looking affable and a little lost. She had a great many small teeth, and most of them were pointed. It wasn't a Stationer's smile, but it wasn't Teixcalaanli either, and Mahit felt, for one dizzying instant, the width and breadth of the galaxy—how *far* a jumpgate might take a person. How the people on the other side might be people, or might be something that looked like people but *weren't*—

That was how a Teixcalaanlitzlim would think. She was getting very good at it, wasn't she.

"Send me an invitation," Mahit said. "I'm sure the politics of Dava are of interest to the politics of Lsel."

Gorlaeth's expression did not so much change as harden: the sharpness of her teeth sharper. Mahit wondered if it was the fashion on Dava to file them to points, or if it was an example of an endemic trait in an isolated population, like the freefall mutants. "More than you might imagine, Ambassador," Gorlaeth said. "Our Teixcalaanli provincial governor hardly ever comes to bother us, save to invite us to events like this one. Your station might take note."

Mahit wasn't sure if that was a threat—*come to our salons, join our little group of ambassadors, and when Teixcalaan eats you too, you'll go down whole and unchewed*—or a genuine offer of sympathy: either way, she was insulted. This woman was from Dava—she still couldn't remember if it was significant for silk or mathematics—and here she thought she could give Mahit *advice*. She'd had enough of advice for one night.

When *she* smiled, she pulled her lips all the way back from her teeth into a grimace. "We might," she said. "I do hope you find a new drink to try, Ambassador Gorlaeth. Goodnight."

The room whirled again when she spun on one heel, but she thought she was still walking in a straight line. She needed to get out of here, before she met someone who could actually do her or her Station harm. She needed to be alone.

There were a multitude of doors out of the throne room of Palace-Earth. Mahit picked one at random, slipped through, and vanished herself into the machinery of the Emperor's own stronghold.

———

Most of Palace-Earth was marble and gold, star-inlay and dim lights, a perpetual state of near-dawn: like the view from the station as they came around the nearest planet again, sunflare and pinpoint stars mixed. There weren't half so many people as Mahit had expected, and almost none of them were guards or police. She didn't see a single Sunlit with their closed gold face-plates, even though they would have gone ever so well with the decor—only a few expressionless men and women with pale grey armbands, leanly muscled and armed with shocksticks, who looked as if they were quite dangerous, or might be if challenged. No projectile weapons in Teixcalaan, even in the palace; some of spacer culture ultimately spread down to the most civilized places. She avoided any door the people with shocksticks guarded, and let herself wander otherwise unimpeded: guided only by where she wasn't *allowed* to go.

She was more sober by the time she found the garden, not dizzy or faintly ill—only buzzed, shimmering-strange—and she was glad of that, both the lack of true drunkenness and the lack of total sobriety, when she realized what sort of garden it was that she had stumbled into, a tiny carved-out heart in the middle of this place. It was a *room* more than a garden: shaped like an enclosed bottle, a funnel that opened onto the night sky. The humid wind of the City slipped down it and was gentled as it went. The air was thick with moisture that dragged at Mahit's lungs, and fed the plants that climbed three-quarters of the way up the garden's walls. Deepest green and pale perfect *new* green, and a thousand, thousand red flowers on vines—and sipping at those flowers, tiny birds with long beaks, hardly longer than Mahit's thumb, that floated and dived like insects would. The beat of their wings was a hum. The entire garden sang with it.

She took two steps into the garden—her feet soundless on the moss that covered the floor—and held up her hand, wonderingly. One of the tiny birds alighted on it, balanced on her fingertip, and took off again. She couldn't even feel its weight. It had been like a ghost. It might not even have landed.

A place like this couldn't exist on a station. It couldn't exist on most *planets*. Even as she walked further into the strange dim sanctuary of it, she peered upward, trying to understand how the birds didn't fly up the funnel and escape into the vaulted Teixcalaanli sky—it was surely warm enough out there for them, though not nearly as sweet—not so many red flowers all at once. Perhaps succor was enough to keep a whole population trapped, willingly.

Succor, and the fine mesh of a net. When she tilted her head to exactly the right angle, she could see it, strung silvery and near-invisible at the funnel's mouth.

"Why are you here?" someone said—a high voice, thin, easy with command. Mahit stopped looking up.

It was the ninety-percent clone. Eight Antidote, the spitting image of Six Direction as he had been at age ten. The child's long, dark hair had come unbound and hung past his shoulders, but otherwise he remained as impeccable as he'd been when he'd stood beside his progenitor while Mahit offered up her wrists. He was not tall. He was not *going* to be tall, unless the 10 percent of his genetics that hadn't been spun from the Emperor's was full of a whole lot of genetic markers for height. What he was was *comfortable*, here in this strange room of trapped and beautiful birds, and looking at Mahit like she was an inconvenient piece of space debris that had to be avoided while inscribing an orbit.

"You're the new Ambassador from Lsel Station. Why are you here, and not at the party?"

For a child of ten he was distressingly direct. Mahit thought of Two Cartograph, Five Agate's little Map, with his orbital mechanics at age six. Children learned what they were expected to know. She had. At ten on Lsel she'd known how to patch a hull breach, how to calculate an incoming ship's trajectory, where her nearest escape pods were and how to use them in an emergency. She'd known, too, how to write her own name in Teixcalaanli glyphs, to recite a few poems; how to lie awake in her tiny safe pod of a room and dream of being a poet like Nine Orchid, having adventures on faraway planets. She wondered what this child dreamed of.

"My lord," she said to him. "I wanted to see more of the palace. Forgive me if I've intruded."

"The ambassadors from Lsel are curious," said Eight Antidote, like it was the opening line of an epigram.

"I suppose we are. Is this—do you come here often? All of the little birds are very beautiful."

"The *huitzahuitlim*."

"Is that what they're called?"

"The ones here are called that. Out where they come from they have a different name. But these are palace-hummers. Lsel doesn't have birds."

"No," said Mahit slowly. This child had known Yskandr. And

Yskandr had filled his mind with some vision of what Lsel Station was like. "We don't. We don't have many animals at all."

"I'd like to see a place like that," Eight Antidote said.

She was missing some vital piece of information. (She was certain she was never supposed to have encountered this child, not alone, not informally.) "You could," she said. "You're a very powerful young person, and if you still want to, when you are of age, Lsel Station would be honored to host you."

When Eight Antidote laughed, he did not sound ten years old. He sounded fey, and bitter, and *smart*, and Mahit wanted . . . something, some emotion she couldn't place. A vestige of maternal instinct. A desire to hold this *kid*, who knew birds and who had been left alone in the palace without friend or minder. (There was certainly a minder somewhere. Perhaps the City itself, the *perfect algorithm*, was watching them both.)

"Maybe I'll ask," he said. "I could ask."

"You could," Mahit said, again.

Eight Antidote shrugged. "Did you know," he said, "if you dip your fingers in the flowers the *huitzahuitlim* will drink the nectar right off your hand? They have long tongues. They don't even have to touch you to do it."

"I didn't," Mahit said.

"You should leave," Eight Antidote said. "You're not at all where you're supposed to be."

She nodded. "I suppose I'm not," she said. "Good night, my lord."

Turning her back on him felt dangerous, even if he was ten. (Perhaps because he *was* ten, and so used to having people turn their backs on him that it was a thing he could order.) Mahit thought about that all the way down the hall, retreating away from the garden and its inhabitants.

They don't even have to touch you to do it.

———

Some kind person, thinking of courtiers and officials on their feet for hours inside the maze of this place, had installed a series of low benches along one of the corridors nearer to the great ballroom and its sun-spear throne. Most of them were occupied, but Mahit found one in a corner that was entirely empty, and sank onto the cool marble. Her hip ached still. She wasn't in the slightest bit drunk anymore, and she was—exhausted, more than anything else, and every time she closed her eyes she thought of Eight Antidote in his garden with his birds.

Does he miss you, Yskandr? she thought, and again the silence inside her mind was an unfillable *gap,* a hole she could fall into. She leaned against the wall behind her, and tried to breathe evenly. The voices of the crowd inside the ballroom were audible a good thirty feet away, a dim laughing roar. *What did you tell him about our Station?*

She hardly noticed when a man sat down on the bench beside her—didn't open her eyes until he patted her lightly on the shoulder, and she startled upright. It was a Teixcalaanlitzlim (of course it was, what else was there), unremarkable: not from a ministry she could identify by uniform, just a man in early middle age in a multilayered dark green suit covered in tiny embroidered dark green starbursts, with a face she was absolutely sure she'd never remember.

"—what?" she asked.

"You," said the man, with an air of great satisfaction, "are not wearing one of those horrible little *pins.*"

Mahit felt her eyebrows knit together, and schooled her face into Teixcalaanli-appropriate expressionlessness. "The larkspur pins?" she guessed. "No. I'm not."

"Fucking buy you a fucking drink, for that," the man said.

Mahit could smell the alcohol coming off of him in waves. "Not enough people here like you."

"Are there not," Mahit said warily. She wanted to get up, but this drunken stranger had wrapped his hand around her wrist and was holding on.

"Not *nearly* enough. Say—were you in the Fleet, you look like you're the sort of woman who's been in the Fleet—"

"I've never served," Mahit said. "Not that way—"

"You *should*," he said. "Best ten years I ever gave the Empire, and they'd like a tall woman like you, doesn't matter there if you're not City-bred, no one will care as long as you follow your *yaotlek* and'll die for your siblings-in-arms—"

"What company did you serve under?" Mahit managed.

"The glorious and everlasting Eighteenth Legion, under the starshine-blessed One Lightning," he said, and Mahit realized she was being given a *recruiting speech*. A recruiting speech for the people who stood in the street shouting One Lightning's name, wanting to unseat the ruling emperor by pure acclamation, by the sound of their joined voices crying out that the attention and favor of the ever-burning stars had turned, and settled on a new person.

"What battles did One Lightning win?" she asked, thinking that she could use this drunkard to try to understand some of the *mentality,* to find the logic behind the acclamations.

"The fuck kind of question is *that,*" the man said, apparently deeply offended by her failure to immediately fall over herself in praise of One Lightning, and got up. His hand was still on her arm, gripping very tightly. "You're—*fuck* you, how dare you—"

No logic, Mahit thought dimly, *just emotion and loyalty, exacerbated by alcohol.* He *shook* her, and her teeth clicked against each other inside her skull. She couldn't decide if shouting *I'm not even one of you!* would make him back off or inflame him more, tried, "I didn't mean—"

"You're not wearing one of those pins but you *might as well be*—"

"One of my pins?" said another voice, urbane, serene. The drunk man dropped Mahit—the stone bench hurt to land on but she was glad of it anyway—and spun to see Thirty Larkspur himself, still resplendent in blue and his partial crown.

"Your Excellency," said the man, and bowed hastily over his hands. His face had gone a shade of nauseous green that didn't match his suit at all.

"I didn't catch your name," said Thirty Larkspur. "I'm terribly sorry."

"Eleven Conifer," he said, still bent over, muffled.

"Eleven Conifer," Thirty Larkspur repeated. "How lovely to make your acquaintance. Is there anything you needed from this young woman? She is, I'm afraid, a barbarian—I *do* apologize if she insulted you—"

Mahit gaped at him. Thirty Larkspur *winked* at her, over Eleven Conifer's bowed head. She shut her mouth. Thirty Larkspur was *dangerous*—smug, and clever, and manipulative, and she understood exactly what Five Agate had meant when she said that Mahit would understand why this man had been made an *ezuazuacat* and then an imperial co-heir after she'd seen him work in person. He was as flexible as a holograph, bending in the light, saying different words at different angles of approach.

"Now then," he went on, "you and I will have a discussion later, Eleven Conifer, and see if we can resolve our differences productively, now that I understand that you're upset enough to commit a crime."

"A crime?" Eleven Conifer asked, with a delicate sort of horror.

"Assault is a crime. But the barbarian will forgive you, won't she? For now."

Mahit nodded. "For now," she said. Playing along. Waiting to see what might happen.

"Why don't you leave her to her own devices and go back to the party, Eleven Conifer? Politics all aside, I'm sure you'll agree with me that there's better drink and quite a bit of dancing in there, and none at all out here."

Eleven Conifer nodded. He looked like a man impaled on a spike, wriggling to get free. "That's true, Your Excellency," he said. "I'll . . . do that."

"You do that," Thirty Larkspur said. "I'll come by later. To make sure you're having a good time."

And that, Mahit thought, was a naked threat. Eleven Conifer scuttled back down the hall, and now she was alone with Thirty Larkspur. *Two imperial heirs in one night, Yskandr. Did you ever do as well?* Her ulnar nerves went all to sparkles again, and she wondered if that was all that was *left* of her imago. An echo of neuropathy.

"I think I owe you my thanks," she said to Thirty Larkspur.

"Oh, it's nothing," he told her, his hands spread wide. "The man was shaking you. I would have intervened no matter who you were. Ambassador."

"Nevertheless."

"Of course." He paused. "Are you *lost*, Ambassador? Out here in the hallways."

Mahit summoned up a Lsel-style smile, all teeth. It managed to discomfit Thirty Larkspur enough that he didn't smile back. "I can find my own way back, Your Excellency," she said, lying through those teeth: "I'm not lost at all."

To prove it, she got up off the bench, and very deliberately walked—trying not to limp where her hip hurt her—back into the roar and noise of the party, leaving the *ezuazuacat* behind her.

There was dancing. Mahit decided straight off that she didn't dance, that her not dancing was part of how she was playing at uncivilization, and also that it was late enough that if she could figure out how to leave (and where she was *going,* when she left—back to Nineteen Adze? To her own apartments?) she *would.*

The dancing was in pairs, but also in interlocking groups that traded partners. It formed patterns on the floor, shifting like long chains, fractals. *Star-charts,* Mahit thought, and then on cue, *These things are ceaseless,* Nine Maize's epigram rising to the surface of her mind.

"There you are," said Five Agate, and Mahit turned to see Nineteen Adze's prize assistant standing just behind her, with one of her hands on Three Seagrass's upper back, steadying. "I've found your liaison, and I've been asked to escort you both home."

Three Seagrass was no longer ebulliently drunk. She was grey-pale at the temples, exhausted. She'd only been out of the hospital for thirty hours, Mahit remembered, and squelched an inappropriate impulse to take her arm. Five Agate, apparently, had the both of them well in hand.

"What did you see?" Three Seagrass asked, as they made their way across the room. Not *where did you go?* but *what did you see.* Not a question which chided Mahit for running off on her own. Not quite.

"Birds," Mahit found herself saying. "A whole garden of birds," and then they were outside, and in a groundcar, and being shuttled back to Palace-North.

chapter NINE

SERVICE RECORD LOOKUP for FIFTEEN ENGINE, ASEKRETA, PATRICIAN THIRD-CLASS (RETIRED).

[. . .] Retired from active Ministry post in 14.1.11 (Six Direction), taking an early pension. Request for retirement made as an alternative to the opening of an inquest into the asekreta's unauthorized connections to local extremists on Odile and surrounding Western Arc territories. The asekreta maintained throughout the process of his retirement that his contacts on Odile were primarily social and incidentally political, and that he reported seditious and anti-imperial sentiment as expected from an Information Ministry agent. [SECTION REDACTED: SECURITY 19] [. . .] nevertheless when offered retirement or investigation he chose retirement without further comment. Monthly reports of cloudhook activity since the asekreta's retirement do not suggest seditious tendencies. Recommendation: continue monitoring at current intensity.

    —//*access*//*INFORMATION*, database query performed

        246.3.11 by *asekreta* Three Seagrass, personal cloudhook

        from secured in-palace location

*   *   *

Stationer contacts with nonhumans have primarily been mediated through the auspices of neighboring polities: a salient example is the extant treaty between the Teixcalaanli Empire and the Ebrekti; as Stationer space shares no jumpgate points with Ebrekt space, the Ebrekt peace agreement with Teixcalaan has been sufficient to normalize Stationer relations with Ebrekti ships—though considerations of Stationer sovereignty in treaty-making with nonhumans continue to be brought up by subsequent Councilors for the Miners and Councilors for Heritage over the past six decades. Nevertheless, barring a nonhuman presence in Stationer space and direct contact, there is likely to be little need for a revision in policy [. . .]

—"Stationer Treaty-Making Across Jumpgate Lines," thesis presented to the Heritage Board by Gelak Lerants as part of his examination for membership; accessed by Councilor for the Pilots Dekakel Onchu, 248.3.11 Teixcalaanli reckoning

THE war came in with the newsfeeds in the morning.

When it began, Mahit was sitting opposite Three Seagrass in Nineteen Adze's dawn-drenched front office, eating porridge with a spoon as if she and her liaison and the *ezuazuacat* were all some sort of peculiar family, while the array of Nineteen Adze's infoscreens hovered over the three of them and played an endless succession of stock clips of Teixcalaanli military ships: soldiers going into them, their magnificently large gunports, the brightly painted sun-gold and blood-red insignia on their grey sides. The newsfeed commentators were effervescent and vague. There was a war; it was a war of conquest, a conquering force sent out to claim more of the vast black void of space for Teixcalaan, the vast black void and whatever bright planetary jewels might be nestled in it, all ready to be subsumed under the battle flag of the Empire. An *accession war.* Everyone was very excited and talking about the trade interests which would benefit most from the Empire being on a wartime footing for the first time in twenty years. Mahit hadn't drunk enough the previous evening to be hung over, despite her efforts, but she wished she had; it would have given her an excuse to feel this queasy. *Steel,* she thought. Steel and shipbuilding and supply lines, and Councilor Amnardbat and Councilor Tarats might be able to renegotiate how much money Lsel got from selling molybdenum to the Empire—it *could* be a useful war . . .

She knew, thinking it, that she was trying to talk herself out of the unstable, shifting-gravity nausea. The certain knowledge that this could not be a useful war, not for Lsel—not with Teixcalaan as it was.

When the newsfeeds had switched from local tabloid updates to the cheery pomp and circumstance of impending military action—it seemed to be a genre, something that Teixcalaanli broadcasters simply knew how to do—one of Nineteen Adze's assistants had appeared at her side with a glass press full of what Mahit recognized by scent as fresh-ground coffee, and spirited away the bowls of tea.

Coffee, a stronger stimulant than tea. *Everyone* was on a wartime footing, weren't they.

"This is not a very informative war," said Three Seagrass pointedly, when the newsfeeds had looped around again to the beginning, the opening of the ships, the marching troops in gold and grey, the phatic commentary of the newsfeed hosts.

Nineteen Adze handed her a tiny cup of the coffee, as if that was an answer. "Wait for it," she said. "Take the breathing room while you can, *asekreta,* there'll be little enough of it to go around very shortly."

"And who," Three Seagrass asked, imitating with uncanny precision the headlong breathlessness of the commentators, "do *you* think will be our commander, Your Excellency? Since you have the enormous honor of being an *ezuazuacat,* and ever so close to the decisions at the heart of the Empire!"

Nineteen Adze, entirely serene, said, "Mahit, your liaison is an actress *and* an interrogator. What rare luck you're having."

Mahit had no idea what to say to that. Three Seagrass was slightly colored through the cheeks, which might imply it had been a compliment. "She's much less straightforward than I am," Mahit said. "I will just ask you who you think will be named commander, and whether it really will be One Lightning and not some other *yaotlek.*"

"It will be," Nineteen Adze said. "You could make double your wager on it, if you weren't so conveniently trapped in my apartments, safely away from the corruption of public betting."

Somehow they had reached a state where Nineteen Adze was *joking* about keeping Mahit prisoner, and Mahit actually found it funny. She wasn't sure there was any sense in which she could take this development as a good thing, aside from how it was— nice, *pleasant,* to not be waiting for imminent death while she ate breakfast. Five Agate had collected her and Three Seagrass at the end of the banquet, and escorted them back into Nineteen Adze's office complex as if there hadn't been any other possible exit: perfectly implacable, all decisions already made. It was a terrible concession to have gone back with her, Mahit knew that it was, but it would have been worse to have *refused* in public—and where would she have gone that was safe, then? After so deliberately getting rid of what allies she had, who would trust her?

And also: Nineteen Adze was publicly tied to *her,* and to Lsel, as much as she was tied to Nineteen Adze.

Mahit licked the back of her spoon. "The salary my station pays me is entirely adequate without recourse to public betting," she said.

"And you had Ten Pearl thinking you were an ignoramus," Nineteen Adze said, amused. "*Adequate without recourse to.* You're *worse* than Yskandr was."

"How so?"

"Yskandr, when I met him—he was perhaps a year, two years older than you? And already a fixture at court by the time I got back from my last military tour of duty and Six Direction made me *ezuazuacat*. Yskandr *liked* Teixcalaan. But you, Ambassador Dzmare, if you weren't an ambassador you'd apply for citizenship."

Mahit didn't flinch; she was proud of herself for not flinching, for saying, "The Minister for Science would never approve such an application," for taking up another spoonful of porridge. Proud also for how Three Seagrass *and* Nineteen Adze both laughed. Their laughter covered how she wanted to squirm, wanted to be grateful for being *not a barbarian* enough that citizenship would have been a possibility and hating herself for wanting to be grateful, all at once.

When the newsfeeds changed over to the starburst glyph of Palace-Sky's internal news service, she was relieved. It would be difficult for Nineteen Adze to interrogate her about her loyalties when all three of them were watching an official announcement. The starburst resolved into Six Direction himself, flanked by a group of Teixcalaanlitzlim that Mahit supposed were the *yaotlekim*, all of the generals who were on-planet and available for publicity. They bristled and gleamed like a thicket of razor-sharp reeds; in the middle of them Six Direction looked old.

The announcement the Emperor read off his cloudhook was short, a tiny and precise rhetorical detonation: *Like a flower turns to the sun or a person takes in oxygen*, he said, *Teixcalaan reaches again toward the stars*—Mahit watched Nineteen Adze's face, her narrowed eyes, the tension in the corners of her mouth. Admiration, she thought, and something in the same region as fear, but not insult. She had probably vetted this speech, or even been consulted on it. (And how long had she known? Since yesterday at the banquet? Since long before then, when she had been pretending to Mahit and Three Seagrass that she was as ignorant of where the war would be as they were?)

We move toward Parzrawantlak Sector, said Six Direction, his face suddenly overlaid with the star-chart of Teixcalaanli space. The City, a golden planet, hovered between his eyes; then the chart shifted, demonstrating the vectors the fleet would take, the points at which they would converge into an unstoppable spearpoint of ships.

Mahit knew those stars. She knew the sector name, too—but she knew it in Stationer, not filtered through Teixcalaanli consonants. *Bardzravand,* "the high plateau," the sector of space that all the Stationers had settled in their long-ago scattering. She'd always seen the vectors on the newsfeed's star-chart inverted, though, looked at them from the other side: an indrawing line that had called her since she was a child. Yskandr had hung the same vectored chart above his bed back in the ambassadorial suite: Lsel looking at the Empire.

Of course it wasn't Lsel that Teixcalaan wanted, though they'd be pleased enough to finally have it: Lsel Station, and all the other tiny stations, were merely in the way of that onrushing tide of ships. Beyond them was alien territory, populated by Ebrekti and species even more foreign, or undiscovered by humanity; beyond them as well were planets to terraform or colonize, resources to extract. The jaws of the Empire opening up again, akimbo, bloody-toothed—the endless self-justifying *desire* that was Teixcalaan, and Teixcalaanli ways of thinking of the universe. The Empire, the world. One and the same. And if they were not yet so: make them so, for this is the right and correct will of the stars.

Lsel itself would be more than an incidental prize, Mahit thought, as clinically as she could manage: one of the oldest continuously inhabited artificial worldlets, replete with the best pilots, a precisely calibrated resource extraction system for mining molybdenum and iron from stellar debris—and a perfect location in a gravity well that controlled most of local space, including the only two jumpgates in the area.

We entrust the outrushing tide to the swift-reaching hands of One Lightning, and name him the yaotlek-nema, *the leader of our legions in this endeavor,* the Emperor finished, to no one's surprise at all.

"Well," said Three Seagrass. "That's . . . certainly that."

"Yes," said Mahit. "It seems to be." She sounded so calm, even to herself.

"Not," Nineteen Adze said, "my first choice of targets. But he doesn't always listen to me." She sighed, squared her shoulders—how could she continue to look so *human,* so much like she was just like anyone else!—and pushed herself away from the table. "But I think you'll find that your value as an ambassador has only *increased* with this news, Mahit. Don't imagine for a moment that I'd toss you out to the wolves."

Still a hostage, then. Still useful to Nineteen Adze as an ally, or as something to be controlled. "I appreciate your continued hospitality," said Mahit.

"Of course you do." Nineteen Adze could sound apologetic if she wanted, like turning on a floodlight of warmth with a switch—and then off again, brisk and bright. "There will be more meetings than anyone can possibly enjoy today. Running a war takes *committees.* Do feel free to use the office if you'd like. Seven Scale will be here if you need anything, and to take care of the breakfast dishes."

She swept out of the room and Mahit sat in horrified, dumb silence in her wake, as if she'd stolen her tongue by leaving.

"Most interesting job I'm ever going to have," Three Seagrass said, like it was a gesture of solidarity—it *was* a gesture of solidarity; she'd patted the back of Mahit's hand, she was trying.

"Ah, so you're not going to ask to be reassigned," Mahit said.

"As if I would. At absolute worst, you're going to be the ambassador who manages your people's integration into Teixcalaan. We'll have a *very* long career together, Mahit," said Three Seagrass.

Mahit could see the way her career on Teixcalaan might curve, now: could see herself becoming like Ambassador Gorlaeth of Dava, trying to find commonality with the other newly conquered. She must have looked stricken, because Three Seagrass said, "Look. We know a lot more now than we did yesterday, and that's not nothing."

Mahit admitted that they did. "I wonder if this is what Thirty Larkspur was trying to warn me about," she said. *"The deal is off."*

"You mean that your predecessor had somehow made an arrangement to keep Lsel Station out of the path of annexation," said Three Seagrass.

Mahit nodded. "And whatever he agreed to was an agreement between him and . . . His Majesty, I suspect. And now that he's dead, the deal is off."

"If I was a suspicious person . . ." Three Seagrass began.

"You are a suspicious person, you work for the Information Ministry," Mahit said.

Three Seagrass composed herself into a picture of innocence, which didn't have any reassuring effects at all. "If I was a suspicious person," she said again, "I would suspect that it is extremely convenient for whoever wanted the fleet to head toward Parzrawantlak that he is dead."

"And if *I* was a suspicious person," Mahit said, "I would agree with you. Three Seagrass, can you get me a *private* audience with His Majesty?"

Three Seagrass pressed her lips together, considering. "Under normal circumstances," she said, "I'd tell you that I could, but there'd be a three-month waiting period and I couldn't guarantee you'd be alone. But under the circumstances, I believe I might just be able to do better than that. You have very good, very official reasons to want to speak directly to His Illuminate Majesty."

"I do," Mahit said. "Arrange it. We have this delightfully equipped office, we might as well use it."

"It's all being recorded," Three Seagrass said, slightly apologetic. "I'd guarantee Nineteen Adze keeps track of every gesture and every glyph."

"I know," Mahit said. "But I don't see us having many *other* options, do you?"

"As long as you know—"

"Arrange it," Mahit said, more firmly, and Three Seagrass nodded, got up, and went to open one of the infograph screens. Mahit instantly felt better. She knew it was a false feeling—the sensation of being in control of the headlong, desperate rush was illusory, even if you took the initial leap under your own power—but she could use whatever comfort she could find.

Every moment she wasn't doing something else, she imagined the vector of ships.

What could she do?

It was a logic problem, or something out of classical physics: given these constraints, what action was possible? Given: that she was trapped in the heart of Palace-North, with only electronic access to her own files and messages, and no access at all to the pile of physical mail which was certainly growing in size and urgency in her own office. Given: that every action she took on an electronic system while here in Nineteen Adze's apartment would be monitored, which further constrained her ability to communicate unguardedly. Given: that Lsel Station would not know yet that the might of Teixcalaan was about to rush over them like the casually outflung loop of a solar flare, and had nothing like sufficient military capacity to meaningfully resist a full Teixcalaanli expedition. Given: that her predecessor had been murdered, perhaps to allow this conquest to proceed in this direction. Given: that her imago's presence as conscious memory was malfunctioning, leaving her with only the ghosts of neurochemical feelings that didn't belong to her, and flashes of memory so vivid they were like living another life. Given: that her imago's malfunction might have been sabotage, and—*think about it, Mahit, let yourself really think about it*—that sabotage might have taken place long before she ever arrived on the Jewel of the World—might, in fact, have originated with her own people, for reasons she didn't understand.

Also given: that if Mahit didn't do something she was going to shatter out of her skin with nerves. By the rosy quartz windows, Three Seagrass was enveloped in a little shell of infographs, murmuring subvocalizations to her cloudhook as if she were talking to an imago herself. Mahit stood up.

Better to take action than to be paralyzed by the thousands of shifting possibilities. Human beings walked and breathed and stepped out of cycling airlock doors to patch thinning places on a station's skin, all without thinking about how their limbs moved, where gravity had caught them, whether the internal bellows of lung and diaphragm had inflated enough or too little. She just needed to—not think. Or, to think, but to keep acting while she thought. Like speaking to Thirty Larkspur at the banquet: there was no *time* for paralysis. At the very least, she needed to make contact with Lsel and give them some idea of what she was dealing with.

She could hope for advice, though she wasn't sure what use advice even would be. She'd already disobeyed her only real directive when she'd admitted the existence of the imago-machines; she wasn't sure if further directives would be any more sustainable. But she'd like to feel a little less alone. To hear any voice from Lsel. Any voice which wasn't the stern and strange warning of Onchu of the Pilots, telling dead Yskandr to beware *sabotage*. That message hadn't been for Mahit anyway. The warning of the weapon wasn't for the weapon to hear.

This was why there were imago-lines for diplomats. So no one would be alone.

Yskandr, please. If you're there at all—

Static, like electric prickles down her arms. The ulnar nerves through the elbow to her smallest fingers. But the imago was just as silent as he'd been since that first hour in the morgue.

No time for cascading neurological disaster either. She'd think about it later. She'd fix it later, somehow. Now Mahit summoned up her own infograph halo and, standing at the opposite end of the office from Three Seagrass, began to compose two messages to the Council on Lsel. She composed them at the same time. They looked like the same message—and how she wished she could show off what she was doing to Three Seagrass, so busily arranging meetings on her behalf. Three Seagrass would understand ciphering a second message inside the first, and she'd admire it.

It wasn't a *good* cipher. It wasn't even a poetic cipher that would require a Teixcalaanli *asekreta* to fashionably decode. It was a book substitution cipher. Mahit had worked it out when she was a teenager, bored and playing at being Teixcalaanli: a master of intrigues and byzantine plots, a person who encrypted everything, and she'd used a Teixcalaanli glyph dictionary as her key. The most common one, *Imperial Glyphbook Standard,* the one which was distributed Empire-wide—and beyond the official borders of Teixcalaan—to teach barbarians and children to read. It had all the useful words, after all: "to hide," and "to betray," and so very many interlocking words for "civilization." She'd picked *Standard* to make her cipher out of simply because it was the most likely to be present in any location. Not even

Teixcalaanlitzlim could possibly remember every glyph in their ideographic writing system. There was a copy in Nineteen Adze's library, and it was the work of only a few minutes for Mahit to go fetch it.

Yskandr had laughed inside her skull when she'd suggested her old cipher to the Council as a method for hidden communication; had laughed *more* when they'd agreed. The ciphering process required that she write in Stationer, which had a thirty-seven-letter alphabet, and that the receiving decoder knew to look at the first letter of each Stationer word for the page number in *IGS*; the second letter for the line number; the first glyph in that table for the meaning. It wasn't meant to be a hyper-secure code; just *enough* encryption to get messages through. A little cover. A shield.

The message she wrote in Stationer she expected to be read, first by Nineteen Adze, then by the Imperial Censor Office, and perhaps even by the captain of the ship that would take it toward Lsel. It contained no more information than the news-feeds had; instead, it recapitulated them exactly, along with— Mahit thought—a relatively reasonable note of distress and concern.

That extra distress and concern gave her enough words to encode the hidden message, an ungrammatical sequence of Teixcalaanli nouns and verbs: *PRIORITY. Former ambassador compromised—movement (self, on foot, round-trip) restricted—memory bad—sovereignty threatened—request Council guidance.*

Even as Mahit was enclosing the double message in an info-fiche stick she doubted guidance would reach her in time for it to matter. But she had asked. And she had provided warning. Even if it was clear from any examination of the fleet's vectors that they were headed toward Lsel space, it was possible that no broadcasts of the fleet vectors would be sent out toward Lsel anyhow—why would the Empire *warn* their prey?

She tucked the stick into the silver basket marked for out-going mail on its table to the left of the office's door, where it sat innocuous with all the others aside from its red-wax marker for urgency, and the red-and-black sticky tab for off-planet communication. Soon Seven Scale would appear on his rounds through the office and bear it away into the City, through the labyrinth of the Censor Office and out.

"Three Seagrass," Mahit said, turning back and thinking of the similar basket back in the ambassadorial apartments, certainly overflowing now with angry messages on their pretty sticks, "is there any useful way I can get access to the work I'm *supposed* to be doing? The infofiche messages?"

"Huh," said Three Seagrass. She considered it. "Maybe part of it. How do you feel about breaking a very minor law?"

"What *kind* of minor law?" Mahit asked.

"The kind a Teixcalaanlitzlim breaks the first time when she's about nine years old. Using someone else's cloudhook."

"I am sure," Mahit said dryly, "that it gets more complicated when the person doing the using is not a citizen."

Three Seagrass reached up to the side of her head and lifted her cloudhook from over her eye. "Absolutely," she said, "but that just means you shouldn't get caught. Come over here."

Mahit came close. "We're being recorded," she said, even though she knew Three Seagrass was well aware.

"Bend down, you barbarians are unreasonably tall."

Mahit bent—thought suddenly and vividly of kneeling in front of the Emperor—and then Three Seagrass was settling the cloudhook over her eye. Half her vision went to data, an endless stream of it that resolved into a list of queries and requests. The interface was surprisingly intuitive: the cloudhook recalibrated to Mahit's own tiny eye movements rapidly, and the structure of the files was a version of the electronic version of her own office, just seen through Three Seagrass's accesses. It was a very *small* amount of cover, but it was cover. If she used Three Seagrass's cloudhook to access her own files, Nineteen Adze wouldn't be able to see that she'd gone in at all. Only that she was wearing her liaison's cloudhook.

"The lower-level requests to the Ambassador's office—visa queries, that sort of thing—are all things you could be telling me to do," Three Seagrass said, "if I wasn't having a fight on your behalf with three protocol officers and a queue system." Her fingers were warm on Mahit's temples. "If you want to do work while I sort out when you get to speak with the Emperor Himself, there's your list."

"Thanks," Mahit said. She straightened. "You don't need it?" She gestured at the cloudhook. Half her vision was *gone,* like she'd had a hemispheric brain injury that had replaced her eye with a to-do list.

"Not for an hour or so. Be useful, Ambassador."

Mahit thought she sounded—fond. Indulgent, even.

It was going to hurt so *much* if she had to stop pretending Three Seagrass was possessed of no agenda but her own ambition and a mild affection for barbarians.

———

The list of queries to the Ambassadorial Office of Lsel Station was approximately half requests to have a visa renewed and half somewhat offensive public interest queries as to "how Stationers conduct their daily lives, particularly with regard to holiday celebrations or other days of local excitement!" Mahit would have been irritated by all of them had they not been a perfectly distracting way of spending the time. As it was, answering tabloid journalists and distressed commercial traders was quite soothing. It took her nearly an hour to notice that there was one particular sort of business query that she had received absolutely none of: no one had written to ask her what she wanted done with Yskandr's body, still nestled in the basement of the Judiciary morgue. It had been more than half a week since *ixplanatl* Four Lever had asked her what she wanted done with it, and yet no one had followed up—not even an undersecretary.

Had they asked, and someone had prevented her from receiving the request? It could be as simple as her lack of access to messages sent on infofiche sticks, but surely someone placed as highly as *ixplanatl* Four Lever would have noticed that the Lsel Ambassador was quite publicly living in the offices of the *ezuazuacat* Nineteen Adze, and *rerouted the mail*. She would assume that if the request had been sent, it had been deliberately mislaid.

Or Four Lever *hadn't* asked, assuming that she would make inquiries first. Or hadn't asked, assuming that until she made an inquiry he could keep hold of Yskandr's body. Mahit thought of how she'd first met Nineteen Adze, sweeping into the morgue without any sort of retinue or reason for being there. Imagined her hands, unerringly reaching for the imago-machine at the base of Yskandr's skull to retrieve it before Mahit could have the body properly burnt. Someone had given her access. Perhaps it had been Four Lever. Mahit could imagine many things an *ezuazuacat* could provide for a Judiciary scientist in exchange for an unsupervised visit to the dead. Worse, she could also imagine many *other* people who could trade favors or influence or money for an hour or two alone with the body of her predecessor and all of his *illegal imported neurological technology*.

It was a problem. It was a problem that couldn't be fixed by simply requisitioning the body, either: Mahit imagined having the undecaying corpse of her predecessor brought into Nineteen Adze's office complex—perhaps she could prop it up on the couch, or lean it against the wall like a coat rack.

That would certainly make Nineteen Adze herself happy.

There had to be a better solution.

"Three Seagrass?" Mahit asked. "How long have you known Twelve Azalea?"

Three Seagrass extricated herself from her whirl of infographs. "Did he write to the office?" she asked, puzzled. "I thought he was entirely enamored of sending you anonymous messages on infofiche sticks."

"He didn't write, no," Mahit said. "But I might write to him. Do you *trust* him?"

"That is a very different question than how long I've known him."

"The one leads into the other," said Mahit.

"Do you trust *me*?"

She could look so calm and ask such personal questions. Maybe it was a Teixcalaanli trait. It reminded Mahit of Nineteen Adze, which didn't exactly make her feel more trusting.

Nevertheless, she said, "As much as I trust anyone in the City," and said it honestly.

"And with us only working together for half a week." Three Seagrass smiled, the corners of her eyes tilting up. "Not that you are spoiled much for choice, considering! I *like* Twelve Azalea, Mahit. We've been friends since we both joined the Information Ministry as tiny ignorant cadets. But he is conniving and theatrical and convinced he's immortal."

"I've noticed," Mahit said dryly.

"So trusting him depends entirely on what you want him to do. What *do* you want him to do?"

"Something he'll probably enjoy, as it's both conniving and theatrical. And . . . secret." Mahit gestured at the infograph screens, and then at her ears.

"Well, he'll like it. Whatever it is. But I can't tell you if he'll do it if I don't *know* what it is."

Mahit said, "This message-task list that I'm using—that's on your cloudhook, isn't it. And a person's cloudhook is private to them."

"Or to whoever is wearing it," Three Seagrass said, pleased. "I think I get the idea. Pass it back over when you're ready."

Composing a message to the Ambassador of Lsel and sending it to *herself* was fairly trivial. Mahit wrote, drawing glyphs in the air with her finger on the cloudhook's projected screen that only she could see: *Twelve Azalea should return to the morgue and retrieve the machine we discussed.* Then she lifted Three Seagrass's cloudhook off her head, blinking at the restoration of the other side of her vision, and gave it back.

After she had read the message, Three Seagrass asked, "Do you want that for yourself?"

"No," said Mahit. "I have one, and besides, that one isn't useful anymore—it's recording decay and nothing else."

"*Could* it record something else?"

Mahit thought about it. "If it was correctly installed, maybe? I'm not sure. I really am *not* an *ixplanatl*, Three Seagrass."

"Mm. Well, Twelve Azalea will do it, I'm sure, and he'll even keep quiet about it, but—" She shrugged.

"But what?"

"You'll owe him a favor. And he'll probably take it apart and make schematic drawings. He'll tell you it's out of his own curiosity, and he won't even lie. Him being curious is how we used to get into half of the trouble we got into."

"How," Mahit asked, amused despite herself, "did you get into the other half?"

"I make friends with terribly interesting people with terribly complicated problems."

"So nothing has changed," Mahit said, feeling on the verge of laughter; feeling again the absolute danger of thinking Three Seagrass was her friend like a Stationer could be her friend.

"I did say you were my first barbarian. So, a little change."

Like that. That unbridgeable gap. Maybe if Mahit hadn't been the ambassador, if she'd met her at an oration contest, in some other life where Mahit had never taken up Yskandr's imago-line but had won a travel visa and a scholarship—maybe in that life she could have argued. Told Three Seagrass more of the truth of what she felt.

"I think I can risk Twelve Azalea's curiosity," Mahit said. "Considering I've already risked your friendship."

Twelve Azalea with possession of schematic drawings was still better than anyone with possession of the actual imago-machine. Mahit could get him to give up the drawings—later. Later, when she wasn't trapped inside Nineteen Adze's apartments. When she wasn't going to have to—somehow (and how had Yskandr done it?—and had it killed him?)—stop the absorption of her Station into Teixcalaan. Later, when she wasn't thinking of how pleased Three Seagrass had looked.

———

Coming back to the spare office that she'd been sleeping in, late in the evening, Mahit saw that the incoming mail had arrived.

Resting in the shallow bowl outside the door were three in-fofiche sticks—an anonymous grey one that surely would be from Twelve Azalea with his answer to her request, and another in a shade she hadn't seen before: coppery metal sealed with white wax, the colors of Three Seagrass's suits. The Information Ministry must have finally decided to tell her who had made sure that a new Lsel ambassador arrived as soon as possible after the old one was—Mahit shook her head wryly—no longer functional. The last was another grey stick, marked with the sticky black-and-red tab for *off-world communication*. Mahit wondered, her heart rate speeding, if Dekakel Onchu had sent another message to dead Yskandr, a second delivery triggered by some event she wasn't quite aware of, something more complicated than her own attempt to log into the Lsel Ambassador's electronic database. She reached into the bowl to pick it up, and found that underneath it someone had left a small branch of a plant she'd never seen before. The stem had been delicately curled around the infofiche stick, but now it lay in a loop of shiny grey-green leaves and a single deep cup of a white flower in the bottom of the bowl.

Mahit scooped it up. It was fresh-cut, oozing a whitish sap that had gotten onto the Information Ministry infofiche and stuck to her fingers. She hadn't seen anything like it in Nineteen Adze's apartments, or even out in the rest of the City, filled with flowers of every shape and color and kind—and yet, it couldn't have been cut more than fifteen or twenty minutes previous.

She lifted it up to her face to see if it had a scent.

"Don't," said Nineteen Adze with a whip-crack urgency Mahit had never heard before. She dropped the flower back into the bowl. Her fingertips felt stinging-hot where the sap had made them sticky. Turning, she saw Nineteen Adze standing in the archway at the end of the hall, and had no idea how long she'd been there. Or that she'd been there at all.

"Did you breathe it?" Nineteen Adze asked, coming to Mahit's side. Her face was more expressive than Mahit had ever seen it, mouth twisted and tense. It was like looking at a mask dissolving. The stinging in her fingers was transmuting to pain.

"No, I don't think I did," she said.

Nineteen Adze snapped, "Show me your hand," like she was addressing a soldier or a disobedient child, and Mahit did. Nineteen Adze took her wrist, the band of her much-darker fingers closing around the bones as if she were gripping a snake behind its head. The touch should have been warm but Mahit felt it as *ice.* Her extended fingers were red where she'd held the flower, and even as she watched they began to blister.

"Well, you won't lose it," said Nineteen Adze.

"What?"

"Come with me," Nineteen Adze said, "you have to get the sap off before you touch any *other* parts of yourself. Or sustain nerve damage." Still holding Mahit's wrist, she stalked off down the hallway, dragging Mahit in her wake.

"What was that flower?"

"A very pretty death." They turned a corner, through a door which had always been closed to Mahit but which slid open to Nineteen Adze's gesture, and emerged abruptly into what could only be the *ezuazuacat's* own bedroom. Mahit caught a glimpse of a tangle of unmade white sheets, a stack of infofiche and codex-books piled on the pristine side of the bed, and then Nineteen Adze had pulled her into the en suite bathroom.

"Hold your hand over the sink but don't turn on the water," she said. "Water will just spread the toxins."

Mahit did. The blisters on her fingers were puffy, glassy-clear, the skin beginning to split. She felt as if her hand were on fire, the stinging spreading up her wrist like the City's electricity had spread up Three Seagrass's. She was still too shocked to feel anything but a distant sort of horror. Who had left that flower for her? How had it gotten into the walled garden that was Nineteen Adze's office complex? Someone would have had to *bring* it—someone less than twenty minutes away, the flower had been *oozing*—one of the blisters on her index finger burst as she watched, and she made a tiny, helpless sound between her teeth.

Nineteen Adze reappeared over her shoulder, an open bottle in her hand. Unceremoniously she poured the contents over Mahit's fingers.

"Mineral oil," she said, picking up a washcloth. "This will

probably hurt a great deal. Hold still." She scraped the cloth over the blisters, stripping the oil into the sink. Mahit was sure she was stripping her skin away with it. She tried not to pull away. Nineteen Adze poured oil and scraped it off twice more. At the end of it Mahit was shaking, tremors up the backs of her thighs. Nineteen Adze took her upper arm in an iron grip and sat her down on the closed lid of the toilet.

"If you fall and crack your skull open," she said, "there will be no point to my having fixed your hand."

Whoever had left the flower couldn't have been Nineteen Adze—why would she have tried to kill Mahit and then dragged her off into the bath and kept her alive? She had been so *sharp,* when she said *don't.*

(So sharp, and so close. Had she been watching? How *long* had she been watching? Had she waited to see if Mahit would actually breathe in the scent of the flower—decided only then to prevent her—)

Did it matter?

Nineteen Adze had gotten down on her knees next to her, and was wrapping her fingers in individual gauze bandages, as attentive as a battlefield medic. Mahit wondered if she'd *been* one, once, fought at the side of the Emperor in person, his sworn companion—she was getting epics into her analysis, Teixcalaan was a modern multiplanetary empire, if *ezuazuacatlim* fought they'd fight from starship bridges.

"What flower is full of contact poisons?" she asked. Her voice caught in her throat, around the edges of the receding pain and the adrenaline shock.

"It's a native planetary cultivar," said Nineteen Adze. "The common name is *xauitl,* for the hallucinations it's supposed to bring you right as you die from breathing in the neurotoxins."

"That's cheerful," Mahit said inanely. She wanted to put her head in her hands, but it would hurt too much.

"Before we had spaceflight, Teixcalaanli archers would dip arrowheads in blooms to poison them," Nineteen Adze went on. "And now the Science Ministry distills the oils into some kind of treatment for palsy. What can kill can cure, if you like that sort of thing. You should be flattered; someone wants you dead *artistically*, Ambassador."

There would be a certain satisfying circularity to the Science Ministry trying to kill *every* Lsel ambassador. Mahit didn't trust it—it was like a ring composition in an oration, the same theme coming around again at the end of the stanza. It was *too* Teixcalaanli, and even if Nineteen Adze hadn't meant her to think of it, she could guess that *she* had come up with it because of exactly that kind of overdetermined thinking. Echoes and repetition. Everything meaning something else.

It was the first time she wondered if Nineteen Adze—if any Teixcalaanlitzlim—could compensate for the sheer thematic weight of how Teixcalaanli logic worked. Wondering felt like being thrown into cold water, shock-bright clarity as the pain in her fingers began to fade. Even if the flower had come from the Science Ministry, it had been brought into Nineteen Adze's office by someone with full access: Nineteen Adze herself, or one of her assistants. At absolute *best* they had decided to allow it to be delivered to her; at worst, one or more of them was actively seeking her death right this moment. Artistically.

Artistically, and flowers. *Blooms,* Nineteen Adze had just said. The same word as the one in Thirty Larkspur's poetic epithet. He'd been solicitous, at the reception—had rescued her from the drunken grasp of that courtier, even—but she didn't trust his motivations. Their conversation had been barbed, apologetic, ever-shifting. And the war was on, now: a war Mahit was fairly sure Thirty Larkspur did not want, or did not want in the hands of One Lightning—the calculus of loyalties had changed—perhaps she was too dangerous to him, alive. (As Yskandr had been?)

Not ring composition, this time, but allusion, wordplay. She was over-reading. It was impossible to over-read a Teixcalaanli text. One of her instructors in imperial literature had said that, at the beginning of the course. It had been meant as a warning and Mahit, age fourteen, had seized it like it was instead a balm.

She looked up at Nineteen Adze's face. Nineteen Adze, who had decided—perhaps at the last possible moment—*not* to let her die. She was watching her, blank and unreadable. Mahit's hand hurt, a low sick pain, and she thought of freefall, of tumbling undirected through space, and then of steering, attitudinal compensation, vernier thrusters. She took a large breath. It didn't hurt to breathe, at least.

"Your Excellency," Mahit said, "since you knew about imago-machines—I do know you knew, you practically told me—what were you trying to do when we first met? In the Judiciary morgue. What did you intend for my predecessor's body?"

Nineteen Adze quirked up one side of her mouth, fractional wry motion. "I keep underestimating you," she said. "Or estimating you differently than you end up being. Here you are, nearly poisoned, in a *bathroom,* and you take this opportunity to ask me about my motivations."

"Well," Mahit said. "We're alone." As if it was an answer. It was, in a way. She wasn't sure she'd have this chance again. (She wasn't sure if she'd have another opportunity to catch Nineteen Adze even this much off-balance. *When* had she decided to save her life? Was she regretting it, even now?)

"So we are. All right, Ambassador Dzmare. Perhaps you've earned a little clarity. I wanted the machine, of course. But you already had guessed that."

Mahit nodded. "It's what made sense. I arrive, I plan a funeral— if you wanted it, you couldn't wait any longer."

"Yes." Nineteen Adze sat back on her heels, composed and patient.

Mahit asked the next question. "What did you want it *for*?"

"When I saw you in the morgue? Then, I wanted a bargaining chip, Mahit. There are many interests at court who might want to control that machine—and control you, through the release or withholding of it."

"Then."

"I hardly need that now, do I?" Nineteen Adze gestured at the bathroom—at the two of them, sitting in it. Mahit nodded, wryly acknowledging. *Having* the Lsel Ambassador was much better than having the means to *buy* the Lsel Ambassador's attention and influence. And Nineteen Adze had a live imago-machine now, the one inside Mahit's skull. Though she'd have to cut her open to get it, and it was malfunctioning badly.

"I imagine," she said, "that I am of less use to you in the current circumstances than you expected I'd be."

Nineteen Adze shook her head. Reached out and patted Mahit's knee, familiar and too, too kind. "If you weren't useful you wouldn't be here. Besides, how often does a barbarian challenge my decisions in my own bathroom? If nothing else, you enliven the experience of daily living. Which is *exactly* like your predecessor. I am finding the similarities very funny, especially after you went to such trouble to inform me of the disambiguation."

Mahit considered what Yskandr would have done; remembered, imago-echo that wasn't hers and wasn't really *anyone's* now, how easy he'd been in his body. How he'd moved hers in fluid, expansive gesture. He'd cover Nineteen Adze's hand on her knee with his, now. Or reach out—

(*his hand flat against her cheek, the skin cool and smooth, she laughs and turns her face inward, her lips against his palm*)

The memory-flash receded. Mahit could repeat the echo, she had her *suspicions* about the nature of the friendship Nineteen Adze claimed with her predecessor, she could reach out and touch her cheek—

Ring composition. Overdetermined.

Instead she met Nineteen Adze's eyes, held them a beat too long, and asked, "What *did* Yskandr promise you, to keep you this interested in us?"

"Not me," said Nineteen Adze. "His Imperial Majesty."

She rocked back on her heels, gathered her feet under her, and stood up, as if she was giving Mahit time to process the unfolding revelation. To remember the sick heat of Six Direction's hands on her wrists, the terrible fragility of him, as if he was being ravaged by some fast-moving disease.

Held out her forearm, so that Mahit was obliged to touch her—to accept the help in standing up, even as she was thinking: *Yskandr, you bastard, you convinced the Emperor of Teixcalaan he would never die.*

CHAPTER
TEN

There is no star-chart
unwatched by her
sleepless eyes, or unguided by
her spear-calloused hand, and thus
she falls, a captain in truth.
Like an emperor she falls, her blood painting the bridge
Where shift after shift she had stood.

> —from Fourteen Scalpel's "Encomia for the Fallen of
> the Flagship *Twelve Expanding Lotus*," the opening of the
> verses on the death of Acting Captain Five Needle

*   *   *

[. . .] we have always been between powers, in this sector—I cannot imagine that our predecessors intended to place us in such a way so that we are required to bend first this way toward Teixcalaan, then that way toward the systems of Svava or Petrichor-5 or Nguyen, depending on who is most ascendant on our borders—but we hold the only access to our jumpgates, and we are thus a narrow and significant road that all these powers must travel upon. Nevertheless I cannot help imagining a more indigenous sovereignty for us, where Stationer power belongs to Stationers and is not in service to our survival [. . .]

> —TARATS//PRIVATE//PERSONAL//"notes toward a
> new Lsel," entry updated 127.7.10-6D (Teixcalaanli
> reckoning)

WEARING a pair of disposable gloves, the sort Mahit would have used to handle refuse back on the Station, Seven Scale disposed of the *xauitl* while Mahit watched. He'd been waiting for her when she came back to the door of her room—approaching the bowl of infofiche sticks again as if nothing of the last hour had happened, the only difference being her bandaged hand and the blazing realization of what Yskandr had sold to the Empire. Hardly any *visible* difference.

Seven Scale put the *xauitl* inside a plastic bag, paused to consider, and then added the bowl itself.

"I'm not sure I know how to wash it correctly," he said, apologetic.

"What about the infofiche sticks?" Mahit asked. "Can you wash *them*?" She wasn't about to lose access to the scraps of information she'd managed to get the City to give her.

"Probably not? But if you wore gloves, you could break them open and read them before I put them through the disposal with the autoclave and the furnace."

As opposed to the regular disposal, Mahit assumed, grimly amused. "Give me yours," she said. "And wait outside, I'll only be a moment."

Seven Scale stripped the gloves off and held them out, pinched gingerly between his fingertips. "There are more in the kitchens," he offered uncertainly.

Mahit took the contaminated ones, and then the infofiche sticks. "These are fine. I'll be one minute. Stay."

He stayed. It was a little terrifying; did Nineteen Adze keep him around for unquestioning obedience? (Did he, ubiquitous, carry in the flower he was now so assiduously disposing of? It'd have been simple. No one would notice Seven Scale carrying flowers. He probably did it all the time.)

Mahit closed the door on him. Carefully she put on the contaminated gloves. The latex caught on the bandage around her hand and she winced, but it was still better than how the sap had felt. The infofiche sticks broke easily in her fingers, one after the other, cracking along their wax seals. She could still exert pressure. The muscles and tendons and nerves running down her palm were undamaged. The toxin hadn't spread that far. She assumed she had Nineteen Adze to thank for that, Nineteen Adze and her speedy intimate mercy. Her *rethinking*.

The stick from the Information Ministry exuded a pretty graphic announcing itself as an official communication and then presented Mahit with a single-line answer to her question: just four glyphs, and two of them were a title and a name. She'd asked who authorized the rapid arrival of an ambassador from Lsel.

Authorization given by Imperial-Associate Eight Loop.

Which—was unexpected. At the banquet, Eight Loop had been the only one of the three presumptive heirs who had entirely ignored Mahit. All Mahit knew about her was what was on newsfeeds and encomiastic biopics of the Emperor. His crèche-sib, who had been the Minister for the Judiciary before her elevation. An agemate. The particular glyph she used for her name's numerical signifier was the same as the glyph the Emperor's ninety-percent clone was using in "Eight Antidote," which said *something* about what loyalties the Emperor owed her, but not anything about why she'd want an ambassador from Lsel Station as soon as possible. Unless she knew what Yskandr had sold to the Emperor, and . . . had wanted it to happen, and wanted it to happen even if Yskandr was dead and she'd have to import another ambassador to accomplish it? Wanted to *revoke* it, by virtue of replacing Yskandr with an ambassador who had different ideas of what might be traded away to Teixcalaan, even in exchange for keeping the open maw of the Empire pointed at some other prey?

Even if Yskandr had to betray Lsel's interests, he could have found some way to do it that wasn't so *horrifically* Teixcalaanli. An imago wasn't a re-creation of a single person. An imago of the Emperor wouldn't be the Emperor, not entirely. Didn't he *know?*

None of that explained Eight Loop's involvement. Except that she was Judiciary Minister, and Yskandr's corpse was in the *Judiciary* morgue, not any other morgue in the City—perhaps she'd arranged that . . .

Mahit broke open the second infofiche stick, one of the two in anonymous grey plastic. Twelve Azalea hadn't bothered with verse this time. The message he'd sent was unsigned, simple— as if he'd composed it on a street corner and dumped the sealed infofiche stick into a public mailbox.

The message read: *Have what you asked for. Might have been noticed on the way out. I can't hold on to it. I'll be at your suite at dawn tomorrow. Meet me there.*

The last stick was the one with the *off-world communication* sticky tab. The one which might be another secret message, a warning for a man who was already dead. A rumor of distant conflicts, tremors on Lsel that would have existed no matter what sort of madness the succession crisis of the Teixcalaanli Imperium might cause—or might already be causing. Mahit found herself afraid to open it, and inside that fear, did so all at once: cracking the stick hard enough that it nearly tore the plastic film, printed in familiar alphabetic letters, that was cradled inside.

This message was shorter than the previous one had been, and dated forty-eight Teixcalaanli hours later: 230.3.11. Still long before she'd arrived in the City, but after she'd left Lsel on *Ascension's Red Harvest.* It was titled "For Ambassador Aghavn from Dekakel Onchu, Councilor for the Pilots." Mahit felt strange, reading it. Like she was eavesdropping, a child snuck unsupervised into a meeting she oughtn't to have overheard.

This message will be delivered if there was no response to previous communication. The Councilor for the Pilots hopes that you are well and repeats her warning: Tarats for the Miners and Amnardbat for Heritage have sent a replacement for you to the Empire, at the Empire's request. If the replacement is loyal to Tarats then she may be trustable; if she is not, or if she is obviously a victim or an engineer of sabotage, the Pilots suggest that you look to Heritage for the source of opposition and—though it gives me no pleasure to refer to it as such—enemy action.

Be careful. I am unable to discern the precise nature of the sabotage if it exists, but I suspect Heritage has made use of her access to the imago-machines.

Destroy this communication.

It was short, and it was *worse* than the previous one. Mahit wished she could find some way to talk to Councilor Onchu— to tell her that her messages weren't falling into a blank and silent void, that Yskandr was dead but his successor was listening. But Onchu wouldn't want to hear it, from her. If she was *sabotaged*. If she was an unwitting, unwilling agent of Aknel Amnardbat, not just politically supported by her but . . . if she'd . . . if she'd *damaged* her imago-machine, somehow . . .

But she couldn't yet understand *why* Heritage would do that. What it'd be for. And she'd thought that really, she *had* been Amnardbat's choice of successors for Yskandr, so maybe it wasn't really sabotage, maybe she was just—fulfilling some function that Amnardbat wanted to accomplish within Teixcalaan.

But if the malfunctioning of her imago wasn't sabotage, she was *damaged,* and it was her own fault. So which one of the options was *really* worse?

Suddenly she needed very much to meet Twelve Azalea and reclaim the dead Yskandr's imago-machine. Even if everything else went wrong, Lsel was annexed, she was thrown into a cell in the Judiciary—if she could get hold of it, she could at least keep that *secret*, hold it in stead, salvage what was left of her predecessor. That might be a kind of penance, if she truly was broken, and the Yskandr she was supposed to have was gone for good.

Mahit burned the plastic sheet, and wiped all the sticks—they were designed to be easily erased—before opening the door of her room again. Seven Scale was still standing in the hallway, holding his garbage bag, as if he hadn't moved at all in the ten minutes she'd been reading. It was unsettling. Even an expressionless proper Teixcalaanlitzlim wasn't *as* expressionless and submissive as Seven Scale could be. If she didn't know better, Mahit could think he was an automaton. Even an artificial intelligence had more immediately apparent volition.

"Here," she said, holding out the emptied sticks. "I'm finished with these."

He held out the bag. "The gloves too," he said. "I am awfully sorry about your hand."

"It's fine," said Mahit. "The *ezuazuacat* fixed it." If Seven Scale had been the person who had left the *xauitl* for her, he'd know that his mistress had prevented it from killing her—but there was no change in his expression. He merely nodded, serene, as if Nineteen Adze administered first aid as a matter of course. Maybe she did.

"Is there anything else?" he asked.

I need to escape this very pleasant and very life-threatening prison of an office complex before dawn, in order to receive an illegal machine looted from the corpse of my predecessor. Can you help me with that?

"No, thank you," Mahit said.

Seven Scale nodded. "Good night, Ambassador," he said, and disappeared down the hall. Mahit watched him go. When he'd turned the corner she retreated back into her office. The door hissed gently shut behind her. She stared mutely at the window-side couch with its folded blanket, thought of lying down and closing her eyes and banishing all of Teixcalaan. Thought also again of going out the window and attempting to escape through the gardens. It was a two-story drop. She'd probably break an ankle, to go along with her bandaged hand and the bruises on her hip from when the restaurant had fallen on her.

She was still trying to come up with a feasible plan that would get her back to Palace-East by dawn when someone knocked at the door. It was past midnight—the City's two moons had both risen, tiny distant disks in the sky outside the window. Mahit had thought that everyone else was long asleep.

"Who is it?" she called.

"It's Three Seagrass. Open the door, Mahit, I have good news!"

Mahit could not imagine what could qualify as good news that would also necessitate the news being delivered at this hour. As she got up to open the door, she imagined Three Seagrass standing surrounded by a small cohort of Sunlit, ready to arrest her; or accompanied by Ten Pearl, ready to *kill* her. All sorts of possible betrayals.

But it was only Three Seagrass on the other side of the door, hollow-eyed and exhausted and sparkling like she'd never stopped drinking coffee. Or something stronger. Maybe she hadn't.

She ducked under Mahit's arm without asking if she could come in, and waved the door shut herself.

"So you wanted a private audience with His Illuminate Majesty, right?"

". . . yes?" Mahit said dubiously.

"Do you have anything better to wear? Though I guess this

is clandestine and we probably shouldn't treat it like an actual formal audience. Still. Something! But only if you've got it, we don't have much time."

"Why does the Emperor want to talk to me in the middle of the night?"

"I am not omniscient, so I can't answer you exactly," Three Seagrass said smugly, "but I *am* the sort of person who spends fourteen hours wading through bureaucrats and patricians third-, second-, and first-class so that eventually I have a personal conversation with the Keeper of the Imperial Inkstand, and *he* says that His Illuminate Majesty is, in fact, very interested in meeting with the Lsel Ambassador, and understands the need for both haste and discretion and would we please go *now*."

"I'm going to assume this is both unusual and has the absolute force of imperial command," Mahit said. Just a few hours previously she would never have thought that a meeting with the Teixcalaanli Emperor would feel most like an opportunity for *escape*. But if she could manage to slip away into the City before coming *back* to Nineteen Adze's offices, meet with Twelve Azalea, and then return before anyone really knew she was gone . . . She'd have to let Three Seagrass in on it. It wouldn't work, otherwise. (And also she wasn't sure she could find her way back to Palace-East without her.)

"Yes and yes," Three Seagrass said. "Nineteen Adze already knows—I think she's going to escort us in. There's a level of misdirection I'm not sure who's responsible for, Mahit—if we are being brought into the palace as if we're an *ezuazuacat*'s entourage, as *cover*—"

"Of course we accept the invitation," Mahit said, cutting her off. "Even if it's secret—maybe especially because it's secret—"

"Were you *trained* for intrigue? On Lsel." Three Seagrass was smiling as she said it, but Mahit was equally certain she meant it, and as a gentle barb.

"Just wait until I explain what we're going to do after we see His Illuminate Majesty," she said. "Then you'll really think I was taught deception along with languages and protocol."

The imperial chambers reminded Mahit more of Nineteen Adze's office complex than the starry brilliance of the oration-contest ballroom: they were a warren of white marble shot through with gold veins, patterned like ruined—or fantastical—cityscapes under lightning-arc skies. Nineteen Adze knew them well enough to smile and exchange pleasantries with most of the people they passed; she practically matched the marbling where her jacket wasn't an even brighter, even colder white. Mahit and Three Seagrass ghosted in her wake. If Nineteen Adze had opinions about the Emperor's request to meet Mahit in private she hadn't shared them. She'd only tugged her boots on over bare feet, looked Mahit over as if she was evaluating her suitability in an entirely new fashion—there was a naked intimacy in that evaluation that Mahit thought originated somewhere between when she'd had the impulse to reach out for Nineteen Adze in the bathroom and when she'd rejected that impulse—and then whisked them away into the depths of Palace-Earth.

It was like climbing down into the heart of the world: chambers opening like the valves between atria and shutting tight again behind them as they passed through. Even after midnight the innermost parts of the palace pulsed with a headlong rushing; the soft tramping of slippered feet, the whisk of some patrician's suit around a corner. Distant low voices. Mahit wondered if the Emperor slept. Maybe he slept in snatches. Up every three hours to do another hour of work, read another night's worth of reports from all of vast Teixcalaan.

The Keeper of the Imperial Inkstand met the three of them in an antechamber whose walls had deepened from marble to antiqued gold tapestry. He was short—as short as Three Sea-grass, who barely came up to Mahit's shoulder—with a thin face and a fashionably low hairline. He and Nineteen Adze raised their eyebrows at each other, like partners sitting down on opposite sides of a familiar game board.

"So you *are* keeping her in your offices," he said.

"Make sure to give her back once His Brilliance is done with her, Twenty-Nine Bridge," Nineteen Adze said, and waved Mahit forward before she could form any polite protests as to having come here by her own designs and with her own liaison.

Three Seagrass said, perfectly metrical, "The honor of meeting you in person, Twenty-Nine Bridge, is like stumbling upon a fresh spring in the mountains," which had to be an allusion if not an outright quotation.

Twenty-Nine Bridge laughed like he'd been given a present. "Come sit with me, *asekreta*, while your Ambassador has her meeting. You must tell me how you managed to defeat all of my sub-secretaries in only one day."

"Careful," said Nineteen Adze, "that one is sneaky."

"Are you actually *warning* me of something?" asked Twenty-Nine Bridge. His eyebrows touched his hairline when he raised them. "What under starlight did this child manage to do to *you*?"

"You'll find out," Nineteen Adze said, smug as a cat. Then she turned to Mahit, tapping her on the wrist, right above the bandage she'd wrapped there.

"You don't have to do all of what he asks," she said, and spun on her heel to sweep out of the room before Mahit could try to determine whether that "he" had meant the Keeper of the Imperial Inkstand or Six Direction Himself.

"I appreciate your help in arranging this meeting," Mahit said to Twenty-Nine Bridge, trying to take some control of the proceedings. "And I hope we are not keeping you from your rest."

He spread all his fingers apart by his sides, a Teixcalaanli gesture that Mahit read as nonchalance. "It isn't the first time. Not for a Lsel ambassador and certainly not for me. Go in, Ambassador Dzmare. He's blocked out an entire half hour for you."

Of course Yskandr had been here before her. Promising eternal life and continuity of memory. Mahit found herself wishing, for what might have been the first time in her life, that she didn't *know* Yskandr so well. That she didn't see quite so clearly how he might have made the choices he'd made. But imago-recipients were chosen for psychological compatibility with their predecessors, and she and Yskandr—if only they'd had enough time!—at the beginning of their partnership had been so *very* fluid. She did understand.

But she was alone, and that was Yskandr's fault. Both of him: the dead man and the vanished imago. His fault, even if there had been sabotage from Lsel. Mahit bowed from the chest and left Twenty-Nine Bridge to entertain (or be interrogated by) Three Seagrass, and went through the last door between herself and the Emperor Six Direction.

Only as she blinked against the change in ambient light—the antechamber had been dimmed for the hour, but the Emperor's receiving room was ablaze under full-spectrum dawnlamps—did she remember the intensity of her imago-inflected limbic system reaction to the Emperor at the oration-contest banquet. She felt shimmering with nerves, like she was about to meet an examination committee or a secret lover, and here was another reason to wish that she didn't know Yskandr, didn't have the afterimages of his neurochemical memory echoing through hers.

The Emperor was sitting on a couch, like a person. Like an old man still awake in the small hours of the morning, his shoulders more stooped than they'd been at the banquet, his face drawn and sharp. His skin was greyish and translucent. Mahit wondered just how ill he *was*—and in what way, whether it was one of the waves of minor illnesses that marked old age or something that was deeper, worse, a cancer or an organ system failure. From the look of him she suspected the latter. The dawnlamps were probably for keeping him awake— full-spectrum light could do that to a person if they were sensitive—but they surrounded him with a mandorla of sunlight that Mahit thought was deliberately reminiscent of the sun-spear imperial throne.

"Ambassador Dzmare," he said, and beckoned her closer with two fingers.

"Your Imperial Majesty." She considered dropping to her knees, genuflecting, letting the Emperor wrap his hot hands around her outstretched wrists again. Wanted it, and in the wanting found reason enough to discard the impulse. Instead she squared her shoulders and asked, "May I sit down?"

"Sit," Six Direction said. "You and Yskandr are both too tall to look at properly, standing up."

"I'm not him," Mahit said. She sat in a chair pulled up next to the couch. Some of the dawnlamps, noticing the presence of another breathing person in the room, obligingly rotated to shine on her.

"My *ezuazuacat* told me you'd say that."

"I'm not lying, Your Majesty."

"No. You're not. Yskandr wouldn't have needed to be escorted past the bureaucrats."

Brazenly, as a panacea against feeling poised on the verge of drowning, Mahit said: "Forgive me. It must be difficult, meeting your friend's successor. On Lsel, there's more support for the transition down the imago-line."

"Is there," said the Emperor. It was less of a question than an invitation.

Mahit wasn't ignorant of how information-gathering worked.

She knew she was injured, exhausted, immersed in a culture-shocked numbness that she couldn't see the edges of, and talking to a man who controlled a quarter of the galaxy, whether or not he was dying by inches; she'd like to crack open like an egg and leak out words. How much of that was good interrogation technique and how much of that was limbic-system echo of trust wasn't even a useful question.

"We have a long tradition of psychological therapy," she said, and stopped, hard, like biting down. One sentence at a time.

The Emperor laughed, more easily than she'd expected. "I imagine you need it," he said.

"Is that based on your impressions of Yskandr or of me?"

"On my impressions of human beings, of which you and Yskandr are only one interesting set of outliers."

Mahit took the hit, smiling—too wide, close to the feeling of Yskandr's smile—and spreading her fingertips apart in that same Teixcalaanli gesture that Twenty-Nine Bridge had used. "And yet there is no comparative tradition in Teixcalaan."

"Ah, Ambassador Dzmare—you have only been with us for four days. It is possible you've missed something."

A great many things, Mahit was sure. "I would be fascinated to hear about Teixcalaanli methods of coping with psychological distress, Your Brilliance," she said.

"I do think you would be. But that isn't why you asked so insistently for this meeting."

"No."

"No. Go on then," said Six Direction. He laced his fingers together. The knuckles were age-swollen, deeply lined. "Make your case for where else I should send my armies."

"How are you so sure that's what I came here to ask?"

"Ah," he said. "It is what Yskandr asked me for. Are you *so* different, then? To care more for some other cause than your station."

"Was that the only thing he asked you for?"

"Of course not. That's just what I said yes to."

"And will you say yes to me, if I ask?"

Six Direction looked her over, with a patience that felt infinite—didn't they only have a half hour, couldn't she get away, the muscles in her side where the falling wall had bruised her ached with holding so still, and she could feel her heartbeat pulsing in the wounds on her hand—and then he shrugged. The motion was almost lost in the complexity of the lapels of his jacket. "I wonder if you are a failure-state or a warning," he said. "It would be useful to know before I answer you. If you are able to say."

He must have meant *was she a failure of the imago process.* Was the fact that she wasn't Yskandr *on purpose* or a mistake. And if it was a mistake, was it a *purposeful* mistake—did the Emperor know about the sabotage? He couldn't have. He wouldn't have, if he'd asked if she was a failure or a warning. Mahit imagined, abruptly, Six Direction's expression on the unlined child's face of Eight Antidote. The same patient calculation. The child was a ninety-percent clone; his face would grow into this face, given muscle memory. The idea was repulsive. A child couldn't stand up to an imago. He'd drown in the older memory; a child hardly had a self to hold on to yet. That was probably what Six Direction wanted.

"If I were a failure-state," Mahit said, "here to show you the uncertainty of imago-transfer, I certainly wouldn't tell you that I was."

And if I am a warning, I don't even know it. She shied away from the concept—she couldn't think through it, here, and even the edges of the idea, flavored with Onchu's secret messages to the dead, made her furious. That Lsel would have sent her, flawed, to prove some sort of point to Six Direction, a rebuke, a *broken* thing—but she couldn't be furious. Not now. She was alone with the Emperor.

He was asking, "Would you demonstrate it, instead?"

"I imagine I wouldn't have a choice," Mahit said. "So it's really up to you to decide, Your Illuminate Brilliance, exactly what I am."

"Perhaps I will continue to see what you'll do." When he shrugged, the sunlamps orbiting his shoulders moved with his motion, as if he and they were some cohesive machine, a system much larger than a man that responded to a man's will. "Tell me one thing, Ambassador Dzmare, before we return to negotiations and answers. Do you carry Yskandr's *imago,* or are you someone else's memory altogether?"

"I'm Mahit Dzmare," Mahit said, which felt quite like lying by omission, a small betrayal of Lsel, so she went on: "And I've never carried any imago but Yskandr Aghavn."

The Emperor met her eyes, as if he was evaluating just who was behind them, and did not let her look away. Mahit thought, *Yskandr, if there ever was a time for you to start talking to me . . .*

Imagined him saying, <Hello, Six Direction,> dry and archly removed and suffused with recognition. She knew the precise tone he'd use.

Didn't say it.

The Emperor asked, "When we discussed the Western Arc families, and what to do about their demands for exclusive trade, what was your opinion?"

Mahit had no idea what Yskandr had thought. Her Yskandr had met the Emperor socially, but had never been so highly regarded as to discuss policy with him. "That was before my time," she said, evading.

She was still being *observed.* Evaluated. The Emperor's eyes were such a dark brown they were nearly black—his cloudhook a stripped-down net of near-invisible glass—she wanted to knot her hands together in her lap, to stop them from having a chance of shaking. It would hurt too much, if she did.

"Yskandr," said the Emperor, and for a moment Mahit was not sure if she was being addressed or if he was talking about her predecessor, "made many arguments and offered any number of things, trying to sway me away from expansion. It was fascinating, to see a mind so fluent in our language try so hard to convince us to act contrary to all the millennia of our success. We spent hours in this room, Mahit Dzmare."

"An honor for my predecessor," Mahit murmured.

"Do you think so?"

"It would be one for me." She wasn't even lying.

"So the commonality goes that far. Or perhaps you are merely being ambassadorial."

"Does it matter, Your Brilliance, which one?"

Six Direction, when he smiled, smiled like a man from Lsel had shown him how: wrinkled cheeks drawn up, teeth visible. A learned motion, but one which felt shockingly familiar, even after just four days seeing only Teixcalaanli expressions. "You," the Emperor declared, "are as slippery as Yskandr was."

Mahit shrugged, deliberately. She wondered if the few sun-lamps which surrounded her were responding to her motion, too.

He leaned forward. The light around him was warm where it spilled onto her shins and knees, as if his fever was *mobile*, could touch her. "It doesn't work, Mahit," he said. "Philosophy and policy are conditional—multiple, reactive. What would be true for Teixcalaan, touching Lsel, is simultaneously untrue for Teixcalaan touching some other border state, or Teixcalaan in its refined form here in the City. Empires have many faces."

"What doesn't work?"

"Asking us to make exceptions," he said. "Yskandr did try. He was very good at trying."

"But you told him yes," Mahit said, protesting.

"I did," said Six Direction. "And if you will pay what he promised, I'll tell you the same."

Mahit needed to hear him say it. To be sure; to get out of the endless loops of her conjecture. "What *did* Yskandr promise you?"

"The schematics to Lsel's imago-machines," the Emperor said, quite easily, like he was discussing the prices for electrical power, "and several for immediate Teixcalaanli use. In exchange for which I would guarantee the independent sovereignty of Lsel Station for as long as my dynasty holds the Empire. I thought it was a rather clever bargain, on his part."

It was in fact clever. *For as long as his dynasty holds the Empire.* A series of imago-emperors would be one single dynasty—one single man, endlessly repeated, if Six Direction really thought that the imago process was *iterative* instead of *compilatory*—and thus Lsel technology bought Lsel independence. In perpetuity. And Six Direction would escape the illness which was killing him, and live again in a body unmarked by age.

Yskandr, Mahit thought, reaching, *you must have been so self-satisfied when you came up with the terms.*

"Perhaps," Six Direction went on, "you'd like to add some of your Lsel psychological therapists. I suspect their contributions to Teixcalaanli theories of mind might be quite fascinating."

How much of Lsel did he want to *take*? Take and devour and transform into something that wasn't Lsel at all, but Teixcalaan. If he wasn't the Emperor, she might have slapped him.

If he wasn't the Emperor, she might have laughed and asked what, exactly, the Teixcalaanli theory of mind involved. *How wide is the concept of you?*

But he was the Emperor—grammatically *and* existentially—

and he thought of all fourteen generations of Lsel imago lines as something that could *contribute* to Teixcalaan.

The Empire, the world. The same word, benefiting equally.

She hadn't said anything for too long. Her head was full of the trajectories of all those Teixcalaanli military transports, rattling against how furious she was, how suddenly, miserably trapped she felt. Against the sick pain-pulse in her damaged hand, beating in time with her heart.

"It took Yskandr years to come to such a decision, Your Brilliance," she managed. "Allow me more than one evening of the honor of your company before I make mine."

"You would like to come back, then."

Of course she would. She was sitting in private audience with the Emperor of all Teixcalaan, and he was a *challenge,* and he took her seriously, and he'd taken her predecessor seriously, and how could she *not* want this? Even through the misery, she wanted it.

What she said was, "If you would have me, Your Brilliance. My predecessor was clearly—of interest to you. I might be, as well. And you do me considerable favor, to talk so clearly."

"Clarity," said Six Direction, still smiling that very Lsel smile, the one that made her want to grin back at him, conspiratorial, "is not a rhetorical virtue. But it is very useful, isn't it?"

"Yes." In a particular sense, this was the clearest conversation Mahit had *had* since she came to the City. She took a steadying breath—set her shoulders, trying to neither echo Yskandr's body language nor mirror the Emperor's—and took the offered conversational bait. "With your gracious permission to continue to fail at rhetoric, Your Brilliance: What made you want our imago-machines? Most people who aren't Stationers find imago-lines quite . . . inexplicable. Inexplicable at *best*."

Six Direction closed his eyes and opened them again: a long, slow blink. "How old are you, Mahit?"

"Twenty-six, by Teixcalaanli annual time."

"Teixcalaan has seen *eighty years of peace*. Three of your lives, stacked up, since the last time one part of the world tried to destroy the rest of it."

There were border skirmishes reported every week. There'd been an outright rebellion put down on the Odile System just a few days back. Teixcalaan was not *peaceful*. But Mahit thought she understood the difference Six Direction was so fixated on: those were skirmishes that brought war to *outside* the universe, to uncivilized places. The word he'd used for "world" was the word for "city." The one that derived from the verb for "correct action."

"It is a long time," she admitted.

"It must continue," said the Emperor Six Direction. "I cannot allow us to falter now. Eighty years of peace should be the beginning, not a lost age when we were more humane, more caring, more just. Do you see?"

Mahit saw. It was simple and wrong and terrible: it was *fear*, of leaving the world unguided by a true and knowing hand.

"You have seen my successors," Six Direction went on. "Imagine with me, Ambassador Dzmare, the truly *exceptional* civil war we might have under their care."

The external chambers of Palace-Earth were empty of everyone but Three Seagrass, who staggered to her feet when the irising inner doors spat Mahit back out again.

"Were you asleep?" Mahit asked, wishing she could nap on a couch, even for ten minutes.

Three Seagrass shrugged. Under the dim gold lights of the antechamber her brown skin looked grey. "Did you get what you wanted?"

Mahit had no idea how to answer that. She was buzzing,

shimmering, full up with poison secrets. What Yskandr had sold. Why Six Direction would do anything to remain himself, and Emperor. Nothing she could easily explain.

"Let's go," she said. "Before anyone notices we've misplaced ourselves."

Three Seagrass made a considering noise, hummed between her teeth. Mahit walked right by her, out of the antechamber door. The last thing she wanted to do was to explain herself. Not now.

If she stopped to *think*.

She was doing nothing *but* thinking.

Three Seagrass came up behind her, at her left shoulder, a perfect shadow, just like she'd been at the oration contest.

"Nineteen Adze left a message," she said, just before they exited the Emperor's chambers. "She said to tell you that she wasn't going to stop you from doing anything ill-advised. That she wasn't going to stop you at *all*."

Mahit shivered, knowing she'd been cut loose, and felt pathetically grateful to both Nineteen Adze and Three Seagrass anyhow.

INTERLUDE

AN imago-machine is small: the length of the smallest joint of a human thumb, at most. Even on a station of thirty thousand souls, and ten thousand preserved imago-lines alongside and within them, the entire storage facility for the machines is one small and sterile sphere of a room. It nestles close to the beating power-core heart of Lsel, insulated as far as it can be from the vicissitudes of space debris or cosmic rays or accidents of decompression: it is, Aknel Amnardbat has said, the safest place on the Station. The harbor of all Stationers: where the dead eventually come to rest, for a time, and then go out again, remade.

Amnardbat stands in its direct center. On every surface but the small patch of floor containing her feet and the path from there to the door, the walls of the room are covered in sealed, labeled compartments: numbers. Names, sometimes, on the very oldest or most important containers for imago-lines. If she was to look up over her shoulder she would see a compartment labeled *Heritage,* where her own imago once came from, and where the imago she will become will go.

She used to find this room soothing: utterly peaceful, a perfect reminder that all of Lsel was under her care, extending back into the past and forward into the future. Aknel Amnardbat thinks herself an archivist; if she lived on a green planet she'd call herself a gardener. It is her task to graft plant to plant, mind to mind, to preserve and design and let nothing of Lsel be lost.

She *used* to find this room soothing.

Some little time ago—six weeks, by the Teixcalaanli reckoning the Station has come to use, was using even before Amnardbat was born, it is by *such small degrees* that a culture is devoured, she had not ever known to notice that a "week" bore no resemblance to the rotation of Lsel, facing and unfacing again its sun—some little time ago she had stood here, and with the access granted to her as the Councilor for Heritage, caused one of those little containers to disgorge its contents into her waiting hands.

She'd cleaned her nails with solvent, just before. Cleaned them, filed them to uncharacteristic points.

The machine in her palms, then, had come from a container marked *P-N (T.2)*. In the parlance of Heritage's imago-machine codes, that meant *Political-Negotiation*—a designation of specialty, of *type*—and then *Teixcalaan,* for the imago-line of political negotiators sent to deal with the Empire—and *2,* the second in a chain. The imago-machine that recorded Yskandr Aghavn, fifteen years more out of date than it should have been.

Amnardbat had held it, carefully; lifted it, turned it in the soft light so it glimmered, metal and ceramides, the fragile connecting places where it would slot into the machine-cradle at the brainstem of its host. Thought, as fierce as she had ever been: *You are as corrupt as an arsonist, as an imago-line that would shatter the shell of the station with a bomb. You are* worse *than both of those, Yskandr Aghavn: you want to invite Teixcalaan in. You speak poetry and you send back reams of literature, and more of our children every year take the aptitudes for the Empire and leave us. Leave us bereft of who they might have been. You are a corrosive poison, and a righteous person would crush this machine under her foot.*

She did not stamp the machine to shards.

Instead she took her sharpened nails and scraped them—so lightly, so, so lightly, hardly believing she was doing it, committing a kind of treason of her own, a treason against memory, against the *idea* of Heritage, against the flood of nauseous horror from her imago (six generations of Heritage Councilors, and all of them sick-frightened, sick-intoxicated)—over each of those fragile connections. Weakening them. So that they might snap, under stress.

And then she had put it back and gone to recommend Mahit Dzmare as the next ambassador to Lsel and for *weeks* she'd felt—good. *Righteous.*

But now she stands in her room of memory, her soothing peaceful repository, and her heart races, and she tastes adrenaline and lead, the aftertaste of the displeasure of her own imago, who would never have done the harm she has done to any imago-line, not without doing it officially, in front of the Council, with the Council's full approval. *What else could I touch*, Aknel Amnardbat thinks. What else could she change.

And would it make a single bit of difference, now that there were Teixcalaanli warships pointed toward their sector anyway?

Even this protected room would shatter, float away in so much debris, if a ship like *Ascension's Red Harvest* decided that Lsel Station's Lagrange point was better *unoccupied*. All her intervention into memory, all her scouring-out of poison: it would mean nothing. She was too late.

CHAPTER
ELEVEN

It is commonality that destroys me: I cannot run as the Ebrekti run together in their swifts, quadrupedal and alive to the hunt, but I understand the nature of a swift: how it depends upon its leader for direction, how it becomes one organism in the moment of the kill. I understand this nature because it is my nature, and Teixcalaanli—though perhaps it is not human-universal, to find common purpose like this, to want to subsume the self in a sworn band. I am no longer so sure of human-universal. I am out alone too long; I am becoming a barbarian, amongst these barbarians, and I dream of seeing Teixcalaan in alien claws. I do not think my dreaming is untoward; it is the casting-forward of desire, the projection of a self into the future. An imagining of possibles.

—from *Dispatches from the Numinous Frontier,* Eleven Lathe

* * *

ITEMS PROHIBITED FOR IMPORT (LSEL STATION): fauna not previously listed under PERSONAL EFFECTS (PETS AND COMPANIONS), flora and fungi which are not certified as irradiated by sterilizing electron beam, food items not in packaging (food items may be sterilized at border control at the discretion of border control agents), all items capable of discharging a hard projectile through atmosphere, all items capable of discharging flame or flammable liquids, all items capable of emitting airborne particulates (including recreational substances meant to be inhaled,

"smoke machines" used by entertainers, "smokers" used by chefs
or food preparers) . . .

—from CUSTOMS INFORMATION PACKET, distributed
to ships seeking to dock at Lsel Station

THE City was alien in the dark. Not so much silent as *haunted*:
the boulevards and deep-sunk flower pools in Palace-Earth were
vaster without the sun, the shape of all the buildings uncannily
organic, like they might breathe or bloom. What few Teixcalaanlitzlim were still abroad in the streets met no one's eyes—
they moved like shadows, operating on some palace business
of their own, unspeaking. Mahit followed Three Seagrass and
kept her head down. She felt sickly tired, and everything hurt:
her hip and her hand and her head, aching with what was almost
certainly a tension headache and not an incipient neurological
event. Almost certainly.

Their steps echoed on the marble. On Lsel there was never
an inescapable dark, aside from space itself: *someone* was awake
and on shift, always. The public spaces were no different at any
point in a person's own individual sleep/wake cycle. If you
wanted darkness you went back to your room and turned down
the ambient lighting.

This entire half a planet was sunless, and would be for four
more hours. Mahit hadn't minded the diurnal cycling when
she'd been inside for most of the dark swing. Being out in it was
different. The heavy, dim sky felt pressurized, pushing down on
the back of her neck, making the headache worse. It was as if
darkness conducted sound, dimmed and distorted it, something she knew was impossible.

The golden tracery of the City's self-protective AI was the
only thing that was more visible at this hour of the night than

it was during the day. It ran under their feet in loops and whorls, crept up the foundations of some of the buildings as high as the second story, like some fungal infiltrate, and shimmered in the dimness. Three Seagrass walked across it with such deliberation that Mahit began to suspect she was afraid.

She wasn't wearing her cloudhook. She'd taken it off as they'd emerged from the imperial apartments, stowed it away inside her jacket. *We're not anywhere,* she'd said, and Mahit had taken that to mean that they were going to traverse the City without leaving electronic traces of Three Seagrass's official presence. Now, following her into the widening dark, Mahit wondered if she was putting off some confrontation with the City that had, inexplicably, refused to behave as she'd demanded.

That had set her alight with blue fire instead, like she wasn't even a citizen. Like the *perfect algorithm* that Ten Pearl had been so proud of had designated her something foreign, something that needed to be kept out. An infection, to be burned out with that selfsame blue fire.

It was only that they were sneaking into Palace-East in the middle of the night that was making Mahit come up with imagery like that; Three Seagrass would probably laugh at her if she explained it. It was all of a piece with how unsettled she felt about her meeting with Six Direction—hidden tensions, bubbling to the surface.

Civil war. The City, at war with itself.

And had he been *right,* to want to use an imago-machine to prevent this great devouring animal, this empire, from setting its jaws upon its own flesh?

Palace-East was brighter than Palace-Earth, but no less uncanny: the brightness came from burning neon tubes, red and blue and orange, that lit up pathways across the plazas, glowing guides to one government building or another. Three Seagrass hesitated at a junction where the AI-tracery had condensed itself into a knot—visibly set her shoulders—and turned away from it to hurry down an orange-lit avenue, waving Mahit after her. The white flowers that lined its sidewalks looked as if they had been dipped in flames.

Mahit had been awake too long, clearly, if she was seeing fire in flower arrangements. That was the problem. Not at all that she was hallucinating—she was almost sure she wasn't—but that she hadn't slept and all the adrenaline from the incident with the poison flower and the meeting with Six Direction was draining out of her.

Nevertheless, she asked quietly, "Are you avoiding the City?"

Three Seagrass didn't stop walking. "No," she said. "I'm not taking chances, that's all."

They hadn't talked about what had happened to her in Plaza Central Nine. There hadn't been time, in Nineteen Adze's apartments. Or it hadn't seemed *right,* to talk about it under the all-observing eyes of the *ezuazuacat's* recording equipment. Now, in the dark, Mahit felt either brave or unmoored, or some tongue-untying combination of both. "It's never done that to you before, has it," she said. "Thought you were someone it was allowed to discipline."

"Of course not."

"Patrician second-class, immune from petty justice."

"Law-abiding citizen of Teixcalaan, *Ambassador.*"

Mahit winced. She reached out and brushed Three Seagrass's shoulder. "I'm sorry," she said.

"Why?"

"I can't be sorry for impugning your moral authority?"

"You can," said Three Seagrass, "but it's hardly practical as a use of your time, I'd think. The City . . . I was surprised."

"You were having a seizure, not being surprised."

Three Seagrass stopped short, turned around, and looked up at Mahit. *"Afterward* I was surprised," she said, with an air of resolute authority. "Afterward I had a lot of time to be surprised. There's nothing to do in hospitals, Mahit, once you're finished reciting the hardest political acrostics you know in order to make sure your City hasn't wrecked your long-term memory."

"I shouldn't have brought it up," Mahit said.

"I'm not fragile," said Three Seagrass. "I can handle my barbarian wondering if civilization is going to electrocute me again."

"Is that really what you think I'm wondering?"

"It's what I would wonder." In the dark, Mahit thought Three Seagrass's eyes looked like black stones, pupilless, as alien as the sky. "Oh, and whether accidents like that have happened to *other* people, and under what circumstances. I might wonder that, too."

"Have they?" Mahit asked.

"More than I'd guessed. Eight, in the past six months. Two of the others died."

Mahit didn't know what to say—*I'm sorry* hadn't worked, and *is it my fault* was blatantly begging for reassurance she knew she didn't deserve: it was *probably* her fault. Or Yskandr's fault. Or the fault of that *civil unrest* that Yskandr had somehow been tied up with. The impending collapse of order.

"I told you I was surprised," Three Seagrass said, quite gently. "Come on, Mahit. It's another twenty minutes on foot to your apartments."

All the way there, Mahit felt like the City was watching them, even without cloudhooks to mark electronic traces of their presence; felt it, and told herself she was over-reading again. It was a *problem*—that the City was killing or hurting citizens—but it might not be her problem. It might not be her fault at all. Surely not everything could be. She could get far enough away from the narrative tendency of Teixcalaanli thought to believe that. She could.

———

The man inside Mahit's ambassadorial apartments was a dissolved silhouette between the tall windows: dark clothes, dark hair, invisible in the dimness before he moved. Mahit saw him first as a flash, some instrument in his hand reflecting the hallway light with white fire, and then as a rush of motion toward her. She had come two steps inside through the irised frame of the doorway. Three Seagrass had put her cloudhook back on to talk to the door, was standing to her left, out of the way—

Terror felt like a kick in the sternum. A sensible person would have run. Mahit had always expected that she'd run, faced with direct physical threat—she'd washed out of the combat-oriented aptitudes *early,* on Lsel, too much self-preservation instinct and too much *flinch.* The man—there was something horribly familiar about his face, now that he'd moved into the spilling light from the hall—came at her with the sharp thing in his left hand. It resolved into a needle, thick as a thorn, dull-glinting with some slick fluid on the tip, and Mahit thought *Poison, it's covered in poison* as she twisted away from it, backward, lost her balance and fell to the floor, landing on the heel of her bandaged hand. The shock of pain was bad enough that at first she thought he'd hit her. Still flinching after all.

"The *fuck*—" said Three Seagrass, in the doorway.

Mahit saw the man look up, freeze in evaluation—and in this freezing, she knew him, she recognized how he looked when he was surprised and distressed, she'd seen him look that way when Thirty Larkspur had pulled him off of her in the hallways of Palace-Earth. She couldn't remember his *name.* He'd tried to recruit her for One Lightning, and Thirty Larkspur had *threatened* him and—and now he was in her apartments and lifting his terrible needle to point directly at Three Seagrass. Mahit thought of the *xauitl, contact* poison, and then *or injectable,* racing through all the neurotoxins she knew, all of them bad—her assailant was fast—there was no way Three Seagrass, still damaged from the electrical shock of the City, would escape unscathed if he hit her with that.

Mahit rolled, slammed her shoulder into the side of his knee with as much of her weight as she could leverage. Caught at his ankle, yanked it up off the floor, both her hands wrapped around the leather of his boot, and felt *spectacular* pain—the blisters under the bandage on her hand must have split. Everything below her elbow had gone to liquid fire, molten and dripping. He fell. She felt savage, still terrified, adrenaline like whiteout, a strange sort of bliss—clawed her way on top of him, used all of her barbaric height and the reach of her un-Teixcalaanli limbs.

He cursed and flipped her—*strong,* he'd said he'd served in the Fleet, in One Lightning's own Eighteenth Legion, he would be strong—but she had her good hand in the collar of his shirt, an ankle hooked around his thigh, and he flipped with her, landed on top of her. The tip of the needle approached her neck. It was going to touch her, going to fill her up with paralysis and suffocation, spill into her brain and dissolve *her* and Yskandr and everything they were together. She made a desperate grab for the man's wrist with the hand that was still wrapped in bandages. Held on, even through the scream of pain, blisters bursting.

"You weren't supposed to fight back," he spat, "filthy *barbarian*—"

He hadn't cared very much about whether she was a barbarian when he'd wanted her to join a Teixcalaanli legion, had he.

Mahit bent his wrist back, as hard as she could, shoving his hand toward his neck. The edge of his needle scraped his throat, left a long line there, beaded red—swelling up immediately—going purple, *fuck,* what was in that toxin? The man made a guttural strangled noise. She could feel his body stiffen—spasm—begin to *jitter,* a meaningless, horrible thrashing. The needle fell from his nerveless fingers and landed on the floor by Mahit's head.

Mahit shoved him away, scuttled backward on her ass and elbows. She should have screamed a while back. It was very quiet now; just the harsh scrape of her breathing.

After what felt like the longest minute of her life, she heard the door to the suite hiss shut, and the overhead lighting clicked on. Then Three Seagrass came to sit beside her. Both of their backs were pressed against the wall. In the perfectly normal ambient lighting, the body of the man who'd attacked her looked small, incongruous, not at all like something that had moved and breathed and might have killed her. The needle lay beside him like a quiescent snake. His name came back to her along with the slowing of her breath. Eleven Conifer. A person. A dead person, now.

"Well," said Three Seagrass shakily, "this is definitely a new kind of trouble to be in. Are you all right?"

"I'm not hurt," Mahit said. It seemed wisest to stop there.

Three Seagrass nodded; Mahit could see the motion out of the corner of her eye. She couldn't look away from the body. "Mm," Three Seagrass said. "Good. Have you ever . . . done that before?"

"What, murder someone?" said Mahit, and oh, that *was* what she had just done, wasn't it. She was going to be sick.

"There's a fair argument for self-defense, but sure, if you like. Have you?"

"*No.*"

Three Seagrass reached over and patted Mahit gently on the shoulder, a hesitant feather-pressure. "Somewhat of a relief, really; I was wondering if Stationers were primed for explosive violence as well as carrying around dead people inside their heads . . ."

"Just once," Mahit said, with a sort of desperate and useless frustration, "I'd like you to imagine I might do something because it's what a person *does*."

"Mahit, most people don't—"

"Get ambushed by strangers with terrifying weapons in their own apartments while evading their only political ally in order to have a secret meeting on a *foreign planet*? No. I assume that doesn't happen to Teixcalaanlitzlim."

"That doesn't happen to *anyone*," Three Seagrass said. "Not as a rule."

Mahit dropped her head into her hands, and then jerked away when her damaged palm brushed against her cheek. She wanted, abruptly and with an absurd intensity, to be *asleep*. Asleep inside the narrow, secure walls of a room on Lsel, preferably, but mostly asleep. She ground her teeth together, bit the side of her tongue. It might have helped. She wasn't sure.

"Mahit," Three Seagrass said again, softer. Then she reached into Mahit's lap and caught her good hand in hers, lacing their fingers together. Her skin was dry and cool. Mahit turned to stare at her.

Three Seagrass shrugged, and didn't let go.

"It happens in histories," Mahit said inanely, like she was trying to make a gift of it: an allusion for a Teixcalaanlitzlim. For the sort of woman who would take her hand for no reason at all. "Pseudo-Thirteen River. Not exactly, but this sort of thing. When the *yaotlek* Nine Crimson is ambushed on the edge of known space—"

"It's not *that* bad," Three Seagrass said, but she swept her thumb over Mahit's knuckles. "You only killed one person, and he's definitely not secretly your clonesib defected to the wrong faction of the Empire. Histories are always worse by the time they get written down."

Mahit smiled despite herself, despite the corpse lying across from her, slowly swelling up, purple-red and bloated. She asked,

"Do they teach you that, when they teach you to remember them?"

"Not exactly," said Three Seagrass. "More an observation from experience—whoever inscribes the history has an agenda and that agenda's usually half *dramatics*. I mean, Pseudo-Thirteen River, everyone in that is desperately upset about mistaken identities and communication delay, but if you read Five Diadem instead on the very same expansion campaign, she wants you to think about *supply lines* because her patron was the Minister for the Economy—"

"We don't have Five Diadem on Lsel. Is that actually her *name*?"

"If your name was Five Hat, and you lived during the golden age of epic historiography, where everyone else was getting feted at court and taken out on campaigns as eyewitnesses, you would publish under a loose pseudonym *too*, Mahit."

Three Seagrass was so earnestly serious that Mahit found herself laughing, short sharp bursts of it that hurt her chest. It was possible she was hysterical. It was extremely possible, and a problem. It still took her half a minute to catch her breath. Three Seagrass squeezed her fingers, gently, and she exhaled hard through her teeth.

When she could manage it, Mahit asked, "Do you know why a man who accosted me at the Emperor's oration-contest banquet might have tried just now to kill me?"

"Is that who he is?" Three Seagrass said, and let go of Mahit's fingers. "Do you remember his name?" She got to her feet, and approached the corpse with her hands clasped primly behind her back, as if she was afraid to touch it accidentally. She peered at it, crouching. The panels of her jacket pooled on the floor, like the just-unfurled wings of a new insect.

"Conifer," Mahit said, "I think—*Eleven* Conifer. But I wasn't sober. Neither was he."

"Tell me how you met him," Three Seagrass said. With the tip of her shoe, she nudged the dead man's head, tilting it up so she could see his face.

"He was looking for anyone Thirty Larkspur didn't already own," Mahit said. "And then I insulted him. And he tried to . . . grab me? Hurt me. And then Thirty Larkspur himself called him off—"

"You shouldn't go places without me," Three Seagrass said, but she didn't sound reproving. "So he knows you. At least a little. Enough to dislike you. Now, he's not anyone I know, and he's not wearing anyone's colors or favors—not that an assassin *would,* no matter what people do in poetry *or* histories—"

"You do think *assassin,* then."

She straightened up. "Do you have other ideas?"

Mahit shrugged. "Kidnapper, thief—someone who wanted to intercept this meeting, except I can't think of who would *know*—"

"Except me," Three Seagrass said, only a little bit wry. "And Twelve Azalea, who asked to meet you here."

"Three Seagrass, if I begin by assuming you are trying to kill me, I—"

She waved one of her hands, a falling gesture of dismissal. "Assume I'm not. Didn't we agree on that, the first day you were here? I'm not trying to sabotage you, and you're not an idiot. Killing you counts as sabotage."

That conversation—in this same room!—felt like it had been months ago, though Mahit was entirely aware it had been only four days. Five, now that the sun was beginning to rise.

"Not you, then," she said, "for simplicity's sake. Which leaves Twelve Azalea and . . . anyone who intercepted his message before it got to me. He did say he was being followed."

"A person who can intercept a message on infofiche would

either have to be right there when he sent it, or else Information Ministry, to unseal the stick and seal it up again."

"Information Ministry is still *you* or Twelve Azalea, Three Seagrass."

Three Seagrass looked at her for a long moment, and sighed. "There are a lot of *asekretim*. Some of us probably work for whoever it is that wanted Yskandr dead, or you dead, or wants Twelve Azalea dead—"

"What if it's not interception?" Mahit asked, cutting her off. "Before he—before I—from what he said, he said *you weren't supposed to fight back*, I think he meant to threaten me, get me to give him something. I don't think he wanted to kill me at all. I think he wanted what Twelve Azalea has, the imago-machine, and I think he wanted me to hand it over. Maybe he was *sent*."

"Who would send him?"

Mahit thought of saying *One Lightning*, but that would assume that everyone knew about the imago-machines, everyone in Teixcalaan, not just everyone in the palace; One Lightning was up in a flagship somewhere in Teixcaalanli space—when would he have *heard*?

Instead she said, "Thirty Larkspur? If he exploited what Eleven Conifer did to me. He was very deliberate about pointing out that what he'd done was *assault*, and that he'd be talking to him later . . ."

"And Thirty Larkspur would want an imago-machine? Enough to blackmail a courtier. Well. I wouldn't put it *past* him." Three Seagrass's expression went strange—distant, a little rueful. "Your imago-machines are a *problem*, Mahit."

"Not for us," Mahit said. *Only for Teixcalaan, who wants them this badly. Or wants them to not exist this badly.*

"No," said Three Seagrass. She left off standing by the corpse and came back over to Mahit, offering her a hand up off the floor. "I think they are a problem for you, too—or at least *you* have a problem, having told any of us about them."

Mahit took her hand, even though she was so much taller than Three Seagrass that the offered leverage wasn't much help. "I didn't," she said, getting to her feet. "Tell you, that is. *Yskandr* did, and the Yskandr who did is a man I have never met."

"What is it like?"

"What is *what* like?"

"Not being one person."

It was such a naked question—more straightforward than anyone had *been* with Mahit in her entire time on this planet—that it took her by surprise; she was still standing there, trying to figure out what sort of answer was even *possible,* her fingers twined up with Three Seagrass's, when the door chimed plaintively in that uncomfortable dissonant chord.

"More assassins?" Three Seagrass said, over-bright.

"Twelve Azalea, I hope," said Mahit. "Go open it?"

Three Seagrass did. She stood sharply to the side of the door while she told it to open, as if being simply out of line-of-sight would preserve her from whatever was waiting to enter. But when the door irised open it was only Twelve Azalea after all. Mahit watched him take in the scene: purple-faced corpse on the rug, dawn light coming in through the windows, Mahit and Three Seagrass themselves standing about like children who had accidentally broken a priceless art object.

Teixcalaanli expressionlessness could, apparently, withstand the revelation of recent murder. Perhaps it helped that Twelve Azalea looked like he'd had an equally distressing night. His Information Ministry suit was waterstained, the orange cuffs gone stiff and spotted. There was dirt smeared across one of his cheeks and most of his hair had come undone from its queue.

"You look terrible, Petal," said Three Seagrass.

"There is a dead man on your rug, Reed; *how I look is not important.*"

"It's my rug, actually," said Mahit. "Now would you come in so we can close the door?"

When the door was safely locked behind him—the three of them closed in with the dead man, a small secret to go along with all of Mahit's enormous other ones—Twelve Azalea reached into his jacket and produced a bundle of cloth. It looked like one of the sheets from the morgue, folded into a neat packet. He held it out to Mahit.

"You owe me, Ambassador," he said. "I have spent six hours being *stalked,* and then another three hiding in the bottom of a half-drained garden. This entire business was very entertaining while we were exchanging coded messages, but it is markedly less entertaining now. Not to mention the fact that you've come up with another corpse while I wasn't paying attention—has anyone called for the Sunlit, are you just going to *stand here?*"

"Petal, we were going to," Three Seagrass said, which was news to Mahit.

She unfolded the cloth. In the center was the small steel-and-ceramide net of Yskandr's imago-machine. It had been excised very carefully with a scalpel, she thought: the feathered fractal edges of the net, where the machine interpenetrated with neurons, were delineated quite far, and then sharply cut off when the edge of the blade had become too unwieldy to keep going on a microscopic level. But Twelve Azalea hadn't known how to decouple the fractal net—the portion of the machine which was like a shell, an interface—from the central core, which contained Yskandr. That was, she thought, still intact, unharmed by even the most delicate of scalpels. The machine might still be usable. (For what? To record someone else? Or to try to reach that Yskandr, the dead Ambassador? Whatever was left of him. She wondered, and decided to not mention the idea to anyone yet.)

Mahit took the machine from the sheet Twelve Azalea had disguised it in—it was no longer than the last joint of her thumb—and slipped it into the inside pocket of her jacket.

"I thought," she said, "that we should wait for you to come and bring me the illegally acquired machinery I asked you to desecrate my predecessor's corpse for, first. Before we called anyone." If Three Seagrass was going to lie to her friend about calling the police, Mahit could *help*. It was probably easiest. It might even be easiest *to* call the Sunlit, to report the . . . incident—it was still a dizzying sort of horror to call it murder, to remember the feeling of Eleven Conifer *turning into a corpse* on top of her—report it exactly as it had happened. A man broke into the Ambassador's apartments; they struggled; in the struggle the man was killed by his own weapon.

"Well, you have it now," Twelve Azalea was saying, "and you can *keep* it—I was followed from the instant I left the Judiciary morgue, Ambassador. By the Judiciary's own investigatory agents—the fucking *Mist* were after me, grey-suit ghosts. I thought I lost them when I spent an hour in a water feature, but maybe I didn't—or maybe my message was intercepted, when I wrote to tell you I'd meet you here. Someone with very good intelligence has been keeping an eye on your predecessor's body, and I had to use a public terminal to write my infofiche stick and send it."

It could have been Nineteen Adze. Mahit remembered how quickly she had arrived in the morgue, just hours after Mahit had suggested burning Yskandr's body in a proper Stationer funeral. But it could have just as easily been a multitude of other actors, most especially Eight Loop, if there was some kind of special Judiciary police force that was chasing Twelve Azalea. That was the problem with this entire mess—too many people interested in Yskandr. Too many *more* people interested in Mahit: she'd done that deliberately, she'd made herself an object of attention, in hopes of finding out who had murdered her pre-decessor, and now she couldn't get away from it even if she tried.

Even if she'd done nothing but stay in her apartment and do the work she'd come here to do, people would have been too interested: Eight Loop had summoned a new Lsel ambassador *deliberately*. There wouldn't have been a possibility of neutral-ity, no matter what she did.

"Are they still following you?" she asked.

Twelve Azalea sighed. "I don't know. Practical espionage is not my rubric."

"Only impractical," Three Seagrass said. Twelve Azalea rolled his eyes at her, and she shrugged expressively, which seemed to reassure him.

"I guess we'll find out," said Mahit. "If someone tries to kill you, as well as someone trying to kill me."

"Assassins and stalkers," Twelve Azalea said. "Just what I needed. If I was a more judicious sort of man, Ambassador, I would not only call the Sunlit but imply that you'd blackmailed me into committing . . . oh, there's got to be a crime for steal-ing from the dead. Is there a crime for that, Reed?"

"Plagiarism," said Three Seagrass, "but it'd be a stretch in the courts."

"It's not funny."

"It *is*, Petal, but only because it's awful."

Mahit envied them the facility of friendship. It would be so much *easier* . . .

Easier wasn't what she had. What she had was Yskandr's imago-machine, a corpse, and the Emperor's offer hanging above her like a weight: turn over the imago technology, turn aside the fleet heading for Lsel, and betray to Teixcalaan everything that her Station had spent fourteen generations preserving. She thought of her younger brother, abruptly, imagined him denied whatever imago his aptitudes might have spelled for him to receive, imagined him taken away from the Station and raised on a Teix-calaanli planet—he was *nine,* he was too young to know any-thing but the romance of the idea—not that she was doing much better.

Why did you say yes, Yskandr? she asked: intimate-you, Sta-tioner language, quiet in the hollow places inside her mind where she ought to have had his voice, the voice of the person they were meant to be becoming, all of his knowledge and all of her perspective.

<I have no idea,> Yskandr told her, bell-clear, <but I imagine I'd run out of better options.>

Prickles down all the nerves in her arms, up from the soles of her feet. Like the dead man had gotten her with his poison needle after all. Mahit sat down, hard, on the couch. If Yskandr was actually *back*—maybe all it took was life-threatening amounts of adrenaline to hook up whatever had gone wrong be-tween them. That made no sense physiologically but it was the only thing she could think of.

<You've landed us in a truly remarkable amount of trouble, haven't—> Then static. Cutoff. The sensation was like having her own brain provide an electrical short. And for all she tried to reach him, Yskandr was as gone now as he had been before he'd spoken, and Mahit was dizzy with the sensation of falling into a hole in her mind, the endless drop that was the gap be-tween her and where her imago should be.

CHAPTER TWELVE

THE GAME'S STILL ON!
Come see THE LABYRINTH of Belltown take on the South-Central VOLCANOES in the most hotly anticipated *amalitzli* match of the season! No subway closures can stop our players! Tickets still available via cloudhook or at the North Tlachtli Court Stadium. Come out for a good time!

> —flyer advertising handball game, printed 249.3.11-6D and
> distributed throughout Inmost Province, Belltown,
> South-Central, and Poplar provinces

*   *   *

[. . .] it has been another five years since you last returned to Lsel Station; not only would the Councilor for Heritage very much like to preserve and update to the current state your imago-line for future generations, I myself would like to hear from your own mouth the state of affairs in Teixcalaan; you've become admirably close-mouthed in the last half decade, Yskandr, and I can't complain about your continued successes in the job I chose you for, but indulge my curiosity—come home to us, for a little while [. . .]

> —message received by Ambassador Yskandr Aghavn from
> Darj Tarats, Councilor for the Miners (087.1.10-6D,
> Teixcalaanli reckoning)

THE Sunlit arrived quite quickly once they had been summoned: three of them in their identical golden helmets, faceless and efficient. Three Seagrass had done the summoning, setting up some communion between her cloudhook and the door's alarm system and then executing a credible impression of tremulous, infuriated surprise—an emotion which Mahit suspected was fairly close to how she actually felt, just *expressed*, for a purpose. Whatever vast reservoir of emotions Three Seagrass might possess seemed *only* to be expressed for purpose, or outgassed in vivid bright hysteria. The kind of control she had over herself made Mahit tired to think about.

She could also be tired because she'd been awake for nearly thirty-two hours. Sleep was an unimaginable territory, reserved for people who didn't have dead bodies in their apartments. At least she was unlikely to get herself arrested. The Sunlit seemed collectively distracted, or else they simply *believed* her: she'd come back to her apartment and been set upon by the dead man, and in the ensuing struggle he had been killed by his own weapon. No, Mahit had never seen a weapon like the thick needle before. No, she didn't know how the man had gotten in. No, she didn't know who had sent him, but in this time of unrest, there were surely a multitude of possibilities.

She hadn't lied *once*. And yet they were trusting her.

Yskandr was gone again, but gone *differently*; all through the questioning Mahit's palms and the soles of her feet had been alive with prickles, as if her extremities had been rendered out of flesh and into shimmering electric fire—not quite numbness. The same feeling she'd been having right before the flashes of imago-memory, but continuous now, and without the accompanying visions. Peripheral nerve damage, except she hadn't damaged anything. Unless the imago-machine in the base of her skull was damaging her right now as she answered questions in Teixcalaanli, expressionless, calm. The place Yskandr should be felt like a hollow bubble, a missing tooth. A cavity she could tongue inside her mind. If she pressed too hard on it the sweeping vertigo came back. She tried to stop doing it. Fainting right now wouldn't help at all.

"Patrician first-class Twelve Azalea," said one of the Sunlit, turning toward him like a gyre on ball bearings, machine-smooth, "what brings you to Ambassador Dzmare's apartments so early in the morning?"

Ah. Perhaps they hadn't believed her after all; perhaps they were being subtle. They'd use Twelve Azalea to crack open her story like the vacuum seal on a seed-skiff, and bleed all the protecting atmosphere away.

"The Ambassador asked to meet with me," said Twelve Azalea, and *that* was not going to help at all.

"I did," Mahit interjected. "I was looking forward to a meeting over breakfast with Twelve Azalea to discuss . . ." She cast around for something they could be discussing that was not suspicious in any way. There wasn't much. ". . . requests made to the Information Ministry by Lsel citizens during the period within which there was no acting ambassador." There.

If a golden face-shield could express all the skepticism of a raised eyebrow, this one was. "That sounds like an extremely urgent matter, that must be addressed before business hours."

"Both the patrician and I have very busy schedules. Breakfast suited us. Or it did, before I was set upon by the intruder," Mahit said pointedly. She felt as if she was about to vibrate out of her skin. Neurological fire and the effervescent distant shivering of sleep deprivation. She smiled, Stationer-style, and wondered if the Sunlit had flinched under the shield. All her teeth were exposed. Like a skeleton.

One of the other Sunlit asked silkily, "What happened to your suit, Twelve Azalea? You seem to have encountered a water feature."

Mahit had seen Teixcalaanlitzlim blush before, but never someone employ it as masterfully as Twelve Azalea did then: a spreading embarrassed dull red under the smooth brown of his cheeks. "It's very . . . I've been a little worried, what with the demonstrations . . . I tripped," he said. "I fell in a *garden,* like I was drunk; and it was too late to go home, I'd have missed my appointment . . ."

"Are you quite all right?" the Sunlit inquired.

"Aside from the injury to my dignity—"

"Of course."

Three Seagrass, curled in the corner of the couch with her feet drawn up under her, said, "Will you be removing the body? It is quite hard to look at." She still sounded tremulous and barely controlled; Mahit wondered if *she* had slept, aside from the brief moment when she'd found her napping outside the Emperor's audience chamber. Probably not.

One week since she'd arrived in the City, and hadn't she been quite the agent of destruction. For Three Seagrass at least. (For Fifteen Engine—*Yskandr*—) She wanted to *do* something. Push something until it broke in her favor, for once.

"This is the second time in a week we have been in personal danger," Mahit said. "After the bombing, and the general condition of your City in preparation for the war . . ." She sighed, deliberate. So distasteful, political unrest. "I thought it would be best to have a meeting in my own apartments rather than anywhere we would have the misfortune of being disturbed, and yet *this* has happened."

All three Sunlit looked at her. She stared back at their blank false faces, jaw set.

"We would like to remind the Ambassador," they said—all three at once, a strange choir, and *were they the City, were they the* same AI that ran the walls and the lights and the doors, were they sub-sumed in the Science Ministry's algorithm too—"that the *yaotlek* One Lightning did offer his *personal* protection to you. And you declined."

"Are you insinuating that this unpleasantness would not have happened if the Ambassador had agreed?" Three Seagrass broke in. "Because that is a *fascinating* conjecture, coming from the Empire's very own police."

They rotated, a slick, frictionless shift, to focus on Three Sea-grass. She lifted her eyebrows, widened her eyes to show the whites—*daring* them to do something about her.

"There are procedures," said one of them, perfectly even, "for making formal accusations of that nature, *asekreta* Three Sea-grass. Would you like to avail yourself of them? We are at your service, as we are at the service of *any* of the Empire's citizens."

That was, Mahit thought, a threat of its own; less direct but not even a *little* less predatory.

"Perhaps I will make an appointment at the Judiciary," Three Seagrass said. Her expression changed not a bit. "Are we done here? Will you be removing this unfortunate man from the Ambassador's rug?"

"It is an active crime scene," the Sunlit said. "The entire apart-ment complex. We suggest that the Ambassador make arrange-ments for alternative accommodations during our investigation. We are sure, given this morning's newsfeeds, that she has many options."

Mahit glanced at Twelve Azalea over the Sunlit's shoulder—he was the only one of them who might have seen a newsfeed this morning—but he just shrugged. She didn't know what she had missed. Maybe it was merely an exposé on the Lsel Am-bassador's unseemly attachment to the *ezuazuacat* Nineteen Adze.

"When can I expect to have access to my own suite again?"

she inquired. Still trying for polite, if pointed: they were *all* on edge now, she and her liaison and the Sunlit.

One of the Sunlit shrugged, a remarkably expressive motion. Some neurological ghost of Yskandr flickered through the large muscles in Mahit's own shoulders—he'd shrugged like that—that *kind* of shrug was performative, insouciant, done more with the outer arms (was he here or was he *not,* she wished she had even the slightest true idea).

"When we are done investigating," said the Sunlit. "You are of course free to go. We understand the accidental nature of the man's demise."

So, not arrested for murder. Just exiled, again, this time from her own apartment, from Lsel diplomatic territory . . .

She had the imago-machine, safe inside her shirt, but what she *didn't* have was the *mail.* And with the mail, any instructions that might have come to her from Lsel. Instructions for *her,* not for dead Yskandr being warned about her. Instructions that would take into account the problems of a *live* Lsel ambassador. She turned to Three Seagrass and Twelve Azalea, shrugged herself—trying to keep the motion her own, not a Teixcalaanli imitation—and said, "Let's get out of these officers' way . . ."

If she could just pick up the basket of infofiche at the door. There *was* a communiqué from Lsel there, something *printed* on plastifilm, like orders always were back home, and then rolled into a tube as if the mail-delivery person had tried to make it look like an infofiche stick.

She swept her hand through the bowl as she walked out—caught the tube of paper in her palm.

"Ambassador," one of the Sunlit said, reproving, as she reached. "Don't worry, we will not open your mail. We don't have that kind of access."

But they would have, if they did, she was sure. Mahit left the actual infofiche sticks in the bowl, as if chastised, and smiled with *all* her teeth, not caring if it was rude. "See that you don't," she said, and then the door to what ought to have been safety was irising shut behind the three of them, and they were in the City, alone, with absolutely nowhere to go.

———

"I used to do this when I'd spent all night in the library and couldn't go back home before the next lectures," said Three Seagrass. She handed Mahit a small bowl of ice cream she'd bought from a proprietor who had set up their business in the shell of a motor vehicle under a spreading, red-leaved tree.

"Don't believe her," Twelve Azalea said. "Ice cream in the public gardens is what she used to do after she stayed out all night *clubbing*."

"Oh really?" Mahit scooped up some of the ice cream on the disposable plastic spoon it'd come with—it was thick and smooth, made of cream that had come out of a mammal recently, and Mahit had no intention of asking what mammal. When she turned the spoon in the early morning light, the ice cream glinted pale gold-green. Feeling as if she was completing a ritual, she asked, "Is this going to poison me?"

"It's made of green-stonefruit and cream and pressed oil and sugar," Three Seagrass said, "the latter two of which I'm sure you have on Lsel, and the former of which, again, *we feed to babies*. Unless you're allergic to lactose, I think you'll be fine."

Mahit's primary experience with lactose had been in its powdered milk form, but it hadn't done her any harm. She put the ice cream in her mouth. It was shock-sweet, dissolving to a complex flavor she'd expect to be savory—a *green* taste, rich, that coated the tongue. She picked up more, licked it off the back of the spoon. It was the first food she'd had since before she'd been nearly killed by the poison flower—the *first* murder attempt of last night, what was even *happening* to her—and she could feel her blood sugar struggling out of the hole she'd dropped it into. Being exiled into the City began to seem a little less insurmountable.

Three Seagrass led the three of them out onto the lawn, a manicured hill covered in a bluish-green grass that had no scent at all, and surrounded by more of the same red-leaved trees, their boughs nearly brushing the ground. It was like a tiny gemstone, one facet of the Jewel of the World, glimmering. Uncaring of her suit—it was wrinkled anyway; Mahit assumed that grass stains wouldn't matter—Three Seagrass sat down, and began to consume her own ice cream with a deliberate and concentrated attitude.

"I don't know why I'm even still with you," Twelve Azalea said, flopped on his back in the grass. "I haven't been kicked out of *my* apartment by the Sunlit."

"Solidarity," Three Seagrass said. "And your documented inability to leave well enough alone."

"This is more trouble than we've ever been in, Reed."

"Yes," Three Seagrass said cheerfully.

"That was . . . that *was* odd, wasn't it?" Mahit asked. She kept going over it in her mind. How easy it had been to persuade the Sunlit that she'd acted in self-defense. Their not-that-subtle threat implying that if she'd only gone over into One Lightning's custody at the Ministry of War—the Six Outreaching Palms—none of this would be happening to her. "That they just . . . let us go. Exiled us from my apartment, and didn't ask us to wait in some police station to be questioned. Despite the degree of trouble we are undoubtedly in."

"It's not unusual that they let us go, necessarily," Three Seagrass said. "I don't know how self-defense is adjudicated on your station, but we tend to allow a substantive benefit of the doubt in the favor of the person claiming it."

"What's odd was the part where the Sunlit suggested you

wouldn't have had to commit murder in self-defense if you'd only turned yourself over to the War Ministry," Twelve Azalea added, with an expansive shrug. "Or why Reed here thought it was a good idea to threaten them right back."

Mahit licked the back of her spoon, chasing that green taste. When it was clean, she asked, choosing the words deliberately, as careful as she'd ever been: "Who do the Sunlit serve?"

"The City," Three Seagrass and Twelve Azalea said, together and at once. Rote answer, *memorized* answer—the answer provided by Teixcalaanli narrative about how the world was.

"And who *runs* them?" Mahit went on.

"No one," said Three Seagrass. "No one at all, that's the point, they're responsive to the City-AI, the central algorithm which keeps watch . . ."

"Like the subway," Twelve Azalea added. "They're the City, so they serve the Emperor first."

Mahit paused, trying to find the edges of the question, the right way to ask it. "The subway's algorithm was made by Ten Pearl," she started, thinking of the flash of memory that her imago had given her, *how Ten Pearl had won his ministry—an infallible algorithm.*

"Ten Pearl doesn't control the Sunlit," Twelve Azalea said. "The Sunlit are people."

"People who respond to the City's needs," Three Seagrass said, slow, testing the idea. "People who go where the City tells them they ought to go—and the central AI core *is* run by Science, I assume—"

Mahit interrupted her. "Who controls the Six Outreaching Palms?"

"The Minister of War is Nine Propulsion. She's new—less than three years in the City—but her record in the fleet's *impeccable.* Annoyingly so; I had to look her up in Information's database once."

"Three Seagrass," Mahit said, "could the Minister of War change what is *meant* by the City's needs? For . . . any reason at all, really."

"What a deliciously awful suggestion, Mahit," Three Seagrass said with an exhausted silkiness. "Are you proposing a conspiracy between two of our Illuminate Emperor's ministries to subvert the *police*?"

"I don't know," Mahit said. "But it'd be *one* plausible explanation for this morning."

"Plausible doesn't mean *likely*," Twelve Azalea said. He sounded offended. Disturbed by the idea. It was a disturbing idea. Mahit didn't blame him. She couldn't think of *why* War would do such a thing, even if it was possible. And she didn't much want it to be possible.

How many eyes does the City have on us right now?

Three Seagrass said, "Talk it over with the Ambassador, Petal, I'm taking a *nap*."

"You are?" Mahit said, incredulous.

Three Seagrass, having finished her ice cream, took off her jacket, lay down on her belly in the grass as if making a point, and dropped her forehead into her crossed arms. Muffled, she said, "I've been awake for thirty-nine hours. My judgment is entirely impaired and so is yours. I have no idea what to do about your immortality machines, a possible conspiracy between Science and War, the war in general, the fact that various members of my government want you to die, which I am expressly against for both professional and personal reasons, and you still have not told me what the Emperor said to you—"

"You spoke to His Illuminate Majesty?" asked Twelve Azalea, flabbergasted, at the same moment as Mahit said,

"*Personal* reasons?"

Three Seagrass snickered. "I am taking a nap," she repeated. "Talk to Petal, Mahit, or go to sleep, we look like slumming *asekretim* trainees, no one will bother us in a garden in East Four, and I'll . . . think of a plan when I'm awake again." She shut her eyes. Mahit could see her go limp—whether she was sleeping or just pretending to was somewhat beside the point.

"Was she like this when you were students?" Mahit said, feeling entirely overwhelmed.

"A . . . less terrifying version, yes," said Twelve Azalea. "Did you actually have an audience with Six Direction?"

Eighty years of peace, the Emperor had told her, in that audience. He'd spoken the words with such vehemence, such naked *want.* Eighty years of civil servants feeling so remarkably secure that taking a nap on a lawn was preferable to finding political shelter. The vast arc of the sky was so blue and so endless, and Mahit felt so very tiny under it. She was never going to get used to the unboundedness of planets, even a planet that was mostly a city.

"Yes," she said. "I did. But I can't talk about it now."

"How long have *you* been awake?"

"About as long as she has, I guess." Longer, possibly. Mahit had lost track. That was a bad sign. Her fingers were still prickly, almost numb. For the first time she wondered what it would be like if she was like this *forever*; if she was damaged in an unfixable way. If everything she would ever touch again would be dim electric fire, and not sensation.

If she could learn to live with that. She wasn't sure. Abruptly she felt on the verge of tears.

Twelve Azalea sighed. "Much as I hate to say it, I think Reed is right. Lie down. Shut your eyes. I'll . . . keep watch."

"You don't have to," Mahit said, out of some impulse to protect at least *one* person from the spiraling mess that association with anything Yskandr had touched was becoming.

"I already desecrated a corpse for you, and now I sound like a bad holoproduction of *Ninety Alloy*. Go to *sleep*."

Mahit lay down. It felt like giving in. The grass was surprisingly comfortable, and the sunlight was dizzyingly warm against her skin. She could feel the tiny lumps of Yskandr's imago-machine and the Lsel communication lying pressed against her ribs. "What's *Ninety Alloy?*" she asked.

"Military propaganda spun through a remarkably addictive romance storyline," Twelve Azalea said. "Someone is always telling someone else they'll keep watch. Usually they all end up dead."

"Pick a different genre to quote from," Mahit said, and then found herself falling away from consciousness, easily, lightly, the dark behind her eyelids opening up like the soft comfort of freefall.

———

She couldn't stay asleep long, even as exhausted as she was. The garden filled up with Teixcalaanlitzlim as the morning wore on, and they ran and shouted and enthusiastically bought ice cream and strange breakfasts made of rolled-up pancakes. None of them seemed to be concerned with civil unrest or domestic terrorism. They were just *young,* and happy, and there was sunlight and laughing voices in dialects of Teixcalaanli that Mahit didn't know and wanted to. (Some other life. Some other life when she'd come here alone, imagoless in truth, and—studied, wrote poetry, learned the rhythms of other ways of speaking that didn't come out of a textbook. Some other life, but the walls between lives felt so *thin* sometimes.) After a while Mahit couldn't even pretend she was sleeping by keeping her eyes shut, so she sat up. There were blue-green grass stains on her elbows. Some of the prickling nerve pain had died back, but it was still there as an undercurrent, a distraction, a thread underneath the worse pain of her damaged hand.

Three Seagrass and Twelve Azalea were talking quietly, their

heads together, bent over a piece of infosheet; the easy familiarity between them made Mahit feel hideously lonely. She
missed Yskandr. She *kept missing him,* even when she was angry
with him, and she was angry with him almost all the time.

"What time is it?" she asked.

"Mid-morning," said Three Seagrass. "You might want to see
this, come here."

At Three Seagrass's side was a small pile of news: a whole
bunch of pamphlets and plastifilm infosheets, wide transparent
sheets of foldable plastic, covered all over with glyphs. The ones
on top of the pile seemed to be an angry university-student pamphlet on atrocities committed in the Odile System by overzeal-
ous imperial legions, an advertisement for discounted tickets to
a game of handball between two teams from provinces Mahit
didn't recognize but were clearly endowed with a great many
fans, and a broadsheet full of new poetry, most of which was
simultaneously very bad in terms of scansion and very happy
about One Lightning. Mahit thought again about who was
running around so blithely in this garden. *Slumming* asekretim
trainees, Three Seagrass had said. University students. This was
a place young people felt safe, safe enough to be mildly radical.
To pass around pamphlets for just about anything, and not
worry about the imperial censorship boards. Who would censor
kids just learning to be servants of empire?

The infosheet that Twelve Azalea was holding seemed to be
a newsfeed—stories, sketches, headlines. Twelve Azalea ran his
fingers over it, and the text moved under his command: it was
like he was holding a transparent window made of news. Mahit caught sight of a small *Item of Note!* in the lower left: her name
spelled out in Teixcalaanli glyphs, rendered awkwardly syllabic.
LSEL AMBASSADOR MAKES HIGH-PLACED FRIENDS, it read.
*Is the new ambassador from distant Lsel still as close with the Light-
Emitting Emperor as the old one? Surveillance photographs suggest*

SHE IS! Last seen in the company of the ezuazuacat *Nineteen Adze entering Palace-Earth AT MIDNIGHT . . .*

"Delightful," Mahit said. "Gossip."

"Not *that*," said Three Seagrass. "That's fine. It's probably good for your—brand. Look at the headline, that's what I wanted you to see."

IMPERIAL ASSOCIATE EIGHT LOOP ISSUES STATEMENT ON LEGALITY OF ANNEXATION WAR, the headline-glyphs spelled.

"Huh," Mahit said. "Give me that? I wouldn't expect public dissent from that direction—"

Twelve Azalea handed it over. Mahit kept reading: Eight Loop's statement was short, impenetrably layered in references to Teixcalaanli precedent, and composed in unrhymed political verse, which she ought to have expected, considering the woman was head of the Judiciary—but after staring at it for a long moment she thought she understood what Eight Loop was getting at.

While going to war was entirely at the Emperor's discretion (of course it was), a war of *expansion* was legally required to be conducted *beginning in an atmosphere of perfect serenity,* which was—if Mahit was reading the Teixcalaanli legalese correctly—a time in which there were no actual *threats* to Teixcalaan to be faced before the fleet could go off conquering. "What threat is she implying exists?" Mahit asked. "And why would she suggest that Six Direction is not *competent* to run this war, now? Didn't they grow up together?" *Weren't they allies?*

Three Seagrass shrugged, but she looked like she'd been given a present: a puzzle to solve. "She isn't *exactly* saying there's a direct threat to the integrity of the Empire, though there's always some sort of rumor that this is the year some alien species or other is actually going to invade human space. She's just saying that His Brilliance didn't prove there *wasn't* a threat. It's not quite a condemnation of his inaction, more like a suggestion that he's missed something important that he should have thought of. Like he's not fit to rule anymore, if he can't remember things like this . . ."

"I don't like it," Twelve Azalea added. "It's sneaky."

It was sneaky. "She sent for me," Mahit said. "As a further point of data. It was Eight Loop who got a new Lsel ambassador here as soon as Yskandr was dead."

"Was *murdered*; it's all right, we know," Three Seagrass said.

"Was murdered," Mahit agreed. "But either way, *she* sent for me, and now she is doing this, and I want to see her in person."

Three Seagrass clapped her hands together. "Well," she said. "We don't have anywhere *else* to be until your appointment at the Science Ministry, and that's tomorrow. Since we can't go back to your apartments, and I don't imagine you want to call up the *ezuazuacat* for help again . . ."

"Not without a better reason than wanting a shower and an actual bed," Mahit said. "I might get to that point by this evening."

"Then we might as well walk straight into Eight Loop's offices."

"We've napped in a garden and now we're invading the Judiciary?" Twelve Azalea asked, plaintive.

"You can go home, Petal," Three Seagrass said. It had much the same attitude as Eight Loop's little insinuation: *You could go home, but you'd be letting down the side.*

Twelve Azalea got up, brushing off his much-abused suit. "Oh no. I want to see this. Even if the Mist do ask me questions about what I was doing sneaking around in the morgue. And they might not even know it was *me*."

———

They made quite a picture, Mahit suspected: two Information Ministry functionaries and one barbarian, all wrinkled and grass-stained; one with a long tear up the sleeve of her jacket from struggling with Eleven Conifer's awful needle (that would be her) and one looking as if he had hidden in a water feature— which he had (Twelve Azalea); only Three Seagrass seemed to wear her disarray as if it was the height of court fashion. Nevertheless they received little direct opposition on their way into the Judiciary: the doors still opened to Twelve Azalea's cloud-hook, which implied that even if he was being stalked by some sort of Judiciary-specific investigatory force, they hadn't forbidden him from being here, and the functionaries within the Ministry kept a quiet sort of watch on them as Three Seagrass walked them through the layers of bureaucracy separating Eight Loop from the sort of annoyance that came in off the street.

That bureaucracy parted for Three Seagrass like over-irradiated plastic, rotten-soft under pressure. There was something *wrong* with it; they were moving too easily up the great needle-spear of the Judiciary.

Mahit thought about mentioning her growing sense that she was following Three Seagrass into a trap. But if she mentioned it perhaps that trap would close around them, needle-teeth like a thousand Judiciaries pointed inward . . .

Eight Loop could have been waiting for her all along. (Nineteen Adze had suggested as much, when she'd insinuated that Mahit should find out who had sent for her in the first place. But she couldn't afford to use Nineteen Adze's judgment in place of her own.)

An elevator took them up the last few floors to Eight Loop's own offices: a tiny red-crystal seedpod of a chamber, semi-translucent. Inside of it the air felt hushed, charged. Mahit found herself staring at how the light fell on Three Seagrass's face, turning it from warm brown to a ruddy color as if she'd been dipped in blood.

"This is too easy," she said.

Three Seagrass tipped her head back, rolled her shoulders. "I know."

"And yet we are in this elevator—"

"I could make Petal press the emergency stop, but it's a bit late to have second thoughts, Mahit."

"Clearly Eight Loop wants us to have this meeting," Twelve Azalea said. "As we also want to have this meeting, I am not seeing the reason for your distress."

"Eventually," Three Seagrass said, dry and distant and a little regretful, "you might have to do something someone else wants, Mahit."

The part of her that was cued onto Teixcalaanli double meanings, allusion and reference and hidden motives—that part of her which, if she was being honest, was why she was a good politician, why her aptitudes had spelled for *diplomacy* and *negotiation* and came up green, green, green with Yskandr's—that vicious part suggested that it was entirely possible that Three Seagrass had been working for Eight Loop this whole time. If she was so insistent on Mahit keeping this meeting . . .

And would it change anything?

It should. It didn't. It was too late, anyway. The elevator doors opened.

Eight Loop's office was nothing like Nineteen Adze's white-quartz serenity of a workroom: despite being at the very top of the Judiciary tower, it felt tightly enclosed, almost claustrophobic. The pentagonal walls were lined with infofiche and codex-books, overlapping and stacked double on the shelves. The windows—and there were windows centered in each of those faceted walls—were drawn over with heavy cloth blinds.

Daylight crept out from under them and advanced only an inch. In the middle of the room Eight Loop herself sat like the central core of an AI, a slow-beating heart nestled in information-bearing cables: an old woman behind her desk, transparent holoscreens in a vast arc above her. They were all inward-facing: the images on them backward, pointed toward Eight Loop's eyes and not Mahit's, feeding her a dozen views, Cityscape and dense-glyphed documentation and what Mahit thought was a star-chart rendered in two-dimensional flats.

"Good morning, Ambassador," said Eight Loop. *"Asekretim."*

Mahit bowed over the triangle of her hands pressed together. "Good morning. Thank you for agreeing to see us."

Nothing about Eight Loop's expression shifted; she was statue-still, unmoved, flat black eyes lacking either interest or dismay. "It saves time," she said. "You coming to me."

"I came a very long way on what has turned out to be your command," said Mahit. There was little point in dissimulation; she was here to ask *why*. Why Eight Loop had possessed such urgency, two months ago, when Yskandr had died; why she needed a Lsel ambassador at all.

"I appreciate the promptness with which Lsel answered my request," Eight Loop said. "It is admirable; that kind of co-operation will only help your people in the future. I suggest you stick to it."

That sounded like a dismissal: *No, I don't need you after all, go and supervise the entry of Lsel into Teixcalaanli space like a good barbarian.* The *absorption* of her Station into the Empire. *Cooperatively.* Mahit had only just arrived here. What had she done—or not done—in the week she'd been at court that had rendered her useless to Eight Loop? When Eight Loop had wanted her so badly?

Had she never wanted her at all, but instead a Yskandr—or just *any* Stationer, anyone with an imago-machine which could be *harvested* for use—if she was the Emperor's crèchesib, if she'd been in on Yskandr's idea of keeping Six Direction alive through imago-machines, then she would have wanted a new ambassador *right away*, whoever it was, as long as that ambassador could get an imago-machine. Or could have their own pulled out of them.

Anger broke over her like a distant and enormous wave. She felt icy cold.

"Your statement in the newsfeeds this morning," she found herself saying, "didn't suggest that you were in favor of the annexation of Lsel. Or of annexation in general. Quite the opposite, in fact; I found myself quite offended on behalf of His Brilliance's judgment—"

"Mahit," said Three Seagrass warningly.

"Don't concern yourself with your charge's impropriety, *asekreta*," Eight Loop said. "Her confusion is understandable."

"You *demanded an ambassador*," Mahit said. "I'd like to know why. And what I might do for you which does not involve merely my meek cooperation."

Still perfectly, insufferably calm, Eight Loop spread her hands out on the surface of her desk. Her knuckles were gnarled, hugely swollen; Mahit couldn't imagine her holding a stylus. "In the two months it took you to arrive, Ambassador," she said, "the situation here has shifted. I am sorry if you had hopes that I retained some special purpose for you. I am afraid I do not, in our current circumstances."

Helpless, in less control of herself than she thought she'd ever been—worse than when she'd killed the man in her apartment, worse than feeling all of Yskandr's neurochemistry light up in fireworks at the touch of Six Direction's hand, Mahit asked: "What do you want me to *do*?"

She sounded plaintive. Desperate, like an abandoned child. Three Seagrass's hand was on her waist, suddenly, small fingertips pressed to her spine, and she *realized* what she was saying, and shut her mouth.

"Go back to work, Ambassador," Eight Loop said. "There will be a great deal of it for you, no matter who sits on the sun throne or stands behind it. No matter whether Six Direction gets his war and draws One Lightning off with it; or gets his war and fails to do so; or doesn't get it at all. Or points it at some sector you don't care about. There will be work for the Ambassador from Lsel Station. That is enough for any citizen; it should be enough for you."

The elevator doors were open, behind them. Backing into them, Mahit felt as if she was stumbling, hardly able to keep her feet; in the small red-lit chamber of their descent, all she could hear was the harshness of her own breathing.

What had she *missed*? What had shifted? What had made Eight Loop first want someone with access to imago-machines, if that even had been what she had wanted a Lsel ambassador for—but what *else* was one *specifically* good for—and then decide that there was simply no point in having one at all?

Looking at Three Seagrass's and Twelve Azalea's faces, tinted red, concerned, she thought that three hours of sleep in a garden really hadn't been enough; she was *erratic,* she was *alone,* she wanted—she wanted Yskandr. Someone else to hold her up, in the center of the vast machinery of Teixcalaan.

———

Mahit sat on a stone bench outside the Judiciary, her head in her hands, and let Three Seagrass and Twelve Azalea talk over her.

"—we can't go back to her apartments—"

"I know *you* can run on stimulants and bravado for days at a time, Reed, but some of us are human—"

"I am not suggesting she isn't, please do not insult me *or* her

by insinuating that I don't think she's as much of a human being as a citizen is—"

"I'm not, for fuck's sake. Maybe you *can't* hold yourself together with wire and tea and your vainglorious ambition, you're
slipping as much as she is—"

"Do you have a *suggestion* or are you just going to insult
me?"

Twelve Azalea sat down on the bench beside Mahit. She didn't
look up. It was too much work to look up, or intervene. "Come
back to my place," he said heavily. "I'm in this up to my ears anyhow, I'm on every recording the City has of you two for the
past six hours, I have lost even the *shreds* of plausible deniabil-
ity. You might as well."

A long pause. Mahit watched the sunlight track across the
plaza's tilework, making it shimmer.

"Such a noble sacrifice," Three Seagrass said finally. Edged.
A challenge.

"Maybe I *want* to help you," Twelve Azalea replied. "Maybe
I *like* you, Reed, maybe I'm your friend."

A sigh. Mahit thought of how water shimmered too, how
water and light moved the same way, if you thought about physics correctly. Ripples.

"All right," said Three Seagrass. "All right, but if there are assassins at your flat I am giving up and applying to join the Fleet
and get off-planet, for *safer working conditions.*"

The noise Twelve Azalea made was not quite laughter; it was
too choked for that.

———

Twelve Azalea kept a flat farther out from the palace complex
than Mahit had yet been—a forty-minute commute, he said, but
not everyone who worked for the Information Ministry had

such cushy perks as Reed had managed, *some* people had to pay rent on their salary—Mahit thought he was talking just to talk, to hear himself say the normal sorts of things a person might say.

Away from the palace and the central districts the City shifted in tone—there were more shops, smaller, an emphasis on food prepared while the customer waited or organics imported from a long way off, the other continent or off-planet, artisan-made items, everything simultaneously disposable and in imitation of some ideal. Mahit had thought they would be stared at by Teixcalaanli pedestrians: a barbarian and two *asekretim,* all disheveled and on their way into a residential neighborhood, but they weren't the source of tension on these streets. The Teixcalaanlitzlim were managing that all by themselves.

At first she had thought that there simply *weren't that many people,* that the population of Twelve Azalea's neighborhood was at work, or lower than the number of dense, tall, flowerlike buildings would suggest, but the way Twelve Azalea's expression changed from mild serenity to puzzlement to growing dread put *that* possibility right out. There was something wrong. The air felt charged, a psychological echo of how she'd felt right after the bomb in the restaurant. She trudged, following Twelve Azalea around corners. She couldn't remember ever having been this tired.

Three Seagrass said, clipped, "We should take a different street, Petal. This one's got a demonstration at the end of it."

"I *live* on this street."

Mahit looked up. The missing populace was gathered in a protean mass that was spilling out of the sidewalks and into the street itself. Men, women, children-in-arms, holding placards and purple banners. Their faces were Teixcalaanli-still, unreadable, intent. Even the children weren't loud. The hush felt more dangerous than noise would be. It felt *intent.*

"Those people aren't for One Lightning," she said. "Not unless public acclamations have gotten much quieter in the past three days."

"A public acclamation we could walk right through," said Three Seagrass, "as long as you were willing to pretend to like rhyming doggerel long enough to shout anything that alliterates with *yaotlek*—"

"This is *politics,* and I really thought my neighborhood wasn't prone to this sort of thing."

"You should know better, Petal," Three Seagrass said, resigned. "Have you even looked at your demographics? You've moved into a trade sector, all these people are—"

"—are for Thirty Larkspur, they're wearing those flower lapels," Mahit broke in. They'd all stopped moving. The demonstration approached, slow-growing like a fungus. The people that made it up walked together, encroaching. One of the placards had a snatch of poetry on it that Mahit recognized: *These things are ceaseless: star-charts, disembarkments / the curl of unborn petals holds a hollowness.*

Nine Maize's couplets, which had so upset the oration contest.

"Yes," Three Seagrass agreed. "This neighborhood is as wealthy as it is because of outer-province trade and manufacturing, which means that they *like Thirty Larkspur,* who is nominally an imperial heir, and yet these people are waiting for the Sunlit to come and shut them down for being actively treasonous and demonstrating for *peace* against the wishes of the *current* Emperor."

No more treasonous than Eight Loop had been, in her editorial, Mahit thought. She thought she'd figured out part of what was going on. Something had passed between the two imperial-associates, some deal they'd made: Eight Loop and Thirty Larkspur were bargaining.

They seemed to be working together to discredit not only One Lightning and his attempt to usurp the imperial throne by public acclamation, but also to discredit the authority of the sitting Emperor at the same time. One Lightning, in charge of this war now, and relying on it to shore up his support, was judicially suspect, according to Eight Loop's editorial—and publicly unwanted, according to this demonstration of Thirty Larkspur's partisans. And Six Direction? Well, he was failing, mistaken in his attempt to allow a war of annexation in a time *not entirely peaceful,* a time where there might be external threats, whether those were some mysterious alien or just the continued unrest in the Odile System and how it was sparking protest even here in the City—he was misunderstanding the law—and that misunderstanding was being rejected by his own populace, who didn't want a war . . .

The Judiciary and Thirty Larkspur working together. Mahit could—almost—*almost* see the shape of what they wanted.

If she wasn't so tired.

"Is there a back alley into your flat, Twelve Azalea?" she asked. "I have seen enough of the Sunlit today, and I think they will be here *soon*—"

It turned out that there was. They ran for it like they were being chased.

CHAPTER

THIRTEEN

EZUAZUACAT THIRTY LARKSPUR TO BE
MADE IMPERIAL-ASSOCIATE

In light of his continued service to His Illuminate Brilliance the
Emperor Six Direction of All Teixcalaan, the ezuazuacat Thirty
Larkspur will as of 09.30 on this first day of the third year of the
eleventh indiction be recognized as an associate to the imperial
throne, equal in rank and in authority to Imperial Associate Eight
Loop and Imperial Associate Eight Antidote; may the three imperial associates grow stably together, equilateral in desire, and rule
jointly if necessary.

> —Imperial Proclamation, posted in Plaza Central Seven
> subway station, defaced with red spray paint (non-
> holographic) reading ONE LIGHTNING in the center of
> a loosely drawn Teixcalaanli war flag; confiscated by
> Sunlit patrol on 249.3.11, to be destroyed

* * *

There is no useful reason to deny Teixcalaan another ambassador,
despite our uncertainty as to Yskandr Aghavn's fate; we need a
voice in the Empire, and Mr. Aghavn has not been a very com-
municative one even before now. I recommend that a thorough
aptitude test be administered to volunteers as well as to young
persons without imago-line who have particularly high scores on
Teixcalaanli Imperial Examinations, and a new ambassador selected from the most compatible of them with the imago recording

of Aghavn—which, I remind you, we *do* have, despite it being out
of date.

—internal memo from Amnardbat of Heritage to the
remainder of the Lsel Council, public records

LATER, Mahit would remember the rest of that afternoon in
snatches: single moments, disconnected from one another by
how time stretched and denatured itself under the pressure of
exhaustion. Her first view of Twelve Azalea's flat, the walls hung
with artwork—copies of off-world oil and acrylic and ink drawings, mass-produced but of high quality—and how Twelve Azalea
had looked obscurely embarrassed when she'd mentioned how
nice they were, as if he hardly ever had visitors to comment on
his taste. The needle-sharp heat of his shower, and how all the
soap in Teixcalaan smelled of a flower she couldn't place, pep-
pery and foreign-shading-to-familiar. The texture of the loose
trousers and shirt he'd loaned her, rough-silk and too short in
every dimension, hovering halfway up her calves and her
forearms. How lying down on the wide couch had felt absurd,
and then *gone*, texture and sound blinked out to nothing.

The weight of Three Seagrass's back, pressed to her back,
stretched out beside her. Opening her eyes to a blur of motion
on the holoscreen, Twelve Azalea eating some sort of noodle
dish out of a plastic container with long sticks, cross-legged on
a chair as he watched a sanitized version of the end of the protest going on just outside his windows, and hearing the distant
crash of breaking glass, and going *away* again inside her own
mind, just for a little while, into that dark space where Yskandr
should have been.

When she woke properly it was full dark. Twelve Azalea had
fallen asleep at the table next to his meal, his head folded on his
arms, and the holoscreen was still going with the volume turned

down: moving images casting light across his face. Mahit gingerly disentangled herself from both the couch and Three Seagrass, who looked pale and unhealthily grey even asleep (*had she sufficiently recovered from the neurological strike? Mahit couldn't imagine that she had*), and crossed to the window. The street outside was quiet. The golden, blank face-shield of a Sunlit glinted from the corner of the intersection. There were at least four of them, in this quiet residential neighborhood, keeping a threatening watch.

Bombs in a restaurant. Demonstrations. And now riots. If the Sunlit really were under One Lightning's control, their presence here was a sign of how much the *yaotlek* was trying to present himself as the only possible force for order in a rapidly intensifying climate of social distress and anxiety. Mahit thought it was smart positioning. She'd think it was even smarter if One Lightning didn't need to head up a war of conquest to prove his imperial bona fides. Still, the repeated attempts of the Sunlit to get her to surrender, not to the Emperor or to the City, but to *One Lightning,* reflected a deeper wound in Six Direction's ability to control Teixcalaan than she'd expected. How much had he already lost?

She'd never quite thought about how *barbaric*—still a terrible little thrill, to apply that word in Teixcalaan to the language's own speakers—Teixcalaanli modes of succession really were. When it wasn't confined properly to epics and songs, empire claimed by acclamation was a brutal process that cared not at all for the places and peoples who had to succumb to make that acclamation plausible.

The holoscreen was still on the newsfeeds. Bright red glyphs cycled over the bottom half of the screen, arranged in a charming doggerel verse: *Urgently direct your attention! / novelty and importance characterize what comes next / in two minutes on Channel Eight!*

Mahit nudged Twelve Azalea on the shoulder, and he startled into consciousness. "—what?" he said, rubbing a hand over his face. "Oh, you're up."

"How do you change the channels on your holoscreen?" Mahit asked.

"Uh. What do you want to watch?"

"The *novelty and importance* on Channel Eight."

"Channel Eight is politics and economics . . . hang on—" His eyes tracked under his cloudhook, tiny micro-adjustments, and the holoscreen flickered, shifted.

Channel Eight! hovered in the right top corner, superimposed on the image of the bridge of some vast ship: a gleaming place, cold metal and pale lights, titanium and steel and the golden Teixcalaanli battle flag splayed on the back wall, blatant in its cluster of sunbeam-spears. In front of it was a dark man, blunt-faced, with narrow lips and high cheekbones. A face like the facets of a stone, made for bludgeoning. His uniform was silver-shot with regalia, medals and honors and rank stripes.

"One Lightning," Twelve Azalea said. "Hey, *Reed,* wake up for this."

Three Seagrass shoved herself upright. There were pressure marks from the couch cushions across one of her cheeks, but her eyes were intent. "—can't sleep through the propaganda, no, it's out of character for me," she said.

"Not at all like Eleven Lathe," Twelve Azalea said, fond, and Mahit *ached,* suddenly; to have friends who could tease her like this. To have *friends,* like she'd had on Lsel.

"Hush, the *yaotlek* is talking, turn it up," said Three Seagrass.

He was. He had a stentorian delivery—not a rhetorician, One Lightning, but a man who could shout effectively over long distances. Mahit could imagine being one of his soldiers—and as he continued, firm and deliberate and with an air of vast and urgent concern, she could imagine why his soldiers would follow him even against the Emperor they were all sworn to serve.

"Even here in orbit, just returned from our successes in the Odile System to the heart of the world, my ship *Twenty Sunsets Illuminated* is aware of the chaos and uncertainty which has boiled up in the streets of the Jewel of the World," the *yaotlek* said, and whoever was in charge of broadcasting on Channel Eight! obligingly began to splice in footage of the protests. Mahit recognized the view outside Twelve Azalea's window, some hours earlier, and wondered where the cameras were, and how many other people were watching through them. Thought again of the City as an algorithm: considered, for the first time clearly, that no algorithm was innocent of its designers. It couldn't be. There was an originating *purpose* for an algorithm, however distant in its past—a reason some human person made it, even if it had evolved and folded in on itself and transformed. A City run by Ten Pearl's algorithm had Ten Pearl's initial interests embedded in it. A City run by an algorithm designed to respond to Teixcalaanli desires was not innocent of those same Teixcalaanli desires, magnified, twisted by machine learning. (A City run by an algorithm designed by Ten Pearl could suddenly rise up against anyone Ten Pearl designated—and if he *was* working with the Ministry of War, if the Ministry of War had . . . what, gone over to One Lightning already, and made some sort of *arrangement* with Science?)

This street wasn't the only one showing up on the newsfeed, full of angry Teixcalaanlitzlim. Apparently there had been a sort of mass outbreak of peace protests all across the sector. The camera unerringly picked out the purple lapel flowers on the shoulders of many of the protestors, in every location.

Channel Eight!, economics and politics, was certainly not on the payroll of Thirty Larkspur, Mahit guessed. Not with that focus, while simultaneously playing One Lightning's anti-protest speech, his voice rolling onward, saying, "I, and all of the brave servants of Teixcalaan I have the honor to serve with, have sympathy for the wishes of the people of the Jewel of the World as they dream of peace and prosperity—but from our vantage point above you, the clarity of our eyes sees what you cannot. Your full-hearted desires have been coopted by the self-serving design of the imperial associate Thirty Larkspur."

Three Seagrass hissed through her teeth, a sharp little intake of breath that fit perfectly into how One Lightning paused for all the watchers to have their own moment of shock.

"The imperial associate cares neither for war nor peace!" One Lightning thundered. "The imperial associate cares for profits! He would not have lent his approval or funding to these pro-tests if our war had been directed toward any other sector of space—but *this* sector threatens his interests!"

"Yeah, come *on*, tell us *how*, where's the punchline," Three Seagrass said. Mahit stole a glance at her; she looked transfixed, alight, her eyes blazing.

"—in this quadrant lies Lsel Station, an insignificant indepen-dent territory which has, unbeknownst to the population of Teixcalaan, been providing Thirty Larkspur with illegal and immoral technology for neurological enhancements. I can only imagine that the annexation of this station would cut off his se-cret supply, and thus he feels compelled to coopt the noble im-pulses of the people we both serve and stir up unrest!"

"Now *that's* interesting," Three Seagrass breathed, at the same time as Twelve Azalea turned the holoscreen off.

"That's a *problem*," he said. "Is it true, Mahit?"

"Not to my knowledge," said Mahit, who could not imagine how One Lightning had decided that it was *Thirty Larkspur* who wanted imago-machines, and not Six Direction, not to mention

how One Lightning had *discovered* them in the first place—
unless it was blatant propaganda . . . She sighed. "And that is
in fact the fucking problem, *to my knowledge* isn't sufficient."

Twelve Azalea sat down across from her, heavily. "To your
knowledge, Ambassador Aghavn did not provide Thirty Larkspur with . . . illegal technology? With neurological enhancements? With *immoral* technology? What's the part you don't
know about, Ambassador?"

Everything about this was abruptly infuriating. Mahit was
so very tired of disambiguating between the tiny shades in
meaning between one Teixcalaanli phrase and another, the
effort it took to rearrange the emphasis of a sentence to render
it accurate. The effort it took to keep straight what she had told
Three Seagrass, what she had told Twelve Azalea, and what she
hadn't told anyone at all.

(The Emperor saying to her, *Who else can provide eighty
years of peace.* Her sick, growing certainty that maybe he was
right, considering the state of his possible successors and how
determined they all seemed to be to rile the people of the
City into destruction and violence for the sake of their own
ascensions.)

Her jaw hurt from gritting her teeth. "Ambassador Aghavn
did not provide *Thirty Larkspur* with anything of the kind. To
my knowledge. Also I am not entirely sure what counts as *immoral* in Teixcalaan—*why* are neurological enhancements such
a problem for you?"

"—but he provided *someone* with them!" Twelve Azalea said,
as if he had come to a satisfying conclusion to a logic puzzle.

"Promised them," Mahit said, resigned, "which actually does
leave me with more leverage than I might have had otherwise.
If he'd actually *delivered* before he got himself killed, I'd have
nothing at all to bargain with."

"Mahit," Three Seagrass interjected, entirely too calm for Mahit's taste, "I am beginning to have certain suspicions about what you discussed with His Illuminate Majesty."

"Hiding anything from you is an exercise in futility, isn't it," Mahit said. She wanted to put her head down on Twelve Azalea's table, and possibly bang her forehead against it a few times.

Three Seagrass touched her shoulder, a brief soothing gesture, and shrugged. "I'm your liaison. Technically we aren't supposed to hide *anything* from one another. We'll work on it."

"Must we?" Mahit said, helpless, and then, when Three Seagrass managed a credible Lsel-style smile with visible teeth, and she found her face echoing it all despite herself, asked again: "What makes technology *immoral*? Tell me that, if you're not hiding things."

"Very little is immoral," Three Seagrass began. "The *yaotlek* is appealing to a very traditionalist, law-and-order-and-triumphal-processions-every-spring sort of person. But there's something *unsettling* about your imago-machines, Mahit. We don't like devices—or chemicals—that make a person more mentally capable than they are on their own merits."

"You took the exams, didn't you?" Twelve Azalea asked. "The imperial aptitudes."

Mahit nodded. They'd been a *delight,* after the endless series of imago-aptitudes; they'd been all Teixcalaanli literature and history and language, and she'd taken them for *her,* and out of the hope that she might win a visa to the center of the Empire, someday.

"So much of who we *are* is what we remember and retell," said Three Seagrass. "Who we model ourselves on, which epic, which poem. Neurological enhancements are *cheating.*"

Twelve Azalea added, "And they are illegal to use in the aptitudes. There's a scandal every few years—"

Mahit was finding it difficult to equate an imago—the combination of persons, the preservation of skill and memory down generations—with *cheating on exams*. "It has to be more complex than that; *cheating* is illegal, but immoral?"

"Immoral is *being someone you cannot hope to emulate*," Three Seagrass said. "Like wearing someone else's uniform, or saying the First Emperor's lines from the *Foundation Song* and planning to betray Teixcalaan all at once. It's the juxtaposition is what's wrong. How do I know that you are *you*? That you are *conscious* of what you're attempting to preserve?"

"You pump the dead full of chemicals and refuse to let anything rot—people or ideas or . . . or *bad poetry*, of which there is in fact some, even in perfectly metrical verse," said Mahit. "Forgive me if I disagree with you on *emulation*. Teixcalaan is all about emulating what should already be dead."

"Are you Yskandr, or are you Mahit?" Three Seagrass asked, and that did seem to be the crux of it: *Was* she Yskandr, without him?

Was there even such a thing as Mahit Dzmare, in the context of a Teixcalaanli city, a Teixcalaanli *language*, Teixcalaanli politics infecting her all through, like an imago she wasn't suited for, tendrils of memory and experience growing into her like the infiltrates of some fast-growing fungus.

"How wide, Three Seagrass, is the Teixcalaanli concept of *you*," she said, just as she'd said before all of this had really gotten started.

Three Seagrass spread her hands apart, a strained, rueful gesture. "I'm not sure. Narrower than the Stationer one. For—most of us."

"Otherwise One Lightning's little stunt on Channel Eight wouldn't be *effective*," Twelve Azalea added. "Just the suggestion that Thirty Larkspur is not only using the populace for his own purposes but that those purposes are . . . *corrupted*, pathetic, anyone who needs enhancements is clearly not worthy of being emperor—"

"I think," said Three Seagrass, "that we are going to have a civil war."

And then, quite abruptly, she pressed her hand over her face as if she was trying to hold back tears.

———

Twelve Azalea had taken Three Seagrass out of the room; Mahit could still hear their voices, rising and falling softly, from around the corner in the kitchen. She had never seen Three Seagrass quite that upset. Not when she had been in danger of her life, not when Mahit herself had been upsetting and alien and frustrating to work with; not even in the aftermath of seizure. But she had crumpled like metal overexposed to radiation, *friable,* when her own considerable powers of analysis had come up with the answer that Mahit already knew: Teixcalaan was hovering on the verge of devouring itself alive.

Mahit thought she could understand, by analogy and longing if nothing else. It was hard for *her* to wrap her mind around— the very idea of Teixcalaan not being *permanent,* irrevocable, eternal. And she was a barbarian, a foreign particle, just a thing that loved (did she? Did she still?) the Empire's literature and culture, it wasn't *home*; it had never been the shape of the world for her like it must be for Three Seagrass, only the shape that distorted the world out of true, the warp of heavy mass pulling at the fabric of space.

The tears dripping out from behind Three Seagrass's fingers had still been awful, and she was glad that Twelve Azalea had walked her off into the kitchen for water and the sort of comfort that old friends could provide. Alone for the moment, she reached into the inside pocket of her jacket and fished out her salvaged prizes from her apartment: the roll of paper shaped into a faux infofiche stick carrying a new message from Lsel Station, and Yskandr's imago-machine.

She lay them both on the table in front of her. Neither was larger than the two joints of her thumb: a silver-pale spider of a machine that had held all of Yskandr Aghavn, and a slim grey tube of paper, sealed with the red wax and red-and-black-striped stickers that marked off-world communication. Carefully, she ran her thumbnail over the wax, cutting through it, peeling back a curl of fragile red. The sealant was far more symbolic than actual: it would be very easy to open the communiqué and close it back up invisibly, if some mailroom official had wanted to. The sealant was *metaphorical,* and here she had to depend on Teixcalaanli beliefs in privacy, in propriety—

Those, and Lsel encryption.

Before she unrolled the paper all the way, she repeated the motion, just her nail sliding against the metal of Yskandr's imago-machine, touching what had touched him. Had been nestled *inside* him. The central rectangular chip, dull now as if the metal had been pickled, and all the long filament-legs stretching from the corners, fractal branches which had infiltrated his brain stem. The base of her skull ached where her own machine rested, sympathetic pain.

Lsel encryption here, too: no one could get to the Yskandr encoded in the machine's memory, with all of his knowledge. Those missing fifteen years that she'd never had access to, not even when the Yskandr in her mind had been functioning correctly. She missed him so *much.*

(Would she like him, the man who had sold Lsel's secrets to Six Direction? She was worried that she *would.* That what he'd done wouldn't matter in the slightest, if only she could have an ally again in truth.)

Mahit cracked the rest of the wax on the communiqué and pressed the roll of paper flat on the table with both of her hands.

What she saw written there was not what she expected. Oh, the message *looked* right—for the first moment she stared at it. Paragraphs, written in an *alphabet,* the Lsel alphabet with all of its thirty-seven letters, shockingly familiar and unfamiliar at once. And the opening salutation signaled clearly that the following paragraph was using her own substitution cipher, the one which depended on a Teixcalaanli grammar. It was the paragraph below that began to worry her—that one was in a cipher she not only didn't *know,* but one she'd never seen.

Well, she had been hoping for good encryption . . .

"Twelve Azalea?" she called, toward the kitchen.

"Yes?"

"Do you have a dictionary? Specifically, do you have *Imperial Glyphbook Standard*?"

"Everyone has *Imperial Glyphbook Standard,*" Three Seagrass called back. She only sounded *mostly* like she'd been crying.

"I know!" Mahit said. "That's why I chose it—so *do* you?"

Twelve Azalea came back in and peered inquisitively at the unfolded paper. "Is that your language? It's got so many letters."

"You say this, and *Imperial Glyphbook Standard* has forty thousand different glyphs."

"But alphabets are supposed to be simple. That's what they tell us in Information Ministry training sessions, anyhow. Hang on, I'll get the dictionary."

At least he had one. She could probably have bought one in any shop, but it was a relief to not have to *find* a shop. Not with the City in its current unsettled state.

Twelve Azalea dropped the book at her elbow with a thud. In codex form it was over four hundred pages long, grammar and glyphs arrayed in tables. "What do you want with it?"

"Sit down," said Mahit. "Watch me reveal some Lsel state secrets."

He sat. After a moment, Three Seagrass emerged—her eyes red—and sat next to him.

It was strange, doing decryption for an audience—but Mahit was, she had realized, committed to these two. They'd stayed with her, they'd *protected* her, they'd put themselves in political and physical danger for her. And besides, she wasn't telling them *how* to decrypt the cipher, just which book to use. It didn't take her long—she'd written this cipher, she knew how to read in it.

The first paragraph of the communiqué identified its sender—Darj Tarats. Mahit was almost surprised: that the Councilor for the Miners would send a message to her, not Aknel Amnardbat from Heritage. But if Amnardbat was responsible, as Dekakel Onchu's secret communiqués implied, for sabotaging her imago-machine, rendering her as damaged as she currently was, perhaps Tarats had . . . intervened? Intercepted the message and made sure he was the one to answer it?

If she believed that, she was taking Dekakel Onchu's suspicions—suspicions she was never meant to have seen—as truth. And Tarats wouldn't have known about Onchu's warning to Yskandr. Tarats would be thinking about talking to a Mahit Dzmare who—might or might not have access to Yskandr Aghavn, her imago, but who certainly didn't know *why* she didn't. If she didn't. Perhaps the *sabotage* was something else entirely, some personal failure of her own, and had nothing to do with a feud between distant Councilors being played out at a remove.

Start from the idea that Darj Tarats wanted to speak to her, whether or *not* he'd known about Amnardbat's sabotage, if Amnardbat's sabotage was even real. The Councilor for the Miners was almost always concerned with issues of *defense and self-rule*; it won him votes. If this message came from Tarats, the threat a Teixcalaanli expansion war posed to Lsel sovereignty was being taken seriously, at least.

Start with what she could absolutely be sure of, and entertain fantasies of sabotage (wouldn't it be *nice* to have the cascading neurological failure not be her fault?—an unworthwhile thought if she'd ever had one) later.

Mahit pieced together the rest of the decipherable paragraph, glyph by glyph. It acknowledged her message (that was one glyph), thanked her for it (another), and instructed her that the book cipher was not an appropriate level of encryption for the remainder of the message, which contained specific guidelines for action based upon an important point of information to which Mahit had heretofore not been privy. (That took six glyphs, and the last one was damn obscure; she'd never seen it written before. It was a Teixcalaanli word for "secret previously unrevealed to the uninitiated." Of course they had a word for that.)

"Yes, yes," she muttered, *"so how do I decrypt the rest . . ."*

Three Seagrass snickered, and when Mahit looked up at her to glare, she held up her hands, apologetic. "I like watching you work," she said. "You're very fast, even when you're confused. You could learn a real cipher, one of ours, if you memorized the season's fashionable poems—"

"Easily," Mahit said, not mollified. "But they're not real ciphers either, Three Seagrass. I mean—they're not real *encryption*. Substitution ciphers are trivial to break with a decent AI and knowing what the key is. Glyphbook or poem."

"I know," she said. "They're not encryption, they're *art*, and you'd be good at them."

That was a strange kind of sting. Mahit shrugged, and looked again at the last sentence of the only paragraph she could understand.

Cipher || *kept safe/imprisoned/locked away* || *(personal/heredi-tary) knowledge (location within)* || *(belonging-to)*

And then in perfectly clear Stationer letters, *Yskandr-imago.*

The code to decrypt the rest of the message, with its secret-previously-unrevealed-to-the-uninitiated, was located in *Yskandr's* knowledge-base, not Mahit's. And Darj Tarats had expected her to be able to access it. (He must not know about the sabo-tage. Or he'd expected that the sabotage would *fail,* that she and Yskandr would have already integrated enough that any dam-age to the machinery that had brought them together would nevertheless be sufficient to decode this.)

Yskandr, who was *malfunctioning.* Who was half gone, whether through sabotage or her own neurological failure, instead of here with Mahit. Who she had no real way of reaching. There weren't enough curses in any language she knew, and even the worst possible words in *Glyphbook Standard* wouldn't be bad enough. How did she explain *I have lost the other half of myself, and I need him,* to these two Teixcalaanlitzlim who had spent some time a little while ago explaining how things like Yskandr were *im-moral?* How did she even begin?

Helpless with it, she said, "I am so completely screwed," and waited for the reaction.

She got one: Twelve Azalea looked worried, like he wasn't sure what he'd do if the *barbarian* burst into tears, too—and Three Seagrass lost the last of her former expression of misery and returned to absolute and entire focus.

"Probably, but if you tell us why I might be able to offer some unscrewing," she said, and Mahit got, all at once, why it was Three Seagrass and not Twelve Azalea who had been given the cultural liaison assignment. There were aptitudes that spelled for *analysis,* good observation of a situation, information acquisition—and then there were aptitudes that spelled for *determination,* and Three Seagrass was full up with the latter as well as the former.

She squared her shoulders. Braced herself. If she—and Lsel Station—were going to survive the transition of power from Six Direction to his successor unscathed, she needed as much unscrewing as Three Seagrass was willing to provide.

Here we go, Yskandr. This is me, trusting someone from Teixcalaan with our lives. How did it feel when you did this?

She wasn't talking to the silent imago-Yskandr, she realized. She was talking to the dead man, who could only hear her if somehow she got access to whatever imprint of him might still dwell, an unused ghost, on his imago-machine.

"I am supposed to have Yskandr Aghavn, or at least a version of him, with me in my mind; I have an imago-machine just like this one," Mahit began, picking up Yskandr's machine between her thumb and forefinger. "My copy of his memories is from fifteen years ago. Or would be, if he was still with me—he isn't, he hasn't been since I saw his body, the first day I was here. He is—or I am—malfunctioning."

Three Seagrass said, "I'd figured that much out, Mahit."

"*I* hadn't—"

"Petal, you just joined us this morning."

"Do you *really* have one of these inside you? What is it *like?*"

He said it like he'd say *Does it hurt?* to a person with a blistering burn. Blank absurdity.

Mahit sighed. "Irrelevant to the current problem, Twelve Azalea, except that usually it's *nice* and presently it is *not working* and I need it to be . . . I need him."

"Because of what's in your encrypted message," said Three Seagrass.

"Because he has the key to it, and I need to know what my government wants me to do."

There was a short silence. Mahit wondered if Three Seagrass

was waiting for some further revelation, some actual useful piece of information that she could use to give Mahit some cultural-liaison help. But there wasn't anything else. There was the message, and Mahit, and the hollow electric silence in her head.

Then Three Seagrass said, "What about the Yskandr in *there?*" and pointed at the imago-machine resting on the table between them all. "I suspect he'd know just as well."

It hit Mahit in a flash of psychosomatic ache: the tiny scar at the base of her skull opening, the new weight of an imago-machine nestled against the pink-grey folds of neurological tissue. All of that, *again*.

She closed her palm around what was left of Yskandr Aghavn, murdered Ambassador, as if to hide him from Three Seagrass's observant Teixcalaanli eyes.

". . . let me think about it," she said.

CHAPTER
FOURTEEN

28. EXT. DAY: chaos and smoke of the BATTLEFIELD of GIENAH-9. Track in past TANGLED BODIES marked with carbon scoring, churned mud, to find THIRTEEN QUARTZ lying half conscious in the shelter of an overturned ground-car. HOLD on THIRTEEN QUARTZ before cutting to 29. EXT. DAY: same as before only POV of NINETY ALLOY. Pull back past NINETY ALLOY's shoulder to watch as they FALL TO THEIR KNEES beside THIRTEEN QUARTZ—who OPENS THEIR EYES and SMILES FAINTLY.

> THIRTEEN QUARTZ (weak)
> You came back for me. I always . . . knew you would. Even now.

(Track around to see NINETY ALLOY's face.)

> NINETY ALLOY
> Of course I came back. I need you. Where else am I going to find a second-in-command who can win half a war on their own before breakfast? (sobers) And *I* need you. You've always been my luck. Stand down, now. I've got you. We're going home.

—shooting script for *Ninety Alloy* season 15 finale

*   *   *

Panel Three: long shot of Captain Cameron on the bridge of his shuttle. All eyes are on him; the rest of the crew look terrified, eager, impatient. Cameron's consulting his imago, so have the colorist emphasize the white glow around his hands and his head. He is looking at the enemy ship, floating in black space, super ominous and spiky—the ship's the focus of the panel.

CAMERON: I learned to talk to Ebrekti, back when I was Chadra Mav. This isn't even going to be hard.

—graphic-story script for *THE PERILOUS FRONTIER!* vol. 3, distributed from local small printer ADVENTURE/BLEAK on Tier Nine, Lsel Station

MAHIT thought about it all through the rest of the evening, while Three Seagrass and Twelve Azalea did laundry, washing their grass-stained clothes, and they all watched the newsfeeds on the holoscreen replay One Lightning's speech and the protest footage. Mahit thought about it *obsessively,* to the counterpoint of troop movements and political exhortations, tonguing the idea like it was a raw sore place in her mouth she couldn't leave properly alone. She'd put Yskandr's imago-machine back inside her jacket pocket. The small weight swung there like a pendulum heartbeat.

There were a lot of ways to misuse an imago-machine.

No, better: there were a lot of ways to use an imago-machine that made Mahit, Lsel-raised, Lsel-acculturated down to the blood and bone all despite her pretentions toward loving Teixcalaanli literature, feel the way Three Seagrass and Twelve Azalea had described feeling about *cheating on the imperial exams.* There were a lot of ways to use an imago-machine that were, for lack of more specific vocabulary in either of her languages, *immoral*.

For instance, a person could take up an imago of their lover who had died—tragically, usually, this was a daytime-entertainment holovision plot—and carry them around instead of allowing that imago to go to the next aptitudes-identified person in the line, and destroy both themselves and the knowledge of generations in the process. That felt *immoral*. And then there were all the smaller variants: new imago-carriers coming back to the widows of the dead, trying to resume relationships which had ended. That actually *happened*, everyone knew someone, there were good reasons that Lsel had built psychotherapy into a science . . .

Make it worse, she told herself. The kind of misuse that makes you *squirm*, not just the kind that makes you sad.

An imago installed in a weak mind, one who passed just *enough* aptitudes for compatibility, but not enough to create a new, real, functioning person out of the two original personalities. An imago that *ate* the mind of the successor.

That one was bad enough that she didn't want to think about

(how that was exactly what His Brilliance Six Direction wanted to do)

what it would feel like.

Good work, Mahit. You found something that you like less than what Three Seagrass suggested you might do.

Three Seagrass thought she should take Ambassador Aghavn's machine and extract an updated Yskandr-imago to overwrite the one which fluttered, broken and useless and only half here in flashes, in her mind. Thought that if she needed that code so badly—and she did, she *did*—it was the only logical course of action.

Three Seagrass, for her part, was not volunteering for what would end up being experimental neurosurgery. Experimental neurosurgery on a planet—in a culture—which *didn't like* neurosurgical intervention. Which found the entire concept *squirmy.* Immoral. Three Seagrass was volunteering *Mahit.*

Hey Yskandr, you could fix this, she thought, for the hundredth time, and got nothing back but silence except for the peripheral nerve buzzing. Who knew if she could even *handle* another imago? This one might have gone wrong because *she* was broken, unsuitable, incompatible; and even if she wasn't, she remembered what the first time had felt like: the dizzying double overlay of perception, the sense of standing on the edge of a high precipice. The slightest movement and she would fall into the hugeness of someone else's memory, and they hadn't had enough *time,* to be a new person, to be Mahit-Yskandr, and the ghost of whoever Yskandr had absorbed when he was young, Mahit-Yskandr-Tsagkel . . .

That name, floating up from the shards of the imago in her mind; the echo of how it had felt when she'd looked it up in Lsel's records, trying to trace back the line she was joining. Tsagkel Ambak, who had not been to the City but had negotiated with Teixcalaan from the bow of a space cruiser, ensuring the continued independent rights of Lsel and the other stations to mine their sector, four generations back. Mahit had read her poetry and thought it was *dull,* pedestrian, all about *home,* and had thought—had thought three months ago—that she could do better.

Maybe the new imago could tell her more about the imago he'd absorbed into the person she'd met when he entered her mind.

She was going to try it, wasn't she. She'd already decided, without even realizing she'd come to the conclusion; she was going to try it because she was alone, and because it needed to be done, and because she wanted to be whole, part of the long line of ambassadors from Lsel—the line she *should* be part of, the line she'd been inducted into and was still reeling from the loss of. If she had been sabotaged she wanted to undo it; she wanted her imago-line back, she wanted it preserved. She wanted to be a *worthy* inheritor of memory. To safeguard it, for the people she was meant to be serving here, as an extension of Lsel Station's sovereignty. For the people who might follow after her, and carry *her* mind and memory onward on her Station.

Patriotism seemed to derive quite easily from extremity.

Mahit supposed that was true for all the rioters in the City's streets, too.

She found Three Seagrass in the kitchen, doing something incomprehensible to a plant: hollowing it out and stuffing it full of another substance, a paste made of rice and what looked like ground meat.

"Is that food?"

Three Seagrass looked over her shoulder. Her face was drawn and set. "Not yet. Wait about an hour, and it will be. Do you need me?"

"I need a neurosurgeon," Mahit said. "If such a thing exists on this planet."

"You're going to do it?"

"I'm going to try."

Three Seagrass nodded, once. "*Everything* exists in the City, Mahit. In one form or another. But I'm afraid I have absolutely no idea where to find someone who would be willing—and able—to cut open your brain."

From the other room, Twelve Azalea called, "You don't, Reed, but I bet you anything you can find someone who does."

"Stop eavesdropping and get in here," Three Seagrass shouted, and when Twelve Azalea appeared in the doorway, she affixed him with a pointed stare. "And *where* shall I find this person? I want my Ambassador alive afterward."

"While you go see the Science Minister I will pursue someone via *less official means,*" Twelve Azalea said smugly. "I *am* attached to the Medical College as my Information Ministry post. Aren't you glad you got me involved in this conspiracy?"

"Yes," Three Seagrass said, "for several reasons, including the use of your flat as a safe house—"

"You are only fond of me for my material possessions, Reed."

"And for your persistent connections to people outside of the court and the ministries. That too."

"You could have just as many, if you wanted," Twelve Azalea said carefully. "If you were interested in branching out."

Three Seagrass sighed. "Petal. You know that's a bad idea. It's *been* a bad idea."

"Why?" Mahit found herself asking. She couldn't think of what would be *bad* about having out-palace contacts, for an *asekreta*.

"Because I'd use them as *assets,* Mahit," Three Seagrass said, sharp, almost self-castigating. "*Just* as assets. And Petal here has actual friends, some of whom I'd probably find my way to reporting as anti-imperial, eventually. When it seemed appropriate or useful."

"You consistently do yourself a disservice," said Twelve Azalea. "All vainglorious ambition and—"

"Not enough empathy, I know," Three Seagrass replied. "Wasn't this conversation about *you?*"

Twelve Azalea sighed, and smiled, his eyes dark and wide, and Mahit realized they'd had this conversation a hundred times; it was *settled,* this thing between them, a carefully tended corner of their friendship, where Three Seagrass didn't ask about what Twelve Azalea did outside of work and Twelve Azalea didn't try to get any of his—what, peculiarly anti-establishment medical friends?—involved with government business in the form of Three Seagrass. They knew what lines not to cross, the two of them; knew them and kept them, and what Mahit was asking for was going to blur every single one. And yet they both seemed to be willing.

She hoped she deserved it. (Lsel Station deserved it—there was that patriotism again, she couldn't get over how it was becoming a strange reflex—but her *asekretim* weren't doing this for Lsel.)

"Yes," Twelve Azalea was saying. "All about me, and how useful I am, and how much I'm helping you. I'll get this done while you're at your appointment tomorrow."

———

Travel across the City was bad and getting worse, even in the clear light of the next early morning. Mahit was almost sure that she and Three Seagrass were being followed, as they left Twelve Azalea's apartment building and headed back inside the subway: not by gold-masked Sunlit, but by shadows, the ghosts of people in grey. The *Mist,* Twelve Azalea had called the Judiciary's own private investigatory force. If these were them—if these were *real*—the name was appropriate.

She could be imagining it. Paranoia was a very understandable response when a multitude of people were, in fact, out to get you. They'd taught that in the psychology classes on Lsel, and Mahit had less and less reason to disbelieve it. Besides, half of the subways were on delay or closed entirely, and angry commuters were not contributing to anyone's sense of safety or well-being. The borders between the six-pronged palace complex and the rest of town were visible as *borders,* now, as they hadn't been when Mahit and Three Seagrass had left Mahit's confiscated crime-scene apartments with Twelve Azalea. There were Sunlit standing in a line, checking the cloudhooks of each Teixcalaanlitzlim, verifying identities. Behind them was the shimmering glass and wire wall of the City itself, irising open and shut for the approved visitors. It seemed like more of a direct threat than ever.

She was carrying the encrypted paper communiqué from Lsel under her freshly laundered shirt, attached to her ribs by virtue of an elastic sports bandage that Twelve Azalea had found in the back of one of his drawers, before they'd left him to find someone to perform back-alley neurosurgery and headed back toward the palace complex. Twelve Azalea had it because he'd twisted his ankle while playing some form of team sport with a ball and net, the same sort of thing which had been advertised on the flyer they'd been given in the garden. Twelve Azalea had been more willing to enthuse about it—apparently he played in an intramural team once a week—than Mahit had been willing to listen, but it hadn't mattered: the bandage was conscripted into use, and now she felt like she was smuggling secrets across enemy lines. Even if they were her secrets to begin with, legally and morally.

"Think we're going to get arrested?" Mahit asked.

Over-cheerful and under her breath, Three Seagrass said, "Not yet." In her clean Information Ministry suit, she looked like a very fine, very precise edged weapon, and Mahit was not in fact sure what she would do without her.

"If not now, when?" she said, with a certain bleak amusement of her own, and then they had come up to the wall of gold-mirrored helmets. Three Seagrass presented herself and Mahit easily, unaffectedly—the very picture of a cultural liaison supervising the movement of her charge through closed doors. The Sunlit asked her for her cloudhook—she handed it over. The Sunlit asked her where they'd been—she explained, without deception or guilt, that they had spent the night at the house of her former classmate and good friend.

Mahit wondered again if the Sunlit shared one enormous

mind with the City—whether this one was right at this moment considering the work of its fellows, in her apartment. It certainly was taking its time. It looked up, and behind Mahit and Three Seagrass—another of those flashes of mist-grey, a reflection in the smooth gold faceplate, something behind Mahit for the Sunlit to look at for too long, an endless little stretch—and down again. Perhaps it was consulting *through* its fellows with the Six Outreaching Palms. Conspiracy on conspiracy. She *was* being paranoid. No one was following them and Science wasn't colluding with War to unseat the Emperor and there weren't protests in the streets and the bomb in Plaza Central Nine had been an *accident of circumstance,* not for her at all, for something unrelated to her, a representative gesture for the people of Odile—surely.

The Sunlit waved her and Three Seagrass through, so abruptly she was actually surprised: adrenaline-drop prickles, hot and cold, slipping down her spine. Walking through the door opened in the City's internal wall felt like climbing into the mouth of an animal. It shut behind them and Mahit thought of the circular teeth on the maws of some station-dwelling parasites, the kind which lived in crawlspaces and battened on to power cable insulation.

The palace complex was, in daylight, much more serene than anywhere else. Walls did that. Walls kept out the visible signifiers of unrest. The walk to the Science Ministry was easy, and the air smelled of the ever-present Teixcalaanli flowers, peppersharp and rich white musk, and there was a chilly sort of sunlight, and yet Mahit could not get her heart rate to come down to something lower than a thrum.

"I'd vastly prefer it if we came out of this one without declaring war, allegiance, or getting you kidnapped by Ten Pearl's best *ixplanatlim* for experiments on your brain," Three Seagrass said.

"I can promise you a lack of declarations of war," Mahit told her, looking up at the silver-steel bloom of the Science Ministry, its pearl-inlaid relief decorations showing the tracks of subatomic particles, the shapes of proteins. "I don't have that authority."

"Wonderful. We'll be fine."

Inside, there was an episode of the now-familiar dance of high-court Teixcalaanli protocol. Three Seagrass made introductions and confirmed their appointment with Ten Pearl; Mahit bowed over her fingertips; inclined her body to a degree that felt right, and whether that was her own instinct or the leftover flickering presence of Yskandr didn't really matter.

She and Three Seagrass were escorted to a windowless conference room, bland pale chairs around a bland pale table, no decoration except for an unobtrusive stripe of that same pearl-inlaid relief circumnavigating the walls right underneath the light switch panels. There they waited.

Three Seagrass tapped her fingernails on the table, a nervous gesture Mahit hadn't noticed her making before. For her own part, Mahit had taken to fiddling with Yskandr's imago-machine inside the pocket of her jacket, unconsciously, and had to make herself stop more than once, and she kept thinking that the communiqué bound under her shirt would crackle if she breathed too deeply, even though it wasn't making any noise at all. The advent of Ten Pearl through the conference room door was a relief. She could *do something*, now that he was here to talk to. Waiting was . . . not working, right now. It wasn't working at all.

"Minister," she said, standing to greet him.

"Ambassador. A pleasure. I'd heard you were missing!"

Ah. So this was how they were going to play this out. Fair enough—the last time she'd seen Ten Pearl she'd played him for the benefit of the newsfeeds at the Emperor's oration-contest banquet. She probably deserved having to fence her way through whatever interpretation of her absence from the palace Nineteen Adze had concocted.

"I've known where I was the whole time," she said, and realized as she said it that she was going to abandon her previous pose as a barbarian and a rube; there was no point to that smokescreen now, and it hadn't worked anyway. Two people at least had tried to kill her, once with a poison flower and once by ambush in her apartments. Being a barbarian—performatively, like a shield—hadn't made her any less vulnerable than being a political operator would. She might as well be honest now. A *clever* barbarian, like Nineteen Adze had called her.

Ten Pearl laughed politely. "I'm sure you have! What a charming way of putting it. How can I help you, Ambassador?"

When Mahit had set up this meeting, she had intended to try to figure out if Yskandr had really been so obvious about his intention to sell imago technology to Teixcalaan as to run afoul of Science—a question which hardly mattered now. Yskandr was dead, and the person he'd sold the imago tech to was the Emperor. What she needed to know now was far more along the lines of *who Ten Pearl supported for succession,* so that she could figure out if he wanted anything to do with the annexation of Lsel, and if he could be manipulated in her favor to stop it.

"I don't want to linger on unpleasant subjects," she began, using just as many tenses as she wanted, no pretense of ignorance between her and the Minister now, "but I would like very much to know—for the sake of my own interests and health, you understand—what it was that you and my predecessor discussed on the night of his death." She could feel how Three Seagrass sat up straighter next to her; the careful focus she had acquired.

Ten Pearl interlaced his hands. All his rings glinted, even under this bland fluorescent lighting. "Are you concerned you might make a similar mistake, Ambassador?" he asked. "Your predecessor ate something unpleasant, that's all. Unfortunate. Our conversation was on very different topics than his eating habits. I'm sure you could avoid consuming such things, if you were careful."

Mahit smiled, with all her teeth. *Barbarian*. But persistent. "No one will be specific as to what he ate," she said. "It's a fascinating omission."

"Ambassador," Ten Pearl said, the word drawn out slow, like he was coaxing her. "Have you perhaps considered that there is a *reason* for that omission? There are all sorts of other subjects we could profitably spend our time on right now. Perhaps we might discuss hydroponic nutrition factors, compared between small and large populations? We have so much to learn from each other, Lsel and Teixcalaan."

It was inconvenient, Mahit thought, being furious. It dulled the edges of her vocabulary. And yet, here she was. Just as furious as she'd been in Eight Loop's office.

She looked him straight in the face. "Ten Pearl, I'd like to know why my predecessor died under your care." It wasn't quite an accusation. (It was an accusation, just not a *direct* one.) Three Seagrass had put her hand on Mahit's knee, warning and warm.

Ten Pearl sighed, a little resigned exhalation as if he was preparing to do something unpleasant and necessary, like disposing of rotten food. "Ambassador Aghavn's activities and proposals were unsuitable; he implied, over an entirely civilized meal in which he was given multiple opportunities to renege, that he was prepared at any moment to flood the Teixcalaanli markets with technology which would upset the functioning of our very society, and that he seemed to have suborned or influenced our Glorious and Brilliant Imperial Majesty—it was my responsibility, as Minister for Science, to deal with the threat he represented."

"So you killed him," Three Seagrass said, fascinated.

Ten Pearl regarded Three Seagrass evenly. "Given the current situation," he said with an encompassing little gesture toward Mahit, as if to include and circumscribe her in the general state of Teixcalaanli diplomatic affairs, and then to dismiss her with them, "I see little reason to deny that, while he was dying, I did not intervene medically. If Ambassador Dzmare would like to bring that up during an inquiry into *medical* malpractice, I am sure she could begin such an inquiry at the Judiciary."

Had her influence fallen *so* far, in two days of unrest in the City and the government, that Ten Pearl could not only blithely admit to disposing of his political opponent—"did not intervene medically" was for Three Seagrass's legalistic ears and nothing else, Mahit knew what he meant when he said it—but also be assured that Mahit had no pull with *anyone* at court who would be willing to punish him for doing so? Clearly Ten Pearl believed that the Science Ministry was beyond the reproach of *whoever* was going to inherit the imperial throne—

—and just as clearly, he believed that Six Direction was no longer, without Yskandr Aghavn and his promised technology, willing to defend Lsel Station, or any of its citizens. And thus he had no use for Mahit, if she wasn't going to try to flood the market with immortality machines—no use except the use he'd have for any ambassador from a small satellite-state on the edges of Teixcalaan.

The deal, as Thirty Larkspur had said at the oration contest, meaning—as she hadn't understood then—the deal between the Emperor and Yskandr, *is off.*

She managed to keep her voice even, her vocabulary pristine, and launched a test satellite into the orbit of the conversation: "I wouldn't begin at the Judiciary, Minister; I'd begin with the

Emperor's own *ezuazuacatlim,* if I needed advice. I've found such safety there."

"Have you?" Ten Pearl said. "I *am* glad; that's a change."

"*Is* it?" Mahit asked, and waited for it: she was beginning to suspect that Ten Pearl wanted to talk, wanted to make her feel powerless with his talking. Three Seagrass's fingers were going to bruise her thigh, they were gripping so hard.

"Your vaunted hostess, Her Excellency Nineteen Adze, stood by precisely as I did," Ten Pearl said. "At that dinner I may have defended the interests of my ministry, and thereby all of the Empire, but *she* let me do it."

Mahit felt an icy clarity. She remembered Nineteen Adze saying *he was my friend* to her over tea—remembered the visceral, neurochemical *familiarity* of Mahit's reaction to her, how what of her was Yskandr wanted to be near her and have a good time and feel challenged and safe at once—remembered how Nineteen Adze had watched her in the hallway of her office complex, watched her pick up the poison flower, bend her head to it as if to breathe. She could have so easily remained in the archway, still and silent in her white suit, and not *intervening* at all.

But she had. She had, for whatever reason, saved *Mahit's* life. Even if she had not saved Yskandr's.

"I do appreciate the warning," Mahit managed to say. She was lying through her teeth. She could lie a little more. She aimed for tremulous, confused, upset. (She *was* upset.) "There have been certain unpleasant incidents—a flower given to me with toxic effects—do you think—"

"I," Ten Pearl said, cutting her off, "am not about to be framed for floral assassination. I am a modern man, and the Science Ministry is not *merely* botanical."

"We were not about to suggest," said Three Seagrass, "that the Science Ministry was merely botanical."

The resulting pause dragged on endlessly, and Mahit wondered which of the three of them was going to break first, either into shouting or into hysterical laughter.

"Is there anything you *would* like to suggest, Ambassador? Considering that I have *not* sent anyone with a flower to do away with you," Ten Pearl said at last.

"You've made my position quite clear," Mahit told him. "I'll be in touch when things have calmed down, if we do end up having something to say to one another. Hydroponics. I'll remember that."

———

In the aftermath of their summary exit from the Science Ministry, Three Seagrass took Mahit to a restaurant. Mahit let her do it with only a token protest—*Last time we tried this there was an act of domestic terrorism*—and got *Last time I made reservations; no one knows where we are, we'll be fine* as a response. It was nice to sit in the dim cavernous space, tucked in close to the wall of a booth, and have strangers bring her and Three Seagrass food.

She only thought about being poisoned briefly, when her soup arrived, and decided she didn't care just this moment.

"Really, I thought you did very well," Three Seagrass said, carving off a thin piece of meat from her meal, which seemed to be a side of an entire animal. Mahit was horribly tempted by the smell of it, and a little horrified at the same time: *that* had too much blood in it to have been grown in a laboratory. That had been a living thing, which breathed, and now Three Seagrass was eating it.

"I'm not sure what else I could have done, while he simultaneously confessed to Yskandr's murder and informed me that absolutely no one cares about it," Mahit said.

Three Seagrass wrapped the meat in a large purple-white flower petal. She'd ordered a stack of them, and was treating them like thin little breads—a conveyance for the flesh from the plate to her mouth. "Wept," she said. "Swore revenge. Attempted immediate violence."

"I'm not a hero in an epic, Three Seagrass." Mahit resented how saying so made her feel ashamed, inadequate: she shouldn't *still want* to want to be Teixcalaanli, *emulating,* a re-creation of literature. Not after this week.

The petal-wrap got smeared with a deep green sauce that seemed to be both condiment and structural glue, and then bitten into with gusto. Around her mouthful, Three Seagrass said, "I said you did *well,* all right? You did. I don't know what you're planning to do next, but you managed that meeting like someone born to the palace, or at the very least like a trained *asekreta.*"

Mahit felt color rise in her cheeks. "I do appreciate that."

The pause between them—Three Seagrass smiling, eyes wide and warm and sympathetic, Mahit exquisitely aware of how her cheeks were *red,* red like flower petals or the meat Three Seagrass was eating—felt charged. Mahit swallowed. Found *something* to say.

"All aside from the murder confession," she began, and was gratified when Three Seagrass sat up a little straighter, paid a little more attention—*there's work to be done here*—"Ten Pearl's overly interested in hydroponics. Ours are *good,* but they're not the sort of thing that feeds a planet. I can't think of why he'd want to talk to me about them, unless something has gone peculiarly off with the City's food-growth algorithm . . ."

And found that what she'd found to say was *interesting,* now that she was saying it. "As off as the City's security algorithm is."

"You mean City-strikes. Like what happened to me in Plaza Central Nine. And . . . whatever is going on with the Sunlit. If something is going on with the Sunlit."

Mahit nodded. "Ten Pearl became Minister *because* of his

perfect algorithms. First the subway, when he integrated all the disparate lines into one algorithmic AI-controlled system, and then the City's security apparatus. Yes?"

"Yes," Three Seagrass said. "How did you learn that, anyway? It happened . . . oh, I wasn't even out of the crèche yet."

Mahit shrugged. "If I say *imago-technology, but not functioning as I expected,* will you be surprised?"

"Not anymore." Another one of those strange, warm smiles.

Mahit couldn't quite keep eye contact when she was doing that. "You said that there'd been eight City-strikes in the past year. When we were walking back, two nights ago. How many *more* is that than the year before?"

Three Seagrass tilted her head slightly to the side. "Seven more. Are you suggesting that the algorithm is faulty?"

"Or it's being used faultily. An algorithm's only as perfect as the person designing it."

"Oh, that's *clever,* Mahit," Three Seagrass said, delighted. "If you want revenge on Science for a murder, murder Science's *reputation of impartiality.*"

It was so utterly *satisfying* when Three Seagrass understood what she meant, without Mahit having to laboriously explain. "Ten Pearl's reputation specifically," she said, agreeing, "since it won him the Ministry, designing this algorithm, which is now hurting *perfectly normal citizens of the Empire.*"

"I like it," Three Seagrass said. "We'll need some data science people—an *ixplanatl* to make the statement look good—and someone to release the report widely—especially if it *is* connected to War, that'll be an interesting needle to thread . . ."

"We'll thread it. After I'm allowed back into my apartment. After this all is—quieter."

Three Seagrass winced, and reached out to pat the back of Mahit's hand. "What *do* you want to do right now? Still . . . what we talked about before? With the machine? I got a message from

Twelve Azalea, while we were ordering, he's come up with some medical person half a province away. "

That felt like the first good news Mahit had heard in a long time. Her skin went prickly, relief and excitement and a kind of intoxicating fear. "Yes," she said. "I need to have access to that cipher even more now. I need to *do* something. Change something. Make the situation *otherwise*."

Three Seagrass considered her, head tilted just slightly. Mahit wanted to look away. She had just suggested that she was preparing to *intervene* in the current political chaos. If there was a point where her liaison would balk, back away . . . but Three Seagrass merely nodded, and said, "I would be terrified."

"Who says I'm not?"

"But you've done it before."

"Under far more expert care than whoever Twelve Azalea has found for us."

Three Seagrass looked like she wanted to bristle at that insult to Teixcalaanli medical technology, but she turned it into a shrug, instead. "He knows a lot of people. All kinds of people. I'm sure this person has at least some idea of what they're doing."

"If I die, or wake up scrambled," Mahit said, "I want you to tell the next ambassador from Lsel—if there *is* a next ambassador—absolutely everything. As much as possible, all at once."

"If you die, the Information Ministry is not going to let me near the next ambassador from Lsel, nor any other ambassadors."

Mahit had to smile. "I'll try not to."

"Good," said Three Seagrass. "Do you want one of these?"

"What?"

"A *sandwich*; you keep staring."

Mahit's mouth filled with saliva. "Was it an animal? Before it was food."

". . . yes?" Three Seagrass said. "This is a *nice* restaurant, Mahit."

She was probably going to die of experimental brain surgery, all of her allies save two Information Ministry agents were either vanished or suspect, and Teixcalaan would most likely eat her home alive with bloody starship-teeth.

"Yes," she said. "I want one."

The meat, when she tasted it, bloomed on her tongue with juice.

CHAPTER
FIFTEEN

Jewel of the World Central Traffic Control Supervisor Three Nas-
turtium to Imperial Flagship *Twenty Sunsets Illuminated*: PLEASE
CONTACT CT APPROACH CONTROL AT ONCE YOU HAVE
ENTERED CONTROLLED AIRSPACE WITHOUT CLEAR-
ANCE OR COMMUNICATION DECLARE INTENTIONS AND
VECTORS FOR CTC TO ROUTE TRAFFIC AROUND YOU
CONTACT CT APPROACH ON FREQUENCY ONE EIGHT
ZERO POINT FIVE AGAIN IMPERIAL FLAGSHIP *TWENTY
SUNSETS ILLUMINATED* YOU HAVE ENTERED CONTROLLED
AIRSPACE WITHOUT CLEARANCE OR COMMUNICATION
PLEASE ACKNOWLEDGE

—satellite communication, 251.3.11-6D

* * *

>>QUERY/auth:ONCHU(PILOTS)/last access
>>Imago-machine 32675(Yskandr Aghavn) last
  accessed by Medical (Neurosurgery), 155.3.11-6D
  (Teix.Rec.)
>>QUERY/auth:ONCHU(PILOTS)/all access
>>field too large
>>QUERY/auth:ONCHU(PILOTS)//all access *.3.11
>>Imago-machine 32675(Yskandr Aghavn) accessed
  by Medical (Neurosurgery), 155.3.11-6D (Teix.Rec.);
  Medical (Maintenance), 152.3.11-6D; Aknel
  Amnardbat for Heritage, 152.3.11-6D; Medical

(Maintenance), 150.3.11-6D; Medical (Maintenance)
50.3.11-6D [. . .]

—record of queries made to Lsel imago database by
Dekakel Onchu, 220.3.11-6D (Teixcalaanli reckoning)

BACK into the subway, and past another checkpoint—the Sunlit all still, all golden and observant. They were less concerned with people *leaving* the palace complex than they had been with people coming in, which wasn't surprising, but Mahit was nevertheless profoundly nervous passing through them. She wondered if an algorithm could sense plans, could *feel* the anticipatory thrum of guilt; if an algorithm, even one which was made up of people who had at least at one point been Teixcalaanlitzlim, could have observed the conversation she and Three Seagrass had had in the restaurant, and act to stop them before they could do anything more. And oh, how she wanted to have time to find out if the Sunlit still *were* Teixcalaanlitzlim, considering the stated Teixcalaanli attitude toward neurological enhancements, and how all of the Sunlit nevertheless turned to look at her and Three Seagrass as they passed, a collective rotation like the inevitable swing of a satellite around a star, seven golden helmets rotating together.

Mahit was braced for them to at least want to ask her more questions about the dead man in her apartments—he was two days dead, now, and surely someone like Eleven Conifer, who had been able to show up at the Emperor's oration-contest banquet, would have had family, associates, old friends from the army. Someone to make a fuss, someone to demand justice.

But the Sunlit only paused, and seemed to consult with one another, and let them go without a word. Perhaps she was being protected? If the algorithm was controlling the Sunlit, there might be more than one person influencing it—not just whoever it was in War, or Ten Pearl himself, but . . . someone else. Those glimpses of grey, the Judiciary agents (or the Judiciary *mirages*), occurred to her again, and Mahit glanced around. She couldn't spot them, but that didn't mean they were gone. Walking faster now, keeping pace with Three Seagrass with quick little steps, she considered jurisdiction in Teixcalaanli law. If the *Judiciary* was following her, perhaps the Sunlit wouldn't dare intervene. She really ought to have studied the intricacies of the legal code for *criminal* law, not just the laws governing the movement and activity of barbarians.

She should have done a lot of things. In the subway, with Three Seagrass directing her toward the central train station, Mahit could still feel the racing of her pulse in her fingertips, beating there along with the ever-present hum of the peripheral neuropathy.

"Not arrested yet," she murmured again.

Three Seagrass's expression was caught somewhere between laughter and what looked like a desperate desire to tell Mahit to *hush*. "Not yet," she said. Mahit grinned at her. Hysteria was catching. She felt like a child, suddenly, playing in the corridors of the Station with her friends, holding on to a secret that the adults weren't supposed to see. When she breathed deeply the wrapped bandage holding the encrypted communiqué around her ribs pressed into her, a reminder.

The central transportation hub for the Inmost Province—the province which contained seventeen million Teixcalaanlitzlim, the palace, the Central City, the province where Mahit had expected to spend the majority of her ambassadorial career—was an enormous, monumental building. It hove into view as they climbed the long staircase up from the subway: a huge edifice crowned with a dome that ate half the sky, surrounded by thorn-spiked towers: a thistle of a building, concrete and glass. Behind it would spread the tendrils and loops of maglev tracks, like a huge system of twisting vines spread in a fan. Mahit knew the verse from *The Buildings* which began the description of this station: *indestructible, many-faceted, the eye that sends out / our citizens, observing.* It did look something like an eye, the eye of an insect—the facets gleamed. When Teixcalaanli literature talked about *eyes* it was often talking about *touch,* or the ability to affect—an eye sees, an eye changes what it sees. Half quantum mechanics, half narrative.

All narrative, on Teixcalaan, even if quantum mechanics helped.

"Where are we meeting Twelve Azalea?" Mahit asked. It would be so easy to get lost in this building—to vanish into the stream of constant motion, Teixcalaanlitzlim traveling in and out, a flow like water.

"In the Great Hall, by the statue of *ezuazuacat* One Telescope," Three Seagrass said. "It'll be obvious; that statue was done during the period where statues were *extremely shiny,* and also very large—two hundred years back, it was a fad, One Telescope is basically all mother-of-pearl."

An enormous statue covered with the insides of shells, that had to have been harvested from an actual ocean. Slowly. Over time. Mahit wanted to laugh, again, and couldn't quite feel *why,* why she couldn't calm down, why everything was edged with this sense of hurtling toward an inevitable crash. *You're about to have experimental neurosurgery, that might be why,* she told herself, and nodded to Three Seagrass. "Let's go, then."

They spotted the grey-suited Judiciary agents, spotted them in truth and not just in Mahit's imagination, at the entrance. They loitered there, too casual, too observant, as they walked in. Mahit wasn't sufficiently dazzled by the sudden clear arc of the Great Hall, the cantilevered glass dome stretching impossibly wide, to not notice that everyone who came through those doors was being taken careful note of. When she spotted another one of them, pacing like a distracted commuter in front of the ticket kiosks but never buying a ticket, she nudged Three Seagrass in the shoulder.

"The Mist. Do you think they followed us?"

". . . I'm not sure," Three Seagrass muttered, almost soundless in the din of Teixcalaanlitzlim searching for their trains. "There might have been one on the street outside Twelve Azalea's apartment who was following us, but if that one even existed they'd peeled off by the time we came out of Science—and these ones were here before we got here . . ."

There were a lot of reasons the Judiciary might be looking for people who looked like her and Three Seagrass, beginning with *Eight Loop has reconsidered how useful I am* and heading on down to *illegal desecration of Yskandr's corpse*. Though that latter action had been mostly Twelve Azalea.

"I don't think they're looking for *us*," Mahit said. "They're looking for—" She didn't want to use his name. "For Petal. Because of the machine."

Three Seagrass cursed quietly. "And they only followed us because we came out of his apartment, and then—We were innocuous, we went to an appointment and out to lunch, we're not the targets."

Again, Mahit considered *jurisdiction*. Maybe they hadn't been the targets of the agent who'd followed them, but they'd been *followed*, and that might have kept the Sunlit from arresting them right then. She found herself in a state of simultaneous gratitude and fury. (She was getting used to the combination: that *doubling*, the strangeness of being grateful for something she should never have had to experience in the first place. Teixcalaan was full of it.)

"Maybe we're not," said Mahit. "Can you see *him*? Petal." She gestured toward what must be the statue of One Telescope, an enormous woman with a barrel chest and wide hips, glowing in swirling ocean-pearl colors from the top of her pedestal. She couldn't spot Twelve Azalea anywhere nearby.

"Let's go around back," Three Seagrass said. "As if we have no idea what's going on here. Be easy. Match the pace of everyone else."

It was very like being in a bad spies-and-intrigue holovision show. Strange people loitering in a transportation center, and Mahit and Three Seagrass trying to be *unobtrusive*—how could a barbarian and an *asekreta,* still in cream-and-flame court dress, be *unobtrusive*—but perhaps they were simply trying to look *unconnected* from the very person they were trying to locate. That might be manageable.

Twelve Azalea wasn't behind the statue of One Telescope. Three Seagrass leaned against its base, perfectly nonchalant, so Mahit leaned as well—leaned, and waited. Tried to see if she could find any visual trace of him in the sea of moving Teixcalaanlitzlim. She couldn't. There were too *many,* and too many of them looked like Twelve Azalea: short, broad-shouldered, dark-haired and brown-skinned men dressed in multilayered suiting.

"Don't react when I move," Three Seagrass murmured. "I see him. Follow me on a thirty-second count; he's in the shadow by the food kiosk, two gates over—between gates 14 and 15." She gestured with her chin, and then set off, wandering with apparent aimlessness toward the kiosk. It was gleefully, loudly, holographically advertising SNACK CAKES: LYCHEE FLAVOR! as well as SQUID STICKS: JUST IMPORTED! Mahit couldn't imagine wanting to eat *either* of those. Three Seagrass bought something from the kiosk, and vanished into the shadows beside it just as Mahit counted *thirty* and began to make her own way over. She avoided the kiosk entirely and skirted around its back, where the holographic advertisements provided substantial visual distraction.

Twelve Azalea was dressed in the most casual clothes Mahit had ever seen him in: a long jacket over a shirt and trousers, all in shades of pink and green. His face was pinched, distracted. The Mist *were* after him, then, or at least they were following him. They didn't seem terribly inclined to arrest him, at the moment.

"Pity there isn't another water garden for us to hide in," Three Seagrass was saying, soft under the chatter of the SNACK CAKES jingle. "I assume these are your stalkers?"

"My stalkers multiplied," Twelve Azalea replied. "There was only one before, when I snuck out of the Judiciary."

"They must have been watching your flat," Mahit said. "We think they followed us too, when we left, but they gave up when we didn't do anything peculiar."

Twelve Azalea laughed, a nasty choked noise, rapidly over. "You must have leashed Reed very tight, Ambassador, to not have done anything *peculiar*. It's been hours and hours."

"Do you think they spotted you?" Three Seagrass asked, graciously ignoring everything else he'd said.

"Yes—but they don't get close. They're not trying to *catch* me, they want to know *where I'm going,* and follow us out to—"

To the unlicensed neurosurgeon. If they were tracked all the way out there, Mahit was sure, the entire plan would collapse under a pile of Teixcalaanli legalities and arrests.

"—and they're between us and the kiosk. I can't let them see me buy the tickets," Twelve Azalea finished.

Three Seagrass was utterly calm, completely focused: that shimmering crisis-energy and determination that Mahit found so frustratingly admirable about her. "I'll get the tickets. No one is watching me. You and Mahit meet me over at gate 26, two minutes. Let her walk in front of you, she's *much* more visible, even if you are stupidly pretty and wearing *bright colors.*"

"I didn't dress for practical spywork," Twelve Azalea muttered, "I dressed for going out-province."

Three Seagrass shrugged, gave him and Mahit both a dazzling Teixcalaanli-style grin, her eyes huge in her thin face, and shrugged out of her *asekreta's* jacket. She turned it inside out, revealing the orange-red lining, shook her hair out of its queue to hang in a curtain around her shoulders, and flung the now-red jacket over one arm. "Be right back," she said.

"*She* seems equipped for practical spywork," Mahit said dryly.

"Reed might be a conservative at heart," Twelve Azalea said, not unadmiringly, "but her conservatism extends as far as thinking about the Information Ministry as an infiltration and extraction unit, like it was before it was a ministry."

Mahit began walking, slowly. Ambling, really, making herself noticeable. A tall barbarian, in barbarian clothing. She made herself move like a Stationer, like someone used to less gravity than this planet: someone *slowed down,* and felt an echo of Yskandr's own time getting used to the pull of the earth, like a reassuring muscular ache. "What was Information before it was a ministry, specifically?" she asked, keeping her eyes on the grey-clad Judiciary officials. They weren't looking at her. They were looking for Twelve Azalea, who was hidden behind her taller shadow. She wasn't important. Not here. Not now.

"The intelligence and analysis arm of the Six Outreaching Palms," Twelve Azalea explained, under his breath. "But that was hundreds of years ago. We're civilians now. We serve the Emperor, not any one *yaotlek*. It helps to reduce the number of usurpation attempts . . ."

Gate 26 announced a departure of a commuter train from Inmost Province to Poplar Bridge, calling at Belltown One, Belltown Four, Belltown Six, the Economicum, and Poplar Bridge. Mahit and Twelve Azalea stood at the side of the gate.

Twelve Azalea was pressed against the wall, Mahit standing in front of him, facing him, hiding him as best as she could from view. The gate announced the departure of the train in two minutes. She could feel the eyes of the Judiciary people pass over her—heard approaching, directed footsteps, chanced a look over one shoulder. There was Three Seagrass, looking entirely like a young woman off home to an outer province from university and not like herself, coming toward them—and a set of the grey-clad Judiciary investigators, converging on them in the other direction.

When Mahit made the decision, she made it all at once. She was *getting on this train,* she was going to find Twelve Azalea's secret neurosurgeon, she was not going to be denied access to her predecessor's memory and ability if she could have it at all. And those Mist agents might know what train they were going to get on, but they absolutely weren't going to know *where they'd get off.*

"Run," she said, "run *now,*" and grabbed Twelve Azalea's sleeve, pulling him through the gate and toward the waiting sleek black-and-gold capsule of the commuter maglev. She had to trust Three Seagrass to run after her—*fuck* her hip hurt when she did this, it still hadn't healed properly—

The doors of the train irised open for them, easily; irised closed behind them. "Up," Mahit said, and Twelve Azalea followed her to the second level of the capsule. A moment later she heard the first announcement of impending departure—*doors will be closing, please stand clear*—and hoped that Three Seagrass had made it on, and that the Judiciary agents *hadn't* and—

—and was gasping with exertion still when the capsule began to move, a graceful soundless *shift,* frictionless, and Three Seagrass came up the stairs.

"They didn't make it, they didn't have tickets," she said, "look, they're on the platform," and fell into a seat, her chest heaving. Mahit looked. There were two men in grey, there, rapidly decreasing in size as the maglev accelerated away.

"That was more exciting than I strictly expected," said Mahit, out of not knowing what else to say. Now that it was . . . not *over,* but paused, she was exquisitely aware of just how much she hurt. Not the best shape to undergo experimental surgery in.

"That could describe my entire week since you arrived, Mahit," Three Seagrass said, and handed her a ticket. Mahit choked a little, trying not to laugh.

"So," Three Seagrass went on, blithe and determined, "how far out are we going? And does this person we are going to see have a name, or are we continuing the amateur spies theme and loitering on a street corner with a pass-phrase?"

"She goes by Five Portico, and we're going to Belltown Six," said Twelve Azalea, and Three Seagrass hissed a bit through her teeth.

"*Six,* really," she said. Outside the train windows the City rushed by in a glowing mess of steel and gold and wire. Mahit stared at it, and listened without listening too hard—the sort of casual cultural immersion which she knew from all of her Lsel psychotherapeutic training was one of her best traits. To let go—to float in the newness, absorb it, internalize when necessary. She needed the rest. She needed to be as calm as she could.

"Yes, Belltown Six, she's an unlicensed *ixplanatl,* where do you *think* she'd live? Somewhere with *good* property values?" Twelve Azalea said. He sounded defensive.

"If I wanted to get plastic surgery I could find an unlicensed *ixplanatl* in *your* neighborhood without going halfway across the province."

"It's a little trickier to find someone who will carve open the Ambassador's skull, thanks."

A little pause. The train made a soft thrumming noise as it

ran, a comforting sort of repeated *ka-thnk,* just on the edge of Mahit's hearing.

"I do appreciate you, Petal," Three Seagrass said, sighing. "You know that, right? It's merely . . . it's been a *week.* Thank you."

Twelve Azalea shrugged, his shoulder moving against Mahit's. "You're going to buy me drinks for about a year. But it's all right. You're welcome."

After nearly an hour, the train exited Inmost Province—the heart of the City, the only place Mahit had expected to go for at least the first three months of her tenure as Ambassador (tourism was for once she was settled, she thought, a distant sentiment from some other Mahit Dzmare, in some other, more hospitable universe)—and entered Belltown Province. At first there was hardly any noticeable change, aside from in the composition of passengers: a slight difference in ethnic group, Mahit thought, a little taller in general, a little paler than Three Seagrass and Twelve Azalea. But slowly the composition of architecture changed as well, as they passed through Belltown One and Three and into Belltown Four, outward in an expanding fan shape of districts—the buildings were no lower but they were *darker,* less airy—the constant motif of flowers and light, the gossamer webwork of the Central City all replaced by tall oppressive spears of buildings, swarming with identical windows. They blocked most of the light.

To Mahit's eyes, used to the narrow corridors of Lsel Station, the lack of blue sky-vault felt strangely comforting, like she could stop keeping track of some small nagging task, and set it down; not having to think about the sheer *size* of the sky. She wondered what the Teixcalaanli thought of it. It was probably a sign of urban blight, all these people close together, blocking out the sun.

Belltown Six was closer-packed still, a spear-garden of

buildings in grey concrete—dim from the moment they stepped out of the train station. The sky above was a bluish sliver. Three Seagrass had her shoulders up by her ears, hunched against a nonexistent chill, and that right there explained most of what Central City denizens thought of *this* province.

"How *did* you find this Five Portico?" Mahit asked Twelve Azalea as he led them down the narrow streets.

He lifted one shoulder in a shrug. "Reed knows this already—she used to tease me—but I tried for Science before I tried for Information, and didn't make the cut on the entrance exams. There's always groups of disaffected students, after an exam cycle. Angry people talking in cafés, on semi-legal cloudhook message nets—I still keep in touch with a couple of them."

"You have—unexpected depths," said Mahit.

Three Seagrass snickered, a sharp little noise. "Don't underestimate him because he's *pretty*," she said. "He didn't get Science because he scored too damn high on Information to go anywhere else."

"*Regardless of that*," Twelve Azalea said, "one of my old friends knows Five Portico and I trust her to not send us to a complete charlatan. All right?"

"Only a *partial* charlatan for us," said Three Seagrass, and then Twelve Azalea was stopping them at the central doorway of one of those enormous spear-buildings. It didn't have a cloudhook interface, like the doors in Central City and the palace—it had a push-button dialpad.

He leaned on one of the lower buttons with his thumb. It made a whining, blatting sound like a tiny alarm.

"Does she know we're coming?" Three Seagrass asked, just in time for the huge door to click and swing open.

"That'd be a yes," Mahit said, and walked in like she wasn't even the slightest bit afraid.

Five Portico's apartment was on the ground floor, the only

open door in the entirety of the corridor: a deep-grey slice of dimness. The woman herself stood in it and watched them come down the hall with no expression on her face save a patient sort of evaluation. Up close, she looked very little like how Mahit had imagined an unlicensed *ixplanatl* would look. She was spare and of middle height, with the Teixcalaanli high cheekbones pressing tight against bronze skin gone ashy with middle age and lack of vitamin D. She looked, in fact, like someone's eldest sib, the sort who neglected to fill out their reproductive quota forms and didn't have the genetics to make the Station's population board annoy her into doing so.

Except: one of her eyes wasn't an eye at all.

It might have been a cloudhook, a very long time ago. Now it was a metal and plastic section of her skull, the edges of it obscured with long-healed twisted skin, and in the center, where the eyeball should have been, was a telescoping lens. It glowed faintly red. As Mahit came closer, the aperture widened.

"You must be the Ambassador," Five Portico said. Her voice matched neither the middle-aged normalcy nor the artificial eye. It was mellifluous, lovely, like she'd been a singer in some other life. "Come in and shut the door."

———

Five Portico's household was not given to the rituals of courtesy. No one made Mahit and her companions overdetermined cups of tea—she thought of Nineteen Adze, and fleetingly regretted the absence of even a prisoner's sense of sanctuary—nor were they invited to sit down, despite the presence of a couch, upholstered in threadbare turquoise brocade. Instead, Five Portico paced a quick circle around Mahit, as if inspecting her general health, and stopped in front of her, square-shouldered, her head tilted up to look her in the face. The technology where her skull should have been glittered where it wasn't transparent, and in the transparent parts Mahit could see through to the yellowish bone and the bright red-pink of blood vessels, sealed away from the air.

"Where's the machine you want installed in you?" she asked.

Three Seagrass coughed, a gesture toward politesse, and said, "Perhaps we might introduce ourselves—"

"This is the Lsel Ambassador, the boy is the one who contacted me, and you are a high-palace Information Ministry official who hasn't been out-province since you had to take school excursions. I'm who you hired. Are you satisfied?"

Three Seagrass widened her eyes in a Teixcalaanli formal smile, viciously pained. "To be sure," she said. "I didn't expect *hospitality* from you, *ixplanatl,* but I thought I might make the attempt."

"I'm not an *ixplanatl,*" Five Portico said. "I'm a mechanic. Think about it, *asekreta,* while I talk to your Ambassador."

"There's already a machine in my head," Mahit said. "Here, where the brainstem meets the cerebellum." She tilted away from Five Portico, twisting to show her, and ghosted a thumb over the tiny scar-ridge at the top of her neck. "I want you to install the new one exactly where and in the same fashion as that one is now. The central portion unweaves—and can be woven back together, the connections to the outer machine resoldered."

"And what precisely does this machine do, Ambassador?"

Mahit shrugged. "It's a form of memory amplification. That's simplest."

That was not simplest, but it was as much as she was willing to share on three minutes' rude acquaintance. Five Portico looked both intrigued and dubious, and both expressions seemed natural to her face. "Is the current version damaged?" she asked.

Mahit hesitated, and then nodded.

"Can you describe *how?*"

The questions Five Portico was asking were subtly different from the sorts of questions Mahit had heard from Twelve Azalea or Nineteen Adze or even the Emperor Himself when she talked about the imago-machines: they felt oblique, shifting, *hinting* at the actual purpose, but not outright *pushing* for Mahit to reveal it. Mahit realized that she must ask them all the time to all sorts of people who didn't want to reveal *why* they needed illegal neurosurgery, and felt peculiarly comforted by not being anything like Five Portico's first patient.

"I don't know what you'll see when you open me up," she began. "The damage might be mechanical and visible. It might . . . not be. The machine is not functioning properly, and I am also having what I can only describe as the symptoms of peripheral neuropathy when I try to access it."

"And at what point in the extraction and replacement would you like me to abort, Ambassador?" The red-glowing center of Five Portico's artificial eye widened, telescoping. It was like looking into a laser housing's white-hot heart.

"We would prefer the Ambassador not be *damaged*," Three Seagrass said.

"Of course you would. But it isn't you whose skull I am cracking, *asekreta*, so I'd have it from the Ambassador herself."

Mahit considered what disasters she was prepared to tolerate. None of them—tremors, blindness, cascading seizures, death—seemed terribly important, in the face of all Teixcalaan pointed at her station, wide jaws akimbo. She'd never felt like this before: untethered from everything. A tiny mote of a person, on this enormous and teeming planet, about to try an experiment that even Lsel's own vaunted neurologists wouldn't approve of.

"I'd like to live," she said. "But only if I am likely to retain most of my mental faculties."

Behind her, Twelve Azalea made a protesting noise. "Really," he said, "I'd be a little more conservative, Mahit—Five Portico takes a person *seriously . . .*"

Five Portico tapped the tip of her tongue against her teeth with a small, considering snort. "That vote of confidence is appreciated," she said, with such dryness that Mahit was not entirely sure if she was offended or pleased. "Alive and mentally agile. All right, Ambassador. And how are you prepared to pay for this little adventure?"

Dismayed, Mahit realized she hadn't even *thought* of how she would be paying. She had her ambassadorial salary—as yet uncollected, and she possessed some doubts that she'd ever receive a single paycheck, if the Teixcalaanli government devolved any further—and she had a currency account on a credit chip that wouldn't even be *read* by anything but a Lsel bank machine. And she'd come out here, somehow thinking that this surgery would be like the restaurants in the palace—someone else's largesse, or someone else's political bargain. It was *stupid.* She hadn't thought. She'd been behaving like—

—oh, like a Teixcalaanli noble, perhaps.

Fuck it.

"You can have the machine you remove," she said. "And you can do with it whatever you like, as long as whatever you like is not handing it over to a member of the Science Ministry or the Emperor Himself."

"—Mahit," Three Seagrass said, shocked.

Mahit looked at her, and set her jaw against the way all the lines of Three Seagrass's face curved into betrayed disappointment. Had it really mattered to her, so much, that Mahit had been respecting Teixcalaanli values, going along with the modes and functions of Teixcalaanli bureaucracy and palace culture? And here she was giving away what Yskandr had tried so hard to sell. Yes. Yes, it probably had, and she didn't want that to be true but here it was (no friendship after all, no chance-found ally, only self-interest, and that *hurt* and there wasn't a thing to be done about it right now), and she did not have the time or energy to explain herself, or to try to make that disappointment go away.

But Five Portico said, "Done," and looked as if Mahit had given her a rich-flavored dessert to bite into. Mahit felt ill. "A little piece of technological piracy from a culture that actually *practices* neurosurgery is worth more than just one expedition into your head, Ambassador. Anything else you need done? Vision enhancement? Reshape your hairline into something even the *asekreta* here would think is attractive?"

"That's not necessary," Mahit said, trying not to flinch. Trying not to let her expression change at all. Perfectly Teixcalaanli, serene. Like Yskandr had taught her. (Was she killing him, her imago, her other-self? Was that the real price she was paying: destroying the person she was supposed to have become, even if she intended to replace him with himself?)

"As you like," said Five Portico. "Barring events beyond my control—even out here in Belltown we're not immune to Sunlit raids, Ambassador, and I'll hand over your machine if it means my life—I promise none of your off-world technology will get back to the people who want it most."

"This was a terrible idea," Three Seagrass said to no one in particular, and Twelve Azalea put his hand on her arm.

"I know," Mahit said, "but I don't exactly have a better choice."

"I imagine you *don't*," said Five Portico. "Or you'd never have ventured out here. Come on into the surgery. Let's get started. You'll have her back in three hours or so, *asekretim*—if you get her back at all."

CHAPTER
SIXTEEN

CURFEW 22.00-06.00—DUE TO INCREASED CIVIL UNREST THE SUNLIT HAVE INSTITUTED A CURFEW IN THE FOL-LOWING PROVINCES: CENTRAL-SOUTH, BELLTOWN ONE, BELLTOWN THREE [. . .]

> —public announcement on cloudhook and newsfeeds,
>
> 251.3.11

*   *   *

[. . .] in light of current circumstances, the Teixcalaanli Imperium requests the services of a new ambassador from Lsel Station. Message ends.

> —diplomatic communiqué delivered by a courier from
> *Ascension's Red Harvest* to the government of Lsel Station

ASIDE from sterile cleanliness, Five Portico's surgery bore no resemblance to the white plastic suites Mahit remembered from Lsel. It consisted of a polished-steel table on an adjustable platform, surrounded by a forest of mobile instrumentation arms and complicated restraints. She felt dreamlike, entirely unreal as she stripped out of her jacket. She left her shirt on, with her Lsel secrets still bound to her ribs underneath it. Five Portico did not seem to care; she briskly guided Mahit to lie on her belly on the table and secured her head with a cage of padded bars and straps. This was absurd. She was going to let a stranger rip her imago-machine out of her in a back room of an apartment complex on another planet. She had said yes, over and over.

Yskandr, she thought, one last desperate reaching-out, *forgive me. I'm sorry—come* back, *please—*

Still silence. Nothing but that nerve-damage flicker down her arms to her outermost fingers.

Five Portico came at her with a needle, the tip beading with anesthetic. The iris of her artificial eye yawned, a shutter-spin of metal expanding outward; the needle's sting in Mahit's upper arm was a sharp afterthought in the face of the white-laser heart of that eye.

She was dizzy. Five Portico's hands were on her arms. She could feel all of her bones where they pressed against the steel. That laser eye slipped wider—she could feel its heat—*was she going to use the eye to cut—*

————

Blank. Slow decay, a winding-down wound backward, wound up again, the memory of a closing dark, *descent,* and then—he woke to un-startled flesh, a flicker of oxygen drawn easily, slowly through the throat—relief, first, dizzying profound relief, *breathing,* the intense joy of lungs perfused with air where no air had been able to come—

(he had been on the floor, on the floor and choking, the carpet-pile pressed into his cheek, and now his cheek was on something cold)

A breath, slower still, drugged-slow—

(—*not his cheek,* the lungs too small, the body narrow and brittle-bright with youth and exhaustion easily mixed and *had he ever been this young,* not for *decades*—other-body, a new small self, *he was dead, wasn't he—dead and an imago, in a new body—*)

His mouth was making keening, absurd sounds. He couldn't figure out why.

It didn't matter. He was breathing. He sank back into blackness.

————

Sunrise on Lsel Station happens four times in a twenty-four-hour cycle. Sunrise across the backs of his (unlined, square-nailed) hands, resting on tempered grey steel, cold. His fingers prickle with adrenaline like stinging needles. Across from him is Darj Tarats, (from somewhere distant, a voice he doesn't recognize: this Darj Tarats is absurdly young, he looks more like a person than the mobile cadaver that someone else is remembering him looking like) grave-faced under the tight speckled-grey curls of his hair, saying, "We are going to send you to Teixcalaan, Mr. Aghavn, if you're willing to go."

He says <as he remembered himself saying> (as *she* had said), "I want to. I have always—"

And the rush of bright desire, the naked shameful want for the thing that was not his by right. Was this the first time he felt it?

(Of course not. It hadn't been the first time for her either.)

"Your wanting to is not why you are being sent," says Darj Tarats. "Though it might mean the Imperium finds more flesh on your body to feast on, and doesn't spit you back out at us for a while. We need *influence* in Teixcalaan, Mr. Aghavn. We need you to get in as far as you can go, and be indispensable."

He says, "I will be," with all the arrogance of his youth, and only then does he ask, "Why now?"

Darj Tarats pushes a star-chart across the steel table. It is fine and precise, and Yskandr knows these stars: they are the stars of his childhood. At one edge of the chart there are a series of black spots, marked-out coordinates. Places where something has *happened*.

"Because we may have to ask Teixcalaan to preserve us from

something *worse* than Teixcalaan," he says. "And when we ask, we want them to love us. Need us. Make them love you, Yskandr."

"What happened at these places?" Yskandr asks, one uncalloused fingertip resting on those spreading black spots.

"We are not alone out here," says Darj Tarats. "And what else is out here is hungry, and nothing else but hungry. They have only been *quiescent* thus far, but . . . that might change. At any moment. When it does, I want you to be ready to ask Teixcalaan to intervene. At least a human empire only eats a person from the heart outward."

Yskandr *shudders*, angry and afraid at once: pushes back the anger, the insult, the feeling of *what you love makes you despicable* in favor of asking a useful question. "We've met aliens before— why is this different?"

Darj Tarats's face is serene and composed and utterly cold. Yskandr will dream of it, in bad moments (knows he will, remembering forward), will dream of him saying this: "They do not *think*, Yskandr. They aren't *persons*. We don't understand them and they don't understand us. There is no reasoning or negotiation to be had."

Dream it, and wake the kind of cold no heavy blanket or warm-fleshed bedmate can dispel. And think, to himself: Why didn't Tarats tell the Council? Why was I his weapon of choice? What does he want for Lsel Station to become, to risk this danger for some unknown stretch (<twenty years,> someone murmurs) of time?

He'd known, even then, that Tarats wanted something larger than the military *protection* of Teixcalaan, but then he'd been on the City, at court, and it hadn't—mattered—

I am remembering this for the second time.

<*I am remembering this for the second time.*>

(*I am remembering what I have never seen–*)

I've seen this. I am this. *Who are* you?

(An inward turn, searching, to find that foreign voice—to look at her, inside themselves. A turning-in, and in turning they see *one another,* doubled—)

––––––

<I'm Yskandr Aghavn,> says Yskandr Aghavn.

Yskandr Aghavn is twenty-six years old and has been in Teixcalaanli territory for just over thirty-two months. Yskandr Aghavn is <dead! dead, I saw you dead on a *plinth* in a *basement! I'm dead because you're dead!*> forty, almost forty-one, and knows the minor inevitable physical tragedy of middle age, the sag around the middle and the jawline.

I'm Yskandr Aghavn, says Yskandr Aghavn, and you are an imago I sent back to Lsel fifteen years ago. Who the *fuck* was stupid enough to put an imago of me into me?

That would be me.

(Again that turning-inward, turning *sideways,* and seeing: high-cheekboned woman, short-cropped hair, tall and narrow with a sharp prow of a nose and grey-green eyes, bloodshot exhausted.)

I'm Mahit Dzmare, says Mahit Dzmare, and I am both of you now.

Blood and *starlight,* says Yskandr, each of him, both of him, exactly the same tone on the Teixcalaanli curse, why did you do *that?*

Laughing inside one's own mind is uncomfortable, Mahit realizes as she does it, or maybe what's uncomfortable is trying to fit three minds into one mind, and she/they are going to break apart right along the fault line where the other two are too much alike and she is . . . not, she is female, a generation younger, four inches too short, she likes the taste of processed fish-flake powder on her breakfast porridge and they are re-pulsed, tiny stupid things like that and she is *falling* inside her own mind, feeling like an echo the place where she is being carved open and made into something she's not under alien and impersonal hands—

———

Lsel Station has a long tradition of psychotherapy because if it didn't, everyone on board would have decompensated into identity crisis a long time ago.

In the earliest stages of integration with an imago, during the most difficult part where the two personalities are sorting out what is valuable about the imago-structure and what should be discarded, what is necessary for the host personality to keep as self-identity and what can be edited, written over, given up— in those early stages what a person is supposed to do is consider a choice, a small choice, an unimportant one where the imago and the host choose the same way. To focus on that choice as a still place, a conflictless heart. Something to build out from.

<Mahit,> says one of the Yskandrs. She thinks it's the young one, *her* imago, the one who is more than half her already. <Mahit, remember how you felt when you first read Pseudo-Thirteen River's *Expansion History,* and you came to the de-scription of the triple sunrises you can see when you're hanging in Lsel Station's Lagrange point, and you thought, *At last, there are words for how I feel, and they aren't even in my language*—>

Yes, Mahit says. Yes, she does. That ache: longing and a vio-lent sort of self-hatred, that only made the longing sharper.

<I felt that way.>

We felt that way.

Both of their voices, almost the same. Electric fire in her nerves, the sweetness of *being known.*

—————

Abruptly and sickeningly, Mahit was aware in a way she never wanted to have been aware of the movement of air currents on the *internal structure of her cervical vertebrae*, a sickeningly inti- mate caress that transmuted into a cascade of nerve impulse, fingertips and toetips lighting up with shimmering pressure that flipped over, the shunt of some massive switch, to sudden pain.

Why wasn't she unconscious?

What was Five Portico *doing to her?*

Mahit tried to scream, and could not: whatever drugs were supposed to be keeping her under the threshold of uncon- sciousness were paralytic (at least *something* works, she thought horribly, at least she wasn't going to thrash and tear out her own nervous system on the points of Five Portico's microsur- gery rig).

Waves of electric feeling, up from her extremities in a help- less rush—

—————

There are two of them. They see each other; one is dead and one decohering, young face a half-remembered sketch, filled in with Mahit's eyes, green instead of brown; the *wrongness* of be- ing in an unfamiliar sensorium, this body's sense of smell more acute, her stress-response hormones *different*—more tolerance of greater pain, and some Yskandr (it doesn't matter which) re- members that female-hormonal bodies are simply better at deal- ing with pain than male-hormonal ones, thinks *At least that'll be easier* but it hurts so *much,* what is happening to her. Them. Her.

Flicker-shuffle; memory scraps like drifting debris in zero-g, caught in some sun-glint and illuminated to the point of visual pain:

(—*sunglare through the window falling on the back of his hand; there are too many lines there, the veins prominent. He'd never thought he'd get* old *on Teixcalaan but here he is, writing in cipher on paper in his apartment, informing Darj Tarats that it is unsafe to send further imago-copies of himself by any channel, and he will not be returning to Lsel again to leave his imago-machine in safekeeping and have a new blank installed to continue recording. It isn't true: what's not safe is letting anyone from Lsel know what he's prepared to do in order to keep them all safe. He feels not just old but* ancient, *a decaying conglomeration of choices made in extremis—in extremis and out of passion, a terrifying combination—but* extremis and devotion *would be worse, and might be truer—*)

("*—in extremis, we must ensure that the Emperor's wishes for his successor are respected,*" *says Eight Loop,* "*and therefore I propose I adopt the ninety-percent clone as my legal heir.*" *Yskandr stares at her, thinks* Nothing I will do to this child is as bad as what his own people have planned for him—they will control every aspect of his life, they made him, they choose for him. Is giving him to the Emperor to dwell inside so much worse?

Then he thinks, Yes, it is, and I'm doing it anyway.)

(—*the Emperor Six Direction is resplendent on his sun-spear throne, a casual intensity on every plane of his face, and Yskandr's stomach flips over in giddy anticipation, a wave of electric feeling that lodges in the base of his throat:* He wants to talk to me, I've shared enough interesting maybe-secrets, this is going to work—I know what I could offer, what he won't say no to—)

(—*his last bite of stuffed flower lodges in the base of his throat; he cannot breathe or swallow. The place where Ten Pearl had stabbed his wrist is a bright spike of heat. Ten Pearl looks at him critically from across the table, and sighs: a faint melancholy sound, resigned.* "*I did try to come up with a better way to keep you out of our Emperor's mind,*" *he says,* "*and so did Nineteen Adze—do forgive her, if your religion grants you the sort of afterlife that involves forgiveness—*")

The flutter of memories coalesces. Collapses. Mahit follows it down, down into the center of the three of them. There is a flicker of resistance—(*No one should know, I can't, it's—you're dead,* thinks Mahit—<*I'm dead,*> thinks the other Yskandr, the young one)—before:

———

"Was the Emperor in bed with you when he asked you to make him immortal?"

Nineteen Adze, sprawled across Yskandr's naked chest, props her chin on her hands and looks up at him with deadly seriousness. She's slick all over with fine sweat. Yskandr should stop finding her erotic at any point now, considering what she's just asked him, but it doesn't seem to make a bit of difference. He wishes he was surprised at himself. He trails his fingers through her hair, gets them tangled in the dark silky strands of it. The Emperor's hair is like this, but silver-grey. The texture is the same.

(The other Yskandr is a flicker: mostly libido, prurient interest that Mahit feels as a pulse low in her groin, an acknowledgment of desire. It almost shields her from an explosive realization: the answer to Nineteen Adze's question is *yes.*)

(<*You got her to notice you,*> says Yskandr to Yskandr.)

(*I was ten years older than you that night and she started taking me seriously about two months before it,* says Yskandr. *Shut up and let me remember this, this was . . .*)

(<Enjoyable?>)

(*No,* says the Yskandr whose memory they're in. *No, this was* important.)

(Mahit is flooded with the memory of Nineteen Adze in the bathroom in her office complex, the strange tenderness of her hands on Mahit's hands, the brisk sudden *care* of her. She tries to recall if the want had been her own or Yskandr's or both of theirs—says to the both of them, watching this memory, *Blood and starlight, what made you think this was a good idea.* She makes the echo vicious. Viciousness does not cover the revelation that she is not at all surprised that Yskandr had seduced—been seduced by—either Nineteen Adze or the Emperor himself. Both of them.)

In that remembered bed, Yskandr averts his eyes from the calm and even gaze of Nineteen Adze, and says, "It's not immortality. If that's what you're asking. The body dies, and that really does matter. Most of personality is endocrine."

Nineteen Adze considers this. Her nakedness seems to make no difference to the cool evaluation in her face; it is the same expression she'd worn before she'd taken him to bed. "So you match for endocrine compatibility?"

"We match for personality; there are a lot of different endocrine systems that can produce very similar *people*, and it's whether the personalities can integrate that matters. But it's easier when there's a degree of physical similarity, or similarity in early life experience."

"His Brilliance wants to have a clone made."

Yskandr shudders at the idea, and tries not to let Nineteen Adze see him do it. (Yskandr shudders. Yskandr-Mahit shudders. Some taboo seems to be indelible, no matter how many Teixcalaanlitzlim one is seduced by or how long a person marinates in the culture of the palace. One doesn't put an imago into a clone of the predecessor; there's too *much* congruence. The personalities don't integrate. One of them *wins*, instead, and whatever the other self had to offer is lost.) "We don't use clones for imago-hosts, Nineteen Adze. I don't have any idea how a clone body will change what happens to the expression of Six Direction *as* an imago."

She clicks her tongue against her upper teeth. She is plastered against him; she can feel his revulsion just fine, he suspects.

"If I think about it as *re-use* of His Brilliance, it disturbs me less. But it still disturbs me," she says.

Yskandr says, "I'd be surprised if it didn't. It disturbs *me*, and I suggested that he use an imago-machine in the first place."

"Then why did you suggest it?"

Yskandr sighs, and shifts them over in the pillows. When he lies on his side, Nineteen Adze fits in the hollow cup made by his hip and chest; a small bony *presence*, indelible. "Because Teixcalaan is an enormous, hungry thing, and His Brilliance Six Direction is neither crazy nor power-hungry nor cruel. There aren't all that many *good* emperors, Nineteen Adze. Even in poetry."

"And you love him," she says.

Yskandr thinks of waking up, wrung out and pleasantly ach-ing, an hour or so after he'd fallen asleep in the Emperor's bed, and finding him awake, a stack of infofiche on his bare knees, working. He'd curled around him, then, made a warm curve of himself as a brace to work from. It was such a small thing and Six Direction had left one hand cupped to Yskandr's cheek, lingering—he'd wondered, then, if he *ever* slept, and heard, an echo like a cloudhook in his mind, a verse from Fourteen Scal-pel's "Encomia for the Fallen of the Flagship *Twelve Expanding Lotus*": the verse describing the captain of that ship, how she had died with her people. *There is no star-chart unwatched by her / sleepless eyes, or unguided by / her spear-calloused hand, and thus / she falls, a captain in truth.* Sleepless emperors. Seduction's a matter of poetry. Of a story he wants to be true.

"And I love him," Yskandr says to Nineteen Adze. "I shouldn't, but I do."

"So do I," she says. "I hope I still will, when he's not himself any longer."

———

Are we ourselves?

One of them is asking. One of them thinks this is a rhetorical question: there's continuity of memory, and that makes a self. A self is whoever remembers being that self.

One of them corrects: *Continuity of memory filtered through endocrine response.*

One of them corrects: *We all remember being that self, and we are not the same.*

They see each other, that peculiar internal triple-vision. Mahit does not remember seeing Yskandr the first time she did this. Yskandr—her imago, her other-self, a tatter fading now, never quite cohesive, the parts of him that exist now are only the parts which were already written into her neurology—he does not remember it either, and does not know (a miserable confessional spill of not-knowing) if he has forgotten or if he has simply remembered what Mahit remembered, or what Yskandr (the other Yskandr, dead, caught up on the point of his dying like a man impaled) remembered.

(—his last bite of stuffed flower lodges in the base of his throat; he cannot breathe or swallow—)

Stop it, Mahit says. You were dying and now you're us.

She is still reeling from his other memories, from knowing the depth of his mutual seduction with Teixcalaan, but she has enough sense of herself still (it is *her* body they are part of) to not want to feel again the strangling poison administered by Ten Pearl.

You were dead, and now you're not, and I *need you,* she says. I need *your help,* Yskandr. I am your successor and I need you now.

Her-Yskandr, a torn rag: *I'm sorry.*

The old man, dying, in love: a gasp, an attempt to breathe—to control the lungs he lives in now—

————

On that steel table, grit-teethed and straining into a convulsed, tonic-clonic arch, Mahit (or Yskandr) (or Yskandr) came to horrified consciousness for a second time since Five Portico had begun the surgery. The terrible sensation of her nervous system being open to the air was gone—tiny mercy; at least there were no more instruments inside her skull, at least if she was going to have convulsions she was going to fry her brain with anomalous electrical activity, not tear it up with blunt-force trauma—

Her lungs seized. Yskandr breathed differently than she did, was used to larger lungs, or lungs that were currently frozen in neurotoxic paralysis. Most of her vision went to sparkles, blue and white, encroaching fizzing grey at the edges of her visual field, and she tried not to panic, tried to remember how to get *this* endocrine system to breathe, to calm down, to *stop*—

Yskandr, I need you, we have work, you don't get to be finished—

The hand which had been burnt by the poison flower slammed into the steel table—and for a dizzy moment she couldn't tell if the pain was her own or the memory of Yskandr dying with a needle stabbed into *his* hand, radiating poison heat. She felt that same electric rush down her ulnar nerves which had been signaling the malfunctioning of the imago-Yskandr she'd shared her mind with.

What if all of this pain was *useless,* what if it wasn't the imago-machine that had been sabotaged, but Mahit herself, the malfunction was in *her* nerves, what if she'd had Five Portico break her open for *nothing*—

<Mahit,> said a Yskandr. The internal voice was peculiar, twinned. Patchy. But *there*.

Her spine was a horrible arch that she couldn't release. *We're not dying unless you make us die,* she told that voice, and tried to believe it.

There was a stinging needle-stick, this time in the flesh of her buttock. *Five Portico,* Mahit thought, *that's Five Portico trying to fix me.*

Flat darkness swallowed her up like a thunderclap. It was a reprieve.

INTERLUDE

A MIND is a sort of star-chart in reverse: an assembly of memory, conditioned response, and past action held together in a network of electricity and endocrine signaling, rendered down to a single moving point of consciousness. Two minds, together, each contain a vast map of past and present, a vaster projected map of futures—and two minds, together, however close, however entwined, have their own cartography, alien to one another. Look now at Darj Tarats and Dekakel Onchu, erstwhile friends, longtime colleagues, deeply suspicious of one another's motives—here they are meeting together in the quiet private space of Onchu's personal sleeping pod. Their knees, folded up, almost touch. The soundproofing is on.

Look carefully at the points at which their universal cartographies do not correspond.

Onchu has brought Tarats her reports on the great three-wheeled ships that are moving through Stationer space and eating Stationer ships and Stationer pilots; she has brought as well the frisson of gravity-skewed fear that her imago-line has instilled in her as a response to the incomprehensible. It costs her some of her pride to admit these things to Tarats, but the Miners and the Pilots are allies of old: the two points of Lsel's government which send men and women out into the black outside the Station's metal shell.

She does not expect what Tarats brings her in reply: that he has known about these incursions, by rumor and hint and suppressed report, for the better part of two decades. Has known, and kept a secret map, and a network of spies and informants to supply that map's points of data. The cargo captain who had come to Onchu made a stop at Darj Tarats's office, afterward.

Onchu is angry at him, for that. But it is not a useful anger, nor one she can spend time on harboring, since Tarats goes on, a spill of confession like a weight released after long hours bearing it up: amongst the constellation of his plans for Yskandr Aghavn, gone to Teixcalaan so many years ago to serve there, was to prepare for an alliance wherein the one empire, as human as the Stationers but more hungry, might be cajoled into throwing itself open-jawed into the maw of an empire vaster and more strange, when the time came. That such an empire might be devoured there, just as it has devoured so much and for so long.

"You are using us as *bait*," says Dekakel Onchu. "A clash between Teixcalaan and these aliens will happen right on top of us—"

"Not *bait*," Darj Tarats replies. "I am making us something worth preserving, in our current form, to a polity which has constantly threatened to absorb us. The clash will not happen *here*—Teixcalaan's fleet will go through our Anhamemat Gate, and through all the rest of the jumpgates where these ships have been showing up—and out into wherever the aliens are coming from."

Onchu imagines Tarats's mind: he must think of Teixcalaan as a tide, a sort of thing that could wash through and pull back again, and leave the ocean the same. She's seen an ocean once. She's seen what a *high* tide does to the shoreline.

Tarats does not think of tides. He thinks of weights: of pressing his thumb down as hard as he can on the scale of the galaxy, making a little indentation, a tiny shift. The sort of tiny shift that might happen if a man were to go to Teixcalaan, and love it with all his heart and mind, and seduce it as much as he himself had been seduced: and thus guide it to its death.

"What do you *want* from this?" Onchu asks, in the quiet of her pod.

"An end," says Darj Tarats, who has grown quite old while pressing his fingers down onto the scale. "An end to empires. An immovable object to crash an impossible force upon, and break it."

Onchu hisses through her teeth.

chapter SEVENTEEN

PATRICIAN THIRD-CLASS ELEVEN CONIFER
DIES AFTER A SHORT ILLNESS

Patrician Third-Class Eleven Conifer, who bravely served the Imperium in the Twenty-Sixth Legion under yaotlek One Lightning, died yesterday after a short illness, according to his nearest genetic kin, forty-percent clone One Conifer, who was reached by this reporter at his place of employment at the Central Travel Authority Northeast Division. "My genetic ancestor's death was unexpected," said One Conifer, "and I will be undergoing a full battery of tests in order to determine if I carry the gene markers for stroke as well . . ."

—TRIBUNE broadsheet, obituary feed, 252.3.11-6D

*   *   *

Movement of Teixcalaanli vessels detected en route to our sector—please advise—intercept unlikely due to sheer numbers—this is at least a legion on the march—

—communiqué received by Dekakel Onchu in her capacity
as nominal head of the Lsel Station defense, from Pilot
Kamchat Gitem, 252.3.11-6D (Teixcalaanli reckoning)

MAHIT woke to dim light, the scratchy comfort of rough fabric under her palms and cheek, and the worst headache she had ever had in her life. Her mouth felt like a polluted desert—too dry to swallow, and tasting of filth. Her throat was raw from screaming, and her left hand was a dull throb, almost as strong as it had been right after the episode with the poison flower—and she was *not dead* and she was thinking in full sentences.

So far, so good.

Yskandr? she asked, warily.

<Hello, Mahit,> said Yskandr, weary. It was mostly the voice of the other Yskandr, of Ambassador Aghavn: older, rougher, than the Yskandr she'd known and lost.

Mostly, but not entirely. Her Yskandr seemed to exist in interstices and cracks—the imago-machine which had housed him was gone, but he'd been a presence as much as she had been in the fantasia of memory and image that had followed that removal. They'd inhabited the same neural architecture and endocrine system for a little over three months. It wasn't enough time for *integration*—if it had been, she'd never have needed to replace him—but she could still feel him, remember *his* versions of Yskandr's memories, fifteen years younger and inflected differently.

They were her memories now. Thinking about them made her feel dizzy and sick with doubled recall—this was why, she guessed, that adding a second version of the same imago, even a later recording, was such a bad idea and never done.

Hello, Yskandr, she managed, thinking past the nausea. The corners of her mouth tugged into that wide smile that was his, and she chided him, gently (they were going to have to *start over* on so many things and oh *fuck* she missed her own imago), *get out of my nervous system.*

<I miss him too,> Yskandr said. <Who wouldn't miss being twenty-six?>

It's not the same thing, Mahit thought.

<No. I assume it's not.>

Mahit sighed, and even sighing hurt her throat. She must have screamed a lot. *I know,* she thought. *We have each other now. We're all there is of our line—first and second Ambassadors to Teixcalaan.*

<You have gotten us into even more trouble than I did,> said Yskandr. She could feel him shuffle through the past week of her life, like a flipbook of infofiche. <I'm actually impressed.>

We would not be in this sort of trouble had you not gotten us into it in the first place, she said. *And now I need your help. And we need to . . . figure out who we're going to be. My priorities are not yours—*

A flash, an emotional *spike* just below her sternum, of how she'd felt while talking to the Emperor. <Aren't they?>

No, she repeated. *And stay out of my nervous system, I told you. You're dead. You're my imago, my living memory, and we are the Lsel Ambassador—*

<I do like you,> said Yskandr. <I always have.>

Flickers, in the interstices, of the version she knew. Nevertheless she felt invaded, heavy with the unfamiliar mental weight of someone *else,* someone who had more life than her, had seen more than her, who knew Teixcalaan better—she thought, helpless and sudden, of how that ninety-percent clone would feel if he ever had all of Six Direction stuffed into his ten-year-old head, and ached with sympathy.

The Yskandr-sense—heavy weight and bright rag both—backed off. That might be some kind of apology.

Mahit mustered her courage, braced for the inevitable physical consequences, and opened her eyes. The headache spiked immediately along with the light, as she'd expected it would, but she didn't vomit and she didn't have another convulsion or experience any immediate visual distortions. Could be worse.

She was lying on a turquoise couch, just like the other turquoise couch Five Portico owned, the one in her front room.

The fabric under her cheek was upholstery fabric. Maybe Five Portico had an entire set of turquoise furniture. Maybe she'd bought them all on sale. The last time Mahit had woken up from brain surgery she'd been in the medical center on Lsel, in a sterile and soothing silver-grey room. This was . . . different.

<Quite,> said Yskandr, bone dry. Mahit snickered, which *did* hurt.

Moving carefully, and feeling like every part of her body had been desiccated in vacuum, she sat up. Neither Five Portico nor Three Seagrass and Twelve Azalea were in visual range. That gave her a long moment to brace herself for the nauseating process of standing up and walking toward the only visible door. Her ribs felt constricted when she tried to take a full breath—*oh,* that was the sport bandage, still wrapped around her lower floating ribs exactly where it had been before the surgery had begun.

It was strange, the things which could make you trust someone: Mahit felt profoundly grateful to Five Portico for not having done more to her than she'd asked for. Only the *requested* violation, thank you: she still had the letter from Darj Tarats, and now, with Yskandr's help, she could read it.

If the others were outside that door, waiting for her to wake up—probably wondering *if* she'd wake up—this might be the best time to decrypt it, while she was alone.

As alone as she was ever going to be again.

<We'll get used to it,> said Yskandr. <We were getting used to it before.>

And then you vanished on me, Mahit told him. *All right. Show me how to read this, if you can.*

She lifted her shirt and unwound the wrapping. The communiqué was wrinkled from how she must have rolled on it, curved to the shape of her ribs, but still whole and still entirely readable with her own book cipher, except for the encrypted section at the bottom. *It says you have the encryption key. Or you did, fifteen years ago.*

<I still do,> Yskandr told her, and she knew he felt the wash of relief that spilled over her as strongly as she did. <It's the one Darj Tarats gave me, in secret, right before I got onto the transport ship to come here. If it's in his cipher, the message is from his hand directly.>

Show me, said Mahit.

Yskandr did.

Sharing *skill* with an imago felt like discovering an unexpected and enormous talent; like she had sat down to do the Station's orbital calculations and suddenly realized she had been studying mathematics for decades, all the correct formulas and the experience to use them arrayed at her fingertips; or being asked to dance in zero-g, and automatically knowing how her body should *feel,* how to move in space. The cipher was mathematical—which must have been Darj Tarats's preference, as Mahit was aware that Yskandr had had to *learn* to do the matrix algebra which formed the basis of generating the one-time decryption key. She was glad *she* wasn't learning it, just feeling it unfold inside her like a blooming flower.

<It's easier with paper,> Yskandr said, <and a pencil.>

Mahit laughed a little, gingerly—laughing hurt her throat and her head. She reached up to touch the back of her neck. There was a bandage there, covering the surgical site. By touch she guessed the wound was as long as her thumb, and tried to imagine what the scar would look like. Then, still careful, she pushed herself up to her feet and tottered toward anything that might contain a writing implement. Five Portico was just anti-establishment enough that she might have actual pens on her desk, not just holographic infofiche-manipulators.

There weren't pens, but there was a drafting pencil resting on top of a bunch of mechanical sketches. Mahit didn't flip through them—Five Portico hadn't removed her shirt, she wasn't going to look through her papers—but even a cursory glance at the top sketch was enough for her to recognize it as a schematic for a prosthetic hand.

And why would a person have to come all the way out here for a prosthesis?

<It's Teixcalaan,> said Yskandr, <neurological fixes aren't the only adjustments of the body which are *unfair*.>

She wished she could tell whether he was being dryly sarcastic or expressing a genuinely held opinion—but *that* wasn't new. That confusion was inherent to every Yskandr, from the first moment she'd had him in her head, back on Lsel.

Here's a pencil, she thought at him. *Teach me how to read what Tarats wants me to do about having an annexation force pointed at our station.*

They—*she,* she with Yskandr's prior knowledge flooding her, opening unexpected windows in her mind—decrypted the message, letter by letter, through the sequential matrix transform that Yskandr had memorized twenty years ago, on his way into Teixcalaan: how *he'd* spent those long weeks in transit. She caught a flash of memory, a spinning scrap—Yskandr on his first night in her (his) ambassadorial apartment, burning the piece of paper Tarats had handed him, that he'd learned from.

Mahit was working so hard on the *process* of decryption that she hardly paid attention to the contents of the message until the entire thing existed in plaintext. It wasn't long. She'd known that, before this entire terrible adventure—it *couldn't* be long, there weren't enough characters, there wouldn't be the sort of elaborate instructions that she wanted. No one would tell her how to get out of what was happening. There would only be advice.

What advice there was terrified her.

*Demand re-route of annexation force; claim certain provable
knowledge of new-discovered nonhumans plotting invasion at
points as given below; withhold coordinates until confirmation
given.*

<Can you memorize numbers, Mahit Dzmare?>
She felt a little like Yskandr was the only thing holding her
up. Her head ached viciously. *Yes,* she thought. *I know all of
Pseudo-Thirteen River, I can memorize a coordinate string.*
<Do it. And then destroy the plaintext.>
How?
<Eat it. It's paper.>
Mahit stared at the coordinate string for a full minute—set
it to rhythm and meter in her head, held it like she'd hold a
poem. And then she tore the strip of paper she'd written the
plaintext on off the original communiqué and stuffed it in her
mouth, thinking the whole time: *We eat the best parts of our dead.
Whose ashes am I consuming now?*
She had to chew to get the paper to go down, and chewing
hurt the surgical site. She did it anyway. It was something to do,
while she considered her options.
Who was she supposed to demand this *of*? The Emperor?
<Yes.>
You're biased, Yskandr.
<Biased, but right.>
Maybe he *was.* Maybe what she should do was exactly what
Yskandr would have done if he wasn't dead, and march into
Palace-Earth with these coordinates on her tongue like a string
of pearls to trade for peace.

———

When she finally made her way into the front room of Five Portico's apartment—giving the surgery door a wide berth—both

Three Seagrass and Twelve Azalea were sitting, side by side like children in a waiting room, on the *other* turquoise couch, and Five Portico was nowhere to be seen. Three Seagrass was on her feet the instant Mahit came through the door. She ran to her and threw her arms around Mahit in a tight hug that broke every personal-space taboo held by Lsel *or* Teixcalaan. Mahit could feel the racing of her heart through the wall of her ribs.

"You're alive!" Three Seagrass said, and then "—oh fuck did I hurt you?" before letting Mahit go with nearly the same degree of force as she'd embraced her. "Are you—*you*?"

". . . yes, not any more than I hurt already, and that *still* depends on the Teixcalaanli definition of *you*, Three Seagrass," Mahit told her. Smiling also hurt the surgical site, but not as much as chewing.

"And you can talk," Three Seagrass went on. Mahit wanted to stroke her hair back behind her ears; she hadn't put it back up in its queue since they'd run away from the Judiciary officials, not even during the time between when Mahit had gone into the surgery and now—whenever *now* was, Mahit wasn't sure of the hour—and with it loose Three Seagrass looked devastatingly young.

"I think I retained *most* of my higher faculties," she said to her, as neutral-Teixcalaanli as possible.

Three Seagrass blinked several times, and then *laughed*.

"I'm glad," said Twelve Azalea from the couch. "But did it . . . work?"

<You have made fascinating friends.>

"Yes," Mahit said, out loud and internally at once. "At least it worked *enough*. I decrypted the message."

"What does it *feel like*?" Twelve Azalea asked, just as Three Seagrass said, "Good. Given that, what would you like to do *next*?"

Mahit would have liked to sit down, if she had a preference.

Possibly to sleep until everything was over, and there was a new emperor, and the universe returned to normal. If she slept that long she would probably be dead. Sitting down, though, that she could do, at least for a moment. She made her way to the couch, Three Seagrass at her elbow—keeping a *decorous* foot of distance now, which Mahit vaguely regretted—and sat.

"I need," she said, "to get back to Palace-Earth and speak with His Brilliance Six Direction."

<Thank you,> Yskandr said, a whisper like fire behind her eyes.

"Must have been some message," Twelve Azalea said.

Mahit very gingerly put her head in her hands. "An annexation force is headed for my home, the Empire is on the verge of civil war, and I *requested immediate guidance from my superiors in government,* did you expect a neutral statement of affirmation?"

"I'm not an idiot," said Twelve Azalea. "I got you here, didn't I?"

"You did," Mahit said. "Forgive me. I've been mostly unconscious for . . . I don't know how long, what time is it?"

Three Seagrass patted her lightly on the back, once. "Eleven hours. It's around one in the morning."

No wonder Mahit felt this *ill*. She'd been under anesthetic for a *long* while. "How much of that was surgery? And where is Five Portico? I'd like to thank her, I think."

"She went . . . out," Twelve Azalea said, "about an hour back; but you were only in the surgical suite for three, maybe four hours."

"We weren't entirely sure you'd wake," Three Seagrass said, all too evenly. Mahit could hear the remnants of distress in her voice, and she wondered again about how badly hurt *Three Seagrass* had been, when she'd been hospitalized after the City's electric-strike. "Five Portico was the opposite of reassuring."

"I don't think I was being very reassuring myself," Mahit said.

"Is there . . . could I have some water?" Her throat was still dry enough to hurt when she talked, and she didn't expect to *stop* talking as long as Three Seagrass and Twelve Azalea were awake to talk back to her.

"Of course," said Twelve Azalea, "there's got to be a kitchen in this apartment somewhere." He levered himself off the couch, with the effort of someone who had been sitting in the same place for a very long time—Mahit felt a little guilty, but not much—and disappeared around a corner.

She and Three Seagrass were alone. The silence between them felt strange, charged again like it had been in the restaurant: until Three Seagrass asked, quietly, "*Are* you still you? I . . . can I talk to him? Is that a possible thing?"

"I'm me," Mahit said. "I've got continuity of memory and continuity of endocrine response, so I'm as me as I am going to get. It's not—a second person, inside me. It's me, with adjustments."

<We can talk to her if you'd like,> Yskandr whispered inside her skull.

We are talking to her, Yskandr.

"All right," Three Seagrass said. "I think the entire process is terrifying, Mahit, and I also think you ought to know that, but I intend to treat you exactly as I did before, until you behave differently."

Mahit suspected Three Seagrass was trying to say, *I trust you still,* and not quite managing to get there. She smiled at her, Lsel-smile, even though it hurt, and got a wide-eyed Teixcalaanli smile back.

Before she could say anything else, there was a commotion of voices from the direction Twelve Azalea had gone—Five Portico, returning, and with company.

"Who is he? Five Portico, you didn't say you had clients." A woman's voice, pointed.

"He's not the client, Two Lemon, he's the client's contact. Come in, he's not the only one."

"This is not the time for *clients*," said Two Lemon, "the *yaot-lek's* just landed a military force at the port—" and then the whole lot of them poured into the room where Mahit was sitting. There were five, mixed in genders and in age; none of them wore cloudhooks. (None of them wanted to be watched by the City and its algorithmic heart.) Twelve Azalea, water glass clutched in one hand, was swept along in the middle of them.

"That's a barbarian," said one of the newcomers.

"A *foreigner*," another one said, as if making a weary correction he'd made a hundred times.

"Foreigner, barbarian, I don't care," said Two Lemon—a plump woman with a straight spine and steel-grey hair in a perfect queue—"what's next to her is a *spy*. Five Portico, why is there Information Ministry here?"

Three Seagrass had become very still, poised and frozen at once. Mahit wondered if they needed to run. She wasn't sure she could.

"She came with the barbarian, and when the barbarian arrived," said Five Portico, and no one bothered to correct *her* on the use of the word, "they had an interesting problem and were willing to pay for it to be solved. Two Lemon, you know very well that I deal with who I want to deal with."

"You could have warned us before we came to your house," said one of Two Lemon's companions, the one who was so interested in *foreigners*, "to have an emergency planning meeting for actions tomorrow—"

Two Lemon affixed him with a flat stare. "Not in front of the spy."

"I am not a *spy*," said Three Seagrass, faintly indignant, "and I do not care what you are planning, or who you are. My assignment in the Ministry has nothing to do with *any* of you."

"Oh, but you are a spy, *asekreta*," Five Portico said, "though I think you might get better, with proper treatment."

"Is that a threat?"

Mahit put her hand on Three Seagrass's arm. "The *asekreta* is here with me," she said, "and I claim her for Lsel Station. She is my responsibility."

<That is amazingly illegal,> Yskandr said admiringly.

Yes, and they don't know that.

Two Lemon peered at Mahit down the slope of her nose. "You're the Lsel Ambassador, aren't you."

"I am."

"The newsfeeds from the Judiciary do *not* like you," Two Lemon said, with very grudging admiration.

"I wouldn't know," Mahit told her, "I was unconscious most of the day. Ask Five Portico." Under her hand, Three Seagrass trembled faintly, all adrenaline.

Five Portico snickered, and shrugged when Two Lemon looked at her. "The Ambassador isn't wrong."

"Is she going to die if she isn't under medical supervision?" Two Lemon asked.

Mahit thought this was a very good question, and that she'd like to know the answer herself, and had to clamp down on the urge to giggle inappropriately.

"Eventually," said Five Portico. "But not because of anything I did."

<How reassuring your *mechanic* is,> Yskandr noted.

"I want her out of here, Five Portico, and her Information Ministry with her," Two Lemon went on. A brief, pleased murmur emerged from her companions, and was shut down with a glance. "We have actual work to do."

So do I, thought Mahit. *Though I wish . . . I wish I knew more about the work being done here. And whether these are the same people who set bombs in restaurants and in theaters, or if they have other methods—are these the people for whom the City is not the City?*

<Teixcalaan is more than the palace and the poetry,> Yskandr murmured, <even I realized that by the end. If we get through this . . . >

If we get through this, I will remember Two Lemon, though I suspect that's the last thing she wants from me.

"We'll leave," Mahit said, cutting off further speculation. "I do wish you luck. With whatever *actions* you are planning." She got to her feet, and didn't even stagger. She might make it back to the train station before she fell over, if someone would *actually* give her water, instead of standing there with the glass like Twelve Azalea was doing, helpless in the middle of the group of . . . whatever they were. Resistance leaders. (Resistance to *what*? To the Empire, to Six Direction specifically? Were they the people who put up the posters in the subway stations in support of the Odile System's breakaway attempt, or were they concerned with some policy choice that Mahit had no idea about and never would? To the presence of One Lightning, or any *yaotlek*, on the City's soil?)

"I'd go fast," said Five Portico, "One Lightning has legions in the streets already."

Three Seagrass cursed, a sharp single word that Mahit had never heard her use before. Then she said, "All right, thank you. Come on," and stood to leave, taking Mahit's elbow as she did.

"Give me five minutes with my client," Five Portico said pointedly. "I try to make sure of my work, and last I saw her she was quite thoroughly unconscious."

Mahit nodded. "In private," she said. "Five minutes in private." Gently she detached Three Seagrass from her arm, and walked—trying not to stagger or shake or reveal anything of how sick her headache was making her feel—back into the room where she'd woken up.

Five Portico followed her, and shut the door behind them. "That bad, mm?" she asked. "You don't want your friends to know?"

"It could be worse," said Mahit. "I seem to have most of my neurological function intact. I want to know what you found. On the old machine. Was it damaged?"

"A few of the nanocircuits were blown out," Five Portico said. "On first glance. They looked weak to begin with. It's a very fragile thing—just touching the circuits could have introduced a short. I'd have to take it apart to know more. A process I am very much looking forward to."

"That's *interesting*," Mahit managed. It was . . . something. Maybe sabotage. Or maybe just mechanical failure.

"Very. Now let me look at you."

Mahit stood still, and let Five Portico peer thoughtfully at the surgical site; followed her directions through a basic neurological examination, no different from the ones she'd had on Lsel. It took less than five minutes. Closer to three.

"I'd tell you to rest, but there's no point," Five Portico said when she was finished. "Go get out of my house. Thank you for the *fascinating* experience."

"Not every day you operate on barbarians?"

"Not every day a barbarian leaves me with barbarian technology."

<You are playing such *games*, Mahit,> Yskandr said in the back of her mind, and she could not tell if he was angry or impressed at what she'd done, in giving away what he'd used to buy an emperor's favor.

A short while later the three of them were huddled in the shadow of Five Portico's building, exiled from even that limited safety. Mahit leaned on Three Seagrass, and wished she'd gotten to ac-

tually drink the water before they'd left. Her throat ached with
dryness. Belltown Six in the small hours between midnight and
dawn was simultaneously silent and raucous: the distant sounds
of shrieky laughter, breaking glass—a shout, quickly muffled—
drifted over the buildings, but the street they stood on was entirely empty, and lit only by the faint neon tracery of the building
numbers, written in a glyph font that even Mahit found old-
fashioned. New fifty years ago, and not vintage yet.

"When, Petal," Three Seagrass asked, her voice a narrow,
tight murmur, "were you going to tell us that your unlicensed
ixplanatl was involved with anti-imperial activists?"

Twelve Azalea had no expression on his face; an insistent,
deliberate blankness. A *hurt*. "She's an unlicensed *ixplanatl* in
Belltown Six. I don't know why you thought she *wouldn't* be.
You're Information Ministry, Reed, *act like it*."

"I am acting like it," Three Seagrass spat. "I'm questioning
the connections of and influences on my own *dear friend*, is
what I'm doing—"

"Stop it," Mahit said. Talking hurt. Talking was going to hurt
more, every time she did it, unless she could keep quiet for a
while. "Tear each other to pieces somewhere else, sometime
else. How are we going to get back to the palace?"

In the pause after her question, she could hear nothing but
the two sets of breathing next to her, and how they blurred into
each other.

Then Three Seagrass said, "We can't take the train; there
won't be trains until the morning. The commuter lines don't
run at this hour."

"And if One Lightning is actually landing troops off the car-
riers at the port, there won't be trains at *all* by morning," Twelve
Azalea added.

Mahit nodded. "There. Look at you both being *useful*." She
sounded exactly like Yskandr would have. Whether that was a

problem or not wasn't something she felt particularly capable of dealing with at the moment. "If we can't get back the same way we got out, what else can we do? Can we walk?"

"In a strictly technical sense, we can," said Twelve Azalea, "though it would take a whole day to get back to the Central provinces."

"*We* can," Three Seagrass said, correcting him. "*Mahit,* on the contrary, is like as not to fall over before we have been walking an hour."

Mahit had to admit to herself that this was true. "My state of health notwithstanding," she said, "a whole day is too long. I need to see the Emperor *tonight.* Before dawn, if we can figure out a way." She was shivering. She didn't know when that had started. It wasn't *cold,* exactly—and she had her jacket—she drew her arms tightly around her chest.

Three Seagrass exhaled, slowly, a hiss through her teeth. "I have an idea," she said, "but Petal will not like it."

"Tell me first," said Twelve Azalea, "before you make more judgments about what I will and will not like."

"I call our superiors at the Information Ministry, and I inform them that we are stranded whilst engaged in recognizance on those anti-imperial activists, and request a pickup and retrieval," she said. "If you like, I can call them from somewhere not near this address. As a *courtesy* toward Five Portico not killing my Ambassador."

"You're right," Twelve Azalea said, "I *don't* like it. You're burning *my* contacts."

<Consider what reasons she will provide to explain *your* presence here,> Yskandr added, a nagging whisper inside Mahit's mind.

I don't have many allies, Yskandr.

<How many allies does your liaison have?>

Not enough. But I'm one of them.

<So far.>

"We're standing on the street," Mahit said. "I would rather be picked up by the Information Ministry than either wait for Twelve Azalea's Judiciary stalkers to find us again or try to make our way back inside the Inmost Province during an attempted military coup."

Three Seagrass winced. "It's not a coup yet. Though it might be by the morning—I don't know how this happened so *fast*."

"Come on, then," Mahit told them both. "Let's walk to the train station, and call from there."

———

The walk was bad. There were more people on the street, even in the dark; gathering on corners, talking in low voices. Once she thought she saw a brandished knife, a curved and ugly thing, shown off between a group of young men in shirts emblazoned with that graffiti-art of the Teixcalaanli battle flag defaced. They were laughing. She put her head down and watched Three Seagrass's heels move step by step and kept walking. By the time they reached the station, Mahit's headache felt large enough to devour small spacecraft that had flown too close to its center of mass. She sat on one of the benches outside of the locked doors and drew her knees up to her chest, resting her forehead on them. The pressure helped, a little—it *distracted*, while Three Seagrass made her call, murmuring subvocalizations into her cloudhook.

Twelve Azalea sat next to her, and didn't touch her, and she wanted—*oh*, she wanted the easy comfort of Three Seagrass's attention, and that was the most useless desire she'd had in hours. Days, even.

<Breathe,> said Yskandr, and she tried. Even breaths; counting to a slow five on the inhalation, a slow five on the exhalation.

Three Seagrass finished her call, said, "Someone will be here in fifteen minutes," and sat on Mahit's other side. And didn't touch her either. Mahit kept breathing. The headache backed off a little, enough for her to raise her head when she heard the sound of the approaching groundcar's engine, and to not have the world spin too badly.

It was a very standard groundcar: black, not ostentatious. The person who got out of it was a young man in Information Ministry suiting, orange cuffs and all; he bowed over his fingertips, and asked, "*Asekreta*? Are these all your companions?"

"Yes," said Three Seagrass, "this is all of us."

"Please get in. We'll have you back in the City proper before you know it."

It all seemed far too easy. Mahit suspected it *was*; and she also knew she couldn't do much else but allow it to happen. The backseat of the groundcar was blissfully dark, and smelled of cleaning products and upholstery. The three of them fit in it thigh to thigh, and Three Seagrass patted Mahit's knee, just once, as they began to drive away; and that small, kind touch she took with her into helpless and exhausted sleep, lulled by the motion of the wheels.

CHAPTER EIGHTEEN

ALL CIVILIAN OFF-PLANET TRANSPORT CANCELED—
INMOST-PROVINCE SPACEPORT CLOSED—SOUTH POPLAR
SPACEPORT OPERATING AT EMERGENCY/CARGO CAPACI-
TIES ONLY—MAKE ALTERNATE TRAVEL ARRANGEMENTS—
THIS MESSAGE REPEATS
> —public newsfeeds, 251.3.11-6D

* * *

... as I am, as you said, quite occupied with the business of keeping our Station valuable but not too valuable to a vast and mostly
heartless Imperium, you will have to continue excusing my absence; when it is more settled here I will certainly enjoy taking a
long and deserved vacation back home, but the point at which I
could leave the constant development of political action at the
Teixcalaanli court alone for four months at least is relatively unimaginable just now. Forgive me for staying away. Do recall that if
you need to contact me you yourself provided private means . . .
> —from a letter written from Ambassador Yskandr Aghavn
> to Darj Tarats, Councilor for the Miners, received on Lsel
> Station 203.1.10-6D

THE first checkpoint between Belltown Six and the Information Ministry's building in Palace-East woke Mahit from that
state just beyond consciousness. All she wanted in the world was

to sink back into the grey silence behind her eyelids, and until now—a perfect fifteen, twenty minutes—no one, not Three Seagrass nor the driver nor even Yskandr in her mind, had pushed her awake. The voices and the lights at the checkpoint changed all of that.

Blinking, she sat up. The groundcar had slowed to a stop, and the driver had peeled down one of the windows. Outside the air was lightening to dawn, a smear of grey-pink—and something smelled of smoke, acrid—

Low voices. The driver did something with his cloudhook, projected an identification sequence. Whoever was on the other side said, "We can let you through on that permit, but you don't want to go. They're marching from the skyport, and the citizenry is marching to meet them. You *really* don't want to do this."

Yes I do, Mahit thought, and didn't know if it was Yskandr's thought or her own.

"Yes," Three Seagrass said, "we do. I have *vital intelligence to report to my Ministry.* Sir."

The driver shrugged, expressively, as if to say, *I'm just here to help.* Through the opened window Mahit heard a low *thump,* as if somewhere, not very far away at all, someone had set off a bomb.

(—Fifteen Engine, studded with shrapnel, blood leaking from his mouth, his blood like tears running down Mahit's face, and that *noise,* the hollow explosion-noise—)

She swallowed hard. The window rolled up. They kept moving. Inside the groundcar it was difficult to see what they were driving *through*; all sound was muffled and the windows were privacy-tinted dark. She kept thinking that she was hearing more of those sounds, the way that a bomb going off made a kind of *collapse* in the air.

"Did you know," she found herself saying, right out loud,

bright and brittle and uncontrolled, "that the worst thing on Lsel, the absolute worst thing, is fire—fire eats oxygen—fire *rises*—fire extinguisher drills are every other day, they start when we're two or three years old, whenever we're big enough to hold the extinguisher—fire is bad and *explosives are worse*."

"I don't know why there'd be bombings at all," Twelve Azalea said. "This isn't—no one wants to hurt the *City*, it's about who gets to *have* the City, right?"

The groundcar slowed again, but there was no halt at any checkpoint. Just a crawl, like they'd hit traffic. "Make the windows transparent," Mahit said. Nothing happened.

Three Seagrass's teeth were gritted very tightly. Mahit could see the tension in her jaw. "Petal," she said, "it's the Fleet. Bombing massed civilian uprisings is how the Fleet *works*. You know that." And to the driver, "Turn the opacity down, would you?"

This time, the driver did.

Through the groundcar's windows—smoky glass, paling to clear—what Mahit saw at first made very little sense. People didn't *break* things, on Lsel—not property, not with cavalier abandon. The shell of a station was fragile and if some part of the machinery of it snapped, people would die: of breathing vacuum, of icy chill, of the hydroponics system shutting down. Casual vandalism on Lsel was a matter of graffiti, elaborate hacks, blocking off hallways with the hull-breach-repair expanding foam canisters. But here in the streets of the City she was watching a Teixcalaanli woman, in a perfectly reasonable suit jacket and trousers, swing what looked like a metal pole into the window of a shop, and shatter the glass there. Do that, walk onward, and do it *again*.

Other people were running—they were in the streets, which was why the groundcar had slowed so much. Some of them had the purple larkspur pins, and some of them had no identificatory marks at all to show their loyalties, and some were Sunlit, gold and terrifying and moving in sharp little triads, like scout-ships diving gravityless through descending orbits. There was smoke in the air, drifting in from over one heartbreakingly lovely many-spired building. The groundcar's driver had taken on an expression of grim and serene determination, pushing forward in spurts that made all of Mahit's insides slosh against her abdominal wall with every jerk of acceleration.

"I don't see legions," Twelve Azalea said, leaden.

Three Seagrass had crawled out of the backseat and into the front, beside the driver. "We're not close enough to the skyport. This is—spillover—"

They heard the shouting—two sets of shouting, back and forth, rhythmic and poetic like the beating of a heart but out of *time,* not together, a heart in fibrillation—before they managed to get much farther. It was a wave of sound, punctuated at unpredictable moments by the *thump* of another explosion. The driver, seeing some opening that Mahit couldn't spot, floored the acceleration and shot the groundcar around a corner—Mahit was thrown half into Twelve Azalea's lap—they raced down an alley—and then the street opened up, a blooming, easy roadway, into a plaza. And there they were: two massed groups of Teixcalaanlitzlim, screaming at one another. The car stopped. There wasn't a way forward through that seething mass.

Where the two groups touched, violence erupted like fungal growths after a long, wet spring. Blood on the face of a woman with a larkspur pin tied to her arm like a mourning band, blood from how she'd been *punched,* and the woman who'd punched her—so close to the groundcar that Mahit could hear everything—shouted *For the Emperor One Lightning!* and smeared her bloodied hand across her forehead, like she was a person in a historical epic marking the sacrifice of her enemy.

They didn't look like Teixcalaanlitzlim, Mahit thought. Drifting thought, absurd, disconnected. They looked like people. Just like people. Tearing each other apart.

There was another one of those terrible *thud*s of collapsing air, much closer this time. An answering *bang* from a group of Sunlit, who were abruptly surrounded by quick-spreading white smoke—the people fighting near them began to cough, ran away from the gas, uncaring which side of the street riot they were on. They ran right by the groundcar, eyes streaming, red. Some of the gas began to seep in through the sealed doors, the windows.

"Fuck," said Three Seagrass. "Cover your mouth with your shirt—that's crowd-dispersal gas—we can't *stay* here—"

Mahit covered her mouth with her shirt. Her eyes burned. Her throat burned.

<You need to get out of the car,> Yskandr told her. She was suddenly calm—clear-calm, poised, everything *slow*. Yskandr doing *something* to her adrenal glands. <You need to get out of the car, and you need to go around this, and you need to do it now. Go, Mahit. I'll show you the way.>

"We can't stay here," Mahit said out loud, and opened the door. The white gas billowed in. "Follow me."

She couldn't breathe—the first breath she took was fire, blazing in her lungs, and Yskandr said, <Just run, breathe later,> so she ran—not knowing how she was running, not knowing how it was possible for her body to run. Not knowing if anyone was following her at all. Yskandr seemed to know some secret path—some familiar pattern in the horrible swirl of blood and white smoke, and she saw for the first time a Fleet-uniformed legionnaire, grey and gold, a squadron of them—Yskandr spun her, rotated her from the hip, a pivot, and raced her away at an angle. There were footsteps behind her. Rapid ones, matching her pace. She looked back: Three Seagrass, and Twelve Azalea. The driver, too.

They skirted the edge of the plaza, raced down a street Mahit was sure she'd never seen. *How many times did you come this way,* she thought, through the pounding of her heart, the way she was gasping for air only when Yskandr thought she couldn't bear not to gasp.

<Enough times. I *lived* here. This is my home—was—>

After another two minutes they slowed to a walk. Mahit was entirely sure she'd faint if Yskandr wasn't making her keep going. No one spoke. The sounds of the riot receded to a dim roar. They reached the demarcation of the palace from the rest of the City—no one guarded the tiny pathway they followed inside, no Sunlit and no Mist and no legions. Yskandr led them all onward, following muscle memory years old and dead now.

And then, like a curtain parting, they turned one last corner and Mahit found herself in front of the Information Ministry, which looked entirely unscathed. A clean thing, out of a former world.

<There,> Yskandr said. <Go in. Sit down before you fall down.>

Everything looked so familiar—two minutes of walking would get her to the entrance of the building containing her ambassadorial apartment (that is, if she could go there at all without the interference of the Sunlit and their *investigation*). But all the tracery of the City's vast AI was lit up under the plaza tilework, as if the entire palace was a curled beast, preparing to strike.

"I don't know how you did that," Three Seagrass said to Mahit. "When we got into the car you could hardly walk."

"I didn't," Mahit said. "Not just me. Not exactly. Are we going to go in?" Her voice was a rag. Now that Yskandr wasn't controlling her breathing she felt like she couldn't get *enough* air. Her chest heaved with each breath.

Three Seagrass looked at their driver, who wore an expression of utter shock: a man *undone,* a man in a world which no longer made sense. "Are we?" she asked.

". . . yes?" he said, and started for the door.

Neither Mahit nor Three Seagrass put their feet on the traces on their way into the Ministry building, even when it made walking awkward and strange.

Inside, there was nothing but the clean and lovely spaces of a Teixcalaanli ministry early in the morning. No sign of distress. Nothing amiss. Mahit found herself on the verge of tears and didn't know why. Three Seagrass's driver led them all into an innocuous beige-shaded conference room, complete with a U-shaped table surrounding an infofiche projector, fluorescent lighting, and a plethora of moderately uncomfortable chairs. It was the least Teixcalaanli room Mahit could remember being in since she'd arrived, but she assumed that places where interminable everyday meetings occurred were much the same throughout the entire galaxy. She'd sat in rooms like this on Lsel, in school and at government functions. She sat in this one now. Dimly—so very dimly, through the thick Ministry walls—she heard another explosion. And then silence. Perhaps the riot had been dispersed. The legions were massing elsewhere. Closer to the skyport.

The arrival of a carafe of coffee and a basket of some kind of bread rolls was *not* standard practice for conference rooms, but perhaps Three Seagrass had pulled some strings for them. The coffee was shockingly, blisteringly good: hot but not hot enough to scald, the paper cup warm in Mahit's palms. It had a rich, earthy taste that wasn't anything like the instant coffee on Lsel, and in some better moment Mahit thought she'd really like to drink it *slowly* enough to think about all the different qualities of the flavor—

<There are *varieties*,> Yskandr said, <and they all taste different. It's fantastic. But the important part is the caffeine.>

He was right. Even in the few minutes Mahit had been drinking the coffee, she felt more *present*, more acute, conscious of a faint thrumming in her skin.

<Slow down a little. I may have exhausted your adrenal glands, just then.> It was close to being an apology.

Twelve Azalea was on his second cup. "Now what?" he asked Three Seagrass pointedly. "We wait for a debriefing? I thought we needed to be getting the Ambassador to the Emperor immediately, if that's even *possible* considering what's happening to the City outside."

We. It hadn't been very long since she'd asked Twelve Azalea to help her steal Yskandr's imago-machine from his corpse, and yet after only such a little bit of time, here he was committed to at least a semblance of ideological unity with a barbarian. Then again, he had known where to find Five Portico and her anti-imperial activist friends—ideological unity was flexible. Mutable, under stress. Mahit looked at Three Seagrass, who was as *under stress* as she had ever seen her: grey at the temples, a raw place on the side of her lip where she must have gnawed it open.

"We do," she said. "But I owe the Ministry *some* courtesy, since they came to get us."

They came to get us. They drove us through a riot. They brought us coffee and breakfast. The world functions as it ought to, and if I keep behaving as if it will continue to, nothing will go wrong. Mahit knew that line of thinking. She knew it intimately and horribly, and she *sympathized* (she sympathized too much, this was her essential problem, wasn't it?), and Three Seagrass was still wrong.

Mahit said, "I don't think we have any time at all—the whole City is going to go up like an oxygen chamber with a spark fault."

Three Seagrass made a noise surprisingly akin to a hissing

steam valve, put her head in her hands, and said, "Just give me one minute to think, all right?"

Mahit figured one minute was within parameters. Probably. Maybe. Everything was very shimmery and surreal. She wondered what level of sleep debt she'd actually reached. There had been the thirty-six hours before she'd slept at Twelve Azalea's apartment—and possibly being unconscious after brain surgery counted—

<It doesn't,> said Yskandr, and that was all *her* Yskandr, the light, quick, bitter amusement of him. <Especially after getting through a riot like that.>

"All right," Three Seagrass said, so Mahit looked at her, keeping her face perfectly Teixcalaanli-neutral, trying not to visibly need her liaison's support as much as she actually did.

Three Seagrass spread her hands, a helpless little gesture. "I'm going to go ask to report directly to the Minister for Information—and she is undoubtedly exceptionally busy just now, so we'll have an *appointment*—and we'll come back when that appointment is scheduled." She got to her feet. "Don't go anywhere. Central Desk is just down the hall, on this floor, I'll be five minutes."

It was an incredibly transparent ruse. But transparency had worked for them before; transparency seemed to have its own gravity when placed alongside the Teixcalaanli overcommitment to narrative. It bent the light. Mahit nodded to Three Seagrass, said, "Try it," and followed that with "And don't worry about us going anywhere. Where would we *go*?"

Twelve Azalea and Yskandr laughed, in simultaneous eerie echo, and then Three Seagrass was gone, slipped out the door like a seed-skiff squirted from the side of a cruiser.

They waited. Mahit felt naked without Three Seagrass, *alone*. More and more exposed, the longer she was gone—especially as the time stretched from two minutes to five, to ten. She could hardly feel anything but the low, anxious thrumming of her own heart, transmitted through her chest to weigh heavy on the spot just between the arcs of her ribs. Most of the peripheral neuropathy was gone—just the occasional shimmer in her fingertips, and she had suspicions that might be permanent. She didn't know how that made her feel. So far she could still hold a stylus, even if she couldn't necessarily feel the pressure of it. If it got worse again—

Later.

When the door to the conference room reopened, and Three Seagrass was there behind it, the release of tension was like being kicked—and then Mahit saw that she was not alone, and the person with her was not wearing Information Ministry white-and-orange at all, but had a spray of purple flowers pinned to the collar of his deep blue jacket. It was fresh; live flowers, cut within the last day. When all of Thirty Larkspur's supporters had been wearing these at the oration contest, they had been fashion, amusements, Teixcalaanli political signaling on symbolic channels. When they had been wearing them in the streets it was a way to take sides in a war. Now this one looked like a badge of office, or of party loyalty.

"Sit down," said the newcomer to Three Seagrass, and gave her a *push*. Mahit was half out of her seat immediately, angry, gathering her breath to speak—but Three Seagrass sat down as she'd been told to. She was flushed across the face, furious, but she waved a hand at Mahit to subside, and she did.

"Ambassador," said their visitor, *"asekretim.* I'm obliged to tell you that you will not be permitted to leave the Ministry building at this time."

"Are we being arrested?" Twelve Azalea asked.

"Certainly not. You are being detained for your own safety."

"I want," Twelve Azalea went on, strident, and Mahit was

proud of him, sickeningly so, "to speak to Minister Two Rose-wood herself about this. Right now. And who are *you*, anyway?"

"Two Rosewood is no longer the Minister for Information," said this person, ignoring Twelve Azalea's request for his name or affiliation. "She has been relieved of her duties during the current crisis by the *ezuazuacat* Thirty Larkspur. I can convey to him your desire to speak to him, if you like. I'm sure he'll get to you as his time allows."

"What?" said Mahit.

"Do you have trouble with your hearing, Ambassador?"

"With my credulity," said Mahit.

"There is nothing to be overly concerned about—"

"You have just told us we cannot leave and that the Minister has been *deposed*—"

"There were questions as to her loyalties," said Thirty Lark-spur's man, and he shrugged. "Thirty Larkspur intends to keep the Empire in safe and steady hands. There are legions in our streets, Ambassador, it is very dangerous to move about just now. Sit tight. Thirty Larkspur will take care of this, and it will all blow over within the week."

Mahit had her doubts. Mahit had more doubts than she precisely knew what to do with: a proliferation of uncertainty, a sweeping tide of being sure that she'd *missed something*. Thirty Larkspur was executing . . . what, a coup in advance of One Lightning's coup? It was possible she was already too late to do anything to turn the annexation force away from Lsel, whether she had tradeable knowledge of impending external threat to Teixcalaan or not. At the oration contest it had been Thirty Larkspur himself—resplendent in blue and lilac, perfectly serene—who had told her that *the deal was off*. If he had gained control of the civil service—he who was apparently willing to dismiss Lsel the instant it wasn't useful to his plans—

"We cannot," said Twelve Azalea, and Mahit was very grateful to him for saying anything that would get her out of her own mind, "stay in a *conference room* for a week. And I still don't know who you are. Sir."

"I am Six Helicopter," said the man—Mahit *stared* at him, and wondered when he'd learned to say his name with not only a straight face but with that degree of smugness—"and of course you won't be spending a week in a conference room, *asekretim*. Ambassador. You'll be moved to a safe and well-appointed location, just as soon as we have got one to put you in."

"And that will be *when?*" Twelve Azalea went on. He had perfected a sort of incredulous, high-pitched stridency: the voice of a person who was being inconvenienced and was going to make a scene about it. Distantly, Mahit found it admirable. Strategic. She didn't interrupt him. "By whose definition of safe? You're implying that there is an attempted *usurpation* occurring as we speak!"

"The *yaotlek*'s little adventure will be over *long* before you could call this unpleasantness an usurpation," said Six Helicopter. "I have a great deal of work to do—I'll make sure someone brings you three more coffee. Please don't try to leave. You will be stopped at the door—this really is a safe place right now. Don't worry."

And with that, he left. The door to the conference room clicked innocuously behind him. Three Seagrass promptly, and disturbingly, broke into laughter.

"Did that actually just happen?" she asked. "Did some jumped-up bureaucrat without an inch of training in protocol just tell us that the Information Ministry is under the control of the *ezuazuacatlim*? Because I think that was what just happened, . and I am at a complete loss; do forgive me, Mahit, this is not within my fucking portfolio of plausible scenarios that I might encounter while acting as cultural liaison to a foreign ambassador."

"If it helps," said Mahit, "it isn't in my portfolio of plausible scenarios I might encounter *as* a foreign ambassador, either."

Three Seagrass pressed her palm over her face and exhaled, deliberate and forced. Stifled snickering still escaped from between her fingers. ". . . no," she said, "I can't imagine it would be."

"If we can't leave," Twelve Azalea said, "how are we going to get the Ambassador to the Emperor? Even just across the palace grounds, even if that riot *doesn't* spill over. In the best-case scenario."

And will there still be an emperor for me to get to, once we're there? Mahit thought, and then had to bite the inside of her cheek against a rush of grief that mostly wasn't hers; it was Yskandr who felt that impending loss like heartbreak, not her. Not— entirely her. (And yet she remembered the pressure of Six Direction's hands across her wrists and hoped—useless, biochemical ache in her sternum—that His Brilliance would somehow survive this insurrection, even if he wouldn't survive much longer than it.)

But who else could she bargain with?

"What if we aren't trying to get to His Brilliance," she said. "What if we were trying to get the attention of someone who could get us *to* him?"

"From inside this conference room," said Twelve Azalea skeptically, gesturing toward the carafe of coffee. "You know they're monitoring our cloudhooks, and you don't even have one—"

"Yes," Mahit snapped, "I am still aware that I am not a citizen of Teixcalaan, I have not forgotten even once, you don't have to *remind me*."

"That wasn't what I meant—"

Mahit exhaled hard enough that she could feel it in her surgical site. "No. But it is what you said."

Three Seagrass had taken her hands away from her face, and the expression which was growing there was one that Mahit had seen before: it was Three Seagrass focusing inward, preparing to bend the universe around her will, because all other options were untenable. It was the expression she'd worn when they'd eaten ice cream in the park, before invading the Judiciary. The expression she'd worn in Nineteen Adze's front office, determined to walk off physical insult and trauma.

"There are all kinds of things a person can do with a cloudhook, no matter how monitored," she said. "Mahit—whose attention do you want?"

There was really only one answer to that question. "Her Excellency the *ezuazuacat* Nineteen Adze," said Mahit. "Her rank is the same as Thirty Larkspur's, which means that she probably can walk right in here the same as he did—and I think she still likes me."

<She liked me,> Yskandr murmured. <She liked me very much, and she let me die.>

She liked you very much, and she saved my life, Mahit thought. *Let's find out why, shall we?*

"All right. Nineteen Adze, she who terrifies me even after all of the other terrifying events currently taking place," said Three Seagrass. She'd become very cheerful, in the time between having had an idea—whatever that idea would turn out to be—and announcing it. Mahit understood *that,* too. The power of having any sort of plan, no matter how absurd or impossible. And weren't all three of them rather emotionally labile, just recently? "For Her Excellency—Mahit, how do you feel about writing some very *pointed* poetic verse? And posting it on the open newsfeeds."

"And you said *I* read too many political romances," Twelve Azalea muttered.

"I'm not going to leaflet Palace-East to announce my endless love for the Third Judiciary Under-Minister," Three Seagrass said, her eyes sparkling. "*That* would be a political romance. This is a known poet posting her newest work in response to current events. With an encoded statement in it."

"Do you *often* post poems on open newsfeeds?" Mahit asked, fascinated.

"It's a little gauche," said Three Seagrass, "but these are difficult times, and that exquisitely boring Fourteen Spire won the imperial oration contest last week. Clearly *anyone* can be gauche, and be feted in public."

"And you think that Nineteen Adze will, what, come get us, if we appeal to her in verse?" It was too *clever* to be practical; it was all Teixcalaanli symbolic logic and Mahit didn't trust it.

"I don't know what she'll do," said Three Seagrass. "But I know she'll read it, and then she'll know where we are, and what we need. You saw how her staff monitors the newsfeeds— Nineteen Adze *pays attention,* that's the first thing in her Ministry briefing file."

Mahit caught her eyes, shoving away an entirely inappropriate impulse to reach out for her. "Three Seagrass," she said, knowing she needed to find out how far Three Seagrass was prepared to go for her, if they set out down this trajectory, "how wide is the Teixcalaanli definition of 'we'? You don't even know what I need to tell His Brilliance. Are we a 'we,' here?"

"I'm your liaison, Mahit," Three Seagrass said. She almost sounded hurt. "Haven't I made that clear enough?"

"This is more than you opening doors for me," Mahit told her. "This is my goals in your words, on the public newsfeeds, in the public memory of Teixcalaan, *forever.*"

"Sometimes I swear you could be one of us," Three Seagrass said, quite softly. She smiled a tremulous but creditable Stationer-smile, all her teeth visible. "Now, help me write this, won't you? I know you have at least a *rudimentary* sense of scansion, and we need to get this done before Thirty Larkspur's man-on-the-spot remembers we have cloudhooks." Then she *did* reach out to touch Mahit, her fingertips like a ghost, brushing over her cheekbone. Mahit shivered helplessly, and went very still: like she was waiting for a blow.

"*Reed,*" Twelve Azalea said, theatrically scandalized, "flirt on your own time."

Mahit wished she wasn't pale enough that blushing was visible on her cheeks; telltale scarlet flushes, and the heat burning there. "We're not," she said. "Flirting. We're discussing strategies—"

<You have been flirting with her since the morning you met,> Yskandr commented, and Mahit wished profoundly that she could get him to shut up. At least when he'd been defective he hadn't been able to be so . . . *revelatory,* in his commentary.

"We're *writing poetry,*" Three Seagrass said, and managed, by maintaining an expression of perfect serenity, to make the activity sound profoundly intimate.

<And she has been flirting back,> Yskandr went on. <When you're not in the middle of a coup attempt, you might want to do something about that.>

———

Mahit had written poetry in Teixcalaanli before: she'd written it alone in her capsule room on Lsel, scribbling in notebooks at age seventeen, pretending she could imitate Pseudo-Thirteen River or One Skyhook or any of the other great poets; framing her own unformed ideas in language that didn't belong to her twice over: she was too barbarian, and too *young.* Now, sitting with her head bent next to Three Seagrass's, adjusting scansion and carefully selecting which classical allusions to foreground, she thought: *Poetry is for the desperate, and for people who have grown old enough to have something to say.*

Grown old enough, or lived through enough incomprehensible experiences. Perhaps she was old enough for poetry now: she had three lives inside her, and a death. When she wasn't careful she remembered that death too *much,* her breath coming shorter and shorter until she reminded Yskandr that he was neither dying now nor in charge of her autonomic nervous system.

Three Seagrass, for her part, composed verse like putting on a tailored suit jacket—a process she knew how to make look good, that made her look good in return. Her mental library of glyphs and allusions was vast, and Mahit envied it viciously: if only *she'd* been raised here, had spent her whole life immersed, she could turn phrases from pedestrian to resonant in a minute's work, too.

The poem they'd come up with was not long. It couldn't be— it needed to move quickly through the open newsfeeds, be quotable and express itself clearly: clearly to the populace, and then in a more nuanced, layered fashion to Nineteen Adze and her staff. Mahit had begun it with an image she knew Five Agate would recognize: Five Agate had *been* there. And Five Agate, clever and loyal and trained in interpretation, would know how desperate Mahit truly was—and tell her *ezuazuacat* everything.

> *In the soft hands of a child*
> *even a map of the stars can withstand*
> *forces that pull and crack. Gravity persists.*
> *Continuity persists: uncalloused fingers walk orbital paths,*
>   *but I am drowning*
> *in a sea of flowers; in violet foam, in the fog of war—*

Two Cartograph, in the library at dawn with his mother, playing with a map of a star system. The first signal: *You know who I am, Five Agate: I am Mahit Dzmare, who understood your love for your son, and for your mistress.* The second: *I am under threat, and the threat is from Thirty Larkspur: flowers, violet foam.*

"Fog of war" was hardly an allusion. That was more of an inevitable and presently occurring truth, and besides, it fit Three Seagrass's scansion scheme.

The rest of it was brief: an ekphrasis of the Information Ministry building, all of its architecture described in detail, imagined with garlands of larkspurs thrown over it like a funeral—*that* was an allusion to a section of *The Buildings*—to tell Nineteen Adze where they were; and then a promise, in a single couplet:

> *Released, my tongue will speak visions.*
> *Released, I am a spear in the hands of the sun.*

Come rescue us, Nineteen Adze. Come rescue us, and help us preserve the sun-spear throne in its correct and proper orbit.

Mahit looked over the poem one last time. It wasn't bad. To her eyes—and she knew she was untrained—it looked *good*, looked effective *and* elegant. "Send it," she said to Three Seagrass. "I don't think we're going to do better in this limited amount of time."

"I'd send it *now*," Twelve Azalea added. "I've been watching the newsfeeds while you've been working. This is getting very bad, very quickly—One Lightning's legions are shooting at the customs officials, claiming that the people need them in the City proper, to quell the rioting. I don't know who is going to stop them—how do we stop a *legion*? Our legions are unstoppable."

"It's sent," Three Seagrass said. "Under my byline, on every open feed I can find, and a few of the closed ones—the poetry circles, one of the Information Ministry internal memo feeds—"

"Is that a good idea?" Mahit asked. "Thirty Larkspur's people are reading that one, I'm almost sure."

"Thirty Larkspur's people will be monitoring our cloudhooks for *any* messages, if they're even the slightest bit good at their jobs," Three Seagrass said. "*I* would have confiscated them first thing."

"How useful that you're on our side and not theirs, then," Mahit told her, and found herself smiling despite everything.

"How long do you think we have?" Twelve Azalea asked.

"Before the legions storm the palace or before we no longer have a broadcast platform?" Three Seagrass inquired, all too cheerfully. "Stop watching the news, Petal, and come see how this poem spreads while I've still got access."

She unhooked her cloudhook from its customary position over her right eye and put it on the conference table in front of them, changing its settings so that it acted as a very small info-screen projector. Mahit watched the poem they'd written spread through the information network of Teixcalaan—shared from cloudhook to cloudhook, reposted and recontextualized, like watching ink spreading in water.

"How much longer?" she asked softly.

"I'd guess three minutes—this is moving *quickly*—" Three Seagrass said, and then the door of the conference room flew open with a bang. Six Helicopter stood there, and behind him were two more people—but his companions were dressed in Information Ministry cream and orange. Three Seagrass bowed over her fingertips at them.

"How lovely to see you, Three Lamplight, Eight Penknife," she said. "How is your afternoon of being suborned by a non-ministry politician going?"

Helplessly, Mahit broke into laughter, even as Three Lamplight and Eight Penknife wordlessly took both Twelve Azalea's and Three Seagrass's cloudhooks and handed them to Six Helicopter.

"You realize," he was saying, "that what you just did—sending unauthorized political poetry on the public feeds—might be construed as *treasonous*? Particularly considering where you were picked up and how Belltown Six is *full* of anti-imperial protestors this morning, not to mention the *rest* of the mess in the City?"

"Take it up with the Judiciary," said Twelve Azalea. Mahit was *proud* of him. They were all going to die, or . . . *something* and yet—they were a *we*. By whatever language's definition.

"I have written political poetry appropriate to the current moment of my experience," said Three Seagrass. "If that's treason, take it up with our two thousand years of *canon*. I'm sure you'll find more treason there."

Six Helicopter tried not to sputter; failed. With his hands full of cloudhooks, he couldn't gesture properly, but Mahit could see in the tension of his shoulders and his jaw how much he wanted to wave his hands, or *shake* Three Seagrass, who sat serene, with her chin cupped in her palms, elbows on the table.

"I am arresting you," he said finally. "I am . . . directing these Information Ministry officials to detain you, as acting representative of acting Minister Thirty Larkspur."

"Bloody *stars*," Twelve Azalea said, ignoring Six Helicopter in favor of Three Lamplight, who had visibly winced. "Are you two really going to do that?"

"If you attempt to leave you'll be stopped," Three Lamplight said. "That much I guarantee."

Eight Penknife added, "And your privileges as *asekretim* are revoked until they might be reviewed by whoever becomes Minister next—"

"I'm terribly disappointed in you, Eight Penknife," said Three Seagrass with an exquisite little sigh. "You were always such a *partisan* of Two Rosewood's policies—"

"Enough," Six Helicopter snapped. "We have work to do. You do not. *Asekretim.* Ambassador." He turned smartly on his heel and left, his Information Ministry loyalists following at his heels. They were alone in the conference room again, with nothing to do, nothing to see—blinded without the cloudhooks and their newsfeeds, confined in windowless fluorescent lighting. Even the carafe of coffee was empty.

Mahit looked at Three Seagrass, and at Twelve Azalea, one on either side of her. "And now," she said, with far more confidence than she felt, "we wait."

———

The waiting was not pleasant. Mahit had the sense of being inside a sealed capsule, protected from radiation and decay, but tumbling over and over in free space—with no guarantee that there would *be* an outside world to come back to once the capsule was cracked open. There was nothing to see in the Information Ministry's conference room; no noise from outside, no shouting of soldiers or marching of booted legionary feet. No flooded City streets glittering with the helmets of the Sunlit or a carpet of purple flowers . . .

Three Seagrass had put her head down on the folded platform of her forearms on the table. Mahit didn't know if she was napping, or just trying to not *think*. Either way, she envied her. Not thinking was the province of other people. Not thinking was impossible, and she rather wanted to claw her own skin off. She kept imagining all of the reasons that Nineteen Adze, *ezuazua-cat* or not, wouldn't challenge Thirty Larkspur for the sake of one Lsel ambassador. The worst of those possibilities was that she and Thirty Larkspur were already allies and she'd merely go along with his decisions about the Information Ministry. The second worst would be if Nineteen Adze had weighed the balance of power, seen that challenging Thirty Larkspur had no chance of success, and opted to stay quiet and ride out the coup, no matter *who* won . . .

She probably wouldn't do that second thing. It didn't seem *like* her. That certainty bubbled up in Mahit like a warm tide: not entirely hers, but a composite of Yskandr's memories and her own, making an evaluation.

"I feel like someone's cut off my hands," Twelve Azalea said, into the dull silence. "I keep reaching for the newsfeeds and they're not *there,* there's only me, not the whole Empire ready at a touch."

<It is lonely, being Teixcalaanlitzlim and without all of Teixcalaan,> Yskandr whispered to Mahit. <It is the one thing I do not envy, without a shred of regret.>

We're never alone, Mahit thought. *You and I. Never again in this life.*

<Or the next.>

If there's a Teixcalaanli ambassador after me.

<If there's a Teixcalaanli ambassador after you, and our imago-line is worth preserving for them.>

Mahit hoped, a small leaden heated ball in the pit of her stomach, that it would be. That something of this week, of her, of her and Yskandr together, would not go to waste. That what she *knew,* now—the external threat to Teixcalaan that she carried in her mind like her very own poison flower, the coordinates of massing alien ships—enough of an *external threat* to cancel any war of annexation—that it would not die with her and Yskandr. Be silenced with her and Yskandr.

Nevertheless she hated the waiting. She could so easily imagine what was going on outside—a hundred different versions of it, assembled from epic poetry and terrible film and the contraband documentary footage of Teixcalaanli annexation wars on planets on the edge of known space. It wouldn't be different here in the heart of the Empire, once they started shooting. It wouldn't be different at *all*. That was the problem. Empire was empire—the part that seduced and the part that clamped down, jaws like a vise, and shook a planet until its neck was broken and it died.

———

The first Mahit knew of the end of that long terrible abeyance of time, drifting formless in the blank, unchanging light of the conference room, was a commotion down the hallway— shouting voices, the sound of a door slamming. A pause, and then a great clatter, as if everything on a desk had been swept onto the floor.

"—do you think?" Three Seagrass was saying, getting to her feet.

"Even if it's not for us, it's *something*," Mahit said. "Something is better than waiting. Let's go see."

"We're arrested," Twelve Azalea mentioned, off-hand reminder. "But—fuck it. Let's unarrest ourselves."

Mahit laughed. Inside her skull, behind the endless ache of the surgical site and the pulse of her blood in her damaged hand, the shimmer of damaged nerves and the endless sour ache in her hip, she almost felt *good*.

<Adrenaline is a *hell* of a drug, Mahit,> Yskandr said. <Let's take advantage while we can.>

Outside the conference room—they hadn't even *locked* it, which felt simultaneously insulting and like Mahit had been a willing participant in her own incarceration, a tiny flare of guilt—and halfway down the hallway leading to the exit, there was a central information desk, staffed by what looked like Three Lamplight, by the height and the haircut. It was this desk whose contents had just been pitched onto the floor, a scatter of infofiche sticks and office paraphernalia, and the destroyer of this small harmony—resplendent in white, and *oh*, Mahit would never get over how much she loved the symbolic valence of everything the Teixcalaanlitzlim did, however utterly contrived, white because it was Nineteen Adze's signature—was Five Agate, Nineteen Adze's best aide and favored student. Her plain face was serene and cold, and she carried in her hand a shock-stick: a slim metal rod, crackling with electric energy. Behind her was another Teixcalaanlitzlim in pure white who Mahit had not seen before, and he carried the same weaponry.

It was a cavalry, of sorts. A cavalry in *livery*, not a single pur-ple spray of flowers amongst them. And it was specifically Five Agate come to find them, which meant that Nineteen Adze might have understood what Mahit and Three Seagrass had been trying to say with their poetry—

"I see them now," Five Agate said, her voice sharp and ring-ing. "Those three. Come over here, Ambassador—the *ezuazua-cat* Nineteen Adze recognizes that your claim of sanctuary with her has not ended."

"They never claimed formal sanctuary," Three Lamplight began, "that won't stand up for a moment in the Judiciary."

"Neither will Thirty Larkspur's palace intrigue," Five Agate snapped, "so we're even. I don't want to cause an *incident*. Let them come here."

Mahit began walking down the corridor, Three Seagrass and Twelve Azalea flanking her. For a moment she thought that they would make it, that they would be safe in Five Agate's hands with absolutely no problems, Nineteen Adze's soft power unsheathed—

—and then Six Helicopter burst out of an office behind them, farther down the hall back the way they'd come. Mahit stopped dead, turned to stare at him. Instead of a shockstick like Five

Agate's, in his hand was what Mahit recognized, with icy horror, as a *projectile weapon*—outlawed on Lsel, those things could cause hull-breach—and he was shouting. Mahit froze, trapped between Six Helicopter and Five Agate, mid-escape.

"Don't you fucking dare—like fuck you jumped-up demagogues are going to get to do whatever you want, there's *legions in the streets, you can't do this anymore*—you have got to *listen to law and order!"*

Inside the horror, Mahit almost found it ridiculous: this petty little man, so angry at losing what little power he'd managed to acquire.

Calmly, Five Agate raised her shockstick, blue-green energy crackling at its end, and began to walk toward Six Helicopter.

The report of the projectile weapon going off was louder than any noise Mahit could remember. There was a scream to her left, short and sharp—and then more bangs, a series of them in a row. She was running down the hallway toward Five Agate without having decided to run, all of her paralysis broken. Three Lamplight had ducked out of view behind the desk, and Five Agate's support staff was advancing past it, his shockstick glittering.

Another shot, and a bloom of red on Five Agate's upper arm, spreading in threads, the red pooling in the white of her tunic, her face gone ice-pale. The sound of her shockstick hitting the floor, *crackling* electricity. Mahit kept running. She reached where Five Agate was—still standing in perfect serenity, as if in shock—grabbed for her other arm, the one that wasn't bleeding, and pulled her after her.

How many projectiles are in that thing?

<Enough.> Yskandr, in her mind, a tight presence. <Enough to kill you. Keep running. Don't look back—>

Mahit looked back.

Three Seagrass was on her heels, right at her shoulder as she *always was,* but Twelve Azalea was not—was a tumbled pile in the hallway, unmoving, bright blood pooling around him.

Five Agate's white-clad attendant shoved his shockstick directly against Six Helicopter's open mouth. Blue fire went through his skull. There was another report from the projectile weapon—a hole opened up in the attendant's gut like the staring eye of a singularity—

"Run!" Three Seagrass screamed, and so Mahit did. She ran, one hand clenched around Five Agate's arm, until she had run right out of the Information Ministry and into the street.

CHAPTER
NINETEEN

Stillness and patience create safety
the Jewel of the World preserves itself.
Torn-up flowers die in unskilled hands
and perverse gardeners flourish
exclaiming on the merits of barren pools.

　　—poem attributed to Five Diadem, later in use as a public
　　　safety message throughout the Imperium

*　*　*

If these legionary warships destroy us, I will have you unseated
in whatever government replaces the fifteen generations of our
Council. You and Amnardbat both. The appeaser and the isola-
tionist. I will have you unseated and your imago-lines destroyed.

　　—note signed *D.O.*, hand-delivered to the offices of Darj
　　　Tarats, 251.3.11-6D

FIVE Agate shook Mahit's hand off her, shook her whole body
in a sharp shudder of adjustment. The blood from her shoulder
was still spreading, red tendrils down her white sleeve. "There
isn't time," she said, which didn't make much sense to Mahit.
Nothing was making a great deal of sense.

"—I have to go get him," Three Seagrass was saying, "he's
dying in there—"

"There isn't *time*," Five Agate repeated, and now Mahit

understood: Twelve Azalea in the pool of spreading blood. Twelve Azalea, her friend. Three Seagrass's friend.

Her chest felt narrow and hot, as if it was her who had been hit by a projectile weapon; like she *was* a projectile, about to shatter apart.

"I don't care about *time*," Three Seagrass said.

"And I don't know how many other projectile-spewing illegal weapons are inside the Ministry," Five Agate spat—Mahit could hardly reconcile this woman with the efficient, quiet aide-de-camp from Nineteen Adze's office. "Nor how many of Thirty Larkspur's partisan hacks were *also* waiting for the moment they could happily *shoot someone*—fuck my shoulder hurts and I'm sorry about your friend—I'm sorrier about Twenty-Two Graphite, fucking *starlight* I'm sorry—but you called for help— they're *singing* that goddamn verse in the street—so *come on and let's get out of here like you wanted.*"

"They're singing?" Mahit asked helplessly.

"The ones who aren't shouting *UP ONE LIGHTNING* at the top of their lungs, yes," Five Agate said, and stalked down the plaza.

Mahit took Three Seagrass's hand in hers. The palm was slick and clammy with sweat. They followed. Five Agate moved at a rapid clip, her shoulder stiff and held high, not even trying to disguise the active bleeding. There didn't seem to be immediate pursuit—perhaps Six Helicopter was dying on the ground next to Twelve Azalea, and oh, that hurt to think, Twelve Azalea deserved better than this—to distract herself, Mahit tried to track where they were headed. She thought she knew the way to Nineteen Adze's offices but everything looked *different* in the full light of day, and the last time she'd come, she'd come in a groundcar escorted by the Sunlit.

The sky was that impossible blue again. An endlessness, bound only by the faint strictures of buildings marring the horizon. Mahit could fall right off the face of the planet. She squeezed Three Seagrass's hand. There wasn't any response.

As they turned the corner, heading away from the central plaza of Palace-East and toward the series of buildings that Mahit thought probably contained Nineteen Adze's offices—the flicker of rose-colored marble was surely where they needed to be—they nearly ran into a platoon of Sunlit. They had appeared like an eclipse: there, abruptly, blocking out the light, twenty faceless people in gold helmets.

"Hold there," said one of them. She wasn't sure which. They all had the same voice. Five Agate drew to a halt. Her chest was heaving.

"You are injured," said a different Sunlit; one of the closer ones, from the volume of their voice. "It is dangerous to be outside; the Emperor has called for a curfew of citizens. Are you attempting to reach a hospital?"

"I—" Five Agate began, "I am attempting to return home— I work for the *ezuazuacat* Nineteen Adze—"

"It is imperative that you not be in the streets," said a third Sunlit.

"The curfew is enforceable by whatever means we deem appropriate," a fourth added—and all twenty Sunlit moved forward toward them together, like automata.

Is personal or institutional violence more threatening?

And then: *Can I fool the algorithm?*

She took a step forward. Voice shaking, she broke in: "We have been shot at." She tried for hysteria—and relied on Yskandr's inherent knowledge to pitch her voice to *accentless* Teixcalaanli. Just for this one moment, let her not be an obvious barbarian. "We were in the Information Ministry—it's been *taken over,* by *mad people*—we—it's horrible, my friend is probably *dead*—"

On cue, Three Seagrass burst into tears. They looked genuine to Mahit. They probably *were* genuine—just held in abeyance until this moment, when they would be useful.

The Sunlit closest to them spoke again, a little softer. "What sort of mad people?" they asked. "Please, citizens, give us information."

"The man who shot my friend," Three Seagrass said, through the tears running down her face, "worked for Thirty Larkspur—he said they'd taken the Ministry because the Minister was compromised—" She wiped at her nose, her eyes. "Forgive me, I'm not like this normally. I'm really not."

"Compromised *how?*" inquired two Sunlit at once; and then a third, repeating it, like an echo rippling through an AI, the algorithm adjusting itself: "Compromised *how?*"

"I don't know," Mahit said, lying through her teeth. "Just—compromised—maybe the Minister liked the *yaotlek's* policies? It's so confusing—and they *shot at us*—"

The whole platoon seemed to turn at once toward them, focusing down: a drift of iron filings drawn into formation by a passing magnet. All their hands were still on their shocksticks. Mahit waited for the blow; for the inevitable weight of institutional violence in the form of electricity, the mobile part of the City's grid attacking her like the still part had attacked Three Seagrass days ago—but if this *worked*, if they could send this platoon *away* from them to intercept whatever might come *out* of the Information Ministry in pursuit—then it would be worth the risk.

"Can we go inside?" Five Agate said. "I don't want to disobey an imperial curfew. My son is inside—I just want to go home—it's right over there." She gestured with her good arm toward the building Mahit assumed was where Nineteen Adze's offices were, or close enough to it.

That, at last, seemed to be enough. One of the Sunlit on the edge of the platoon detached themselves, took a few steps away from the rest. "Go," they said. "We will investigate the situation at the Ministry. One of us will escort you." Once separated from the group, the individual Sunlit almost seemed like a person. Mahit wanted so badly to know how a Teixcalaanlitzlim *became* one of them.

<If you find out,> Yskandr told her, <you'd be doing one better than I ever did.>

The rest of the platoon moved fluidly along the path that the three of them had taken out of the plaza. Mahit imagined, vividly, that they were following the scent of Five Agate's spilled blood, a hunt in reverse.

The remaining Sunlit waved one hand, and the three of them—Mahit still holding Three Seagrass's hand, Three Seagrass still weeping uncontrollably—followed that gesture onward: and in this fashion Mahit came to the door of Nineteen Adze's offices under police escort a second time.

Ring composition, she thought. *Around we go.* And came back once again to that improbable piece of information: they were singing her verses in the streets?

<Nothing is untouched,> Yskandr murmured—the young Yskandr, *hers,* that familiar flickering static-bright voice. <Nothing you make is unmarked by Teixcalaan. Even *I* learned that.>

Nineteen Adze had turned her front office into a war room. She stood—as she had before—in the center of a vast sea of holograph projections, arcs upon arcs of them; but what had been an orderly information-gathering enterprise was now populated by a group of exhausted-looking young men and women, trading images back and forth with gestures, writing—by hand, on *paper*—notes, talking in rapid low voices through their cloudhooks to people somewhere else.

In the middle of the chaos, Nineteen Adze was a pillar of

white, still immaculate, though the dark skin of her cheeks had gone grey under the eyes, and the eyes themselves were reddened. Mahit's first thought was that she had been crying, and hadn't slept at all—wondered how much of the rush of concerned sympathy was hers and how much was Yskandr's. Decided that didn't matter, just as Nineteen Adze caught sight of them, dismissed the cloud of projections around her head with one sharp gesture, and went right to Five Agate.

"You're hurt," she said, taking both of Five Agate's hands in hers.

"—a little," Five Agate said, and Mahit could see in her face: she would have walked right back into Six Helicopter's line of fire, for just this moment with the *ezuazuacat* she served. "It doesn't matter, really. I lost Twenty-Two Graphite—"

"You both volunteered. He knew as well as you what might happen. Go into the back," Nineteen Adze said, with that same stunning, strange gentleness she had turned on Mahit in the bathroom after the incident with the flower. "You've done so well. You did what I asked. Sit down, drink water, we'll get the *ixplanatl* in to look at your arm."

You've done so well. Even in the face of losing one of her people, Nineteen Adze could provide comfort to the remaining ones. The ache in Mahit's throat couldn't be hers alone. Yskandr would have wanted to hear that, wouldn't he? Especially from her— (a sharp flicker of what Nineteen Adze had looked like naked, ten years ago, and Mahit didn't even feel *lust* so much as *desire*, wanting to touch, to *be with*).

<No,> Yskandr told her. <I wanted her to *agree with me.* You want her to look at you like you've been righteous.>

". . . what a prize you are, Mahit Dzmare," said Nineteen Adze then. "What a price I am apparently willing to pay for you. Did you write that poem all by yourself?"

"Three Seagrass wrote most of it," Mahit said. She was still holding Three Seagrass's hand, and now, her liaison squeezed her fingers.

"My dear *asekreta*. Eloquent as always."

Three Seagrass made a terrible choked little noise, and said, "Your Excellency, please do not call me eloquent when I am covered in *snot*."

Nineteen Adze looked like she was trying to laugh and had forgotten how; mirth had abandoned her entirely. Instead she shrugged, with a peculiar half smile, and said, *"Released, I am a spear in the hands of the sun.* It's *catchy.* Go sit down, will you? I have to decide what to *do* with you."

"I need to speak to His Brilliance," Mahit said. "That's what you should do with me. After that you can do whatever you want."

She walked over to the couch—the same one she had sat on the first time she'd been interrogated by Nineteen Adze. Thought again, *Ring composition.* Her legs felt like water. They spilled her down onto the cushions. Three Seagrass came with her, a satellite in orbit; when she sat next to Mahit, their thighs touched. Mahit wished she had a handkerchief to offer her, to clean up her face, get some of the tears gone. Give her back some modicum of dignity, which was in fairly short supply just now.

Nineteen Adze watched them go; watched them sit. She seemed, for a long and awful moment, *rudderless*—all of her direction and drive sapped. Then she straightened from the top of her head, her spine a long arc, and strode across the office to stand in front of them both.

"I can't just walk you in to him," she said. "He's under guard. And he's not well. You know that, Mahit."

"He hasn't been well for a long time," Mahit said. "Which *you* know. And he knows, and *Yskandr knows*."

"Knows?" asked Nineteen Adze, tilting her head fractionally to the side.

"Knew. It's . . . complicated. More so now. I—Nineteen Adze, Your Excellency, the last time I was here I told you truly that you could not speak to him, since he was *gone*, no matter what he or my government had intended; now I can just as truly say differently. I've—we're—it's a long story and involved surgical intervention and I have the worst headache of my life and *hello—I've missed you*—"

Stepping back; letting that part of her that was Yskandr take, for just a moment, the muscles of her face, shape them to his broader smile, the way his eyes had crinkled up at the corners in smile-lines that her younger skin hadn't had time to develop.

A mobile flush swept across Nineteen Adze's face, like forged metal glowing and going out again.

"Why would I believe you now?" she said, but Mahit already knew she did.

"You killed me," she said, Yskandr said. They said. "Or you let Ten Pearl do it and didn't stop him, and that's much the same. But I miss you anyway."

The breath Nineteen Adze took was huge, dragged through her lungs, a resettling gasp barely controlled. She sat down on the opposite couch, carefully, folding like she thought she might fall if she didn't. "I assume you want to talk about it—you always *did* want to talk about decisions—"

"Maybe," said Yskandr in Mahit's mouth, and she had not known he could be so gentle, "after this is over. We hardly have time, do we, my dear?"

"We do not," said Nineteen Adze. She took another one of those enormous breaths. "Be Mahit again; I had not quite imagined how disturbing this would be. Your *expressions*. You're like a ghost."

"Really it's the wrong analogy," Mahit said, "ghosts—"

<Hush,> Yskandr told her. <She doesn't need that right now.>

And you were accusing me of flirting—

<We have an empire to preserve, Mahit.>

Oh, is that what we're doing? I thought we were saving our Station from being annexed—

This kind of back-and-forth talk wasn't good for them, Mahit knew. She felt nauseated, the headache gathering in her temples, and both Nineteen Adze and Three Seagrass were looking at her like she had quite gently slipped off an edge into a great pool of insanity.

"I have information," she said, trying to pull herself together, be Mahit-who-was-once-Yskandr and not a terrible hybrid of both of them, "which I have obtained at great personal cost to myself and possibly to my people on Lsel Station, which *needs the ear of His Brilliance* right now. I have been trying to get back to him. I've been detained, my friend has been shot and is probably dead, I have had to negotiate with Sunlit—you seemed like my *only* possibility of getting close—"

Nineteen Adze cursed softly. "Please accept my deep condolences about your friend. I hope he is in better shape than you fear."

Mahit remembered the spreading pool of blood around Twelve Azalea, how *much* of it there had been, how arterial-bright, and thought: *Hope is insufficient.*

"So do I," she said. "He is . . . he has been more generous to me than a barbarian would expect of anyone."

Three Seagrass made a peculiar noise, something caught between a snicker and a sob. "What he's done is got himself killed for you, Mahit," she said. "If he hadn't been *my* friend he'd never have gotten himself into this mess at all."

With the wave of a hand, Nineteen Adze summoned one of her aides; the young man materialized by the couches as if he himself was a hologram. (He was not Seven Scale, who had disposed of the poison flower. Who might have *brought* the poison flower. Mahit needed to ask about him, about everything that had happened that night, about *why Nineteen Adze had tried so hard to save her life*.)

"Would you get the *asekreta* a glass of water and a handkerchief," Nineteen Adze asked the aide, "and bring all of us some brandy; I think we will need it."

He vanished as swiftly as he'd appeared. Nineteen Adze nodded, as if confirming something to herself, and said, "If—and I do mean *if,* Mahit Dzmare—I am to bring you to His Brilliance in this time of absolute unrest and uncertainty, risking my own position and possibly my life to do it, you had better tell me what you are planning to tell him. In the same amount of detail. It has to be *worth it,* Ambassador. More worth it than an immortality machine which makes ghosts and double-persons out of your oldest friends."

At that moment, the aide returned with a tray bearing three glasses of dark copper spirits and one of water, and Mahit had never been more glad to see alcohol in her life. She picked up the nearest glass. The spirit clung to the sides when she swirled it, a viscous oilslick shimmer.

"Please, Three Seagrass, tell me this won't taste like violets."

Three Seagrass, gulping water like she'd been dehydrated for hours—she *had* been, Mahit realized, she'd been crying and running at the same time—put her glass back down, took an appraising look at the brandy, and said, bone-dry: "That will taste like fire and blood and the smell of soil turned over in the spring after a rainstorm, if it's what I think it is—are you trying to get us drunk, Your Excellency? I promise I don't need much help at this point."

"I wanted," said Nineteen Adze, "to be civilized for a moment." She picked up her glass, raised it in a small and silent toast. "Drink."

Mahit drank. *To living through the next twelve hours,* she thought as the liquid slipped down her throat, bright and hot and rich; plasma fire and soil burning. A peculiar type of petrichor. *To Lsel Station remaining Lsel Station.*

<To us,> Yskandr whispered, somewhere she could barely feel. An upswelling of emotion more than a voice. <And civilization, if that is something that remains.>

Mahit put the glass down. She felt warm all through. It would work as a substitute for courage.

"All right, Your Excellency. I will tell you. But first I would very much appreciate if you would explain why you kept *me* alive, and not my predecessor. I need to know if I trust you because I *have* to—and I do trust you, but I am compelled by lack of other options—or if I might trust you because I want to."

"Which of you is asking?" Nineteen Adze asked. She'd drunk her brandy like a shot, all of it at once.

"It's not a good question, Nineteen Adze. *I'm* asking." Mahit did not specify further.

She sighed. Folded her hands in her lap, dark against the bone-white suit. "Two reasons," she began. "First: you—*were*—not Yskandr Aghavn. And what you wanted was not what he'd wanted; he wanted to give Six Direction what I can only understand, after a great deal of questioning and research and thinking, as an immortality machine—a machine that would put my friend, my lord, my *Emperor* in the body of a child, make him into something that was—not even human, and might do him irreparable harm. Might do *all* of us irreparable harm, with that child on the sun-spear throne."

Mahit nodded. "I did not come here to trade imago-machines for my station's freedom, no." They were reversed; she realized quite suddenly that *she* was leading this interrogation. That it was an interrogation. Or a negotiation.

<They're the same species of thing.>

"What was the second reason?" Mahit went on.

"I couldn't do it twice," Nineteen Adze said. "I couldn't—
watch it twice. I'm not a squeamish person, Ambassador, I've led
my share of planetary conquests. But you were *enough* my friend,
even if you weren't sufficiently him to want what he wanted.
And you hadn't done anything yet worth that death. It would
have been very painful."

Mahit felt like it was she who was being exposed, carved
open, all nerves hypersensitive to the air like they'd been on
Five Portico's surgery table, even though the person who was
talking wasn't her at all.

"Who sent me the flower?" she asked. Distantly, she registered that Three Seagrass had put her hand on the small of her
back; a kind pressure.

"It was a gift," said Nineteen Adze, "from the household of
my fellow *ezuazuacat* Thirty Larkspur to my household. What
I did with it was of course up to me."

Which meant—which meant that Nineteen Adze had *first*
decided that Mahit should die, and watched her nearly breathe
in the poison of that flower, and then changed her mind *while
watching*. Which meant that Thirty Larkspur had *dared* Nineteen Adze to get rid of the new Lsel Ambassador like she'd
allowed the old one to be gotten rid of.

Thirty Larkspur didn't want *Yskandr* dead; that had been Ten
Pearl, and perhaps also Nineteen Adze. Thirty Larkspur hadn't
cared about Yskandr. Thirty Larkspur wanted *Mahit* dead, and
thought that Nineteen Adze, who had helped dispose of one Lsel
Ambassador, might do it again.

He'd decided Mahit was too dangerous to have around—he'd
probably decided that *anyone* who could give Six Direction an
imago-machine was too dangerous to have around. An imago-
machine, especially as imagined by a Teixcalaanlitzlim, an *immortality* machine, would mean Six Direction on the throne
forever. Thirty Larkspur would never be able to use this moment

of political unrest to dismantle the tripartite association of imperial successors and claim the throne entirely for himself—that *was* what he was doing, she couldn't interpret how he'd taken over Information in any other way—if Six Direction was still Emperor. It wouldn't matter that some jumped-up *yaotlek* was trying to acclaim himself the rightful star-blessed ruler. The moment Thirty Larkspur needed would be *gone*, if Six Direction had access to an imago-machine.

She was abruptly astonished that they'd escaped the Information Ministry at all, and blamed that fragile success entirely on Six Helicopter being a power-drunk politician and not the sort of person who actually asked his boss what to do next.

"One last question," said Mahit, "and then we can go on. How many people in His Brilliance's government knew you allowed Yskandr to be killed?"

Nineteen Adze's smile was Lsel-style, and small; a quirk of the mouth that made Mahit want to mirror it with the patterns of Yskandr's own smiling. (They'd liked each other so *much*. The endocrine response activated even after confession to murder.) "Everyone who mattered," Nineteen Adze said. "Including His Brilliance; I think he is still very angry with me, though he understands why. He always does understand why I do things."

Mahit remembered the fever-dream of Yskandr and Nineteen Adze in bed: Yskandr saying *I love him, I shouldn't but I do,* and Nineteen Adze telling him *So do I.*

So do I, and then *I hope I still will when he's not himself any longer.* No danger of that anymore. His Brilliance would be himself. There were no more imago-machines on Teixcalaan save the one inside Mahit's skull—and the one she'd given to an anti-imperial activist medic.

She'd think about *that* later. It was out of her hands.

Three Seagrass was staring at the *ezuazuacat* as if she'd grown a second head or another pair of arms. "I am terrified of you, Your Excellency," she said, using the word for "terror" which, in poetry, could also mean "awed." The sort of adjective that was applied to atrocities or divine miracles. Or emperors, which Mahit assumed were in many ways both at once.

"The perils," said Nineteen Adze ruefully, "of getting to know someone." She looked at her brandy glass, as if she wanted to drink the empty air there. Shut her eyes for a moment. The lids were grey with the faint tracery of visible veins. "Now. Enough of this. Tell me what you want to tell my Emperor."

Mahit framed what she was about to say before she actually said it: tried to say it simply and directly, without pretense or insinuation. The facts. (The politics would come *after* the facts; would devolve from the nature of the facts, as politics tended to do.) "The Lsel Councilor for the Miners has sent me—under multiple layers of encryption—the locations of increased, threatening, and pernicious alien activity—the sort of activity that presages a conquest—in both our quadrant of local space and two others. The aliens are of a sort unknown to us, and we have not established communication. They are hostile. Both we on Lsel Station and you in all the vast starfield of Teixcalaan are in considerable danger."

Nineteen Adze clicked her teeth together and made a small, inquisitive noise. "And *why* did the Lsel Councilor for the Miners want you to know this information?" she asked.

"I believe," Mahit said carefully, "that Darj Tarats would prefer the beast we know, the empire we have negotiated with for generations, than a force beyond our control in Lsel space."

"That's why he wants you to *tell us*," Nineteen Adze said. "I'm asking why he wanted you to know."

What she was asking was closer to *By what method did Darj Tarats think you could use this information to influence us?* Mahit leaned back against Three Seagrass's hand. Her eyelids felt heavy; her tongue was still a little brandy-numbed. "I wouldn't have figured it out," she said conversationally, "if there hadn't been all those newspaper articles a few days ago about Eight Loop."

"Go on," said Nineteen Adze.

"The ones where she was questioning the legality of the annexation war," Three Seagrass said, sudden and bright: she'd gotten it. Of course she had.

Mahit nodded. "The ones where she was questioning the legality of the annexation war *because the borders of Teixcalaan are not secure*," she said. "She could have meant just that . . . business you all are having, in Odile. I think that's what she meant, when she said it. But *I* know—an actual alien threat is worse than some internal insurrection. If the borders of the Empire are not secure, an annexation war cannot legally be justified, and even a strong emperor at the height of his powers might be overruled by council and ministers and *ezuazuacatlim*. And now, with this information, I can prove that there is an active threat to the borders of Teixcalaan. We are *all* in danger from these aliens. And the Councilor for the Miners would like me to use this loophole in Teixcalaanli law to get the Empire to leave my homeland alone. No secure borders, thus no annexation war, and Lsel remains independent. That's simple language, *ezuazuacat*. I'm being as clear with you as I can be. As I know how to be."

It left out entirely whether or not Aknel Amnardbat had tried to sabotage her, and why. That wasn't for Teixcalaan, Mahit thought. That was for Lsel. For her and Yskandr to think about together, if they lived through this week. She could keep that one thing for herself, in this terrible burst of confession. If she mentioned it now she'd destroy her own credibility. Besides— Amnardbat couldn't have known Yskandr was *dead* when she'd sabotaged her. It should have been Yskandr all along, doing what she was doing, carrying this message to Nineteen Adze, a last-ditch effort to save Lsel from annexation.

<I wish I could ask her what she was thinking, doing this to us,> Yskandr murmured, and the bright flash which was all that was left of the *other* Yskandr raced down Mahit's arms like a static charge.

You and me both, Mahit thought. *When she spoke to me she said we were a perfect match: we understood Teixcalaan. I thought it was a compliment—*

<From Amnardbat? No. Amnardbat *hates* the Empire,> Yskandr said, fascinated, intrigued, and then . . . interrupted.

"That's *extremely clever* as well as somewhat disturbing," said Nineteen Adze, "whether or not it's true."

"Let me tell Six Direction," Mahit asked. She could talk to Yskandr about sabotage *later.* "Take me to him. Please. For the sake of what we were, and what he and Yskandr were, and for both of our peoples."

"You do realize that I can't just walk you in after dark, like last time," Nineteen Adze said. "He isn't even in Palace-Earth—it's too *dangerous* there for him right now."

"I *do* realize. I know I'm asking you for something very large," Mahit began, and was interrupted by the return of the aide who had brought the brandy. He was empty-handed, this time, and his face was expressionlessly grave even for a Teixcalaanlitzlim.

"Your Excellency," he said, "forgive me for interrupting."

"Did I or did I not give standing orders that any further developments were *not* interrupting, Forty-Five Sunset?"

The briefest flicker of a smile; his eyes gone wide, and then blinking back to standard. "You did. Your Excellency, I regret to tell you that the *yaotlek*'s forces are in the city center and marching on the palace; there have been reports of multiple civilian deaths. I have feeds if you need them."

Nineteen Adze nodded; a short, sharp movement. "The clashes, are they partisan?"

"They're being instigated by flower-bearers, yes."

"*Must* we use Thirty Larkspur's propaganda language, Forty-Five Sunset?"

"My apologies, Your Excellency. Thirty Larkspur's agitators, with their purple larkspur pins, are primarily responsible for provoking the *yaotlek's* soldiers."

"Thank you," said Nineteen Adze. "I assume it's fractionally better if it's Thirty Larkspur and not the whole mess of people who want to sing your poetry, Three Seagrass. We might still have their loyalties. I'm not sure."

"Who is *we?*" asked Three Seagrass, and Mahit felt the echo in her bones: *What is the Teixcalaanli definition of* we?

"*We* are people who would like to see Six Direction on the sun-spear throne for as long as he lives," said Nineteen Adze.

"I'll swear to it," said Three Seagrass. "Right here, if you like. With blood."

It was an old Teixcalaanli custom: one of the oldest, from before the Empire had been multicontinental, let alone multiplanetary. For luck, for proof of an oath. To swear fealty or bind a person to a task. Blood in a bowl, mixed, and that bowl poured out as a sacrifice to the sun.

"How traditional," said Nineteen Adze. "Mahit—would *you* so swear?"

Did you ever, Mahit asked Yskandr, quiet in her mind.

<The once,> Yskandr said, and Mahit remembered the long, curving scar on his hand, below the place where Ten Pearl had stabbed him with his poison needle. <Six Direction asked me if I wanted to, and I told him I wouldn't be bound to him, that if I served I wanted to serve freely, in what respect I did serve— but that I wouldn't lie to him, and I'd swear so.>

Will I be bound?

<You'll find out, won't you.>

"Bring the bowl," Mahit said, and with a wave of Nineteen Adze's hand it was done. A little brass bowl, and a short steel knife that Mahit could imagine Nineteen Adze using all too easily. A *claw* of a thing. Three Seagrass took it by its handle and pressed her forefinger to the edge, cutting deep so that the blood welled quickly, dripping into the bowl. It was harder for Mahit to do; her fingers shook on the knife's handle, but the edge was microscopic and slit her finger open with next to no pressure and hardly any sting. Nineteen Adze was last. Their blood mingled, all the same shade of red.

In the oldest version of this custom, Mahit knew, they would all *drink* the contents of the bowl. So much for Teixcalaanli squeamishness about the consumption of the revered dead. They ate people who were still alive.

"May His Brilliance Six Direction reign until he no longer breathes," said Nineteen Adze, and Mahit and Three Seagrass echoed her.

Nothing *happened*. Somehow Mahit had expected something would; that blood sacrifice would be magic, or sanctified, or—

<Or like it is in the poems,> Yskandr finished, and she was forced to agree.

There was a little breath of silence. Then Nineteen Adze stood up, holding her bleeding finger safely away from the fabric of her suit, and said, "We'll get some bandages, and then, Ambassador, *asekreta*, I believe we will go see the Emperor."

CHAPTER
TWENTY

I carry exile in my heart. It animates my poetry and my politics; I will never be free of it, having lived outside of Teixcalaan for so long. I will always be measuring the distance between myself and a person who remained in the heart of the world; between the person I would have been had I stayed and the person I have become under the pressure of the frontier. When the Seventeenth Legion came through the jumpgate in bright star-snatching ships and filled up the Ebrekti sky with the shapes of my home, I was at first afraid. A profound discontinuity. To know fear in the shape of one's own face.

—from *Dispatches from the Numinous Frontier,* Eleven Lathe

*   *   *

What, my dear, is worth preserving? Your joy in work? Mine in discovery?

—private letter from Ambassador Yskandr Aghavn to the *ezuazuacat* Nineteen Adze, undated

THEY were keeping the Emperor in a bunker under Palace-North. It took forty-five minutes to walk there, Mahit and Three Seagrass and Nineteen Adze and one of the aides—the young man, Forty-Five Sunset. They went through tunnels, avoiding the curfew, the roving bands of Sunlit. The entire palace complex was riddled with them, deep under the ground. At her left,

Three Seagrass murmured, "The rumors are that the palace sinks as many roots into the ground as it does blooms into the sky; we daylight servants of the Empire see only the flowers— justice, science, information, war—and the roots which feed us are invisible but strong." Mahit liked hearing her talk. It was how they'd started this, barbarian and liaison, Three Seagrass decoding Teixcalaan for her. She liked it, and at the same time she knew that Three Seagrass was doing it to keep herself calm.

Nineteen Adze moved them through checkpoints, guarded first by the shimmering AI-walls of the City—opened by Nineteen Adze's cloudhook—and then by ever-increasing numbers of Teixcalaanlitzlim, dressed very simply in grey tunics and trousers with armbands bearing the imperial crest on their left arms. Mahit was reminded of the Judiciary forces who had been chasing Twelve Azalea, and thought of Eight Loop, who was Six Direction's crèchesib, who might have given him a secret personal guard of Judiciary-trained people. They all had shocksticks. Some of them—more, as they went deeper—had projectile weapons, and one woman carried what Mahit would swear was a laser which should have been mounted on the prow of a small warship. None of them wore the full-face cloudhooks of the Sunlit.

The innermost guards wore no cloudhooks at all, and they took the cloudhook Nineteen Adze was wearing from her. She gave it over easily.

One Lightning's infiltration of the City's AI-algorithm—One Lightning, working through War—must have gone very deep, to have the Emperor guarded only by people who would be guaranteed free of any influence of it: left as naked and abandoned by the vast flow of Teixcalaanli literature and history and culture and moment-to-moment news as Mahit had been naked and abandoned when she had lost contact with her imago.

Nineteen Adze spoke to some of them; others simply nodded

to her. Mahit wondered how many times she'd come this way before—whether she was new to this level of disaster and threat, or if there had been other times in the long history of her service to Six Direction that he had been forced to hide down here in the strange heart of the Empire.

<I never knew about it,> said Yskandr.

He might have slept with you, but you weren't his, Mahit told him.

<I didn't *want* to be anyone's. I loved him. That's different.>

How can you love an emperor like you'd love a person, Yskandr? Unspoken: *How could I? Would I?*

She never had. That was all Yskandr. She'd met the Emperor *twice,* once in public and once in private—and been impressed, had felt the echoes of Yskandr's familiarity all through her nerves and limbic system, but that wasn't *her.*

Maybe it was *them,* though, the combination of her and both Yskandrs, integrating together—and that might be a problem. She wanted to stay as objective as she could.

Beyond the last door and the last guards was a small room, by imperial standards, flooded with sunlamp light—the whole ceiling was made of full-spectrum lamps. It was *warm,* like basking in solar radiation on a viewport couch was warm, and bright enough that Mahit thought no one in here would ever sleep again. More grey-uniformed guards stood in the corners, and one of them stepped forward to take Three Seagrass's elbow and gently separate her from Mahit and Nineteen Adze. She left willingly.

Six Direction himself sat in the center of the room on a divan, dressed in resplendent red-purple and gold, and while at home in Palace-Earth he had borne a halo of sunlamps, here in the deep places under the City he was surrounded by a scintillating fortification of information holographs, a migraine aura composed entirely of reports. He looked terrible. His skin had gone to a grey-brown crepe, translucent purple under the eyes, and while the smile he turned on Nineteen Adze—and then on Mahit herself—was brilliant and sharp enough to make her heart flip over in her chest, she was *scared* for him. Viscerally.

<He wasn't this bad when I died,> Yskandr said to her.

I don't think the past three months have done anyone any favors, including His Brilliance. Dying men die faster when they aren't allowed to rest.

<Emperors don't sleep.>

"Your Brilliance," said Nineteen Adze, "I've brought you trouble again."

"So you have," said the Emperor. "Come sit beside me once more, Mahit, and let us see if we get any farther than we did in our last conversation."

Mahit went, drawn forward by invisible strings: desire, hers and not-hers. Obedience to imperial authority. All the effort and sacrifice she had put into making this meeting possible. She sat, becoming part of the fortification-aura of information. Just one more piece of data surrounding Six Direction. There were visible bruises, this close up, on the Emperor's wrists, over the veins; inelastic skin and thin-walled vasculature insulted by what must have been countless injections. She wondered what was keeping him alive.

"I also have come to bring you trouble," she said.

"I hardly expected any less, from Lsel Station." Six Direction smiled *at* her, Lsel-smile, with mouth and teeth, and she didn't know what to do with how *much* she felt, all at once. It would be so useful if she felt nothing. If she could be purely a political tool, purely an instrument of preventing Teixcalaan from annexing Lsel. It would be so easy, to be cold and clear and—

<*Talk,* Mahit, or I will.>

For a moment Mahit considered slipping, letting Yskandr *have* her, letting Yskandr talk to his Emperor one more time— and then she felt sickly horrified. *Get the fuck out of my neurology and out of my limbic system, Yskandr. I am not you reborn. That is not how we are.*

A hiss, like static on a wire. Then: <Talk.>

"Your Brilliance," Mahit began, "I have received actionable intelligence from my government on Lsel which describes a grave threat to Teixcalaan; graver, I am afraid to say, than the current unpleasant chaos outside this room."

"Do go on," said Six Direction. "I could use a distracting problem, one slightly less intractable than my current situation. However *grave*."

Mahit went on. She explained the entire message—explained it as she had to Nineteen Adze, including its blatant political maneuver. And then she waited, to see what the Emperor would say.

He was quiet for the space of a few breaths. She could hear the faint bubbling in his lungs. Then he looked to Nineteen Adze. "And do *you* think our latest Lsel Ambassador is as credible as the last one?" he asked her.

Nineteen Adze, standing next to Three Seagrass nearer the door, nodded. "I wouldn't have brought her here if I didn't believe her. I think she's reporting exactly what she was told by her government, and I think she's reporting her biases honestly. If this was at any other moment, my lord, I'd suggest she was coming to us for *help*; a fair diplomatic trade, vital information for her Station's continued lack of being *formally* Teixcalaanli."

"It is not any other moment," said Six Direction. He turned back to Mahit. "I will ask you what I asked you before, Mahit Dzmare, and with appreciation and thankfulness at being informed of this danger—will you agree to what your predecessor agreed to? Give me what *Yskandr* would have given me if not for my lovely friend Nineteen Adze and the arrayed forces of Science and Judiciary; trade me my life reborn, and you will not even need this danger to protect your interests in Lsel."

"Can't we be done with this, Six Direction," Nineteen Adze said, and there was an aching, exhausted anguish in her voice. "I want you to live and to hold the throne forever; I will miss you all the days of my life when you are gone, but the sun-spear throne is not a barbarian medical experiment and should not be—*look* at Mahit, your Brilliance. She has Yskandr in her and she is not Yskandr."

The Emperor affixed his eyes on Mahit's. She felt like she was drowning. All the supernatural power she'd imagined a blood ritual to evoke for her was right here, and all it was was reflected limbic system response, a trick of neurology. And yet there was a soapbubble–thin hook behind her sternum, an *ache*. Six Direction lifted one of his hands—they did not shake, and she had time to wonder at his strength—and cupped her cheek in his hand.

She let Yskandr—the sequence of responses, continuity of memory and its reflection on emotion, on pattern, that used to be Yskandr—lean into that palm. Let him shut her eyes in a deep, slow flutter.

And then took it all back, sat up straight with her eyes wide open, and said, "Your Brilliance, he loved you. I have met you *thrice*."

In the shocked little silence that followed, she went on: "Besides. I do not *have* an imago-machine for you. And I cannot—even in a better situation than this—get you one in time to preserve your memory before your life is over. I am *sorry*, Six Direction. But my answer is no."

The Emperor smudged his thumb along the curve of her cheekbone. "There's one in you," he said, "isn't there."

"If you wanted," Mahit told him, swallowing hard against bright fear, he was the *Emperor*, if he wanted to carve her open he could wave a hand and one of the grey-clad guards would do it right here on the floor, with Five Portico's surgical scar to guide them, "you could put me and Yskandr—two versions of Yskandr, even, it's complicated, it's all so very fucking complicated—into your mind. Or into the mind of anyone you like. But there is no imago-machine, Your Brilliance, which will bring you and only you into another person's mind. None for two months' worth of travel."

Six Direction sighed, and let her go. She felt the afterimage of his hand like a brand, glowing-hot, hypersensitive. "It does not change very much, I suppose," he said. "I have not been counting on the hope of resurrection since your predecessor's death. I was not expecting you to bring me hope. I had only . . . wished for it." He waved a finger, and Nineteen Adze came to him, sank to the floor at his side on her knees. He put a hand to the back of her neck, and she leaned up into it.

Mahit had thought of her as an enormous tiger, clawed and dangerous, and yet—she knelt. She leaned into that hand.

<Nothing empire touches remains itself,> Yskandr murmured to her.

Or perhaps that was her own voice, casting itself in a tone she'd be most likely to believe.

"How goes this very stupid rebellion, Nineteen Adze?" asked the Emperor.

"Stupidly," Nineteen Adze said, "but badly for everyone. One Lightning is killing civilians; Thirty Larkspur is trying to unseat you via flat-out internal coup, I *believe* because he thinks if you die Eight Loop and Eight Antidote will cut him out of the government—so he's using One Lightning as an excuse to take preemptive power while you're still alive, and doing it by sending instigators into the streets with his ridiculous little badges of floral honor—we've lost Two Rosewood in Information, she's dead, or as good as, and I don't have much hope about Nine

Propulsion in War; if she hasn't gone over to One Lightning already she *might*, at any time, if she thinks it will get her an *ezuazuacat*'s position in his government . . ."

"Would you like to be Information Minister, Nineteen Adze, since you know everything already?"

". . . I *like* my current title. As I've said, multiple times," said Nineteen Adze. And sighed a little. "If you need me to be, though, I will."

"That's not what I need from you," Six Direction said. Mahit found absolutely no comfort in his phrasing. Neither, from her expression, did Nineteen Adze.

"Where *is* Eight Antidote?" Nineteen Adze asked. "If you can tell me. I am—concerned, my lord, for his welfare."

It would matter very much where the ninety-percent clone was; even at ten years old—*Was he conceived when you and Six Direction finally agreed on your trade, Yskandr, or was he already an insurance policy?*—he was likely to be the first of the three co-emperors, by virtue of his genetic heritage, when Six Direction died. If Six Direction died before the child reached his majority.

"He's down here with us," said Six Direction. "You will protect him, Nineteen Adze. Won't you?"

"Of course I will. When have I *not* acted in your best interests, Your Brilliance?"

<When she killed me,> Yskandr whispered, and Mahit wondered if the Emperor was thinking the same thing.

"Oh, once or twice," Six Direction said, and instead of flinching or being cowed, Nineteen Adze laughed. Mahit could abruptly imagine how they must have been when they'd first met: Nineteen Adze a young military commander, Six Direction come into the high blossoming of his power. The easy friendship that they'd struck up. The successes of their partnership.

Then the Emperor turned back to Mahit, and she felt quite small, and terribly young, and not nearly as simpatico with these two Teixcalaanlitzlim as Yskandr had been. She wouldn't have become part of that strange triangle.

<Are you sure? It took me a decade to fall. You've had a week.>

No. She wasn't sure. She merely wasn't *ready*.

"So, Mahit Dzmare—if you cannot solve the most fundamental problem of good government for me, if you cannot give me eternity and stable rule—what *can* your news from Darj Tarats give me? What shall I do with an alien invasion on the borders of my empire, from down here while I hide from death and deposition in the heart of my palace?"

And just like that, she was being given a *test*. The same way she'd felt on her first day here, suddenly knowing she needed to speak Teixcalaanli, *all* the time, not just in her mind or between friends. She would speak Teixcalaanli now. She knew the phrasings, the shadings. She had all of Yskandr's long history with Six Direction—all the conversations they had had, over tables and at legislative meetings and in bed—to guide her. Everything that ached—her hand, her hip, the endless, endless headache—fell away, and she thought: *All right. Now.*

"You can discredit One Lightning," she said. "*And* you can elevate Eight Loop above Thirty Larkspur."

"Go on."

She was *flying*. "One Lightning is waging an usurpation—an attempt to be *acclaimed* Emperor—and has he won victories? No. Is he even trying? *No*, he is leaving the edges of Teixcalaan open to alien threat. A *barbarian* had to bring this message to you, which is a shameful failure on the part of your *yaotlek*, who should have *known of this danger first* but has put himself and his vainglorious ambition above the safety of the Empire." She had to pause for breath. Behind her, she could feel Three Seagrass's eyes on her, and wished that her liaison was with her, close enough to hold her hand. "And . . . Eight Loop warned the entire City that the annexation war—which Thirty Lark-spur supports, has supported in public at your last oration contest—was of dubious legality, *due to the possibility of these threats.* She fulfills her role as Judiciary Minister; Thirty Lark-spur is exposed as using his position of influence upon you to put you in political danger."

She winced a bit. "It does ask you to admit that you may have been led astray by your *ezuazuacat,* I have to confess."

"A small price," Six Direction said. "I am an old man, and eas-ily persuaded by interests foreign to me, am I not?"

<Never *easily,* my lord,> Yskandr said, and Mahit had to clamp her jaw shut on the words. Instead, she shrugged, spread-ing her hands wide. Better to not say anything. Better to make this case for Lsel Station, in Teixcalaanli words.

Six Direction looked down at Nineteen Adze. Some commu-nication passed silently between them. She nodded. His hand came off the back of her neck and she got up to her feet, fluid and graceful for a woman in middle age who probably hadn't slept for a day and a half at least.

"We'll have to broadcast it," she said. "On every feed. Impe-rial override; emergency message. And it will have to be *you* saying it, Your Brilliance—no one will believe a proxy right now. You saying it, and the Ambassador prerecorded and spliced in as appropriate."

"As ever, Nineteen Adze, I *do* trust your judgment."

Nineteen Adze's smile was more like a flinch. Mahit sus-pected she was thinking of how she had allowed Yskandr to die, and doomed Six Direction at the same time. It would be like a thorn in her, a *goad.* Six Direction must like that, to have some-thing to *twist*—

"Ambassador Dzmare," said Nineteen Adze. "Mahit—will you record your statement from your government for us?"

If this was the plan, this was the plan. "Yes," Mahit said, "I will. Where should I go?"

"Oh, we have everything we need right here," said Six Direction. "Emperors have *lived* down here, for months. A holograph recorder is nothing." He waved a hand toward some of his grey-uniformed attendants, and they swung into motion: some left the room, others approached Mahit and the Emperor on the couch, with some wariness.

"She looks like she's been dragged through the riots," said one of them. "The blood on her—I think we should keep it. It suits the gravity of what she brought you."

"Even barbarians can make sacrifices," said Six Direction. "We could all take note of that."

As the attendants helped her up from the couch and led her into a room which looked identical to the imperial briefing room Mahit had seen on the newsfeeds when she'd watched the annexation war being announced from Nineteen Adze's breakfast table, she tried very hard not to feel *filthy*. Corrupted. Made *useful*. It didn't work.

It didn't work, and it didn't stop her from telling her secrets again, this time to the recording cameras, as clearly and persuasively as she could.

———

The Emperor and Nineteen Adze had a brief, vehement argument about where they would broadcast the announcement from—Nineteen Adze was for everyone remaining hidden underground, but Six Direction waited her out, let her say all sorts of flattering things about his welfare and fragility, and then proclaimed that he was, in fact, the Emperor of all Teixcalaan, and he would make this announcement, fearlessly, from the sun temple at the top of Palace-North, and that she would come with him and stand beside him while he did it. There was no real arguing with him. Mahit could feel the weight of his authority, even diminished and under threat—the long shadow of his *eighty years of peace* stretching out to shape even this moment.

After the argument was over, there was the usual administrative chaos of orchestrating a complex public appearance on no notice—a rapid twenty minutes of imperial attendants talking briskly to one another, sending messages. The Emperor and Nineteen Adze vanished under heavily armed escort. Mahit caught sight of the child, Eight Antidote, being whisked off into the chaos of that escort, and thought of how many times he might have been moved similarly: relocated at the whim of one political moment or another. He looked at her, as he went— a small, thin boy, observant, straight-backed. Mahit thought of the birds in the garden in Palace-Earth. *They don't even have to touch you,* Eight Antidote had said, then. He'd been talking about the birds—she'd thought at the time—but it was true. They didn't touch him. They moved him without laying hands on him at all.

She herself was taken into another room, smaller, more private—strewn about with infofiche and print-books, half-erased holoprojections still up on screens. A workroom. There was a couch in the middle of it, and Mahit sat down on it. Someone brought her a warm washcloth to wipe the blood and dust off her face; someone else brought her Three Seagrass, who was bemusedly holding a large cup of tea, and the two of them ended up sitting on the couch next to one another, watching the swirl of activity around them. Mahit felt unmoored, entirely cut away from the world. All her tethers gone. Even Yskandr in her mind was a banked, quiet presence.

Half the wall in front of them was taken up by an enormous holoprojection, the only one still active. It had begun broadcasting the imperial seal and flag, with a countdown timer superimposed—forty-eight minutes until the Emperor would speak to his people. At thirty-seven minutes the attendants, save for a guard at the door, all vanished, the great machine of imperial work lifting away and alighting somewhere else. Mahit had played her part. She'd given her secrets up. There was nothing she could do now but wait.

Three Seagrass put her empty teacup down on the floor. Thirty-five minutes. The quiet was velvet-soft. Mahit couldn't stand it.

"What do you think they're doing?" she asked, just to hear sounds that weren't her own breathing or Three Seagrass's, lighter and more rapid.

Three Seagrass swallowed, pressed two fingers between her eyebrows, as if she was shoving back tears. "Oh, I'd guess they're finding Eight Loop," she said, and her voice was not at *all* steady—Mahit turned, looked at her with real concern. "For the visual impact of imperial authority, all of them standing together—"

"Three Seagrass, are you all right?"

"Oh, *fuck*," Three Seagrass said, "no, I'm not, but I was so hoping you wouldn't notice?"

They were alone. The door guard was guarding the *door*, looking away, a silent and still presence. They were suspended out of time, out of the inexorable forward flow of events. Mahit reached out—horribly conscious that this gesture wasn't hers, wasn't even Yskandr's, but belonged to the *Emperor*—and cupped Three Seagrass's cheek in her hand.

"I notice," she said.

It was not unexpected when Three Seagrass burst into tears, but it was awful; Mahit felt guilty, like she'd *caused* it, this little shattering. Like she'd tapped too hard on the shell of an egg and it had splintered, held together only by the internal membranes inside. "Hey," she said, "hey, it's—" It wasn't all right, and she wasn't about to say so. Instead, acting on instinct and an up-swelling of *care*, a feeling like her vagus nerve had been expertly struck and was vibrating, she reached to pull Three Seagrass into her arms. She came willingly; the slight weight of her rested against Mahit's shoulder, and her face was pressed into Mahit's collarbone. Hot tears dampened her shirt.

Gently, Mahit stroked her hair, still unbraided from its ha-bitual queue. The world was spinning on and on and on—the countdown at thirty-two minutes—and she couldn't fathom the wrenching depths of what this must feel like to Three Sea-grass, who had looked like she would cry at the very *mention* of civil war, back in Twelve Azalea's apartment.

"I thought I was fine," Three Seagrass said, muffled, "but I keep thinking of all the blood. *Fuck.* I miss Petal so *much*, al-ready. It's been three hours and I miss him so much and that was such a *stupid* way to die—"

Oh. Not civil war at all. Something much deeper, much more immediate. Mahit squeezed her arms around her, and Three Seagrass made a miserable, hiccupping sound. "This is— the whole *world* is changing and I'm crying over my friend," she said. "Some poet I am."

"When this is over," said Mahit, "you'll write Twelve Azalea a eulogy that people will sing in the streets; he will be a synecdoche for everything Teixcalaan is suffering right now, needlessly. No one will ever forget him, and that will be your doing, and—oh, I'm just so *sorry*, this is all my fault—" She was going to cry too, and what good would that do anyone, two people crying on a couch underground?

Three Seagrass picked up her head from Mahit's shoulder, looked up at her, tearstained, red in the face from crying. There was a brief, strained pause. Mahit could swear she could hear the rushing of blood in her own capillaries. They were breath-ing exactly in time.

When Three Seagrass kissed her, Mahit opened up for her as if she was a lotus floating in one of the City's gardens at dawn—slow, inexorable, like she had been waiting a long, long time through the night. Three Seagrass's mouth was hot; her lips wide and soft. One of her hands settled in Mahit's short hair, held on tight, almost tight enough to hurt. Mahit found her hands had landed upon Three Seagrass's shoulder blades—they were sharp under her palms—she pulled her closer, halfway into her lap, without breaking the kiss.

This was a terrible idea. This was *lovely*. It was the nicest thing that had happened to her in hours—in *days*—Three Seagrass kissed like she'd made a thorough study of the practice, and Mahit was *glad* of it, glad that she'd done it, glad of the distraction from everything else.

They broke apart. Three Seagrass's eyes, inches from hers, were very wide and very dark, and red at the corners where she'd wept.

"Petal was always right about me," she said. Mahit tucked a stray strand of her hair behind her ear and let her talk. "I *do* like aliens. Barbarians. Anything new, anything different. But I also—if I'd met you at court, Mahit, if you were one of us, I'd have wanted to do that just the same."

What she was saying was exquisite, a balm and a comfort, and horrible at the same time: *If you were one of us, I would want you just the same,* and Mahit wanted simultaneously to climb back inside her mouth and shove her out of her lap. She *wasn't* Teixcalaanli, she was . . . she hardly *knew* anymore, except that she wasn't Teixcalaanli and wouldn't be no matter how many lovely *asekretim* climbed into her arms, tearstained, wanting to be held. Wanting to be held after sacrificing nearly everything she was for Mahit's sake.

"I'm glad you did," she managed, because she was, because it had been *sweet*. "Come here, let me—let me." Her hands in

Three Seagrass's hair, on the narrow channel of her spine. Holding her.

They didn't kiss again, just breathed together in time, until the holoprojection screen chimed—fifteen minutes—and changed, beginning to show a series of aerial images of the City, what someone might see from the vast height of the sun temple on top of Palace-North. The eyes of the Emperor, opening up.

CHAPTER
TWENTY-ONE

the City rises marching
a thousand starpoints strong
released, we shall speak visions
uneclipsed
I am a spear in the hands of the sun

     —City protest song, anonymous (possibly attributed to

        patrician first-class Three Seagrass)

THE full extent of Teixcalaanli imperial power, even reduced, even under threat from multiple angles, was a crushing on-slaught of symbolism. Mahit felt it three ways: first her own longing appreciation, born out of a childhood half in love with Teixcalaan the story, Teixcalaan the empire of poets, all-conquering all-devouring all-singing beast in the garden of her imaginings; second, the echo of Yskandr-doubled, two versions who had come to live here and make themselves into people who *could* live here, could move in this language and speak and see nothing but Teixcalaan, and still remember Lsel as a distant and beloved home; and last, the quick intake of breath and the full-body tremor of the Teixcalaanli woman Mahit held in her arms as they both watched the theater which was meant to defuse an insurrection.

It began with the Emperor's-eye view of the City, that shift-ing panorama—slowly transformed, overlaid with the flowers and spears and sun-petal-gold glow of the imperial seal, the imperial flags—not the battle flag, the peace flag, the one that hung behind the sun-spear throne. There was music. It wasn't martial—it was *old,* a folk song, stringed instruments and a low flute like a woman's voice.

"What is that?" Mahit asked Three Seagrass, and Three Seagrass sat up a little. Her arm was looped around Mahit's waist.

"It's—it's an arrangement of a song from the era of the Emperor Nine Flood, right before we broke solar system—it's *old.* Everyone knows it. It's—fuck, they're being so *good* with the propaganda, it makes me feel nostalgic and scared and brave and I know exactly what they're doing."

The images on the holoprojection resolved to the inside of a sun temple—far larger and more ornate than any Mahit had seen before, in holograph or infofiche-image: the great central chamber shaped like a belled flask, open at the top and crowned with a lens that scattered bright beams of light around the central platform and its dished bronze bowl of an altar. The entire room was jewel-clear, faceted, glimmering: translucent gold, garnet-red. The music died away, and there was Six Direction, standing just in front of the altar. They'd done brilliant work on him with makeup: he almost looked healthy. Almost, except for the shocking prominence of his cheekbones. Eight Loop was nowhere to be seen, but at his left stood Nineteen Adze, resplendent in bone-white—but it was the *same* bone-white suit she had been wearing when they left, complete with a smear of Five Agate's blood on the sleeve. The *ezuazuacat* bloodied in service. At his right was the ninety-percent clone, Eight Antidote. His small shoulders were very straight; his face had those same high cheekbones as the Emperor, but under healthy pads of childhood flesh.

Emperor, and successor, and advisor: all in the heart of power. As an image, it was *reassuring.* As a beginning of a message to all Teixcalaan it was *frightening*: to have gathered them together like this emphasized the seriousness, the *necessary* conveyance of this particular message. That sun temple was at the very top of Palace-North.

<There are Fleet ships in orbit right this moment,> Yskandr murmured to her. Which meant, if One Lightning wanted, he could blow the temple and the Emperor both to nothing, with a single command.

Every other Teixcalaanlitzlim would know that, too.

Six Direction pressed his fingertips together, and bowed over them—greeting every watcher. He did not smile: this was too serious for smiling. The camera hung about his mouth like a caress, waiting for words. When he spoke it was a relief, a tiny burst of relaxed tension, until the words began to make sense: *Through our great work and careful husbandry of civilizations, pruning where necessary, encouraging the flowering of society where it is most beautiful, we have together held this empire, with my hands guiding all of yours—but now, in this moment of fragility, when new blooms are trembling on the verge of unfolding into the light of the stars, we are all endangered. Some of you know this danger in your hearts; some of you have felt it in your bodies, in the sound of soldiers' feet, in the damage inflicted upon our City, the heart of our civilization, by our own limbs—*

Mahit felt like her heart had crept so far up her throat that it rested on the back of her tongue; she was all pulse. This was not the speech she had expected. She had expected a moment of reassurance, and then a quick use of her own footage to prove that there was danger, and it came from *outside*, was alien forces massing on the edge of Teixcalaanli space—not this careful rhetorical construction which approached *renewal* as a theme, a dangerous theme for an emperor under threat from his military and his bureaucracy both.

"What is he *doing*?" she breathed.

"Keep watching," said Three Seagrass. "Keep watching, and wait a minute. I think I know and I don't want to be right."

"You don't want—"

"*Hush*, Mahit."

She hushed. The Emperor kept speaking—asked for calm and for reflection. *Before the dawn there is a quiet moment where we can see the approach of both distant threat and the promise of warmth,* he said. Next to him Nineteen Adze's expression had changed from even neutrality to something Mahit recognized as dawning horror—resignation—and then a schooling of herself again to stillness. Something was wrong, and Nineteen Adze had noticed it. Something was *happening* and Mahit didn't understand it.

Six Direction was talking about Lsel, now—briefly, alighting on it, *a mining station at the edge of Teixcalaanli space, a distant eye that speaks to us of danger observed.* Her own image, then, superimposed upon the frame of Nineteen Adze, Six Direction, and Eight Antidote: Mahit Dzmare, looking *very* barbaric, tall and high-foreheaded and narrow-faced with her long, aquiline nose, explaining the coming invasion from an imperial briefing room. She looked exhausted. She looked honest.

<You did very well,> whispered Yskandr. <Hardly anyone would convict *you* in a court of law, on either side. You walked right down the center line.>

The face of the Emperor was behind her face; as her mouth moved, on the holograph, the Emperor's mouth remained a constant still presence, as if he was commanding her performance by sheer force of will.

The whole image—all of them, the entire sun temple—was replaced by a familiar map: Teixcalaanli space, a grand starchart. The last time Mahit had seen this it had been deployed to show the vectors of the annexation war which would claim Lsel and everything around it. Now those vectors were dimmed, and as she watched, the map lit up with each of the coordinate points Darj Tarats had given to her: the places where the threat was greatest, where the aliens had been spotted in their ships, festooned with weaponry. Inverse stars on that map: bright for a moment and then spreading a deep, dark, *threatening* red, like a pool of blood.

Mahit thought of Twelve Azalea, and was still thinking of him when the map vanished. She misunderstood what she was seeing in the sun temple for long seconds, lost in memory and connotation.

The Emperor was holding a naked blade, a knife made out of some dark, shining material, translucent grey at its sharpest edges. He'd shed his robe; it pooled around his ankles. All of his bones were visible, even through the light trousers and shirt he wore: every bit of emaciation his illness had wrought upon him rendered up for the eyes of the cameras. Eight Antidote had pressed the side of his hand to his mouth, a child's gesture of distress—Nineteen Adze was saying something, Mahit only caught the end of it, a wisp of *my lord, I—don't—*

Six Direction, speaking: *Teixcalaan requires a steady, even hand—a hand star-graced, a tongue prepared, a fist that grasps the sunlight. In the face of what we are about to suffer—I who have served you since I knew what service was—I consecrate this temple and the war which is to come.*

"He's really going to," said Three Seagrass, her voice too real, too loud, and too immediate on the couch next to Mahit. "No emperor has—not for *centuries*—"

I name as my immediate successor and the executor of this war of preservation the ezuazuacat Nineteen Adze, said Six Direction, *in sinecure for the child of my genetics, Eight Antidote, until the time of his majority.*

Mahit had time to think, *What have I set into motion,* and to feel a great onrushing spasm of grief: hers, Three Seagrass's, Yskandr's—

The Emperor took two steps backward, into the center of the raised altar. *With my blood I sacrifice for us,* he said—broadcast, unstoppable, to every Teixcalaanlitzlim in every province, on every planet in Teixcalaanli space. *Released, I am a spear in the hands of the sun.*

Her words. Mahit's and Three Seagrass's, the poetry they'd used as a lure to get themselves free—the poetry that was being sung in the streets—

Six Direction raised the knife, the sun glinting through it— and brought it down again. Two swift cuts, high on the inner thighs: the femoral arteries gone to fountains of red. So much blood. And somehow, in the middle of that pool, two cuts more: from wrist to elbow, and again on the other side.

The knife clattered to the metal floor of the sun temple.

It did not take him long to die.

In the silence afterward, Mahit realized she had been hold- ing Three Seagrass's hand so hard her fingernails had cut into her palm. The only sound in the universe seemed to be the two of them, breathing. In her mind Yskandr was a vast and empty void of triumph and grief. She looked away from him. She looked at nothing at all.

On the screen: Nineteen Adze, soaked in red, her suit stained beyond recognition, had caught up the knife.

The Emperor of Teixcalaan greets you, she said. Her face was *wet.* Blood. Tears. Wet and grim and absolutely determined. *Be calm. Order is a flower blooming at dawn, and dawn is breaking now.*

———

There was quiet for a little while, and then there was the ex- pected sort of chaos; all those grey-uniformed imperial guards, trying to figure out what to do. Where to *go.* How to get to their new Emperor and then move her to some sort of safety, consid- ering there was *still* a legion-leading starship with all of its weaponry pointed at the City, in low orbit. Mahit and Three Seagrass sat in the middle of it—no one seemed to care very much about them. They weren't doing anything. They didn't seem to be an immediate threat to anyone.

"He set her up for it," Three Seagrass said wonderingly. "She didn't know until she was up there next to him. Her Brilliance. The Edgeshine of a Knife. I guess it'll fit. Still."

They'd reversed emotional positions, somehow. Mahit couldn't stop crying for very long; even if it wasn't entirely her own endocrine response, her *body* had decided to dissolve into the weight of grief. Yskandr wasn't *gone*—she didn't think she'd ever feel that hollow blank-space wrongness again—but both versions of him were bleak, scoured-cold landscapes, rooms without air, and Mahit kept *weeping,* even when she wanted to talk.

She wiped at her nose with the heel of her hand. "Of course it'll fit," she managed. "The office will bend around her and she'll bend around it, too, and it'll all be . . . a story. Her Brilliance, the Edgeshine of a Knife. Like it was never supposed to be any different."

That seemed to be comforting for Three Seagrass to hear. Mahit herself felt comfortless, *angry,* blown open and empty: she kept remembering how *much* blood there had been, how Six Direction had said *released, I am a spear in the hands of the sun,* as if she'd written it for him.

For him, and not for her or for Lsel.

Nothing touched by empire stays clean, she thought, and tried to imagine it was Yskandr saying so when it wasn't Yskandr at all.

———

It took thirty-six hours for the insurrection to be over.

Mahit watched most of it on Three Seagrass's Information Ministry newsfeed, lying in what used to be Yskandr's bed in her ambassadorial apartment with the other woman's cloud-hook over her eye like a permanently affixed crown. Getting up seemed both difficult and unnecessary.

One Lightning's soldiers turned out to be more unwilling to slaughter large numbers of marching, singing Teixcalaanlitzlim than Mahit suspected he had counted on. But then he'd been expecting his opponent to be Six Direction—old, failing, his military victories a long time over, beset by an uncertain succession. Not a new-crowned emperor, sanctified by a blood sacrifice like something out of the oldest epics. Before Nineteen Adze's emperorship was a day old the *yaotlek* had recalled all his troops under the cover of *their protection of the City being unnecessary,* and had appeared on a news program standing *next* to Nineteen Adze, to get on his knees and put his hands between hers and swear his loyalty.

There was no mention of the war of conquest.

"That's the Station saved, then," Mahit said to the ceiling. Yskandr's garish and lovely painting of all of Lsel space as seen from Teixcalaan was the only thing that heard her, and she could take its silence as mockery.

Yskandr himself was merely a whisper, a <You did better than I. That says something for the survival of our imago-line.>

Mahit ignored him. When she paid too much attention to him she had crying fits, weeping, inconsolable, on and on until she was physically sick. It made her angry; it wasn't even her grief. She hadn't figured out what her grief was about, yet.

That night she dreamed of Six Direction saying her poetry, speaking her thoughts, and thought she might be getting closer.

If she'd been at home on Lsel, she suspected that the integration therapists would have an absolute field day with her and Yskandr. They'd get a scientific paper out of it. By the next morning even Yskandr found this funny—bright shimmers in her nerves, a bit of actual energy. She got up. She ate noodles and chili oil and a protein cube that tasted almost like a Lsel protein cube, but probably was made of some kind of plant. And then she lay down again, exhausted by that small effort, and watched the newsfeeds.

There was little sign of Two Lemon and the other anti-imperial activists. No bombs in restaurants. No protests. Mahit assumed they'd gone back underground, quiescent for the moment, and wondered—wondered like a person contemplating the impossibility of lifting an enormous rock to look at what grew underneath it—what Five Portico would do with the remains of her faulty imago-machine.

Thirty Larkspur's part of the insurrection took a bit longer to wind to a close—there was a loose détente established, a series of small newsfeed reports that a new Information Minister had been appointed—a man Mahit had never heard of—and that Thirty Larkspur had himself been given some sort of advisory role on commerce.

Not one of Her Brilliance Nineteen Adze's *ezuazuacatlim*. But not out of the government either.

It wasn't Mahit's problem.

She wanted it to be, which *was* part of the problem. It was so difficult to put everything *down,* to trust that anyone, anywhere, would in fact do their jobs. That there was any safety.

She wondered how Nineteen Adze felt about it. About the same, she suspected.

———

On the third day after Six Direction's death, after Mahit had received a beautiful infofiche stick, bone-white—made from some animal—and sealed with the imperial seal, inviting her as the ranking representative of her government to attend the funeral and coronation, she decided that the absolute least she could do was get back to answering the mail. The mail which was three months and *two weeks* late now. There was still a bowl of it, infofiche sticks in every possible color, from utilitarian grey plastic to Nineteen Adze's solid bone-and-gold, and—

And she'd come here to serve Lsel Station, and its people who had come to live in Teixcalaan. Who had just lived through an insurrection and a change in emperorship, too, and probably wanted their permits permitted, and their visas approved.

She sent Three Seagrass a message on one of the utilitarian grey sticks: *You left your spare cloudhook here. Also I could use some help with the mail.* She didn't really need help—Yskandr knew how to do all of this, and so she did too—but they hadn't talked. Since.

Four hours later Three Seagrass showed up with the sunlight slanting through the windows, looking evanescently thin and grey-pale at the temples and around the eyes, but just as impeccable as she'd been when she met Mahit coming off the seed-skiff: every corner of her suit pressed, orange flames creeping up the sleeves. Information Ministry again, undisgraced.

"—hi," she said.

"Hi," said Mahit, and abruptly remembered nothing but how Three Seagrass had felt in her arms, and suspected she'd blushed scarlet. "—thanks for coming."

The air between them felt fragile; more so when Three Seagrass sat down next to her, and shrugged, and quite clearly didn't know what to say.

They'd done better with poetry. They'd done better with politics. Fuck, they'd done better with *kissing,* and that had been a mad reaching-out for comfort. Mahit wanted to do it again; wanted, and immediately thought better of it. They'd been watching the end of an imperial reign, then. Now it was just the two of them, and the slow, outgoing tide of aftermath, and Mahit couldn't quite imagine how to begin such a thing.

"I half thought you'd have gotten yourself made Minister for Information," Mahit said, light, light enough to be joking, "and wouldn't have any time for me."

Some of the tension went out of Three Seagrass's shoulders. "Her Brilliance offered me Second Undersecretary to the Minister, actually," she said, "but I'm still your cultural liaison, if you want."

Mahit thought about it—thought about it while she took Three Seagrass's hand in her hand, and laced their fingers together, and said *thank you* with all the honorific particles she could remember tacked onto the end, so that it became both enormously sincere and utterly hilarious, all at once. Thought about working with Three Seagrass, here in this apartment that had been Yskandr's, and finding her way toward being— what? Something Nineteen Adze, Her Brilliance on the sunspear throne, might *need*? (That would be a way to begin, with Three Seagrass, too.)

<I had twenty years before it killed me,> Yskandr said. <You might get longer.>

She might. And then she remembered Three Seagrass saying *If you were one of us, I would want you just the same,* and felt an echo of that encompassing anger—she *wouldn't* be Teixcalaanli, even if she stayed, even if she did everything Yskandr had done. She wouldn't be a creature that could play, like Three Seagrass played, with language and poetry at oration contests. And she'd never stop knowing it.

"I think," Mahit said, right out loud, once Three Seagrass had stopped laughing and had let Mahit touch her cheek, very gently and just once, "that you should be Second Undersecretary to the Minister for Information. You're too *interesting* for this job,

Three Seagrass. You should do what you planned to do when you got it, which is use me as a stepping-stone toward *vainglorious ambition*. And get back to being a poet."

"What are *you* going to do without me?" Three Seagrass asked. She did not protest more than that.

"I'll think of something," said Mahit.

AFTERMATH

A PERSON could glut themselves on a surfeit of beauty, it turned out, especially if that beauty was enlivened by collective grief and deep xenophilia: the coronation of the Emperor Nineteen Adze, She Who Gleams Like the Edgeshine of a Knife, Her Brilliance, Lord of all Teixcalaan—Mahit mostly remembered it as a sequence of overwhelming snapshots. The procession that wound its way through the City, reflected and replayed on every screen. A hundred thousand Sunlit marching, kneeling at the Emperor's white-slippered feet, rising, moving on. The algorithm readjusted, or merely accepting Nineteen Adze as the rightful ruler of the Empire. The City itself lit up gold and red and a deep, rich purple, blooming, blooming. The interment of the exsanguinated body of Six Direction, buried in the *earth* to rot. Encomia upon encomia; new poets on every corner. The massing of soldiers—young Teixcalaanlitzlim volunteering for the coming war against the aliens, over and over and over. Singing, sometimes, as they went.

There were two new songs that went *I am a spear in the hands of the sun.* One was elegiac and beautiful and a choir sang it at the moment the great imperial crown was placed on Nineteen Adze's head. The other one was bawdy and obscene and relied on a pun in Teixcalaanli that Mahit would have understood if she'd been studying the language only one year: *anyone* could understand how *spear* could be interpreted in a multitude of ways.

Mahit learned that song. It was hard not to.

The way Nineteen Adze's face never changed, not during the interment and not when they put the crown on her—that Mahit learned, too. It was hard not to.

Once the City had exhaled enough ceremony, and felt more like an exhausted runner, leaning out of breath, trying to adjust to the deep ache in its lungs, small funerals bloomed like fungi after rain: there were more and more announcements each day, some arriving by infofiche and some by public newsfeed. Three hundred and four Teixcalaanli had been killed during the insurrection, according to the official reports; Mahit suspected that number was too small by an order of magnitude.

She wore her best mourning-black, black for the void between the stars, Lsel-style—not red for blood given, like a Teixcalaanlitzlim—when she went to Twelve Azalea's. There wasn't a body. He'd donated it to the medical college, which was so like him that it *hurt*. There was only a cenotaph, with the lovely glyph of his signature on it, placed in a wall inside the Information Ministry alongside hundreds of others: every one of them an *asekreta* who had died in service to the Ministry.

She saw Three Seagrass there, and heard her read a poem for Twelve Azalea: a stark, bleak thing, vicious in its grief. An epitaph for worlds ripped out of the sky, for unfairness. For all the senseless deaths. It was beautiful, and Mahit felt . . . *guilt,* when she thought of all the senseless deaths that were still waiting. All those Teixcalaanlitzlim, singing as they signed up for the legions.

All those planets they would touch, and devour.

She had Yskandr's corpse burned—so simple, at the last, to send a request to Judiciary, signed and sealed on infofiche, addressed to *ixplanatl* Four Lever, Medical Examiner. The ashes were waiting for her in her apartments that evening. A box the size of her hand, full of bones and half-mummified flesh, all rendered to dust.

Would you want me to taste? she asked her imago, the twinned strangeness of him.

A very long pause. <I don't think I'd be very good for you. That preservative.> All the young Yskandr, the first one. Hers. And then, <Wait for when you don't need to ask.>

Which was all the old Yskandr, the one who remembered dying. Mahit considered when that would be, when she wouldn't want to make *sure* that she was doing some justice to her imago-line—and put the box of ashes away.

———

She did not meet the Emperor in the imperial apartments in Palace-Earth, and neither did she meet her in Nineteen Adze's office complex back in Palace-East. Mahit imagined the latter had been shuttered.

They met just before dawn, in the plaza in front of the Judiciary, with its pool full of deep-red floating flowers. Mahit was awake by virtue of being summoned by a grey-suited imperial attendant knocking at her door, and wished vehemently for coffee, or tea, or even a nice simple caffeine pill. Nineteen Adze looked as if sleep was something that happened to other people, who happened not to be emperors. It was beginning to suit her; or her face was settling into it. The new hollownesses, the focus of long-seeing eyes.

"Your Brilliance," said Mahit.

They were sitting on a bench. There was one attendant-guard with them, and she did not wear a cloudhook, and she carried a projectile weapon. Nineteen Adze folded her hands in her lap. "I'm almost used to it," she said. "People calling me *Your*

Brilliance. I think when I'm used to it, that will mean he's really dead."

"No one is dead," Mahit said carefully, "who is remembered."

"Is that Lsel scripture?"

"Philosophy, maybe. Practicality."

"I assume it'd have to be. Considering how wrapped up you are in your dead." Nineteen Adze lifted one hand, let it fall. "I miss him. I can't *imagine* what it'd be like having him in my head. How do you make decisions?"

Mahit exhaled hard. In her mind, Yskandr was all fondness, warmth, laughter. "We argue," she said. "A little. But mostly we agree. We're . . . we wouldn't match, I wouldn't be his successor, if I wasn't going to mostly agree with him."

"Mm." Nineteen Adze was quiet, then, for a long moment. The wind ruffled the petals of all the red flowers: a vast confined sea. The sky lightened from dark grey to paler grey, shaded gold where the sun would burn off the clouds.

When she couldn't stand the silence any longer, Mahit asked, "Why did you want to meet with me?" She left off the honorific. She left it a plain sentence: Why did you, one person, want to meet with me, another person?

"I thought I'd ask you what you wanted," said Nineteen Adze. She smiled; that viciously *gentle* smile, all her attention focusing down onto Mahit. "I can imagine you might like to extract some promises from me."

"Are you planning to annex my Station to Teixcalaan?" Mahit asked.

Nineteen Adze laughed, a brutal, shoulder-shaking sound. "No. No, *stars,* I hardly have time. I hardly have time for anything. You're safe, Mahit. You and Lsel Station can be as much of an independent republic as you'd like. But that's not what I asked. I asked what *you* wanted."

In the pool, a long-legged bird had alighted: white-feathered, long-beaked. Two feet high at the shoulder, at least. As it stepped, it didn't disturb the flowers; its great feet slipped between them and rose again, dripping. Mahit didn't know the word for the kind of bird it was. "Ibis," maybe. Or "egret." There were a lot of kinds of birds in Teixcalaanli, and one word for "bird" in Stationer. There'd been more, once. They didn't need more than that now. The one stood for the concept.

She could ask for . . . oh, an appointment to a university. A place in a poetry salon. A Teixcalaanli title. A Teixcalaanli name to go with it. Money; fame; adulation. She could ask for absolutely nothing, and remain in service, the Ambassador from Lsel, and answer mail, and sing a song in Teixcalaanli pubs that once she'd written some of the words to, a long time ago.

Nothing the Empire touched would remain hers. Very little was hers already.

"Your Brilliance," said Mahit Dzmare, "please send me home, while I still want to go."

"You keep *surprising* me," said Nineteen Adze. "Are you sure?"

Mahit said, "No. Which is why I want you to send me home. I'm *not* sure."

<What are you doing?>

Trying to see who we are. What is left of us. Who we might be now.

———

Approached from the underside of the largest of the pockmarked metallic atmosphereless planets that formed the Lsel System, the station hung suspended, perfectly balanced in the gravity well between two stars and four planets. It was small, a dull metal toroid, spinning to maintain thermal control. Rough from fourteen generations of solar radiation and small-particle impact. Thirty thousand or so people dwelling in the dark. More, if you counted the imago-memories. One of them at least had recently tried to sabotage one of those long memory-lines, and would be waiting to see what had come of her attempt.

Mahit watched the Station come into view.

The Emperor's hand—slim, dark-fingered, intimately familiar—had reached out, in the plaza. Reached out and taken Mahit's jaw between her fingers, turned her face. Mahit should have been frightened, or stunned into endocrine cascade. But she had felt—floating. Distant, free.

"We do need an ambassador from Lsel," Nineteen Adze had said, "though it's not terribly urgent at the moment. If I want you, Mahit, I will send for you."

Mahit felt that way now, as Lsel came back into the center of her ship's viewports. Very distant. A certain kind of free.

Not, in the end, quite home.

A GLOSSARY OF PERSONS, PLACES, AND OBJECTS

ahachotiya—An alcoholic drink, popular in the City, derived from fermented fruit.

Aknel Amnardbat—Councilor for Heritage, one of six members of the governing Lsel Council; her purview is imago-machines, memory, and cultural promotion.

amalitzli—A Teixcalaanli sport, played on a clay court with a rubber ball which opposing teams attempt to throw, bounce, or ricochet into a small goal. Versions of *amalitzli* specialized for low- or zero-gravity environments are also popular.

Anhamemat Gate—One of two jumpgates situated in Bardzravand Sector; leads from Stationer space into a resource-poor area not currently under the control of a known political actor. Colloquially, "the Far Gate."

Aragh Chtel—A Stationer pilot assigned to sector reconnaissance.

Ascension's Red Harvest—A Teixcalaanli warship, *Engulfer*-class.

asekreta—A Teixcalaanli title, referring to an actively serving member of the Information Ministry. Plural *asekretim*.

Bardzravand Sector—The sector of known space within which Lsel Station and other stations are located (Stationer pronunciation).

Belltown—A province of the City, divided into multiple districts; for example, Belltown One is a "bedroom community" for Teixcalaanlitzlim who cannot or do not wish to live in the Inmost Province districts, but Belltown Six is a notorious hotbed of criminal activity, urban congestion, and low-income residents.

Buildings, The (**epic poem**)—An ekphrastic poem describing famous architectural achievements of the City, commonly taught as a school text in Teixcalaan.

Captain Cameron—Fictional hero of the Lsel graphic novel *The Perilous Frontier!*

City, the—The planetary capital of Teixcalaan.

cloudhook—Portable device, worn over the eye, which allows Teixcalaanlitzlim to access electronic media, news, communications, etc.; also functions as a security device, or key, which can open doors or give accesses; also functions as a geospatial positioning system, communicating location to a satellite network.

Darj Tarats—Councilor for the Miners, one of six members of the governing Lsel Council; his purview is resource extraction, trade, and labor.

Dava—A newly annexed planet in the Teixcalaanli Imperium, famous for its mathematical school.

Dekakel Onchu—Councilor for the Pilots, one of six members of the governing Lsel Council; her purview is military defense, exploration, and navigation.

Ebrekt/Ebrekti—The Ebrekti (singular "Ebrekt," adjectival form "Ebrekt") are a species of quadripedal obligate carnivores, whose social structure (called a "swift") resembles a pride of lions. The Teixcalaanli Emperor Two Sunspot negotiated a permanent peace treaty with the Ebrekti, clearly defining zones of mutual non-competition, four hundred years ago (Teixcalaanli reckoning).

Eight Antidote—A ninety-percent clone of His Brilliance the Emperor Six Direction. One of three associated heirs to the sun-spear throne of Teixcalaan. Ten years old.

Eight Loop—The Minister of the Judiciary on Teixcalaan. Crèche-sib to His Brilliance the Emperor Six Direction. One of three associated heirs to the sun-spear throne of Teixcalaan.

Eight Penknife—A member of the Information Ministry.

Eighteen Turbine—*Ikantlos* of the Teixcalaanli fleet, currently commanding Battle Group Nine of the Twenty-Sixth Legion, assigned to the Odile System.

Eleven Cloud—A failed usurper, who tried to overthrow the Emperor Two Sunspot, four hundred years ago (Teixcalaanli reckoning).

Eleven Conifer—A patrician third-class, retired from honorable service in the Teixcalaanli fleet at third sub-*ikantlos* rank.

Eleven Lathe—A Teixcalaanli poet and philosopher, best known for his work *Dispatches from the Numinous Frontier*.

Expansion History, The—A history of Teixcalaanli expansion, attributed to Thirteen River (attribution debunked; current literary scholars of Teixcalaan refer to *The Expansion History* as being composed by "Pseudo-Thirteen River," an unknown person).

ezuazuacat—The title for a member of the emperor's personal advisory council; referred to as His, Her, or Their Excellency. Derives from the original name of the emperor's sworn band of warriors, back when Teixcalaan had not yet broken space.

Fifteen Engine—The former cultural liaison to Ambassador Yskandr Aghavn. Currently retired from service to the Information Ministry, and living as a private citizen.

Five Agate—Aide and analyst in the employ of Her Excellency the *ezuazuacat* Nineteen Adze.

Five Diadem—Pen name of the famed Teixcalaanli historian and poet Five Hat.

Five Needle—Teixcalaanli historical figure, memorialized in the poem "Encomia for the Fallen of the Flagship *Twelve*

Expanding Lotus." Died defending her ship after a series of field promotions left her the ranking officer.

Five Orchid—A fictional Teixcalaanli historical figure, the protagonist of a children's novel, in which she was the crèche-sib of the future Emperor Twelve Solar-Flare.

Five Portico—A mechanic, living in Belltown Six.

Forty-Five Sunset—A junior aide to Her Excellency the *ezua-zuacat* Nineteen Adze.

Foundation Song—Teixcalaanli song cycle memorializing the deeds of the First Emperor. Passed through oral tradition; over one thousand versions are known.

Four Lever—An *ixplanatl* in service to the Judiciary Ministry, in the role of Medical Examiner.

Four Sycamore—A newscaster, employed by Channel Eight!

Fourteen Scalpel—The writer of the poem "Encomia for the Fallen of the Flagship *Twelve Expanding Lotus*."

Fourteen Spire—A minor contemporary poet, active at Six Direction's court.

Gelak Lerants—A member of the Lsel Heritage Board, an accreditation body.

Gienah-9—A mostly desert planet, annexed with great force and considerable personnel loss by Teixcalaan, and then lost in a rebellion. Re-annexed; subjugated. A popular setting for military dramas.

Gorlaeth—The Ambassador to Teixcalaan from Dava.

huitzahuitlim—"Palace-hummers," a species of nectar-eating bird.

ikantlos—A military rank in the Teixcalaanli fleet, usually tasked with commanding a battle group within a legion.

imago—An ancestral live memory.

Imperial Censor Office—The office of the Teixcalaanli government tasked with determining what media is spread to which areas of the Empire.

infofiche—A mutable, foldable, transparent plastic which can display images and text. Reusable.

infofiche stick—A thumb-sized container, often personalized, containing a holographic representation of a message which appears when the stick is broken open. It may also contain an actual piece of infofiche.

infosheet—A news sheet made of infofiche.

Inmost Province—The central province of the City, containing the government buildings and major cultural centers.

Inmost Province Spaceport—The major spaceport of the City, seeing 57 percent of inbound traffic.

Inscription's Glass Key—The flagship of the Teixcalaanli Emperor Two Sunspot.

ixhui—A meat dumpling.

ixplanatl—Any accredited Teixcalaanli scientist (physical, social, biological, chemical).

Jewel of the World—The colloquial (and the poetic) name for the City-planet.

Jirpardz—A pilot on Lsel Station.

Kamchat Gitem—A pilot on Lsel Station.

Keeper of the Imperial Inkstand—The title for the Teixcalaanli emperor's schedule-keeper and chamberlain.

Lost Garden—A restaurant in Plaza North Four, famous for its winter-climate dishes.

Lsel Station/Stationers—People living on the primary mining station in Bardzravand Sector. Planetless.

Mahit Dzmare—The current Ambassador to Teixcalaan from Lsel Station.

Mist, the—The Judiciary Ministry's investigatory and enforcement body.

Nguyen—A multisystem confederation near Stationer space, with whom the Stationers have a trade agreement.

Nine Crimson—A Teixcalaanli historical figure, *yaotlek* of the

Third, Ninth, and Eighteenth Legions of the fleet, approximately five hundred years ago.

Nine Flood—A Teixcalaanli historical figure, an Emperor from when Teixcalaan had not yet become a spacefaring power.

Nine Maize—A major court poet at the court of His Brilliance the Emperor Six Direction.

Nine Propulsion—The current Minister of War.

Nine Shuttle—The planetary governor of Odile-1, recently reinstated after an uprising.

Nineteen Adze—She Whose Gracious Presence Illuminates the Room Like the Edgeshine of a Knife, one of Six Direction's *ezuazuacatlim,* formerly a member of the Teixcalaanli fleet.

Ninety Alloy—A Teixcalaanli holoproduction, episodic. Military romance.

North Tlachtli—A neighborhood in Inmost Province.

Odile—A Teixcalaanli planetary system which has recently been the site of insurrection and unrest.

One Conifer—A Teixcalaanli citizen, employed by the Central Travel Authority Northeast Division.

One Granite—The legendary first *ezuazuacat* to the First Emperor.

One Lightning—A *yaotlek* of the Teixcalaanli fleet, much acclaimed by his soldiers, in the service of His Brilliance the Emperor Six Direction.

One Skyhook—A renowned Teixcalaanli poet, often taught in schools.

One Telescope—An *ezuazuacat* from approximately two hundred years ago. A statue of her stands in the central transport hub for Inmost Province, commemorating her achievements.

osmium—A valuable metal, often found in asteroids. One of the exports of Lsel Station.

Parzrawantlak Sector—The Teixcalaanli pronunciation of Bardzravand Sector.

patrician (first-, second-, or third-class)—Ranks at the Teixcalaanli court, primarily representative of personal salaries received from the imperial treasury.

Petrichor-5—A large democratic multisystem political actor near Bardzravand Sector.

Poplar Province—One of the more distant provinces from Inmost Province; an ocean-crossing away.

Pseudo-Thirteen River—The unknown author of *The Expansion History,* who used the name Thirteen River despite not being the Minister of the Judiciary of that name whose treatises on retributive justice are still taught in Teixcalaanli law schools.

Red Flowerbuds for Thirty Ribbon—A Teixcalaanli romance novel.

Ring Two—A designation for provinces in the City which are more than three hundred but less than six hundred miles from the palace. Information Ministry slang.

Secret History of the Emperors, The—A famous (and salacious) anonymous account of the lives of many Teixcalaanli emperors. Often updated. Never imitated.

Seven Chrysoprase—A newscaster, employed by Channel Eight!

Seven Scale—A junior aide to Her Excellency the *ezuazuacat* Nineteen Adze.

shocksticks—An electricity-based weapon, primarily used for crowd control on Teixcalaan.

Shrja Torel—A citizen of Lsel Station. Mahit Dzmare's friend.

Six Direction—His Brilliance the Reigning Emperor of All Teixcalaan.

Six Helicopter—A Teixcalaanli bureaucrat.

Six Outreaching Palms—The colloquial (or poetic) name for the Ministry of War; so named for the reaching out of hands in every direction (north, south, west, east, up, and down) which is the hallmark of Teixcalaanli conquest theory.

Sunlit, the—The police force of the City.

Svava—A small independent multiplanetary state near Bardzravand Sector.

Teixcalaan—The Empire, the world, coextensive with the known universe. (Adjectival form: Teixcalaanli; a person who is a citizen of Teixcalaan is a Teixcalaanlitzlim.)

Teixcalaanli—The language spoken in Teixcalaan.

Ten Pearl—The current Minister of Science.

Thirteen Penknife—A Teixcalaanli poet.

Thirty Larkspur—He Who Drowns the World in Blooms, one of Six Direction's *ezuazuacatlim,* formerly a scion of a major merchant family from the Western Arc.

Thirty-Six All-Terrain Tundra Vehicle—A Teixcalaanli citizen.

Three Lamplight—A member of the Information Ministry.

Three Nasturtium—A Teixcalaanli citizen, Central Traffic Control Supervisor at Inmost Province Spaceport.

Three Perigee—A historical Teixcalaanli Emperor.

Three Seagrass—A member of the Information Ministry, cultural liaison to Mahit Dzmare, the Lsel Ambassador.

Three Sumac—A Fleet Captain of the Twenty-Sixth Legion in the Teixcalaanli fleet.

tlaxlauim—A certified accountant or financial professional in Teixcalaan.

Tsagkel Ambak—A negotiator and diplomat from Lsel Station; formalized the Station's current treaty with the Teixcalaanli Empire.

Twelve Azalea—A member of the Information Ministry. A friend to Three Seagrass.

Twelve Solar-Flare—A historical Teixcalaanli Emperor, who first discovered Parzrawantlak Sector, and thus Lsel Station.

Twenty Sunsets Illuminated—The flagship of *yaotlek* One Lightning.

Twenty-Four Rose—A Teixcalaanli author of travel guidebooks.

Twenty-Nine Bridge—The current Keeper of the Imperial Inkstand, serving His Brilliance the Emperor Six Direction.

Twenty-Nine Infograph—A member of the Judiciary Ministry.

Twenty-Two Graphite—An aide to Her Excellency the *ezuazuacat* Nineteen Adze.

Two Amaranth—A historical *ezuazuacat,* serving the Emperor Twelve Solar-Flare.

Two Calendar—A major court poet at the court of His Brilliance the Emperor Six Direction.

Two Cartograph—The son of Five Agate. Six years old.

Two Lemon—A Teixcalaanli citizen.

Two Rosewood—The current Minister for Information.

Two Sunspot—A historical Teixcalaanli Emperor who negotiated peace with the Ebrekti.

Vardza Ndun—A pilot on Lsel Station, now an imago held by the pilot Jirpardz.

Western Arc—An important and wealthy sector of Teixcalaan, home to major merchant concerns.

xauitl—A flower.

yaotlek—A military rank in the Teixcalaanli fleet; commander of at least one legion, appointed for a purpose or for a long-running multilegionary campaign.

Yskandr Aghavn—The former Ambassador to Teixcalaan from Lsel Station.

On the pronunciation and writing system of the Teixcalaanli language

The Teixcalaanli language is logosyllabic, written in "glyphs." These individual glyphs represent both free and bound morphemes. Teixcalaanli glyphs also can represent phonetic sounds, usually derived from an initial morpheme's pronunciation which has lost its meaning and become purely phonetic. Due to the logosyllabic nature of Teixcalaanli, double and triple meanings are easily created in both verbal and written texts. Individual glyphs can function as visual puns or have suggestions of meaning unrelated to their precise morphemic use. Such wordplay—both visual and aural—is central to the literary arts of the Empire.

Teixcalaanli is a vowel-heavy language with a limited set of consonants. A brief pronunciation guide is given below (with IPA symbology and examples from American English).

a—ɑː—father

e—ɛ—bed

o—oʊ—no, toe, soap

i—i—city, see, meat

u—u—loop

aa—ɑ—The Teixcalaanli "aa" is a *chroneme*—it extends the length of the sound *a* in time, but does not change its quality.

au—aʊ̯—loud

ei—eɪ̯—say

ua—ʷɑ—water, quantity

ui—ʷi—weed

y—j—yes, yell

c—k—cat, cloak (but never as in *certain*)

h—h—harm, hope

k—kʰ—almost always found before r, as in crater or crisp, but occasionally as a word ending, where it is heavily aspirated

l—ɣ—bell, ball

m—m—mother, mutable

n—n—nine, north

p—p—paper, proof

r—ɾ—red, father
s—s—sable, song
t—tʰ—t, aspirated, as in top
x—ks—sticks, six
z—z—zebra
ch—tʃ—chair

But in consonant clusters (which Teixcalaanli favors), t is more often found as "t," the unaspirated dental consonant in stop; l is often "l," the dental approximate in line or lucid. There are many loanwords in Teixcalaanli. When pronouncing words originating in more consonant-heavy languages, Teixcalaanli tends to devoice unfamiliar consonants, i.e., "b" is pronounced like "p" and "d" is pronounced like "t."

On the language spoken on Lsel Station and other stations in Bardzravand Sector

By contrast, the language spoken on the stations in Bardzravand Sector is alphabetic and consonant heavy. It is easier for a native speaker of Stationer to accurately pronounce a Teixcalaanli word than the other way around. (If one wishes to pronounce Stationer words one's own self, and has only Earth languages to go by, a good guide would be the pronunciation of Modern Eastern Armenian).

ACKNOWLEDGMENTS

I began this book in the Cartel Coffee Lab in Tempe, Arizona, in the summer of 2014, two weeks into an intensive language course in Modern Eastern Armenian: my head full of the shapes of words that weren't mine. I finished it in a bedroom in Baltimore in the high spring of 2017, too early for my wife to be awake, watching the light come in slow over the city: thinking about exile, and how a person almost but does not quite ever come home.

Between Arizona and Baltimore there were three countries, four cities, three jobs, and more help in the making of this book than I can easily describe. An acknowledgments section inevitably is a thin shadow of all the thanks which are deserved. But nevertheless: my eternal gratitude to Elizabeth Bear, who was first my friend and then my teacher and then my friend again, and who kept telling me I was entirely capable of writing a novel, and a good one, despite my protestations; to the rest of the 'zoo, on AIM or Slack or in person, for being the best bar, and the best place to learn to be a writer and a human being; to Liz Bourke, who accidentally sold this book, and who understood the project of it; to Fade Manley, who suffered valiantly through having the early chapters copy-pasted at her; to Amal al-Mohtar and Likhain, who gave me the courage to write about assimilation and language and the seduction and horror of empire, and who then challenged me to do better; to the Viable Paradise workshop, without which I would be poorer in friends and poorer in skill; to my brilliant agent DongWon Song, who saw this project for what it was and what it has come to be, all at once (& I promise not to do important business phone calls from Sweden next time); to my editor, Devi Pillai, who told me to go find the rest of this universe and put it on the page for you all.

And also my thanks to Theo van Lint, who showed me Armenia; to Ingela Nilsson, who didn't mind when I wrote an SF novel while I was her postdoctoral researcher and supposed to be writing about Byzantium; to Patrick and Teresa Nielsen Hayden, who welcomed me into both this industry and their hospitality; to my mother, Laurie Smukler, who was the first person who asked me whether I wanted to leave the academy and write instead, and thought it'd be a good idea; and to my father, Ira Weller, who gave me science fiction to begin with, when I was too small to know better—let there always be more "science affliction" for the both of us.

Lastly and most truly: Vivian Shaw, my wife, first reader extraordinaire, who showed me that stories could also be joy—thanks are insufficient, darling, but they're all yours anyway, like everything else.

*Turn the page for a sneak peek at
the next book in the Teixcalaan series*

A DESOLATION CALLED PEACE

Available September 2020

CHAPTER
ONE

. . . INTERDICT SUSPENDED—for a duration of four months,
extensible by Council order, the interdict regarding Teixcalaanli mili-
tary transport through Stationer space is suspended; all ships bearing
Teixcalaanli military call sign are permitted to pass through the An-
hamemat Gate—this suspension does not authorize Teixcalaanli
ships, military or otherwise, to dock at Lsel Station without prior visas,
approvals, and customs clearances—SUSPENSION AUTHORIZED BY
THE COUNCILOR FOR THE MINERS (DARJ TARATS)—message
repeats . . .

> —priority message deployed on diplomatic, commercial,
> and universal frequencies in the Bardzravand Sector,
> 181st Day, 1st Year, in the 1st Indiction of the Emperor
> of All Teixcalaan Nineteen Adze

*   *   *

Your Brilliance, you have left me with all the world, and yet I am bereft;
I'd take your star-cursed possessing ghost, Six Direction, if only he would
teach me how not to sleep.

> —the private notes of Her Brilliance the Emperor Nineteen
> Adze, undated, locked, and encrypted

NINE Hibiscus watched the cartograph cycle through its
last week of recorded developments for a third time, and
then switched it off. Without its pinpoint stargleams and

fleet-movement arcs inscribed in light, the strategy table on the bridge of *Weight for the Wheel* was a flat black expanse, dull matte, as impatient as its captain for new information.

There was none forthcoming. Nine Hibiscus didn't need to watch the cartograph again to remember how the displayed planet-points had winked first distress red and then out-of-communication black, vanishing like they were being swallowed by a tide. No matter how thickly laid the lines of incoming Teixcalaanli ships were shown on that cartograph, none of them had advanced into the flood of blank silence. *Beyond this point,* Nine Hibiscus thought, not without a shimmering anticipation, *we are quite afraid to see.*

Her own *Weight for the Wheel* was the second-closest vessel to the communicationless swath. She'd sent only one ship farther out than she'd take her own people. That was the hybrid scout-gunner called *Knifepoint's Ninth Blooming,* a near-invisible sliver of a ship that slipped free of her flagship's open-mawed hangar and into the silent black. Sending it might have been Nine Hibiscus's first mistake as Her Brilliance the Emperor Nineteen Adze's newest *yaotlek*—commander of fleet commanders, with multiple Teixcalaanli legions at her command. An Emperor made new *yaotleks* when that Emperor wanted to make a war: the one begot the other. Nine Hibiscus had heard *that* old saying the first time when she'd been a cadet, and thought it herself approximately once a week, absent confirmation of absolute observed truth.

Nineteen Adze, new-crowned, had very badly wanted to make a war.

Now, at the very forefront of that war, Nine Hibiscus hoped sending *Knifepoint* hadn't been a mistake after all. It'd be useful to avoid unforced errors, considering *how* new a *yaotlek* she was. (It'd be *useful* to avoid errors at all, but Nine Hibiscus had been an officer of the Six Outreaching Palms—the Teixcalaanli imperial military, hands outstretched in every direction—long enough to know that errors, in war, were inevitable.) So far *Knifepoint* was running as quiet as the dead planets up ahead, and the cartograph hadn't updated in four hours.

So *that* gambit could be going any way at all.

She leaned her elbows on the strategy table. There'd be elbowprints later: the soft pillowing flesh of her arms leaving its oils on the matte surface, and she'd have to get out a screen-cleaner cloth to wipe them away. But Nine Hibiscus liked to *touch* her ship, know it even when it was just waiting for orders. Feel, even this far from its engine core, the humming of the great machine for which she served as a brain. Or at least a ganglion cluster, a central point. A fleet captain was a filter for all the information that came to the bridge, after all—and a *yaotlek* was *more so*, a *yaotlek* had farther reach, more hands to stretch out in every possible direction. More *ships*.

Nine Hibiscus was going to need every one of them she had.

Around her the bridge was both too busy and too quiet. Every station was occupied by its appropriate officer. Navigation, propulsion, weaponry, comms: all arrayed around her and her strategy table like a solid, scaled-up version of the holographic workspace she could call into being with her cloudhook, the glass-and-metal overlay on her right eye that linked her—even here on the edge of the Teixcalaanli imperium—to the great data-and-story networks that held the empire together. Every one of the bridge's stations was occupied, and every occupant was trying to look as if they had something to do besides wait, and wonder if the force they had been sent to defeat would catch them unawares and do—whatever it was that these aliens were doing that snuffed out planetary communication systems like flames in vacuum. All of her bridge officers were nervous, and all of them were tired of being patient. They were the Fleet, the Six Outreaching Palms of Teixcalaan: *conquest* was their style, not massed waiting on the edge of the inevitable, paused in worrisome silence at the very forefront of six legions' worth of ships. Nearest to the danger, and yet still unmoving.

At least when Her Brilliance Nineteen Adze had made her *yaotlek* to prosecute this war, Nine Hibiscus thought, she'd let her keep her own ship as flagship. Each of these officers was a Teixcalaanlitzlim she'd worked with, served with, commanded—each of them she'd led to victory in the uprising at Kauraan System less than three months ago. They were *hers*. They'd trust her a little longer. Just a little longer, until *Knifepoint* came back with some actionable information and she could let them loose a bit. Taste a little blood, a little dust and fire blooming from the death of an alien ship. A fleet could last a long time, fed on those sips of sugar-water violence, as long as they believed their *yaotlek* knew what she was doing.

Or that'd always been how Nine Hibiscus had felt, when she used to serve under Nine Propulsion before Nine Propulsion had gone off to pilot a desk planetside in the City. She'd been Minister of War under the last, dead, lamented emperor, and Nine Hibiscus—who spelled her name with the same number-glyph as Nine Propulsion used, and hadn't yet regretted that late-teenage star-eyed choice—had thought she'd probably be Minister under the new one. Had *expected* that.

But instead, Nine Propulsion had taken retirement almost immediately upon Nineteen Adze's ascension. She'd left the City entirely, and Nine Hibiscus, bereft of the comfort of mentorship (she'd been lucky to have had it so long, if she was being honest with herself) had woken up one shift with an urgent infofiche stick message from the Emperor Herself—a *commission*.

If this war is winnable, I want you to win it. The Emperor's dark cheekbones like knives, like the edges of the flares of the sun-spear throne she sat on.

And now, calling her back to herself in this present moment, a low voice to Nine Hibiscus's direct left: one that wouldn't startle her at that distance. (The only one who could sneak up that close, regardless.) "Nothing yet, then, sir?"

Twenty Cicada, her *ikantlos*-prime, who served as her adjutant and second-in-command. He had his arms folded neatly across the cadaverous thinness of his chest, one eyebrow an expressive arch. As always, his uniform was impeccable, perfect-Teixcalaanli, the very image of a soldier in a propaganda holo-film: if you ignored the shaved head and how he looked like he hadn't eaten in a month. The curling edges of green-and-white-inked tattoos just visible at his wrists and throat, when the uniform shifted as he moved or breathed.

"Nothing," said Nine Hibiscus, loud enough for the rest of the bridge to hear. "Absolute quiet. *Knifepoint*'s running silenced, and at their usual speed they're not going to be back for another shift and a half, unless they're running from something nasty. And there isn't much *Knifepoint* would run from."

Twenty Cicada knew all that. It wasn't for him. It was for how Eighteen Chisel in Navigation's shoulders dropped an inch; how Two Foam, on comms, actually *sent* the message she'd been hesitating over for the past five minutes, reporting continued clear skies to the rest of their multilegion fleet.

"Excellent," said Twenty Cicada. "Then you won't mind if I borrow you for a moment, *yaotlek*?"

"Tell me that we are not still having problems with the escaped pets in the airducts on deck five, and I will not mind being borrowed," Nine Hibiscus said, widening her eyes in fond near-mockery. The pets—small furred things that vibrated pleasantly and ate vermin, a peculiar variant on *cat* that was endemic to Kauraan—had come aboard during their last planetfall there, when she'd still been Fleet Captain Nine Hibiscus of the Tenth Legion, not *yaotlek* yet. The pets had not been a problem—or something Nine Hibiscus had even *known* about—until they had decided to reproduce themselves, and moved into a Deck Five airduct to do it. Twenty Cicada had complained vociferously about how they were disturbing the homeostasis of *Weight for the Wheel*'s environment.

"It is not the pets," Twenty Cicada said. "That I promise. Conference room?"

If he wanted privacy to discuss whatever it was, it certainly wouldn't be good. "Perfect," Nine Hibiscus said, pushing herself upright. She was twice as wide as Twenty Cicada, but he moved around her as if he had solidity enough to match. "Two Foam, your bridge."

"My bridge, *yaotlek*," Two Foam called, and that was as it should be, so Nine Hibiscus went to see what was wrong with her ship—her fleet—*now*.

Weight for the Wheel had two conference rooms right off the bridge—a large one, for strategy meetings, and a small one, for fixing problems. Nine Hibiscus had repurposed the latter from an auxiliary weapon-control station when she'd first been made captain. A ship needed a space to have private *official* conversations, she'd thought then, and she'd been largely right; the small conference room was the best place to solve personnel issues, recorded on the ship's cameras, visible and invisible all at once. She took Twenty Cicada inside, cuing the door to open with a micromovement of one eye that directed her cloudhook to talk to the ship's algorithmic AI.

Twenty Cicada wasn't given to preambles; Nine Hibiscus had always known him to be *efficient,* brisk and clean and mercilessly direct. He preceded her through the door—and to her surprise, did not turn to give his report. Instead he headed directly for the room's narrow viewport, and put a hand up against the plastisteel separating his body and the vacuum. Nine Hibiscus felt a flicker of warmth at the familiarity of the gesture, warmth mixed with uncomfortable dread: Twenty

Cicada touched the ship, too, but he touched the ship like he was longing for space to come in and take his hand. He'd done that for as long as Nine Hibiscus had known him, and the two of them had met on their very first deployment.

Which was long enough ago by now that Nine Hibiscus didn't particularly feel like counting the years.

"Swarm," she said—the nickname he'd gotten back on that deployment, the one she had mostly given up calling him for the sake of officer hierarchy—"spit it out. What's going on?"

"Sir," he said, still staring out at the black, gentle corrective for the cameras, even if the recordings of this room would never be seen by anyone but her: who outranked a *yaotlek*? But he was so *correctly* a Fleet officer, a Teixcalaanlitzlim's Teixcalaanlitzlim, seamless in the role of *ikantlos*-prime and adjutant, a man who could have walked out of *The Expansion History* or *Opening Frontier Poems,* except that the system his people had come from hadn't even been absorbed into Teixcalaan when either of those works had been written. (Except that he still kept up some of that system's peculiar cultural-religious practices— but hesitance wasn't one of *those,* either. At least not one she knew about.)

"Yes, *ikantlos*? Report."

Finally he turned, widened his eyes in wry and resigned amusement, and said, "In about two hours, sir, you're going to get an official communiqué, addressed to you *specifically* as *yaotlek* in charge of this combined fleet, from Fleet Captain Sixteen Moonrise on the *Parabolic Compression* of the Twenty-Fourth Legion, demanding to know what the delay in action is. It will be countersigned by Fleet Captain Forty Oxide of the Seventeenth and Fleet Captain Two Canal of the Sixth. We have a problem."

"The Seventeenth *and* the Sixth?" Nine Hibiscus asked. "They hate each other. That rivalry is two hundred years old. How did Sixteen Moonrise get them both to sign?"

They absolutely had a problem. Her combined fleet was six legions strong: her own Tenth and five more, each with its own Fleet Captain newly subordinate to her authority. The traditional *yaotlek's six,* both tactically effective and symbolically sound. If *three* of those six were already willing to sign an opening salvo against her authority as *yaotlek* . . . She didn't need to say it; both she and Twenty Cicada knew what a letter like this one meant. It was a test, a press to check for weak spots: a light barrage to find the best point to concentrate a wedge attack. It was bad enough that she'd been given both the Sixth and the Seventeenth Legions as part of her fleet, but she'd expected any ensuing conflict to be *between them,* something to carefully manage by doling out the best assignments equally. Not this surprising show of political unity through displeasure.

"From what information I've received from my associates on their ships," said Twenty Cicada, "Sixteen Moonrise appealed on the one side to Forty Oxide's long experience compared to yours, and on the other to Two Canal's vehement wish that *she* had been made *yaotlek* instead of you, and neither of them knew the other one had agreed until right before they agreed to send the message."

There were reasons that Twenty Cicada was nicknamed *Swarm,* and it wasn't just his peculiar name: a name with a living creature in it instead of a proper object or color or plant. Swarm was Swarm because he was everywhere at once: he knew *someone* on every ship in the Fleet, and those someones tended to keep him well-informed. Nine Hibiscus clicked her teeth together, considering. "Politics," she said. "All right. We've had politics before."

Nine Hibiscus had had politics come after her more than once. Anyone who made Fleet Captain did. Anyone who made Fleet Captain and meant to keep the position and win victories for her legion—well, that sort of Teixcalaanlitzlim made enemies. Jealous ones.

(Every time there'd been politics before, though, Nine Hibiscus had also had Nine Propulsion in the Ministry as a threat of last resort. The new Minister of War, Three Azimuth, was no one's friend in particular—or at least she wasn't Nine Hibiscus's friend.)

"Two Canal and Forty Oxide aren't the point anyhow," said Twenty Cicada. "Sixteen Moonrise is. She's the instigator—*she's* the one you're going to have to defuse."

"Perhaps she'd like the point position when we do make our approach."

Twenty Cicada said, dry as processed ship's-air, "So direct, sir."

She couldn't help grinning: teeth-bared like a barbarian, a savage expression. It felt good on her face. Felt like getting ready to act, instead of waiting and waiting and waiting. "They *are* insinuating I'm over-hesitant."

"I can have that order composed. The Twenty-Fourth will be cast shouting into whatever void is eating our planets by shift-change, if you like." One of the problems with Twenty Cicada was that he offered her exactly what she wanted, for precisely long enough for her to remember that it was a bad idea. It was the kind of problem that ended up being one of a thousand reasons Nine Hibiscus had never thought of replacing him with a soldier who came from a more assimilated world.

"No," she said. "Let's do one better. The glory of dying first for the empire's too good for Sixteen Moonrise, don't you think? Invite her to dinner instead. Treat her like a favored colleague, a prospective co-commander. A new *yaotlek* like me needs allies, doesn't she?"

Twenty Cicada's expression had become unreadable, like he was adjusting some value in a vast calculation of a complex system. Nine Hibiscus figured that if he was going to object he would go ahead and object, and went on assuming he wouldn't.

"Fourth shift—that'll give her the travel time to get over to *Wheel.* Her and her adjutant. We'll have a *strategy discussion,* the four of us."

"As soon as the letter officially arrives, sir, I'll send that invitation back—and alert the galley that we're expecting guests." Twenty Cicada paused. "I don't like this. For the record. It's too early for anyone to be pushing you like this. I didn't expect it."

"I don't like it either," Nine Hibiscus said. "But since when has that made a difference? We persevere, Swarm. We *win.*"

"We do tend to." A flicker, again, of that dry amusement. "But the wheel goes around—"

Nine Hibiscus said, "That's why we're the *weight,*" like she was one of her soldiers in the mess, ship-phrase slogan, and smiled. *Game on,* she thought. *Sixteen Moonrise, whatever it is you want from me—come play.*

Over the comms, then, Two Foam's disembodied voice: "*Yaotlek,* I have visual on *Knifepoint.* Three hours early. Coming in fast. Coming in—*hot.*"

"Bleeding *stars,*" Nine Hibiscus spat a quick, instinctive curse, just for her and Twenty Cicada to hear, and then signaled her cloudhook to patch her into the comms frequency. "On my way. Don't fire on anything until we know we have to."

———

Lsel Station was a sort of city, if one thought of cities as animate machines, organisms made of interlocking parts and people, too close-packed to be any *other* form of life. Thirty thousand Stationers on Lsel, all in motion, spinning in the dark in their gravitational well, safe inside the thin envelope of metal which was Station-skin. And like any other city, Lsel Station was—if you knew where to go, and where to avoid—a decent place to take a long enough walk to exhaust yourself out of overthinking.

<A fascinating theory, that one,> said Yskandr, <which you are in the process of disproving at this very moment.>

Mahit Dzmare, by certain technicalities still the Ambassador to Teixcalaan from Lsel, even six months returned in quasi-disgrace from her post, had perfected the art of *thinking* the sensation of rolling her eyes. *I haven't walked far enough yet,* she said to her imago—to *both* her imagos, the old Yskandr and the fragmentary remains of the young one. *Give me time.*

<You've got twenty minutes before Councilor Amnardbat is expecting you,> Yskandr—he was mostly the young Yskandr today, arch and amused, experience-hungry, all bravado and new-won fluency in Teixcalaanli manners and politics. The Yskandr-version she'd mostly lost to the sabotage of the imago-machine which had brought him to her in the first place, nestled at the base of her skull, full up with live memory and the experience she'd needed to be a *good* Ambassador from Lsel, on the glittering City-planet heart of Teixcalaan. Sabotage executed—possibly, she remained unsure—by the very Councilor she was due to have dinner with in twenty minutes.

There was another life, Mahit thought, where she and Yskandr would have been in the City still, and integrated already into a single continuous self.

<There never was>—Yskandr told her, and that was the *other* Yskandr: twenty years older, a man who remembered his own death well enough that Mahit still sometimes woke up in the night choking on psychosomatic anaphylaxis—<any other world but the one we got.>

Mahit was too many people, since she'd overlaid her damaged imago with the imago of the same man, twenty years farther on down the line. She'd had a while to think about it. She was *almost* used to how it felt, the fault lines between the three of them grinding together like planetary tectonics. Her boots made soft familiar noise on the metal floor of the Station corridors. She was out near the edge of this deck—she could just barely see the curvature of the floor, here, stretching up. Walking endless loops just on the inner surface of the Station's skin had started as a refamiliarization tactic and turned into a habit. Yskandr didn't know the geography of the Station any longer— in the City he'd been either fifteen years or three dead months out of date, but here at home he was just a long-exiled stranger. In fifteen years the walls moved around, the decks repurposed, little shops opened and shut. Someone in Heritage had changed all the fonts on the navigational signs, a shift Mahit hardly recalled—she'd been *eight*—but she found herself staring at them, a perfectly innocuous *Medical Sector: Leftward* sign suddenly compulsively fascinating.

We're both exiles, she'd thought, right then, and had hated herself for thinking it. She'd been gone a few weeks. She had no right to the name. She was home.

She wasn't, and she knew it. (There was no such place any longer.) But the walking was a semblance, and she *did* remember where some things were, the shape and rhythm of the Station, alive and full of people—and she and Yskandr both had the same joy in discovering new places. On that, the aptitudes had gotten them entirely dead to rights.

This deck—Heritage offices, eventually, but right now a residential section, everyone's individual pods hanging in warm bone-colored rows, interspersed with common areas—wasn't one she knew well at all. It was full of kids; older ones, three-quarters of the way to their imago aptitude tests, sitting easily on top of bulkheads and clustered in chattering groups around shop kiosks. Most of them ignored Mahit entirely, which was comforting. Six months back on the Station and half the time she ran into old friends, her crechesibs or classmates, and all of them wanted her to *tell them about Teixcalaan*. And what could she say? *I love it; it almost ate me and all of you together; I can't tell you a single thing?*

<Propaganda's fascinating when it's inside your own mind,> Yskandr murmured. <It endlessly surprises me, how good the City is at engendering compulsive silence.>

You died there rather than coming back to share your plans with our Station, and you'd like to lecture me on silence? Mahit snapped, and felt her smallest fingers go to fizzing sparkles: neurological afterimages of sabotage. That side effect hadn't stopped. It was more obvious when she stumbled into one of the places she and Yskandr *hadn't* managed to integrate yet, at all. But her sense of his presence withdrew to a banked and observant simmer. She'd ended up next to one of the kiosks, while she was too busy talking to her imago to notice where she was going. (Probably she should mind those slips more than she did. The slips where she wasn't quite *her,* in her body.) Ended up next to a kiosk, and in a line for what it was selling.

Which seemed to be—handbound literature. The kiosk was labeled ADVENTURE/BLEAK PUBLISHING. Its display was full of graphic stories, drawn not on ever-changeable infofiche but on *paper,* made from flattened rag pulp. Mahit reached out and touched the cover of the nearest. It was rough under her fingertips.

"Hey," said the kiosk manager. "You like that one? *The Perilous Frontier!*"

"The what?" Mahit asked her, suddenly feeling as adrift as she had the first time anyone had asked her a question in Teixcalaanli. Context failure: *what frontier? aren't they all perilous?*

"We've got all five volumes, if you're into first contact stuff; I love it, the artist on volume three draws Captain Cameron's imago like Chandra Mav's only visible in reflective surfaces, and the *linework*—"

The manager couldn't be more than seventeen, Mahit thought. Short tight-curled hair over a bright-toothed grin, eight hooped earrings up the side of one ear. That was new fashion. When Mahit had been that age everyone was into *long* earrings. *I'm old,* she thought, with a peculiar delight.

<Ancient,> Yskandr agreed, dust-dry and amused. He was years older.

I'm old, and I have no idea what kids on Lsel like to read. Even when I was a kid on Lsel I didn't know, really. It hadn't seemed important, before her aptitudes—why bother, when there was so much Teixcalaanli literature to drown herself in? To learn to speak in poetry for?

"I haven't read them yet," Mahit told the manager. "Can I have the first one?"

"Sure," she replied—ducked down underneath the counter and produced one. Mahit handed over her credit chip, and the manager swiped it. "They're drawn right here on this deck," she said. "If you like it, come back on second-shift two days from now and you can meet the artist, we're having a signing."

"Thanks. If I have time—"

<You have ten minutes before Councilor Amnardbat wants to feed you dinner.>

"Yeah," the manager grinned, as if to say *adults, seriously, what can you do.* "If you have time."

Mahit waved, went on. Walked a little faster. *The Perilous Frontier!* fit in her inside jacket pocket like it was a political pamphlet. Exactly the same size. That was interesting, in and of itself. Even if it turned out to be a horribly dull story, *that* was interesting.

The Heritage offices were a neatly labeled warren, seven or so doors on either side of the deck corridor, which had narrowed from the wide residential space to something more like a road. Behind those doors, all the extra space would be full of the offices of people assigned to jobs in Heritage: analysts, mostly. Analysts of historical precedent, of the health of art production and education, of the number of imago-matches in one sector of the population or another. Analysts and propaganda writers.

How Teixcalaan had changed her, and how *quickly*. The last time Mahit had come to the Heritage offices, for her final confirmation interview before she received both her imago and her assignment as ambassador, she'd have never thought about Heritage as being in the business of propaganda. But what else were they doing, when they adjusted educational materials for one age group or another, trying to have the aptitudes in five years spit out more pilots or more medical personnel? Changing how children *wanted* to be.

She was hesitating, poised outside the middlemost door with its neatly signed (*in the new font, and when will I get to stop noticing the fucking new font, Yskandr, it isn't actually a new font*) nameplate reading AKNEL AMNARDBAT, COUNCILOR FOR HERITAGE. Hesitating because she hadn't seen Councilor Amnardbat since that last confirmation interview, and hesitating because she still couldn't understand why the woman she'd met then would have wanted to sabotage Mahit's imago-machine. Ruin her before she could even attempt to do right by the imago-line she was part of. If Amnardbat had even been responsible—Mahit only had the word of a *different* Councilor, Dekakel Onchu, Councilor for the Pilots, on that. And Mahit had that word because she'd received letters, while embedded in the Teixcalaanli court, which Onchu had meant for Yskandr.

She missed, with an ugly and sudden abrupt spike of feeling, Three Seagrass, her former cultural liaison, the woman who was supposed to make incongruous experiences make more sense to the poor barbarian in her charge. Three Seagrass would have just opened the door.

Mahit lifted her hand, and knocked. Called out her own

name, "Mahit Dzmare!", a Lsel-style appointment-keeping: no cloudhooks here, to open doors with micromovements of an eye. Just herself, announcing herself.

<You aren't alone,> Yskandr said, a murmur in her mind, ghost-thought: almost her own thought.

No, I'm not. And Amnardbat doesn't know there are two of you— three of us—which is its own problem—

The door opened, so Mahit stopped thinking about dangerous lies she had told. Not thinking about them made them easier to hide. She'd learned that somewhere in the Empire, too.

Councilor Amnardbat was still slim and middle-aged, her hair worn in a spacer's cut of silvering ringlets, narrow and long gray eyes in a wide-cheekboned face that always looked like she'd been exposed to too much solar radiation—*chapped,* but in a rugged sort of way. She smiled when Mahit came in, and that smile was welcoming and warm. If she'd been working with her staff before Mahit's arrival, they weren't immediately visible. Heritage was a small operation, anyway. Councilor Amnardbat had a secretary, who wrote her correspondence— he'd been the one to send Mahit this invitation through the intra-Station electronic mail—but Mahit saw no one in the office at all. Just chairs, and a desk with infopaper piled all over it, and a screen on the wall showing some camera's view of what was outside Lsel just now. A slow rotation of stars.

"Welcome home," said Councilor Amnardbat.

<Six months, she's been waiting to tell you that?>

It's a gambit, Mahit thought, and felt Yskandr subside into a watchful, attentive hum. More awake than he'd been in a long time. She felt that way, too. More awake, more present. Having a dangerous conversation with a powerful person in their offices. Just like she was supposed to do, on Teixcalaan.

"I'm glad to be here," said Mahit. "What can I do for you, Councilor?"